CROSSOVER

July 29, 2017

Dear Cindy,

I shall always be grateful for the warm welcome that you and Bob gave me.

Much love,

Jessie

CROSSOVER

Did I Miss My Exit?

Jessica Oswald with Margaret E. Furman

Publishing Inc.

ISBN-13: 9780692623350
ISBN-10: 0692623353
eBook ISBN: 978-8-692-6346-8
Library of Congress Control Number: 2016901797
Ararat Ark Publishing Inc., Apple Valley, CA
Published by Ararat Ark Publishing Inc., a California corporation.

To the following people who have loved and supported me, with a grateful and appreciative heart:

Benjamin Specter
Herschel Specter
Michael L. Shapiro
Conrad J. Dumais
Raymond J. Dumais
Everette M. Oswald

Jessica Oswald

A NOTE FROM THE AUTHORS

To our readers:

As you open these pages, allow us to take you on an imaginative journey with our protagonist, Alissa. We hope you will have an occasional chuckle, a tear or two for seasoning, moments of empathy, and perhaps a deeper understanding of womanhood and the way we and our sisters have been molded by circumstances sometimes beyond our control.

With love,
Jessica and Margaret

CONTENTS

INTRODUCTION

It was not to be a traditional funeral. In the background, a recording of "Nessun Dorma" was playing softly. The rendition was by the grandson of the deceased, tenor Daniel Streeter, who was touted as the New York Met's new Pavarotti. A spirit of stoic acceptance permeated the halls of the mortuary. No pictures of the decedent were on display because the bereaved felt none could be found that captured the animated image they held in their hearts. The crowd of mourners roved, mingling as they talked among friends while ignoring the rows of chairs set out for their comfort—they found more comfort in selectively connecting with one another for mutual support.

The simple wooden casket was situated at the far end of the nave, where a large, stained-glass window of the desert allowed sunlight to radiate facets of color through the entire length of the hall. There were no cold marble walls in this nook, just an infusion of warm pink to match the subtle hues of desert and thick green carpeting reminiscent of days when gardens and trees sprinkled the landscape.

The only intrusion into this peaceful place was the noise from the members of the coed Cigar and Cannabis Club which was conducting its weekly meeting at the far end of the grounds. The proprietor of the cemetery couldn't be faulted for bringing in paying customers to keep his business venture in the black; even the undertaking business was suffering from the depressed economic times.

The beige-and-golden-gray rays of light from the window lay across the faces of all who came to say good-bye. The open coffin was blanketed in delicate white mariposa lily wildflowers imported from northern California as part of the final request of the deceased. Were the flowers not covering her body completely, those in attendance would have seen that the corpse was dressed in a cozy, sky-blue, Nantucket Rose-flannel sleeping gown trimmed in eyelet lace. She was clothed for the last time in the style that had become her signature comfort-sleeping attire.

The widower spoke first, followed by warm eulogies from several of those who were gathered. When all who wished to speak finished, air force chaplain Mark Grant closed the memorial service with an inspiring spiritual message in lofty imagery befitting the occasion.

"Dearly beloved, we are gathered here today to honor a mother, grandmother, wife, and friend. Alissa was born in Huntington, Long Island, New York, ninety-six years ago, under the water sign of Aquarius. If Alissa is to be remembered, it will be because her life followed what she referred to as her personalized airplane-oxygen rule: she learned that we must first find who we are as individuals before we can be something for others."

The pastor reached to select one of the lilies. Inspired by holding it, he spoke extemporaneously from his heart about the woman who had also touched him with her uncomplicated openness. But true to his personality, formed when Mark Grant was working on his undergraduate degree in theater arts at USC, he used this opportunity to embellish his remarks with theatrical aplomb.

"Deep inside the interior of this delicate flower are distinctive yellow-and-purple markings that suggest butterfly wings. It is not surprising that this was Alissa's favorite flower. Like Alissa, the mariposa lily lives in the midst of striking contradictions. It is sometimes called the Madonna of the Rocks because its virginal purity is married to a harsh, rocky environment. A true madonna is the blessed woman who holds an untarnished, innocent dignity that is contradictory to evil, chaos, and despair."

"And contradictory to the many times Mom was married," said Josh to his sister in a whisper.

"Because this seemingly delicate flower is able to sustain its beauty in the midst of harshness, that very quality brings a healing balm to all who encounter it. It inspires us by imparting a nurturing essence. It draws the soul into a deep, interior space like the chalice of the flower itself. This is a quality of being held or enfolded in a kind of maternal embrace that allows the soul to feel nurtured in the arms of a higher being, as a child does in a mother's arms, or as a friend draws encouragement, hope, and support from a mystical kinship."

"Oh my god," Katie said in a hushed voice to Josh. "I thought I was weaned long ago."

"The flower has ethereal qualities and sweet and evocative fragrances that are more heavenly than earthly. It deserves its name: the butterfly." He replaced the flower on top of the casket, offering a final prayer requesting support for the mourners left behind when Alissa moved on for the next step of her spiritual journey.

After the service, the mourners were invited to a celebration of Alissa's life around a table of champagne and sugar wafers served as their final earthly communion in the presence of the departed. Eight-year-old Joy Windsor, great-granddaughter of the deceased, took one of the lilies and placed it in her hair. Turning toward the guests, she noticed that some looked sad. Joy personally delivered a lily to each remaining guest one by one, with the assurance that "Grandma Great would like you to have this to remember her."

When Joy approached her mother, Millicent Windsor, Millicent took the child's hand, kissed her, and thanked her for her act of kindness. "You are so like my grandmother. She would be so proud of you. Flowers like these used to grow in my grandmother's front yard when she lived with Roland in northern California. Wouldn't it be wonderful to see this much beauty from your front porch?"

Colonel Calvin Zach lingered alone at the casket, wanting to preserve his last moments with his beloved wife. He could not bring himself to leave. He brushed the flowers from her face, thinking that the theatrical tones of the homily were in stark contrast to the light, lyrical quality of her voice. His wife looked as if she were sleeping. He did not want to believe she would not wake again. Perhaps a kiss would awaken her.

"Thank you for your eulogy, Cal," said Katie, approaching the man who had been her stepfather in recent decades. "I volunteered you when Pastor Mark asked if someone in the family would be speaking before he gave his homily. I told him you were Mom's latest husband."

Cal stiffened. "Just so you didn't say 'late husband.'"

Katie smiled, thinking, "Oh god, please help us. Mom shaped another person who plays with words. I don't know if I can handle this." She stepped closer and took the gnarled, arthritic hand of the ninety-seven-year-old man. They moved out of the chapel to stand on the little patch of Astroturf, where her daughter, Millicent, and granddaughter, Joy, were waiting in the welcome shade of a solitary artificial olive tree.

"Neither Josh nor I could have held it together, Cal. You understood Mom perhaps even better than we did." She broke into a grin. "Do you think it took my mother four husbands to get it right?"

"Get what right?" said Cal, pulling his hand back and stiffening his back in proper military attention. "She always believed she was doing right by everybody, and she was."

"You know what I mean," said Katie, thankful to notice her brother and husband approaching to give her backup assistance if it was needed. But Josh wasn't willing to jump into a conversation that looked like it was going to be somber, and Ken was distant and contemplative as usual.

"Sometimes I thought Mom didn't know who she really was. She seemed to flounder a lot, as if she was losing her bearings. She had so many ups and downs, and I was never sure if I understood her. But she was more together in the later years. She was not so anxious. She seemed to have finally found herself. You didn't know her in the early days, Cal. They were pretty difficult for us, weren't they, Josh? We think it was your influence on Mom that got her anchored and focused. Whatever it was she was looking for, and whoever she thought she was, we think you helped her find it. I want to thank you for that."

"No Ma'am, she helped me," said the old man. "Alissa acted on life and understood exactly who she was. She was not as you describe her. Did you ever ask her who she was?"

"Ask her? I'm going to go out on a limb here. What do you think I should have asked her about, Cal?" asked Josh.

"If you were to ask, Alissa would tell you she was constantly evolving. She wasn't unfocused. She was all-absorbed in each event as it occurred. If you look at her whole life, you can see how it all comes together. The changes you observed were not inconsistencies. She may have appeared different at each stage of her development. I wouldn't be surprised if that were true. After all, it wasn't a smooth path that she traveled. Whatever happened to her had to be just the way it happened. Her essence was being created moment by moment. Don't sell her short. She was very complex."

"I don't understand," said Katie.

"Think of it like an oyster."

"Mom preferred shrimp," said Josh.

"The apple does not fall far from the tree. You have your mother's humor, Josh," said Cal.

"Apple? I thought you were talking about oysters. This conversation isn't going to start getting dirty, is it?" Josh said with a laugh.

"Not from me," said Cal, unwilling to be interrupted. "I am not referring to the reputed aphrodisiac qualities of oysters. I am talking about an oyster's intrinsic value. When a piece of sand or other irritant comes into the oyster, its entire development changes. To the oyster, it's an obstruction—it may even hurt. But when someone finds the oyster and discovers the irritant has become a beautiful pearl, the pearl becomes the focus of value, not the oyster."

"You are telling us that Mom is a pearl?" asked Josh. "I figured that if she was a gem, she was a diamond in the rough. She spent a lifetime enjoying her own impurities."

"No, Josh, I'm telling you that she is the oyster. What she gave us was the pearl."

"I'm going to cry," said Katie. "Cal, you're so sweet. Was Mom that important to you?"

Millicent stepped forward to volunteer her opinion. "I know exactly what you mean. Grandma Alissa and I had many private talks, especially in Sonoma, late in her life. She was my inspiration. She inspired me to reach for the stars. No one encouraged her to do that with her life. She developed a life-support system of people. I hope you know, Uncle Josh, how much you meant to her."

"Josh? What about me?" asked Katie.

"She was proud of you and wanted you to be happy." Cal smiled. "The irritants Alissa experienced were real. Some of them were obstacles, but Alissa had her own particular way of dealing with each of them. She faced life's disappointments head on and with humor. She stood her ground with that hallmark feminine firmness that made her one sexy woman."

"I've never thought about Mom as being sexy," said Josh, thankful for an opportunity to lighten the conversation. "But I think I know what you are getting at. Mom would say she played the hand that was dealt her, but she understood you don't always win at the casino. I had this customer who said that luck is being in the right place at the right time with the necessary knowledge."

"Since when did you get to be a philosopher?" asked Katie.

"I didn't make it up. I'm repeating it. I think it's as old as the hills."

"'Excuse me please,' I heard you say 'old as the hills.' Is this conversation about me?" asked a gray-haired woman, approaching the family with a warm smile.

"Please don't take offense Ma'am," said the always-proper Calvin Zach. "That's Josh's way of lightening up a very difficult day with his humor."

"No offense taken, I'm sure. I'm Catherine Michaels, Roland's sister," she said, taking Cal's hand. "Josh and Katie know me well." She turned to Alissa's children, hugging them. "'Chance favors the prepared mind,'" she said, directing her remarks to Josh. "It was Louis Pasteur."

"What was Louis Pasteur?" asked Josh.

"Your quote—I'd say it in French, but I'm a little rusty. Your customer must have read about Pasteur," Catherine said.

"My customer was Mario Ghirardelli. He'd just gotten off the boat. I'd be surprised if Mario read anything that wasn't on a wine label," said Josh.

"You are being unkind, Josh," said his sister. "I've met Mario. He had a lot of insight. He had a very practical approach to life. I can see him making this up on his own. Wisdom is not necessarily a product of education. Haven't you known ordinary people who had a remarkable insight on life? I have."

"I agree, Katie," said Catherine. "Education may polish us, and culture may make us appear to be erudite in a way my grandmother would call 'breeding.' But your Mario might have the ability to understand the practical world as well as Louis Pasteur."

"Yeah, Mom was always coming up with her own creative observations, too. That is, when you could get her to be serious. But don't let her hear you suggest she wasn't educated. She will roll over in her grave," Josh said.

Catherine laughed. "I'm so pleased to be around you again, Josh, and for this opportunity to meet you, Colonel Zach. It's unfortunate that our meeting has to take place at Alissa's funeral. To tell you the truth, until now, I've always avoided talking in a graveyard, and I find this awkward today. Maybe I am a little superstitious."

"Are you afraid of waking the dead?" said Josh, feigning shock.

"Don't worry about waking up Alissa," said Ken Streeter, Katie's husband. "My late mother-in-law won't be moved by anything other than the force of her own will."

"Actually," said Katie, "I wonder how farfetched that is. People in comas can hear what is going on around them. Watch out, Josh." She stepped forward in contrived aggression. "Be careful what you say about Mom. She may be listening."

"Well, there is a big difference between being in a coma and being dead. It's called no brain function," said Josh.

Cal joined in. "I observed some interesting lack of brain function conditions when I was in the Air Force Office of Special Investigations. They never amounted to much. The OSI couldn't come up with any dead witnesses ready to talk or lawyers who made it to heaven. So since the jury is out on that one," he said, laughing, "let's let it pass."

"Pass or pass on?" asked Josh, unwilling to let a potential pun die. "But you can't pass over Mom so lightly, Catherine. Didn't she tell you she was coming back?"

"I'm sorry, Catherine. There he goes again," said Cal in his most apologetic tone.

"Oh, Josh isn't kidding, Cal. Mom did say that. I remember it, too," said Katie, winking at her brother.

Josh was being reflective. "I wish the minister didn't make those allusions to virginity. It didn't seem appropriate for a service for Mom."

"He was speaking allegorically," Cal said.

"Yes," said Katie, "we understand that, but wasn't it a little over the top? The woman had four married names to tack on to her moniker. She wore those names as proudly as if they were college stoles on her graduation robe. She majored in husbandry. I never figured out her attitude about men. I'm glad Chaplain Grant avoided reciting Mom's litany of surnames. It's embarrassing for those of us less-adventurous types. I'm thankful that he kept everything on a first-name basis today.

I was surprised at all the accolades. Our Mom wasn't important. She wasn't the first woman to go to the moon. She didn't invent anything to stop global warming, write the all-American classic, eradicate world hunger, or even host the evening news. And yet, here were all these people today who couldn't wait for their turn to say something nice about her. It was almost embarrassing. But I have to admit I learned some new things about her, and it is all very touching. Mom's friends are hams, just like her. Put a mike in from of them, and they start talking. It's Pavlovian."

"You should realize this about your mother," said Catherine. "She had a profound influence on us. I have never seen anyone change as much as my brother, Roland, when he married Alissa. She came into his life at the right time with the right gifts. As you may know, they had both been damaged by divorce and were reluctant to try marriage again. It was Alissa's acceptance that helped guide Roland into a relationship that *he told me* was the happiest time of his life."

"I don't get what it was about Mom that caused these people to speak so favorably of her. Next thing you know, I would have expected the pope to show up for the canonization," said Katie. "You would never have heard anything like this from our father. He didn't think they should ever have married."

"I can speak only for Roland. With my brother, his negative attitude was keeping him unhappy and distrustful. He had to get to the point when he could discard his old, bad memories. Until you do so, you are only hurting yourself. Being loved unconditionally brought forth what we French call *joie de vivre*."

"I thought Mom said Roland gave the *joy of life to her*," said Katie.

"I'm so pleased to learn that. You see, Katie? That shows they were right for each other," said Catherine.

"That's prosaic. It almost sounds trite. It doesn't do anything for me. I still don't get it. You are making this sound like Mom had some extraordinary secret."

"It's no secret," said Catherine, "your mother knew that self-contempt and self-pity are sisters. They usually indicate a lack of fulfillment, and they breed anger. Anger will destroy you."

"Yeah," said Josh, "and you'll get no help from Mom; she took her secrets to the grave with her. Oh well, maybe she'll pop up out of her grave and tell us what we missed."

"She's not going into the ground, Josh," said Katie. "She's being cremated. Didn't you know that?"

"Mother, you didn't tell me that," said Millicent. "I assumed that since Grandma was in an open casket, she would be buried."

"What difference does it make?" asked Cal. "She wanted both."

"It makes a difference to me," said Millicent. "If she is to be cremated, I want her ashes. I will have her ashes made into a diamond. Human ashes are carbon based, you know."

"Oh yeah, I think I remember something about carbon-based humans from a *Star Trek*

"The man-made version is a genuine diamond. It has all the sparkle and durability of any from the mines in Africa," said Millicent.

Katie was shocked. "You would use Africa as an example. That's so bigoted. Haven't you heard of the horrible civil wars intensified because they were financed by blood diamonds?"

Millicent paused to reflect on her request for the ashes. "Yes, Mother, I have heard of the blood diamonds. I know about the injustices in the mines, the creation of war lords, and that trading in them is used to finance insurgencies--but this diamond will not be one of those. This diamond will represent my ancestral lineage—my personal blood line. I will wear it proudly."

Josh suspected that his sister and her daughter were headed for an unpleasant confrontation. He changed the subject. "Cremated, excavated, ashes, smashes: what's the difference? Come on, Cal, you were telling us about Mom. We want to know the top-secret scoop. Forget those Air Force Office of Special Investigations restrictions. You can tell us. Pretend we have security clearances. You don't have to keep any secrets," he said ploddingly. "What was Mom's specialty? And don't embarrass us by telling us it was sex—remember there are children here."

"Okay, if you haven't figured it out for yourself by now, I guess I will have to spell it out for you," said Cal with a smile. "Alissa said the secret of life was that you don't always have to have an answer. The difference between wisdom and being a smart aleck is to know when to keep your mouth shut. You could take a lesson here yourself, Josh. Always having to have a comment shows insecurity. Your mother spent a lifetime looking for the clues that showed that kind of insecurity in herself, and she was constantly working on healing the fears that caused it."

"I love it, Cal," said Catherine, giving him a kiss on each cheek. "That is Alissa in a nutshell. But I have to leave this wonderful gathering now. We must keep in touch."

"Do you have a ride?" asked Cal.

"Oh, yes, my niece brought me. She is waiting in the car so I could speak with you alone." Catherine pulled Cal aside. "I almost forgot what I wanted most to tell you. Maybe I shouldn't bring this up after all. Everything was so perfect today, but I think you should have a private talk with the funeral director."

"Why is that, Catherine?"

"Well, when I was leaning over Alissa's body to say good-bye, I noticed something totally unacceptable. It really spoiled an otherwise perfect farewell to our dear Alissa. If I saw it, maybe others did too."

Catherine saw a whimsical smile beginning to form on Cal's face, but she was determined to continue. "There was dust in the casket, Cal. It was quite noticeable. There was a clump of gray house dust as big as my thumb. I've never seen anything like that at a funeral before. Where were they keeping her body? It's disgraceful. I thought I should bring it to your attention."

"That was part of Alissa's last wishes."

"Oh. I misunderstood," said Catherine considering that dust in the casket might be symbolic. It might have something to do with the passage in Ecclesiastes chapter 3 that read, "From dust we came and to dust we shall return." She was embarrassed that she had not thought of the symbolism on her own.

"I'm so sorry. Is the dust there for religious significance?"

"No Ma'am, it's not religious. It's Alissa's idea. She wants to feel at home no matter where she might be going. You know her resistance to tidiness. She tried to convince me that creative people can't be tidy...like cleaning up after yourself might intrude on your talent. I am the neat freak in our household. Since we've been married, I have been the collector and destroyer of killer dust balls. I look at dust balls as predators and invaders. I destroy them all. I have to admit, it was a bit of a feat to grant her this last wish. I had to move the refrigerator to find some to collect for her casket."

"*Mon dieu!*" said Catherine.

"Yes, really," said Josh, stepping up to the plate to help his stepfather in a sneak play. "I saw him with my own eyes. Cal was wearing rubber gloves because of contamination control, and he put the dust he collected into an envelope. Then it was hermetically sealed, and transported in a diplomatic pouch to—"

"Stop...Stop...Stop," Katie interrupted, "it's enough to tell Catherine that Cal and Alissa complemented each other."

"Grandmother Alissa said it was against her religion to be a neat freak. She said that she and Cal were compatible because she made the clutter and Cal cleaned it up," said Millicent.

"I think a good dustup now and then is good for any relationship," Ken said with a laugh. "Don't you, honey?" he suggested putting his arm around Katie's waist, "It clears the air and makes making up worth waiting for."

But Katie was no longer interested in housekeeping jokes. She saw something her brother should know about. "Speaking about right for each other—look who just arrived, Josh. Check out the parking lot. Mr. Wrong just got out of his car. He's late for our mother's funeral. Does this surprise you?"

In a whisper, Josh said, "Sam always was slow. Mom would have been better off if he had been late for their marriage."

"Like fifty years late," said Katie, laughing.

"What are you two snickering about?" asked Cal.

"See that couple over there?" asked Katie pointing toward the path to the entrance of the chapel. "That's Sam Woods and his first and third wives."

"I only see one woman," said Cal.

"Right," said Josh "Meg--she's been recycled."

"He probably doesn't know the service is over. Shall we invite him here to talk to us?"

"No!" said Josh. "Please don't do that. It's better if we ignore him. You'd only find out he has nothing to say and takes forever to say it."

"We should ask him if he brought the money he owes Mom," said Katie.

"Come on. Let's get out of here before Sam sees us. I'll bet he is here to be sure that Mom is dead. If you recall, their divorce settlement stipulated that Mom would inherit his pension benefits. He's probably checking to see if he's finally off the hook."

Seeing no activity on the cemetery grounds, the tardy couple asked directions from two mortuary workers who were on their way to the chapel to remove Alissa's casket to the crematorium.

"Where would I find the memorial service for Alice Woods?" asked Sam.

"There is no Alice Woods service here today," said one of the workers.

"Are you sure you have the right day?" asked Meg with a whimper.

"I'm certain it's today. She must be here somewhere."

"Sorry," said the mortuary worker. "If you check at the office, they can tell you when the Alice Woods funeral is scheduled."

"Oh," said Sam, gathering his wits. "That's right. Sorry about that. I mean Alice Michaels. Where is the Alice Michaels funeral?"

"There is no Alice Michaels here either," said the second worker.

"Let's go home, Sam," said Meg, "It's beginning to rain. There is no funeral here today. I don't see any open holes."

Sam was searching his memory for his ex-wife's current married name. He became irritated. "Do you have an Alice Zach?"

"We have an Alissa Zach. If that's who you are looking for, follow us. We're on our way there now to take things down."

"You mean the funeral is over?" asked Sam, looking more confused than ever.

"Looks like she didn't wait for you, Mister," the second worker said, laughing. "Maybe she would have hung around waiting for you to show up if you knew her well enough to remember her name."

Meanwhile, back at the bed of wildflowers, the door opening to admit the mortuary workers brought a burst of desert wind that caused the petals of the flowers to stir. At least the workers thought it was the wind that rustled the lilies.

Unaware of the scene at the coffin, the last mourners were departing. Katie was considering that her mother could still hear her and was feeling uncomfortable about some of the things she had said about her. Josh was contemplating his mother's promise to return, and he so wished that could happen that he finally gave up the facade of joking and allowed his true grief to rise. He slumped against the exterior of the car and tried to pull himself together, but he could not. He collapsed into an uncontrollable, anguished, heartfelt, primal cry. Ken gently urged Josh to join his wife in the car for privacy. Unable to engage in any conversation about her late mother-in-law because of her tears, Rachel had been grieving for hours in isolation.

Cal was determined to keep her presence with him. He took his leave of the place and walked upright and courageously, no longer in a dress uniform at a military parade, but always maintaining a military posture. The old man pressed forward upon his cane as if it was the only thing left in his life sturdy enough to bear the weight of his pain.

After embraces and promises to keep in touch, Katie, Ken, Millicent, and Joy left for the airport, with Josh driving the rental car, but not before Millicent arranged to have her grandmother's ashes sent to her for reconstitution into a diamond. As the cars left the parking lot, little Joy Windsor called attention to something special. A rainbow with colors as vivid as any she had ever seen suddenly appeared. It was anchored to the mausoleum at one end and floated off into the distant foothills at the other end.

Joy pointed. "Look, Mommy! Is that Grandma Great going to heaven?"

For Cal, the image of the rainbow and the perfume of the mariposa lilies would become the presence of Alissa that would be with him to the end of his days. She would never die.

He left for Sedona alone, driving straight through until he arrived at the home they had shared. Once there, he took the wilted mariposa lily out of his jacket lapel and placed the limp brown remnant into the page of Alissa's Bible, where their wedding verse, Song of Solomon 8:6 (ESV) was found: "Set me as a seal upon your heart, as a seal upon your arm; for love is strong as death." He slumped into his favorite chair on the back patio, watching the sun set on another glorious day as he whispered to the heavens, *Rest in peace, my beloved.*

ONE

Boarding the Ship

All stories have to begin somewhere, and for Alissa Barrett, her story began sixty years before she was born on a day that was filled with hopeful anticipation for her great-grandfather Carolus Baelan, who was proudly bringing his beloved wife and three beautiful daughters to the United States. The invitation to work in New York had come from a colleague Carolus had met when they were chemistry students in Paris.

His was not a family among the "huddled masses yearning to breathe free," for which the Statue of Liberty holds her torch of welcome. Carolus's position as instructor in Matei Basarab, the newly established secondary school in Bucharest, was prestigious, affording his wife, Rozalia, and the girls the social status and the financial means for her to continue to explore her own interests. Carolus's only concern on that day of departure was that his wife was reluctant to leave Bucharest.

Rozalia had been engaged for years working with her cousin Dimitrie Brandza to establish the Botanical Garden at Bucharest. The supervision of the garden was assured by the new director, Ulrich Hoffmann, who was successfully managing the seventeen-and-a-half hectares. It was spring, and the new seedlings were beginning to grow. Soon visitors would be able to tour the gardens that she had conceived--had helped plan.

Rozalia had dreamed of the day when the founders of Gradina Botanica din Bucuresti would begin taking bows for their work. She was more than disappointed that Carolus was pulling her away—she was hostile to the idea. She saw no purpose in leaving all this to go to New York City, where no one would know of her accomplishments. She brooded silently on the train ride to Antwerp, staring out the window of their compartment and making the trip through central Europe seem longer with her disinterest in her surroundings.

Gabi and Elena were as eager as their father to make this trip. They had dreams of their own about treasures that might await them in the United States. *What would the young men be like in New York?* They giggled and whispered at the thought of marrying cowboys or even Indians. Rozalia shuddered at the teenagers' empty-headed chatter.

The Baelan family wasn't escaping Romania. Their life there was comfortable and secure. Carolus had benefited from the financial position his merchant father and providence had provided. His father had the means to pay for a good education for all his sons, and studying in Paris put Carolus in touch with important contacts, among them the young Elizabeth Pauline of Wied who was destined to become the queen of the Romanian Royal House. But Carolus was not a man to rely on others for support. He was by nature independent, confident, and courageous. Teaching was a rewarding profession, and he enjoyed being part of the new school. But his passion wasn't fulfilled in the classroom. He was a true scientist, and the position promised in New York would give him the opportunity to do experimental research. He would have free reign to test theories that he was already tossing around in his mind. He saw a brighter future in the adventuresome opportunity he would have in the United States than the security he was leaving behind. Carolus couldn't wait to board the ship.

"Name?" called out the purser of the steamship *Atlantis,* checking the names of first-class passengers on the May 2, 1877 reservations list.

"Carolus Baelan and Rozalia from Bucharest," said Carolus, showing the purser their Romanian passports and exit papers, "with our daughters.

We bring our baby Elisabeta, eleven months old, and here is our Gabriela," he said, proudly urging Gabi forward. "She is fourteen, and our young lady Elena is age sixteen. She is Ilinca on the application."

Gabi and Elena were blossoming young women. Their dark-brown hair, held back tightly with ribbons, showed off their beautiful features, long eyelashes, and sparkling brown eyes. Any father would be proud to show them off.

As the steamship left its moorings, the girls were at the rails, watching every move through the channel and out to sea. The ocean breeze pulled the ribbons from their hair, they flirted with the young seamen, and they ran from stem to stern as far as the deck was open for exploration. They did not want to miss anything about this adventure, so it wasn't until land had completely escaped their sight that they headed to their cabin, where they would face their mother's admonitions to behave like proper young ladies and remember their social class.

At sea, the voyage became tedious. Carolus passed the time in conversations with fellow male passengers. Men from several European countries were aboard the *Atlantis*, and Carolus, the social butterfly, soon became popular among them. He was fluent in French, Italian, and English from his studies abroad, and German and Romanian were his mother tongues.

But there was nothing to sustain the interest of the girls. To help them adjust to their new home, they read Carolus' German books about this new democratic country of the United States. They helped care for their baby sister--understanding that Elisabeta, born during Rozalia's later years, was a special blessing. But Rozalia put an end to the girls' free range of the decks, leaving them with no one to talk to except their little family. After a few days, discussions about the United States were beginning to get stale.

No one aboard the ship knew, as they were approaching the mid-point of their voyage, that a major Atlantic storm was brewing. It came up suddenly.

Without warning, deck chairs were tossed by the wind. Swells became waves. The captain adjusted the ship's bearing to ride the waves head on.

Passengers who had never before been to sea did not understand how a ship this large could be tossed around like a cork in a bottle.

Carolus found his family huddled in their cabin. Rozalia was especially frightened and held her baby close to her. The tossing and turning of the ship were giving them all a severe case of *mal de mer* (seasickness). Nausea ripped through them as the waves crashed against the ship and erased any enthusiasm they had had a few days earlier. Each rolling movement of the ship caused them to reject any food they had just swallowed, and the stench of the vomit was overpowering. Their bodies weakened.

The storm lasted for days. Carolus cried out in prayer, "Oh God, help my family." *Was I too selfish thinking only of the possibilities of my new career? Have I forsaken my responsibilities to my family? They don't deserve this. A woman like my Rose should not have to deal with these physical conditions. Let us live through this, and allow me to see the joy of my family as they breathe the inviting air of the United States."*

◆ ◆ ◆

Meanwhile, the people below the decks in steerage class had more than an Atlantic storm to contend with. It started with the oldest and the youngest passengers among them developing a croup-like barking cough. It was common for babies to develop the croup, so at first no one was alarmed. But other oddities were noticed. Soon, the healthier immigrants were contributing to the cacophony of harsh coughing. Necks swelled, gray patches developed in throats, and within days some observed blood oozing from faces, arms, and legs. At this point, below the decks, the provincial people were beginning to believe this evil was punishment from god for not being satisfied with what they had left behind in their homeland. Until then, no one had yet died.

Above decks in the Baelan stateroom, Gabriela and Ilinca were complaining of sore throats. When Rozalia examined them, she observed white patches in their throats, and it seemed their necks were beginning to swell. She was uneasy about this but ordered the girls to gargle with salted water and stay in bed to keep warm. This appeared to be an ordinary cold, probably brought on because of their weakened condition from the bout with seasickness. She gave her daughters the handkerchiefs they had embroidered themselves for the sniffles she expected to come.

Rozalia mentioned this in passing to Carolus. But she was not aware of the true nature of the illness or the ordeals and perilous times they would have to face before this voyage was over. She watched her daughters starting to shiver. They complained of painful swallowing and difficulty breathing. She was beginning to become alarmed. By now, all three of her children had taken ill. The baby was the worst, too weak to cry as the wrenching cough of the croup and fever was taking all vitality from her little body.

Rozalia knew she was losing control to something ominous. Days rushed by in a blur as she focused only on trying to nurse her daughters back to health. The coughing got worse.

"Mama, look what is on my handkerchief," cried Gabi as she showed her the blood mixed in her nasal discharge. "I have a nosebleed."

Rozalia knew this was more than a common nosebleed; this specimen was foul-smelling. She asked Gabi to pull open her nightgown. The examination showed ugly skin lesions oozing small amounts of blood on her daughter's arms and legs.

"Carolus," Rozalia cried out in despair, "go among the people we are traveling with to see if there is a medical doctor aboard who can tell us what is happening to my family."

It did not take Carolus long to learn that the mysterious condition was diphtheria, a disease recognized in Europe since the fifth century and known often to be fatal. He had to warn Rozalia.

While the older girls struggled in a hopeless, losing battle, Carolus was left with nothing to do but pray for healing. Rozalia held her frail infant as closely as possible and rocked back and forth, humming a lullaby from her childhood in Romania.

Go to sleep, my tiny baby. Try to sleep and get asleep, till the white dawn breaks the day. Then wake up as a grown child. Get asleep, my tiny baby. Till tomorrow in the dawn.

She knew her baby might not grow to childhood. She fell into desolation and succumbed to an ominous vision. In it, a dark shadow was creeping along the decks. She saw tentacles of the dreaded disease diphtheria traveling from the steerage decks below, where she knew it had taken root, and was now reaching into the staterooms of the passengers on the first and second-class decks. Like the Wagnerian opera *Tannhäuser*, pounding the bombastic message of conflict into an audience, the disease pounded the passengers trapped on a floating deathtrap into submission. Rozalia knew there would be no thunderous applause at the end of this journey. The scourge aboard this ship was triumphant. It was defeating the hopes and expectations of all classes of passengers.

Gabriela broke Rozalia's spell with her faint complaint. "I'll never see cowboys or Indians. Mama, I feel only like I want to die," she moaned.

"Shush, shush, shush," said Rozalia, trying to think of something to encourage her daughter. "Don't speak of such things. The women of our heritage are strong, and this will pass."

"Mama, I feel the same way," cried Elena, almost too weak to enter her protest. "Help us, Mama. Give us something to make us feel better."

Carolus was watching but had nothing to offer his beautiful Gabriela and Ilinca or the baby, who was too young to tell him how badly she felt. He knew the path of the disease and that there was nothing anyone could do to help his family. He quietly slipped out of the stateroom and found his way up the stairs to the main deck, hoping the ocean breeze would bring a whisper from God to encourage him. This was in God's domain, and Carolus knew it. There was no one on the decks to help console him. He stood on the windswept deck alone. No one but he was strong or brave enough to be there while entire families were dying about the ship of death. He wished for the wind to be strong enough to blow away the disease but it brought him only a cold chill. There would be no help. The only insight Carolus received that day came from within his own heart: *Any measure of success I might have accomplished in this New World would be a pyrrhic victory.*

He returned to the stateroom discouraged, despondent, and full of dread, knowing what might lie in store. When he arrived, he was in a stupor of disillusionment and felt naked in his vulnerability to a disease that would run its course, taking some and leaving others.

The sight of his family made him weep openly. There was no longer a need to present a brave front for the sake of his children. The older girls were blue and lifeless. They had passed from this life, showing the pain and suffering on their tightly held lips and their final act on earth--clutching each other in despair.

The baby, still sheltered in her mother's arms, was miraculously still alive. She was crying weakly, showing her mother that she had improved enough to faintly request care. Rozalia looked up to the heavens and said, "No mother should have to lose a child. You have taken two. I won't let you have this one."

Rozalia noticed that her husband had returned. Screaming and crying in rage and despair, she cursed her husband. "Damn your New World." She was almost suffocating baby Elisabeta with her will to keep the infant alive. "Not this child. You can't have this child. I'll tear the eyes out of anyone who harms my baby. Our family is being cursed," she said crying herself into a stupor of sleep.

Carolus gently took Elisabeta from her mother's arms, washed the baby to soothe her, changed her clothes, and laid her on a clean bed, whispering his thankfulness for the blessing of his baby's life.

There indeed was a curse on this family. Carolus created a name for this dysfunction. He called it Diphtheria Affected Crippling Negative Anxiety, or DACNA for short. What he and his wife did not realize was that it would become the causation of dysfunction into future generations of their family.

◆◆◆

Two days after journey's end, Carolus' friend Otto von Stuben arrived in New Bedford, Massachusetts, to take them to the apartment he had arranged for them in New York City. He was shocked with what he saw. Rozalia was dressed totally in mourning black, and her demeanor was of a woman twenty years older than she had looked three years ago, when Otto had last seen her. Carolus was carrying the baby, and he assisted Rozalia into the carriage. She was too weak to walk.

Otto knew about the loss of the girls from the telegraph that Carolus had sent from shipboard describing the epidemic of diphtheria and his thankfulness that the ship was not scheduled to arrive in New York–where the sick passengers would be at risk of being sent back—at the shipper's expense—by the doctors at Ellis Island.

"I'm so sorry, Rozalia," he said, taking her in his arms. "But I thank God you and your baby survived this terrible misfortune. Please allow me to take you to the apartment I arranged for you in New York City. Your travels are not yet over. It will be three more days of travel; however, this part of the trip is not so dangerous."

◆ ◆ ◆

As they approached the city, Rozalia finally succumbed to her fatigue and was able to fall into peaceful sleep. She allowed the gentle swaying of the carriage and the syncopated clatter of the hooves of the horses on the brick streets to relax her. Baby Elisabeta had been fed and was quietly resting in her father's lap while he watched the activity in the bustling city. The sun was setting, and as the rays of the sunset melted into darkness, Carolus hoped the pain of their journey would one day be erased from their memories. But that wasn't going to happen without further distraction.

In the city, a new odor filtered into the cab of the carriage. It grew stronger, and soon it woke Rozalia from her repose.

"What is that?" she asked in disgust.

"Smells like fish, doesn't it?" Otto said with a laugh. "Don't worry; your apartment is not in the city. It's in my neighborhood, near the college. You'll find people there you will be comfortable with."

"I don't speak English," declared Rozalia, not wanting to cooperate with her new conditions.

"That's not necessary, Rozie. In fact, there is another family from Romania there; you will have someone to talk to. But we do have to drive through the city to get there. I timed our journey for the evening so you would not be too alarmed. We have our work cut out for us to improve New York City."

Rozalia sat upright. "It doesn't smell like fish to me. What kind of fish do you have in New York?"

"We have some oyster-processing plants in this neighborhood," said Otto. "We will pass this soon."

"It's making me sick to my stomach."

Smoke from melting tar caused the horses to snort. Fires from burning animal fat lighted the sky. Elisabeta began to cry. Carolus tried to comfort her. Rozalia was angry.

"Now I smell liquor."

"We have many kinds of food being processed here in the city—molasses, sugar..."

"You must have slaughterhouses as well," said Carolus. "And look at that. Over there, ahead, and to the side, I see animals rotting right there in the streets, and there is garbage in the gutters. Good grief, Stuben, this is not a scientific challenge you have here. This is a basic sanitation problem."

Rozalia vomited. This was not from the intermingling of the odors. After the voyage on the ship, she could tolerate sickening smells. But the sight of raw sewage with human excrement flowing into the street, illuminated by the gas lampposts, was more than she could handle. It reminded her of the way the serfs in Romania lived in crowded, primitive shacks. A sudden, overwhelming fear overcame her. Would these surroundings bring her down to that level of existence?

"I'm so sorry, Rozalia," said Otto. "Try to think of this as a challenge. Your husband and I will be well paid to put an end to this."

Carolus was inspired by *Tannhäuser* too. "Rozalia, think of this all as a struggle to be remedied. We will not be waiting only for the staff in the pope's hand to sprout leaves. Otto and I will be instrumental in making that happen."

"I have already lost two daughters," screamed Rozalia. "What more do I have to sacrifice?"

Carolus, filled with guilt, tried to comfort his beloved wife. He took her hand and drew her fingers to touch his lips with a kiss.

But Otto, having trouble keeping the carriage horses under control, was not happy with her outburst. "I'm deeply sorry for your loss," he began, trying to keep his voice low to conceal his exasperation. "But my dear lady, you are not the only woman to lose a child. Our beloved queen and friend, Elisabeta of Wied, lost her young child—Maria has died too. Even the royal family cannot escape grief."

Carolus and Rozalia had not yet heard this news, but Carolus knew it would not be comforting to his wife. Rozalia and Elisabeta of Wied were as close as sisters. Rozalia loved Maria and had been given the honor of being chosen to be the child's godmother only four years earlier.

"But Maria was not killed by diphtheria on a steamship full of serfs," she professed.

"No, Rozalia. Maria died of scarlet fever."

◆◆◆

It was Rozalia's good fortune that her husband's talents contributed to the cleaning of the air in the city of New York. His position was lucrative and allowed them to live in the prestigious district of Lennox Hill on Manhattan Island and for Elisabeta to receive the finest education available to New York City women of the time. Carolus tried to make up for the emptiness caused by the loss of their beautiful daughters by showering Rozalia with gifts at every opportunity.

Whenever Rozalia was in one of her peevish moods, he would arrive with something to try to cheer her up. The gifts did not change her. Even the pair of three-karat diamond earrings did not move her off the couch of despair or out of her black dresses.

◆◆◆

Twelve years later, one of those world-changing events occurred that people often attribute to an act of god. Otto was the one to bring the news.

"Have you heard of the publication of Robert Koch's germ theory?" he asked Carolus one day at work.

Koch had been their classmate years ago, and they both knew their German colleague had been doing a great deal of lab work since graduation. Koch's teacher, Jacob Henie, had postulated as early as 1840 that diseases were caused by microorganisms.

"Herr Doktor Koch has made a breakthrough. Look at this, Carolus. Robert used that microscope of his to discover something they are calling bacteria. It proves` a contagion source of disease. This will be revolutionary."

Carolus knew what this would mean for his wife. She had already been convinced that the immigrants in the hull of the ship had sent the diphtheria to the first-class passengers. Now his colleague Koch had identified both diphtheria and scarlet fever as diseases spread by bacteria. He would never be able to dissuade his wife that the huddled masses in the bottom of the ship or economic slums were the cause of the loss of her daughters as well as the daughter of Elisabeta of Wied. Now Rozie would be more convinced than ever that her psychic experience was a valid interpretation of the disease traveling from the hold of the ship into her stateroom. Carolus decided not to tell Rozalia about the discovery that microorganisms cause disease. Keeping her uninformed might keep her from empowering her vitriol.

Elisabeta's upbringing was influenced by her mother's anger and played out in Rozalia's overbearing attitude that stifled the young child. Rozalia so resented the loss of her two beautiful daughters taken from her in the spring of their lives that she saw the plain, ordinary, and sickly Elisabeta as a poor substitute for the vivacious, beautiful, young women Gabi and Ilinca were growing into while Rozalia watched with prideful joy.

Whenever Rozalia looked at Elisabeta, it reminded her of her loss. Gabriela and Ilinca were clever and smart; Elisabeta was awkward and uninteresting. All rooms brightened when Gabi and Ilinca entered; no one noticed when Elisabeta arrived unless it was to notice her frail stature brought on by the cardiac arrhythmia when diphtheria had weakened her heart. Rozalia indulged her. Neither parent believed she would marry. Carolus thought a good education would help Elisabeta and hoped Hunter College would give her an opportunity to choose a career to her liking.

To her parents' dismay, Elisabeta wasn't suited for teaching because she did not like being around noisy, fussing children. She did not like nursing, as it put her in contact with riffraff (a prejudice learned from her mother), and she wasn't interested in public health for the same reason. Elisabeta was interested only in encouraging her mother's indulgence. She thrived on being pampered, waited upon, and catered to. None of that was being offered at the college.

It wasn't long before Elisabeta came home with the announcement that she had married. Carolus and Rozalia were stunned. In their wildest nightmare, they had never imagined such an outcome would result from their careful sheltering of their child. The young man she had chosen was tall and handsome. He loved their daughter, whom he affectionately called Eli. But that was all he had to offer.

Eli introduced Franz Kiraly to her parents as the former groomsman for the prized horses of the king of Hungary. The young immigrant, who could barely speak English, was no more than a stable hand from Rozalia's point of view--and a horse thief in the eyes of Carolus. Franz moved into the Baelan household. His only contribution to posterity was to sire two healthy daughters, Hester and Jane whom Carolus and Rozalia helped raise.

Jane was the Baelans' favored granddaughter. She was beautiful and talented and reminded them of the two daughters they had lost. So while the older daughter Hester became the housemaid for Eli and Franz, Jane was indulged and pampered in much of the way that her mother had been. But most damaging of all to family dynamics was the fact that Carolus and Rozalia indulged Jane the same way they had indulged Eli (albeit for different reasons). So Jane got a double dose of being pampered, and to add to her status, her father Franz called Jane his little princess and a gift from god. No one had much to say about Hester.

◆ ◆ ◆

Rozalia died as she had lived--full of misery. She was buried in one of her black dresses, requested no music at her funeral, and had instructed Carolus not to let anyone know of her passing. These were easy requests to honor, because the woman had made no friends in the United States, and no one but her family would be at the funeral anyway.

Her passing gave Carolus a new lease on life. He had never overcome the fact that he could never satisfy his wife since leaving Romania. He was relieved that he no longer had to try. As his retirement approached, Carolus had finally achieved the success he had sought in the United States. By now, the scientists in New York had achieved their goal of cleaning the air and water in the city. He had left his mark on history, and along the way he had made many friends and admirers among the people in New York. His gift for languages was valuable to the project as it gave him the opportunity to speak to the ever-increasing immigrant population in their native tongues.

With Rozalia's passing, the mood picked up at the house. Her black dresses were gone, shades were no longer drawn and even the window treatments were changed. Franz (whom Carolus continued to call the former horse thief who escaped from having a rope around his neck) replaced the dark drapes with bright, colorful curtains, which let in the light. He celebrated by buying his first car and used his eye for fashion and the cash from selling some of Rozalia's jewelry to open a gentlemen's haberdashery. As the business became successful, every Christmas Franz enjoyed giving the men in his family a beautiful new tie, thusly creating the family mantra, "Kiraly left hemp for silk."

One Christmas, after Franz had his late mother-in-law's diamond earrings made into two rings, he proudly gave one to his bedridden wife Eli and the other to his current bedfellow, Molly Malone, as a token of his divided love and affection.

TWO

Be Careful What You Wish For

We are all the products of our environment, and some are a casualty of the people who most injured us in our early years. Alissa Barrett was no exception. Alissa was never fed on the milk of mother's love. She was given a daily dose of vitriol from her mother that would disable her and mold her persona into a child without the ability to stand her ground or face painful truths. This was due to the fact that she had a mother who carried into her maternal role anger from her own past. Alissa's mother Hester the housemaid in the Kiraly family, misdirected her malice in an attempt to deflect her own unhappiness and took her vengeance out on her only child. In the early years, when Alissa did not have the ability to decipher the cause of her own unhappiness and wanted only to be loved, the influence of her mother turned Alissa into a child who believed she had no value.

The shadow of Hester's discontent adversely influenced Alissa's self-image almost her entire life. There was no one in Alissa's childhood who was aware of or could have staved off this damage because, while Alissa was experiencing her mother's screaming words of fire, lava, and incessant criticism, Hester presented herself *to everyone she met* as an intelligent and personable woman, while the Jekyll-and-Hyde personality was a conundrum to Alissa. The child came to believe that her mother's criticisms of her must be valid because everyone else seemed to hold Hester in high esteem.

First, Alissa had to become aware of the dysfunction that served to impede her. Initially, this awakening created hatred, but over time as Alissa learned to accept her mother for who she was, the hatred cooled. Alissa's salvation was that she was able to overcome these obstacles and grow into the woman she was meant to be.

Alissa's father George had other issues. He had studied law and sat for the state bar exam, but he received only a passing grade on his first try and his pride would not allow him to settle for anything less than a grand entrance into a new career. Certain he would receive a higher score if he were to take the exam again, George did not apply for licensing. This brought a lot of criticism from his parents. But instead of bowing to their pressure and applying for the licensing he had earned the right too, he chose to prove himself in another way.

He persuaded the most popular girl in town to run off with him to be married. This would have to be done secretly as the couple was young. Hester Kiraly's wealthy father attracted many offers for marriage to her but she accepted George Barrett--perhaps because of his good looks. George Barrett was a proper man who would not have participated in any premarital promiscuity, so marriage before sex was his only option. When the family learned that Hester and George were living together, they insisted on a wedding, and the young couple obliged without ever disclosing that they already were married. It wasn't until years later, when Hester and George were being moved into an old-age home, that George's brother Bill discovered both marriage licenses.

◆ ◆ ◆

In 1938, during the Great Depression, like many young men, George could not find work. He was overqualified for every position he applied for, and employers were not willing to hire a man who would leave as soon as the economy turned around. George knew he was smart and had no problem letting anyone know it. But he wasn't assertive during job interviews, and because he did not have a mind for business, many opportunities slipped by. This may have had to do with the pessimistic attitude of that time. But it also might have been due to his unwillingness to test fate.

George had been raised on literature and loved short stories. His favorite was "The Monkey's Paw," by W. W. Jacobs, and he often quoted the passage "fate ruled people's lives, and those who interfered with it did so to their sorrow." He put this phrase to use whenever he did not want to face disappointment so it was not a surprise that when he finally did sit for the bar exam again, his score was even lower. Anyone else might attribute this to the fact that it had been years since he was in law school, but George attributed it to fate. The fear imposed by Jacobs when the protagonist in his story created terrible conditions by wanting wishes to come true was instrumental in feeding the pessimism in George. He never achieved sufficient courage to work toward achieving his own personal dreams.

Hester wasn't influenced by the Jacobs story and saw her husband's lack of achievement as a personality defect. This became a major source of contention throughout their lives together.

With a baby soon to arrive, George decided to help his father with the family printing business in Huntington, New York. Grandpa Barrett did not have enough money to put him on the payroll, but he was willing to take a chance on an idea he had learned about. He sent George on a trip to Czechoslovakia to contact a man who had developed a more economic printing process, using synthetic ink. This meant Hester was left behind with a small child and no money. Her only income came from the boarders she took in to the large house they rented on Maple Avenue. If anyone asked where her husband was, she would explain, "He's a bouncing check and I'm staying at home to cover it."

To make matters worse, the business contact didn't work out and the trip was to no avail because the Czech printer could not be found.

Whenever George asked about him, people would refuse to talk and would try to hush him up. The trip was aborted when a neighbor of the man in Prague took George aside to say, "Please, go away, if you have any heart. They are rounding up Jews here for God knows why. Asking about his business only draws attention to him." To George's frustration, he returned home empty-handed, in his heart believing again it was fate but in reality it was the product of the times.

◆ ◆ ◆

When a family is poor, food becomes the primary focus of attention. The benefit of Hester stretching her "house money" was that she and the new baby Alissa never went hungry. Sometimes, this meant a menu of cooked cereal and milk for breakfast, a lunch of macaroni and cheese, and an evening meal of soup du jour. Hester's style of cooking was to line up each item on the counter and carefully measure the ingredients over the mixing bowl. She would scrape the top of the measuring spoon or cup with a knife and allow the excess to drop into the bowl. This system played havoc with recipes in which success depended upon a proper mix of ingredients, but it measured up to Hester's insistence on not wasting a crumb of food.

When George returned home without the secret printing process he had sought, he was wearing the twenty pounds Mama had lost on her sparse diet. Hester wondered what he was doing to get fat when these were such lean times in the United States. He certainly wasn't putting any meat on her bones. She figured he must have been eating well in Europe or drinking a lot of the local Pils.

"You look like a bratwurst," she would say.

"And you remind me of sauerkraut," he would respond.

With disrespect like this, it was no wonder their marriage was in a pickle. Thus began years of bickering, taunting, egging on, and unabashed family fights. Divorce was not in Hester's vocabulary. That was no way out. Hester wanted to kill him and systematic torture was her way of accomplishing this. Hester's anger hit the top of the scale when George was so happy to see baby Alissa. He called her a "gift from god," a loving remark that met Hester's ears with hurt and insult. These were the exact words her father had used for her younger sister Jane.

So, while George lavished a young Alissa with attention, Hester openly displayed cold indifference to her or taking out her anger by belittling her child at every opportunity. She would deviously attribute trivial mishaps to Alissa. But these were often fabrications to create an image of a child who was totally inept, mean-spirited, sloppy, and useless. This was Hester's way to get even with both her husband and the child she perceived to be a threat to her husband's attention. Hester was most happy as long as she could keep Alissa unhappy and keep her husband from having any power. She accomplished this by exercising control of the family, whether it was in the form of open hostility or covert manipulation.

As soon as George realized his "gift from god" acclamation annoyed Hester, he used it every time he wanted to bait his wife into a confrontation. Little did he know the phrase went to the core of Hester's embedded anger and hurt her in ways she was unable to overcome.

But even without the status of being employed, George tried to reassume his status as head of the house. This was a sham, because Hester decided how the money would be spent; George wrote the checks, but Hester decided which bills would be paid and what obligations the family would take on.

◆ ◆ ◆

George set admirable standards, but they belonged to a different time and to the age of chivalry that was no longer relevant. Hester was an impenetrable enigma that would take Alissa lifetime to understand. Alissa had no power to influence either of them, and they ignored her needs because they were too absorbed with their own petty issues. Alissa's opportunity to be a child slipped away before she learned how to play and, because she tried early on to understand this complicated social structure, she became more cerebral than was good for her social development.

Alissa was making observations and taking mental notes; but she was getting mixed signals. For example, George instilled the idea of personal privacy by insisting that bathrobes were worn to cover pajamas, doors on the bathroom were closed when in use, and her parent's bedroom door was locked at night. Although these habits were instilled in Alissa long before she was old enough to understand their purpose, she obeyed the letter of the law because, as a typical child, she knew conforming meant acceptance and approval.

One day when Hester was bathing Alissa, Aunt Jane came to visit. This was the first time Alissa had met her mother's sister. Hester disapproved of her sister Jane's lack of responsibility and had not encouraged her to visit. Jane insisted on coming into the bathroom to talk to Hester.

Modesty had been so ingrained in the child that Alissa picked up the hand towel and covered herself as best she could.

Aunt Jane mocked her by saying, "You think you have something different from anybody else?"

The child did not know what the "something" was that her aunt was commenting about, so for the entire time they were in the bathroom, Alissa did not remove the hand towel and wondered why the bathroom door had not locked out this unfamiliar intruder into her space.

Alissa's mother never put up with dirtiness, insisting that Alissa be scrubbed each day, tip to toe. She enforced the good-grooming code by combing Alissa's hair with a small-toothed pocket comb ensuring that all the knots were out of her long brown hair before tightly braiding it and catching each sprout of the natural curls that resisted being captured. Having Hester in charge of personal hygiene often meant pain and suffering would ensue but the ritualized torture impressed upon Alissa that being neat and clean was important indication of being properly raised.

Hester would lower her voice when she wanted her words to bring extra weight. It was as if subconsciously she believed the male voice command more compliance. But rather than sounding like a man, she produced a menacing sound more like the roar of an animal poised for attack of its prey. It was effective and if any of those people who viewed Hester as kind and caring had heard it, perhaps they would change their opinion.

"Go take a bath. You're filthy," she would say with the low raspy roar, giving Alissa a push in the direction of the bathroom.

"It's our fault if something should happen," Hester shouted to her husband after she heard the water running into the tub believing that Alissa was no longer able to hear them. "We are not preparing this child for the real world. All you give her is dreams and philosophy. We should give her tactics to use for survival and a real understanding of the way people are. People are no damn good. They are no damn good. The more people I know, the more I like my dog."

"It's 'The more I know people, the better I like dogs,'" said George, unwilling to look up from his newspaper to acknowledge his wife's concerns.

"What?" replied Hester, regaining the indignant mood that had become her personality trademark in the privacy of her home.

"Your quote—it's Mark Twain. Mama, tell me," he said, knowing he'd really caught her this time, "when have you owned a dog?"

The dog comparison was a serious indictment. She repeated it often; even though she did not like dogs, she liked people less.

But this was more than evil people and dogs. Hester believed her economic woes were caused by spending much of her budget to care for Alissa properly. She did not want to spend a penny of her money on Alissa. Her hatred of the child grew each time George doted on his little princess, and whenever Alissa required Hester's time, attention, and especially, her money, Hester's hatred would grow out of control. *The sight of her is making me sick. If only there was a way I could be rid of her.* Taking a deep breath she was able to calm herself momentarily but as her anger subsided, cold hard indifference took its place.

◆ ◆ ◆

When orders came down to Alissa from those large people with whom she lived, Alissa would concentrate carefully on the details to be sure she followed them to the letter of the law.

The words of her father, *Stay focused, Alissa,* rang in her ears even when he was not home to say them.

Put on your play clothes as soon as you come home from school. Don't bring home any riffraff. What will the neighbors think? coming from Mama's lips became irrevocable rules of conduct to be diligently enforced, not trite suggestions on standards for harmonious living.

Not wearing school clothes or work clothes at home was common practice during the Depression years. Most families, like the Barretts, did not replace things if they could avoid it. They tried to keep their clothing from becoming worn out. It was expensive, and most families wore their clothing until it was threadbare. In the days prior to automatic washers and dryers, doing laundry was a major task. No family would want to give the appearance of being poor because that was a reflection upon the father—the breadwinner—while the cleanliness of the clothing was a reflection on the mother. Both of these prohibitions against exposing the truth of a life of financial difficulty were justified by the anxiety-producing question, "What will people think?" This was reinforced by every parent who said, "We may not be from wealth, but we are proud enough to be clean."

It was as if the family that admitted they were overworked or poor or let their standards down by not being physically clean was admitting that they deserved their unfortunate circumstances. It was as if they were being punished by god, or fate, or luck because of something they might have done wrong. The idea of deserving your status was firmly established by history, custom, society, and the church. But those social constraints were not Hester's and George's reasons for conformity. In the Barrett family, George was inferring that Hester's standard of care of the house, no matter how clean, would never be adequate in his eyes, and Hester was saying, "How can I keep your household properly when you don't provide enough money for me to do so?"

Alissa was not told the reasons for these rules, and she had to work out the logic herself. It didn't help that both Mama and Daddy were inconsistent in their orders, and Alissa's self-image was evolving, so she incorrectly surmised it was because of a deficiency in *her* that rules were to be obeyed without compromise.

That is how Alissa came to believe that she had to change her clothes when she came home from school because she didn't deserve to wear good clothes except in public, when Mama and Daddy's image (not hers) must be maintained. She understood that it was permissible to wear her good clothes only to impress others for her parents. It wasn't because of her self-worth because she had none.

But times were not carefree for anyone during the Depression, and because of the economic tension, many children were being shaped without familial love and security. The Depression retreated from public consciousness to give center stage to a world war. Alissa soon learned of children in other parts of the world who were having a much more difficult time than she was. That was the first clue she had to understand that children are not to be blamed.

THREE

Help Wanted

George Barrett was the recipient of a letter from the government Selective Service. He had the choice of a military career or working as a printer at the US Government Printing Office in Washington, DC. Influenced by a pattern of always being in the red, George chose to entrust his future to the GPO and donate his blood to the Red Cross. Ink before blood, he reasoned. The relocation required him to move his family to a city where they did not know anyone, but it meant a steady salary for him that was sufficient to allow Hester to plan her household expenses with a consistent budget and still have enough to set aside a nest egg in her savings account. It was the richest time in their lives.

George loved the GPO position. He was proud to be following in the footsteps of his father. He would be making a good living with a reliable employer. But he wasn't printing the money. He was printing translation books for the military. At a time when the whole world was going to war, it gave him great pride and satisfaction to know that this job was important to the war effort and may have had the effect of helping humankind.

The house the Barretts rented in DC was a comfortable bungalow with a large swing on the back porch where Alissa spent happy hours reading to avoid the wrath of her mother. When George arrived home from work at the end of the day, he would fill Alissa with stories he heard from coworkers about the progress of the war. George had a special awareness of what was happening to ordinary people from his prewar trip to Czechoslovakia and the combination of these narratives of courage in the face of terror were captivating for the young girl. They presented a theme of possibility and hope, but to Alissa the narrative were no different from the images in her books. These were make-believe and had no connection with the reality of her life.

That year, Alissa won an art competition at school with her entry of a lovely scene of palm trees and water that she copied from a magazine at the dentist's office. It earned her a blue ribbon and a set of pastels. Mama would not allow the chalk into the house because it was too dusty, so the big back porch with the swing also served as Alissa's first art studio, where she could safely be alone with her art.

◆ ◆ ◆

Hester would send Alissa to the store with a quarter when she ran out of cigarettes. It didn't matter that the child couldn't pronounce the brand name. The grocer soon learned what she wanted when she asked for a *pack of old goats.* He would smile and hand her the correct package of cigarettes. Alissa was allowed to spend the change on penny candy, and her favorite was a cherry lollipop filled with a Tootsie Roll. Not every trip to the store was for cigarettes and candy, or Alissa might have grown up to be diabetic, and Mama might have died of lung cancer.

One day after school, Mama told Alissa that she wanted her to deliver a pie to a neighbor who was ill. Hester was a good cook, but her pies left something to be desired. She never learned the delicate balance between rolling the crust thin without breaking it and having it thick enough not to come apart when she transferred it to the pie plate. So she solved the problem by stopping the rolling pin as soon as the crust was the size of the pie plate. This made the crust tooth crushers and almost inedible defeating the care that Hester had taken when she prepared the filling. No one had ever complained to Hester, and George was accustomed to her pies, but Alissa secretly wondered if she would have preferred cow pies.

Hester knew other pie crusts were better than hers, but it didn't cause her to make the effort to improve her technique. The pie was to be delivered by Alissa to the Dutch lady who had befriended Hester with pastries when they first arrived from Huntington. Hester was aware that the Dutch were famous for their pies with crusts that "melt in your mouth."

The following weekend, Alissa overheard her parents having a loud, unhappy conversation. Mama was angry. She was telling George about the Dutch lady who was well enough now to have come to return the pie plate. The Dutch lady, too, had baked a pie and had offered to stay and show Mama a technique to make her crust lighter.

"How do you like that?" said Hester. "My neighbor thinks it's her job to show me how to make a pie. What does she know?"

◆ ◆ ◆

It was incredibly exciting to live in Washington, DC, where the hustle and bustle of city life brought new sounds, sights, and places to visit. Especially interesting for Alissa were the trips to the Smithsonian Institution and the white-marble Jefferson and Washington monuments.

One day, Hester announced that she would be taking Alissa to Woodward and Lothrop, a very nice department store downtown. There was a sale and Alissa needed a new winter coat. But Hester had an ulterior motive for the outing that did not include the purchase of a coat for Alissa. This outing, perhaps, would be the only opportunity to rid herself of the child. They were new to DC, no family members were close by, and Alissa had not yet learned her address. Hester's status had diminished since George was gainfully employed. She was no longer the person who held the family together by controlling the budget. With George home on a daily basis, Hester's anger intensified every time her husband doted on his daughter. She had come to a breaking point. She will rid herself of Alissa once and for all.

Hester conceived of a plan that required a trip downtown and a trolley ride. In DC, as in Huntington, there was no automobile in the Barrett family. Hester knew the route the trolley would take. She knew when the conductor would be changed. She planned to slip out of the trolley as soon as the replacement took place. The new conductor would not know Hester had arrived with a child in hand, and if Alissa was not able to see her mother, she would not notice that Hester was missing until it was too late.

Hester had never scrubbed Alissa so clean—she paid attention to everything, from Alissa's fingernails to starching her dress, polishing her shoes, ensuring she wore white socks, and pulling her hair tightly into braids tied with white ribbons. This was midday and the trolley was not crowded with men going to work. Alissa and her mother boarded, and Hester put the appropriate fare in the motorman's token box. She put a firm hand on Alissa's shoulder and walking to the back of the trolley, she instructed her daughter to take a seat next to a man who appeared to be asleep. "Sit still and behave yourself," she instructed.

Alissa was disconcerted by having to be seated next to a dirty man and apart from her mother. Hester took a seat for herself toward the front of the trolley where she could avoid looking at Alissa by gazing out the front window.

The man's appearance alarmed Alissa, but she kept her eyes focused downward on her shiny shoes. But she couldn't avoid the smell, and out of the corner of her eye, she saw the man flailing his arms and murmuring incoherently. He was no longer sleeping.

In a broad, sweeping motion, the man reached into his coat pocket and pulled out a pencil. He glared at it and then at Alissa. Alissa did not move. He was babbling something to her, and to her astonishment, he reached over and used the pencil to write something on her leg. Alissa was paralyzed with fear and hoped her mother would come to rescue her.

But Hester was sitting with eyes forward, rigidly staring out the window for the stop where the substitution of motormen would take place.

But before the swap that would provide Hester with an escape, the motorman was watching the commotion in his rear-view mirror. Fortunately, at the next stop, the motorman observed a policeman patrolling at the corner. He engaged the emergency brake and jumped off the trolley to report that there was a drunk onboard bothering a child.

The policeman went directly to where Alissa and the man were seated. "You're coming with me," he said to the drunk.

The drunk offered no resistance. "Okay, where are we going?" he said as he got up and peacefully started to exit in custody of the policeman–as if this were a routine he had committed to memory.

"Where's your mother, little girl?" The policeman's strong voice added to Alissa's fears.

Alissa saw her mother approaching. "There she is. There's my Mama."

"Is this your daughter?" asked the policeman. "Why wasn't she seated next to you?"

"When we got on the trolley, it was crowded," said Hester, pulling Alissa close to her as she dragged her to an empty seat near the back-door exit.

The policeman took the drunk off the trolley, saying a few words to the conductor. They each glanced back at Hester with disapproval.

Alissa was too stunned to know what to do, and she was too young to make any sense out of this. All the child knew was that her leg was dirty, and Mama was angry.

"Time for us to get off too," said Hester knowing this was a corner where she could connect to another trolley line.

Alissa began to sob uncontrollably as Hester exited with Alissa in tow. This angered Mama. "I'm dirty, Mama. I'm sorry. That man made me dirty."

Hester grabbed her child and shook her. "Alissa, stop it. We'll wash it off at the department store. Control yourself, or you'll get nothing when I take you shopping."

◆ ◆ ◆

By the time Alissa was eight her parents had become experts in the development of their volatile relationship. They were living away from the extended family and had no reason to put on a public face because there was no one in DC they felt the need to favorably impress.

Alissa escaped many of her fears by reading. Having her nose in a book had another advantage. It kept her from feeling so lonely. The library became her sanctuary, and she would check out books to smuggle into class in her school bag. She read them whenever she could sneak a peek. Alissa was bright enough to understand everything the teacher said without being coached. Lessons did not need to be reinforced with repetition. She would hide a library book on her lap, and while the teacher was helping her classmates, Alissa was filling her time and her mind from the stories on the pages of the books. She could anticipate what the teacher would say, and she learned to read ahead. So her scholastic grades did not suffer from her lack of attention to the lessons, but her citizenship grades were another matter. Her report card of straight As also reported the teacher's comments that Alissa was unfocused and a daydreamer.

It's no wonder she was daydreaming. She was bored out of her wits with schoolwork that was too easy. There were many new arrivals working in DC during that time and some families came from areas that were not as advantaged as Long Island. Alissa found that many of her classmates were dull. The teachers felt they had to adjust their teaching techniques to aim at the slowest students in the class or too many of the students would fail. Alissa felt she was in the wings of the theater and not part of the play.

◆ ◆ ◆

A common game in public schools during the forties was *tag*. A child would hit a classmate (usually on the upper arm) declaring, *You're it. Pass it on*. The recipient of the *tag* would announce the name of the child who had tagged her and tell the next person to pass the punch forward.

Alissa hardly ever participated in this activity because she would be huddled in the corner of the playground, quietly reading the current book of her choice. The kids did not like her nonconformity and would taunt her by calling her a *bookworm*. Alissa did not engage in name-calling with her classmates but she was willingly accepted hers as long as it did not interfere with her reading.

One day while Alissa was reading on the playground, she was interrupted with a punch that came with, "Yucky Karl tagged me. You're it. Pass it on."

She ignored it. She brushed her arm in an attempt to dismiss the disruptive tag and with annoyance in her voice said, "I don't want to play."

Now the children had two people to terrorize. They did this by starting a rumor. "Yucky Karl loves Alissa. Alissa loves Yucky Karl," they teased. It became the mantra of the day, and Alissa covered her ears so she didn't have to hear it.

Karl came to the unfortunate conclusion that Alissa's demonstration of not joining the "Yucky Karl" game indicated that she really *did* like him, and he desperately needed a friend. Now there was someone in the class who wasn't mean to him, even if she was the new kid in class. He was happy to have found what he thought was his first girlfriend.

Still engrossed in her book, Alissa wasn't aware that any of this intrigue was playing out on the playground. So it wasn't until the day Karl followed her home after school and started hitting her and laughing that Alissa realized something was terribly wrong that needed to be dealt with. She had done nothing to bother him. Why did he think hurting her was funny?

When she got home, she told Mama. "This boy, Karl, has been following me and was hitting me all the way home. I'm sorry, Mama. The kids say he is yucky."

Hester dismissed it by saying, "Never mind that. Don't get on your high horse. Boys do that. He probably likes you. Come in and change into your play clothes."

Boys do that. He probably likes you. How did those two thoughts relate to being punched in the arm? There was nothing in the books Alissa was reading that explained Karl's behavior or Mama's explanation. She knew of no males who hit women unless they were grossly evil like the man back in Huntington who had beaten up his Chinese wife. Grandpa helped her and her husband was arrested. She knew that criminals were to be avoided. But no one had explained to her how a child can avoid people, and the only criminals she knew of personally were the man with the pencil on the trolley, whom the policeman took away, and the butcher.

◆ ◆ ◆

Hester was really angry with the butcher. She said he was a criminal because he put his thumb on the scale when he weighed the meat. He was trying to cheat her not only of her money but of the precious ration stamps.

Alissa had been taught not to strike anyone. But she didn't understand why that was always to be true for her, when there were exceptions made for other people.

Just that morning, George defended the owner of a fish market whose court case had been in the paper. He couldn't read it aloud because he was laughing so hard but he managed to relate the story interspersed with chuckles.

"A lady had come into the fish market, pointed to a fish on a bin of ice, and asked if it was fresh.

The owner said 'yes'.

Then she moved to a mackerel in another bin and asked if that one was fresh.

The owner said, 'Yes, they all came in this morning. Yesterday it was in the Atlantic Ocean. Today it is here for you to buy.'

She moved to a third and asked again, and the owner assured her that he never kept fish that weren't fresh. She moved to the fourth and fifth bin, each time asking the same question and getting a similar response, and the owner was beginning to feel insulted. Then she started over. She returned to the second bin for the second time and asked the question again.

That's when the owner lost his temper. He picked up the mackerel by the tail and whacked the lady on the side of her head with it. 'Is that fresh? Or is that fresh?' he said.

The woman stormed out of the fish market, bringing the police back with her and insisting the owner be arrested. The court case was decided in favor of the woman, and the owner was fined one dollar because the judge felt that, under the circumstances, he would have done the same thing."

George said *that even though the story sounded fishy, he would have gladly paid a hundred dollars to have seen it.*

Hester had to make a remark. "It's so like to to approve of a woman being hit in the head with a fish."

So Alissa's dilemma was not resolved. Karl had no reason to hit her. It didn't fit any pattern Alissa could conceive of. It was unfair, it wasn't fun, and it hurt. How could it show that he liked her? Why did Mama sluff this off as unimportant, natural, or acceptable? And why would Daddy think it acceptable for a woman to be hit in the head with a fish?

The more she pondered the conundrum, the more she was slipping into relating to the fish—something used to punish others and without any value for its intelligence, its attractiveness, or its ability to love and be loved. But the fish Alissa was beginning to identify with was not the mackerel on ice at the butcher's. She felt smaller than that. She didn't even have the gills to breathe underwater. She was pliable. She was like the amoeba the science teacher had talked about in school that day. Alissa was identifying with a single-celled organism found in water and in damp soil on land that was a parasite of other organisms and lacked a fixed form and supporting structures.

Alissa ignored Karl from that day on, and eventually he stopped following her and hitting her and laughing. Although the mystery wasn't resolved, Karl did stop. Alissa held on to her conclusion that there was something very wrong about his behavior; she didn't know what. In due time, Alissa would be learning more about boy-girl relationships and the extent to which injustice occurs.

But for now, she accepted life's ambiguities by maintaining a low profile and avoiding confrontations in the hope that somehow, they would go away the same way she could close the book at the end of an unhappy chapter.

FOUR

Smoke and Mirrors

In 1945, the war was over, and so was George's government job. He brought the family back to Long Island, where bad habits continued. Hester modified her routine of salting money away for herself. This time it was *in case bad times came again*. George continued to take this as an attack on his manhood.

One day, when George was going through a dresser drawer looking for a clean shirt to wear, he discovered a crisp, new, one-hundred-dollar bill. It had been placed under the drawer liner, but the edge of the bill was sticking out, giving up its hiding place.

Approaching Hester in an indignant manner, he asked in a demanding tone, "Do you know who this belongs to?"

"No."

"Then it must not belong to anyone. Since I am the head of this household, it belongs to me," he said, slipping the money into his billfold. He left the house without a word of explanation and took the trolley to the most exclusive men's store in town, where, at a time most men would not pay one hundred dollars for a three-piece tailored suit, he spent the entire amount on a silk shirt. He came home wearing the new shirt.

He didn't say anything.

Hester didn't say anything.

She put on her hat and gloves and drove the car to their bank. She withdrew every cent in the joint savings account from the boom days in DC. She purchased a mink stole and arrived home, carrying it in an oversized department store box.

George didn't question what she was carrying. Hester went directly to their bedroom and put the box on the top shelf of her closet right over the spot where his silk shirt was hanging.

The mink was condemned to stay hidden in the closet for forty years until a family member found it when Hester was moved into a nursing home. It had never been worn. Doing so would have invalidated the image she had crafted of herself during the years when she couldn't afford a mink and had told everyone that she didn't like them because minks belonged to the rodent family.

It is interesting to observe the obfuscation that is required when a person acts in a particular way with the sole purpose of something plausible that was done or said in the past. In Hester's case, the mink was another version of what she had done when she was in high school when she purchased an eighteen-dollar pair of silk panties, ordered by mail, from Paris. It's true that the 1920s were a time of excess, when the purchase of expensive panties would not be considered extraordinary. But eighteen dollars for panties was extravagant even then. Her justification was that she needed to spend the money before her father would gamble it away or spend it on her sister, Jane.

◆ ◆ ◆

Jane's and Hester's parents had not treated them equitably. When Hester was old enough, she did the bookkeeping for the family business and was unpaid. On the other hand, Jane was treated regally by their father, given spending money without any requirement, and encouraged to have a good time.

With time, Hester's father, Franz Kiraly, was becoming irritated by the fact that his wife Eli was always sick. He no longer believed it was from the damage to her heart during the diphtheria epidemic. His wife was always in bed and not for his pleasure. To put it in Hester's words, *A man needs a healthy wife in bed – not a sick one.*

By the time her sister, Jane, was born, Hester was already taking care of everything, so there was no need for Jane to help out. Jane took on her mother's personality—without the excuse of being ill. She became spoiled and lazy from the indulgence of her parents. Everyone but Hester accepted this arrangement. Hester became extremely bitter.

As a young woman, Hester was proud to wear the panties. The undergarment was her personal secret, but wearing a mink stole could not be done without being noticed. Both of Alissa's parents had purchased something expensive that they chose not to wear. George didn't have any place to wear a silk shirt. Hester refused to wear the stole. The silk and mink were part of a power play to determine who had control of the money and ultimately the marriage. Mama and Daddy Barrett were the yin and yang of dysfunctional families.

Although neither of them was religious, they were reinventing the biblical myth that was the foundation for marriage in conventional society: if Eve was made from Adam's rib, he was the head of the house. But George wasn't able to exert that power. It would have been useless to say it was god's will, because Hester would have argued that she was god. So he picked at her. He called it ribbing. He would make fun of her in a clever way that his wife wasn't imaginative enough to challenge. That was the only way he found to exercise what he felt was his right as the man of the house. After all, if woman is made from the rib of the man, doesn't he have the right to reclaim this missing body part by ribbing her? It's his property right.

Hester, on the other hand, unable to stand up for herself intellectually, wished that he would choke on his words. If the biblical Adam had choked on the apple, it might have been the end of the human race, but if George choked, it would be okay with her as long as it meant her husband stopped ribbing her.

Hester was unable to give George any extra credit for being the breadwinner. In her eyes, anything he accomplished was ineffective and done only for "show." In her words, she wore the pants, and George, who was often mistaken for the screen actor Robert Young, wore the vest. She meant that because she did all the hard work (i.e., the housework); she wore the pants, whereas George's accomplishments were just a showpiece. He wore the vest, and with it he got all the glory and prestige. This irritated her to the core. It competed with the image she had projected within their small social circle before their marriage, when she was the popular debutante with abundant admirers.

George's background had not been as financially secure as Hester's. Grandpa Barrett's printing business suffered during the Depression at the time George's father might have wanted to bring his son into the family business. George knew he had to make his own way. How different things might have been if Grandpa's printing press had not ultimately been repossessed by the bank when his clients could no longer pay. It's interesting to speculate that Hester might have been a more encouraging and supportive spouse had George been able to provide a higher standard of living or if she had been able to be content regardless of financial security.

Speculation is irrelevant; because the reality of their marriage was that they were stuck in their own misery. Unfortunately, the result of their malfunctioning relationship was that their daughter, Alissa, was observing all this and it caused her to decide early on in her life that the way to avoid the trap they'd made was never to argue with her husband.

◆ ◆ ◆

One Saturday afternoon, while standing on a stool to reach the top of the ironing board, Alissa refused to iron her father's dress shirts. This was not an act of defiance. It was a plea for assistance. She refused because she knew she couldn't do the job well enough to please her mother.

Mama had complained before that Alissa didn't iron his starched white dress shirts properly because she wrinkled the points of the collars and didn't get the area around the buttons properly smoothed. It was futile to protest. Hester would never tolerate insubordination from her daughter. Hester grabbed the hot iron from Alissa's small hand and threatened to mark her for life with the burn she was prepared to inflict in payment for Alissa's act of civil disobedience.

When Alissa reported the incident to Daddy, she hoped he would help her. He didn't. His response was, "I have to agree with your mother because she is my wife, and it is my duty to support her. If Mama drops the shoe she is using to hit you because she has grown too tired to continue, I will see to it that you will pick it up and hand it back to her so she can continue your punishment. You must never displease Mama, Alissa. Remember that."

George's threat was much more severe than anything her parents had ever done to punish her. It had the effect he wanted—Alissa was terrified. And she was nullified. She had no value. Had George known that it also broke the spirit of independence that he should have encouraged, perhaps he would have handled this differently. But the weaker George felt as a human being, the more severe were his demands on Alissa.

Alissa's parents were both so focused on their own daily battles that Alissa was an aside. They weren't interested in what their bickering was doing to her. They also had no appreciation of the confusion caused by the inconsistencies in the rules of the house.

Mama's *Don't bring home any riffraff* rule was memorialized the day Alissa came home with a new school chum who lived on a houseboat. Mama could not know the family because they had floated into town recently. The child was not as clean as Mama's standards demanded because all water had to be brought aboard the houseboat in bottles. When Alissa arrived home with the girl, she thought she could give the girl a big treat by taking her to a real house with running water.

Alissa noticed that Mama had purchased jelly donuts that day from Holmes-to-Homes delivery service, a bakery distribution system common in the day. The housewife could examine the bakery goods when the deliveryman came to the door with his big basket of goodies before deciding if she wanted to make a purchase. It was very unusual for Mama to buy any bakery goods this way, as she considered these items overpriced and said they were not up to her own baking skills. But this day, Mama had made an exception. Mama purchased a half dozen jelly-filled donuts.

For Alissa, this was heaven. She loved the taste of store-bought bakery goods, especially those that had gooey filling. She asked her mother if she could give a donut to her new friend. Hester agreed but not magnanimously. She explained that the friend could have one donut only if Alissa understood that she was giving away from her share. Alissa was content with that. There was enough for everyone to have two.

That night, after the new friend had gone home and Mama was serving desert, Mama took one donut for herself and gave Daddy two. Mama explained that Alissa would have none. She was reminded that if she had not shared hers--with riffraff, she would have had some for dessert, too. The message was clear. Alissa learned that her rewards came only from obedience to Mama's rules, even when the rewards could disappear after the fact. You could get punished even when doing something kind, because it was more important to obey Mama and uphold her definition of riffraff than it was to exercise kindness to the stranger who was less fortunate. After all, being kind to strangers was Daddy's rule.

At dinner, Alissa had none of the jelly donuts, but she did not protest against Mama because she had learned to accept her hypocrisy. The kindness that lived naturally in her heart saw the hypocrisy, but she saw no way to defend against it. Alissa could be brave when she stood up to help others, but to protect herself she would need to invent other strategies. This would take more time than her chronological age provided. She didn't learn to do that until she was an adult.

Years later, Alissa called this skill *the airplane rule*. When the airlines cautioned their passengers to *put the oxygen mask on your own face before you assist someone else with theirs,* they were putting into standard safety rules the truth that you won't be able to help someone else unless you are in a position to help. That means in an emergency, time is of the essence. Your own survival needs must be met first. But Alissa's young life was lived long before it was customary for ordinary people to fly. When she was a child, she did not have the tools or insight to put on her own mask first. It would take years before the compartment that held the mask would automatically send it down when it was needed.

FIVE

The Silenced Song

The influence of her mother would haunt Alissa for many years to come. Like any typical young woman, Alissa wanted to be able to reminisce about her mother as her friends did about theirs. But she had nothing to tell. There were no recipes to describe because Mama kept that information to herself. There were no joyful childhood tales that could be retold. Alissa's mother had trained her daughter to feel that she was unworthy of love. Her mother had poisoned the well. She told anyone who would listen conjured-up stories about Alissa that put her in a bad light while making Mama out to be a martyr for having to put up with an ungrateful daughter.

Hester did more than that. She made Alissa feel dirty, despicable, and dumb. Family meetings for Alissa meant enduring glaring relatives asking why she wasn't a good girl. Unable to defend herself against made-up stories, she stoically sat in a corner with hands clenched on her lap. She trained her mind to drift off into thoughts found in movies or the books she read of cherished mothers who inspired goodness and joy.

It's no wonder that Alissa grew up believing she was incapable of expressing intelligent ideas or of accepting compliments from others describing her as a worthwhile human being. In later years, when she scored very high on intelligence tests and came in second in the state on her college-entrance exam, she asked her friends, *I wonder who came in first.*

Although the school reported the scores to her parents, Alissa never discussed the scores with Mama, as she knew it would make her mother angry. It took years of living away from home for her to come to the place when she could tell Hester about the high test scores--and when she did, Mama's response was, *That goes to show what a bad school that was, if they thought you were a good student.*

When Alissa was in high school, the music teacher told her she had a beautiful voice and set up an appointment for her to be tested for a scholarship. She would be coached by some of the finest voice teachers in the state as they looked for their own ticket to success by discovering the next wunderkind and nurturing that student to become the next opera star. She earned that scholarship and it provided for her first year of lessons. Alissa believed she had found her calling. She performed well and received many encouraging accolades. On the way home from classes, she dared to daydream of a life of music on the stage. But the second phase of the lessons required the signature of her parents on a financial contract. This was to become the most significant battle of Alissa's young life.

Hester said there was no money for lessons, but George had another argument. His was elegant but equally demoralizing.

George teased her. "You are living in a fog. We will provide you with whatever you need. You need only to trust in us. Who would know best for their child if not the parents? Greater minds than yours have confronted this and come to the understanding that parents know best."

Alissa was sobbing. Her father went to the phonograph and placed a 33 1/3-speed record of Franz Schubert's "Opus 1" on the turntable. "Sit down with me and listen to this music," he said. "It's based on a poem by Johann Wolfgang von Goethe. A child is carried through the woods by his father while the father comforts his unwarranted fright. I love this music and this poem because it shows parental love."

Alissa listened intently, but the lyrics were in German, and she did not understand them. She watched George. He became completely absorbed in the sounds and no longer noticed her. She was thinking that she could sing this music. Her eyes filled with tears, and when she could no longer be in the same room, she whispered, *I'm sorry*, as she quietly slipped to her bedroom to cry.

"What are you telling her?" demanded Hester. "Don't you know the child in that poem dies?"

George was stunned. "That's not the point, Hester. The point is the father carried his son through the fog and the frightening images of rustling leaves in the mysterious forest. Are you suggesting we should allow Alissa to take voice lessons?"

"No," said Hester, raising her voice so Alissa could hear her through the door to her room. "She will disgrace us. Besides, we don't have the money for this foolishness. ABSOLUTELY NOT!" she yelled.

Her parents not only blocked her opportunity to reach for her dream; Alissa would soon learn that her parents were also unified in their position not to permit their daughter to leave home until she was married. It was when Alissa earned a scholastic scholarship that her parents took matrimony out of the equation and Alissa realized how much her future was dependent upon the financial position of her family.

She was told that she would have to find work to pay any expenses. Many others had to work to pay for college, so it was all plausible and agreed to. The stage was being set for Alissa to find a way from living under her mother's rule—but Daddy's influence was more difficult to decipher.

Alissa's favorite class in high school was the senior English class studying short stories. She especially enjoyed the works of O. Henry, but her favorite was "Charles," a short story with a surprise ending by Shirley Jackson. It was during this class that she discovered the saying *Be careful what you wish for*, which happened to be her father's favorite quote, from the story "The Monkey's Paw." It was such a scary story. In reading it, one could only feel the helplessness of the White family in the story. There was no way they could remain hopeful. When they wished for money, it came in the form of insurance for their son's death. When they wished for his return, he came back crippled from the injuries that almost killed him, and their only fulfilled wish was to allow him to die peacefully. There was no improvement to their lives, and the wish to improve their conditions resulted in only them living out their lives without their beloved son.

Alissa shivered as she read it. She now understood why her father was reluctant make changes needed for a more fulfilling life. She speculated that his holding her back may not be because he didn't want her to succeed but because he wanted to protect her from the disappointment of failed dreams that had been the pattern of his life.

◆ ◆ ◆

But young high-school girls do not spend all their time thinking about failed lives; they think mostly about high-school boys. Alissa often met with a group of her girlfriends at Stynko's on Main Street to play the jukebox, gossip about the other high-school students arriving in the cafe, and speculate about who was dating whom. As she was hanging out with friends the afternoon of her enlightenment about "The Monkey's Paw", Alissa was still feeling the numbness of her discovery in English class when her mood was interrupted with a "Hi" from Fred Walters approaching their table.

She and her friends had pegged Fred as a spoiled brat, and Alissa did not encourage him as he slid into the booth to sit next to her. She wasn't sure how it happened because she was still focused on being careful about what you wish for, but before she knew it, she had agreed to go with him to see the movie *Roman Holiday*.

In *Roman Holiday*, Gregory Peck played the part of a reporter who was covering the escapades of Princess Ann, played by Audrey Hepburn. Peck's character falls in love with Hepburn's character and chooses not to expose what he learned about her private life. Princess Ann is in love with the paparazzi reporter, but she remains true to her obligations. She knows she cannot relinquish her duties and marry him for love. The movie ratified what Alissa had been taught by George, who encouraged her to be honorable and grounded. But she was thankful that no kingdoms would fall when someday she would find her heart's desire and fall in love.

On the way home from their date, the front left tire on Fred's 1945 black Chevy two-seater coupe had a flat. Many of the boys at Huntington High took auto shop, and it was common for the young men of the day to tinker with their cars, doing tune-ups, oil changes, and minor repairs. The skill to change a tire was expected from red-blooded American boys in the fifties. This wasn't the case for Fred. He was the rich kid who could not be expected to dirty his precious manicured hands.

Fred called home. This meant asking Alissa to walk to the corner to make the phone call for him. Fred remained in the car to protect it. He wasn't expecting his father to come and help. The aversion to menial labor was a trait handed down in the family.

"My dad will send Amos Bigly," announced Fred when Alissa returned to the car.

"For what?" she asked.

"Someone is going to have to change the tire. That will have to be Amos."

"Are you hurt, Fred? Why can't you change the tire? I can help if you want me to."

"Don't be ridiculous, Alissa. I'm wearing a new pair of chinos and suede shoes. You don't want me to ruin them, do you?"

"So, are you allergic to menial work? Will you break out in a sweat?"

"Why should I? This is what we have Amos for."

While they were waiting, Fred asked Alissa for her opinion on a dilemma that was bothering him. "My friend Neil wants to see Paul Newman in *Picnic*. He asked me to go with him. It's playing at the Music Box Theater."

"What's your dilemma?" asked Alissa.

"Problem is, Neil can't afford orchestra seats. He can afford only balcony seating. I would enjoy seeing the show up front. How should I handle this?"

"Why don't you get a balcony seat, too? That way you can sit with your friend."

"I could visit with Neil during intermission. I don't see any reason why I should have to sit way back there to accommodate him."

"Why don't you pool your money and come up with two seats together?"

"That's something to think about," said Fred. "I wonder if he has enough to pay for a loge seat."

"Wouldn't you be able to kick in enough so you both have loge seats?"

Fred looked angry. "Don't try to trick my Alissa. I'm not going to pay for him. If he can't afford a good seat, he should stay where he belongs."

"I thought you were asking me how to handle this, and I gave you several options. It seems to me that having the best you can afford is more important to you than sharing with a friend."

"Well, I don't mind having him as a friend, but I don't have to be a fellow traveler. We can enjoy a Coke together after the show. Thanks for helping me think this through, Alissa, but no thanks."

When Alissa regained her composure after stifling a primal scream, Mr. Walters and Amos arrived, and things went from bad to worse. Fred looked terrorized when he saw his father. Mr. Walters wasted no time in berating Fred for having a flat tire, calling him *stupid and useless*. Alissa's heart sank. She regretted getting involved in their family situation. What kind of people were these Walterses?

Amos was a black man in his early twenties. He was as handsome as the actor Sidney Poitier, whom Alissa had seen on *Kraft Television Theater*. Amos needed no instruction. He immediately went to the spare tire in the trunk and effortlessly and efficiently put the jack under the car. Alissa had never personally known anyone who employed a black man to do manual work. Alissa moved toward him to watch him change the tire.

"Good evening, Mr. Bigly," said Alissa. "Thank you for helping us. I hope your family didn't need you tonight."

Amos lowered his head so he would not look directly into her eyes, but a faint smile appeared as he politely said, "Yes, ma'am."

The date with Fred had nothing to do with George's control over his daughter. Alissa was willing to obey her father's rules. She was always careful not to damage her reputation. Allowing that to be tarnished in the 1950s could classify her as being one of the bad girls who were sought after only by the boys when they were looking for a fast date.

But dating brought out a side of her that had been stifled at home. Alissa was pretty and clever, and her budding sarcasm was received as playful coquettishness by the boys. They thought she was great fun to tease because she did not get insulted. For Alissa, dating was a time for her to do the testing. She was looking for the young man who would be a suitable lifelong, loving mate. She knew there were several who might like to try out. She hadn't entirely written off Fred.

When Alissa saw Fred again at school, he asked for another date. This time he wanted to take her to dinner.

"How was *Picnic*?" she asked before she would accept his invitation.

"Fine."

"Where did you sit?"

"Row B orchestra."

"And Neil?"

"I don't know. I didn't ask him where he sat."

"You didn't sit with your friend?"

"Why should I?"

Alissa didn't argue with Fred but she refused the date. His elitist attitude and his father's display of intimidation of his son frightened her. To Fred, status was marketable. It could be bought and sold.

Alissa's many admirers during her high-school years elicited mixed signals from her parents. Both her parents had been popular when they were growing up, but they kept this information from their daughter so she would have no excuse to copy them. But their hovering over Alissa and their whispered consultations behind her back made Alissa believe she was doing something wrong, when, in fact, she was an innocent, focused young woman simply wanting to find joy in life. If there was guilt, it was planted by Hester and George's imagination.

◆ ◆ ◆

Alissa was an honor student and was good at math, and she considered pursuing science. But girls at her high school were taking chemistry only because they would be the only girl in the class, or they were taking biology so they could be nurses. Dissecting frogs in bio class was repulsive; she didn't like the smell of formaldehyde, especially when the instructor wanted the class to dissect the droppings of the barn owl to see what it had to eat for dinner.

The biology teacher may have been impressed with the owl's digestive system and that owls' favorite foods are mice, rats, and other small rodents, including gophers. He might have cared that they eat their food in one gulp, complete and intact, and have no way to digest it, so that later that night, after about ten hours, they cough up a little ball of fur, teeth, and bones in the form of a pellet. But when the teacher brought these sterilized pellets for the students to dissect to see what the dinner menu for the owl had been, the repulsion was more than Alissa could bear.

She cupped her hand over her mouth, knowing that if her school lunch were to come up, it wouldn't be as a sterile pellet. This would preclude a future career in ornithology. Chemistry was out, too, because Alissa didn't think she could memorize the entire chemical periodic table. Having one period a month was sufficient. But she was attracted to the exploratory aspect of science and continued her quest to find the right science to study.

In the 1950s, women were encouraged to enter only the nursing and teaching professions. Even those choices were considered an advancement of the opportunities for women. It was only as recently as the Civil War that they were accepted as nurses, and most of those women had to work as unpaid volunteers to prove their worth. Alissa was persuaded that science wasn't considered gender appropriate. *They must have forgotten about Madame Marie Curie.* Alissa didn't expect to rise to the level of the Polish physicist and chemist, but she was inspired by the books of Rachel Carson and dreamed of following in her footsteps.

This might have been reaching for goals too high in the fifties. Alissa could count on one hand the number of female scientists, medical doctors, and engineers she knew, and she was aware that most of these women were single.

SIX

Role Reversal

Alissa did not know why Daddy asked her to take a day off from school for "a little trip so they could spend the day together." Even more surprising was Mama's snarky smile as George proposed the plan to Alissa. *What was going on? Was there something she had done to break one of their countless made-up rules on behavior?* George remained silent on the trip, and Alissa had time to contemplate a possible offense she might have committed as George drove all the way into Brooklyn. As she stared out the car window, the area reminded her of the movie *On the Waterfront*, where Marlon Brando's only escape from the neighborhood was to make a living as a boxer.

Alissa didn't know where they were going until the sign read Brooklyn City Limits.

"Why are we going here, Daddy?"

"I have to get seventy-two dollars from a gentleman who has owed me the money far too long."

"You took me out of school for that?"

"Aren't you enjoying the trip? I thought we could have some time together. We've both been so busy."

Alissa was amused. There was no indication of her father being dissatisfied with her, so she settled back to try to enjoy the view.

This was no scenic route. It opened up a whole new world to her. She saw tightly arranged tenement houses, trash and litter on the streets, and people sitting on their front stoops to escape the oppressive heat of their apartments. These were the neighborhoods of the numbers men, the bookies, and the loan sharks. It was all so different from Huntington.

But the question remained, *why here?* And if Daddy wanted this trip as time to spend together, *why was he silent?*

George pulled into a parking lot. "Alissa, I need you to come with me."

"Can I wait for you here?"

"No, this is not a good neighborhood for you to be alone in the car, and besides, it's too hot in the car," he said impatiently, motioning for her to follow him.

They walked to one of the run-down stores with metal gates covering the storefront windows. They rang a bell at the door of Gus's Tailor Shop. A buzzer sounded, signaling the door was unlocked, and they entered to find a dark and musty-smelling shop. In Huntington, Alissa and her father would have looked very much like an ordinary man with his daughter entering a tailor shop to order a custom-made suit. But in this neighborhood, they were out of place. Alissa was feeling uncomfortable, and she pressed against her father for assurance.

Thankfully, the transaction went quickly. The tailor simply opened the cash register as he saw George coming into the shop. He withdrew seven ten-dollar bills and two singles and laid them on the counter as if to count them, but neither man said anything. George swept the bills off the counter, rolled them up, and placed the roll into his right front pocket.

Obviously, George was not here to buy a suit. But Alissa wondered why her father didn't say thank you and why he didn't give the man a receipt for the cash. They left the store quickly and George grabbed Alissa's hand as he hurried her along with him back to the car.

At that moment, Alissa heard a loud, angry male voice calling out her father's name. George ducked down alongside the car. He pushed Alissa's head down with one hand and opened the car door with the other, shoving her into the driver's side.

He didn't need to tell her to hurry—the angry voice and her father's expression of fright told her this was not the movies. She slid into the passenger's side, smelling George's sweat as he came in after her. George took the steering wheel and started the engine.

"Stay down," he yelled as the car started to move. Alissa could not restrain herself. She had to see what was happening. With the car speeding out of the parking lot, she took a peek over the edge of the door and saw two men running toward the car and yelling curse words at her father.

During the drive home, this time Alissa was the one to remain silent. She was processing what had happened.

Meanwhile George was nervously chattering in relief. His day had ended in success. He got the money without being strong-armed by the men in the parking lot. George was elated. His eyes darted uncontrollably. His voice was staccato and a register higher than normal.

"Want to stop for an ice cream? Mama will be glad to see us. I wish I had a camera to take a picture of Gus as he had to part with the money he owed me," he ran on without allowing Alissa to respond. She was thankful for that. She was beginning to feel ashamed of her father. She realized he had put her life in danger. *Had he brought her along only to disguise his mission?*

When they arrived home, Hester was waiting at the front door. "Did you get it? Did you get all of it?"

George smiled and handed the roll to Hester. She counted it out and carefully placed the money in the lingerie drawer of her dresser.

Alissa went straight to her room.

"You don't have to be so huffy," called Hester. "Didn't you have a nice time being with your father all day?"

"She's fussy. It must be her time of the month," said George.

Those were the last words heard by Alissa as she retreated to her room in despair and slammed the door shut. She put her head into the pillow so no one could hear her sobs. But she was unable to see that there might be something untoward in what she experienced that day. That was a bridge too far. She ended her sobs with resolve to live with the matter.

There must be a better way. It's awful not to have enough money to buy groceries.

It was difficult for Alissa to come to the realization that her father had feet of clay. He had taught her to trust him unquestioningly as one would follow the teachings of a guru. But his teachings were high and lofty, higher than the reality of an ordinary human being struggling with himself and needing devoted adoration from a daughter whom he could train to think of him more highly than he thought of himself.

Although her father had many wonderful attributes, this day reemphasized that he was orbiting in the same world as her mother. They were completely self-absorbed. Her father wanted to be a prophet, and her mother wanted to be god. There was no joy in that house. There were unending rules and constant arguing. Their private little world occupied their whole lives.

Ordinarily, people in this situation would choose fight or flight. But Alissa was only sixteen years old. She could not run away because there was no place to go. She could not stay because it would mean annihilation. She was unable to accept the conditions in this house, and she was not able to change them. She was overcome with the desperate urge to utter the primal scream—a scream for grief, for anger, for fear, to be saved. *Was there anyone in the world who could help her find a better place and way of living?* But nowhere in her thinking did she realize it was up to her to save herself. She did not have the skills to do this.

Finding joy was inborn in Alissa, as it is in all babies as they come into the world with only the purest love of all—the ability to unconditionally receive love. She wanted only to share and nurture that birthright. Her psyche needed to find happiness to match her own personal identity but she was not able to understand this. She only knew something was missing. That deep, dark void and abyss was terrifying. *If only she had a hero,* she thought, *who would ride into her world on the white horse and make everything fine.*

SEVEN

Swarthmore and More

Adults the age of Alissa's parents were later dubbed "The Silent Generation." Conformity was the name of their game, and the game was invented by those who had survived the Great Depression and World War II. They taught their children compliance and gratitude, expecting them to appreciate all they had and live their lives as depicted on the pages of *Better Homes and Gardens.*

There was a warning that all was not well between the generations when the signature movie of the day, *Rebel without a Cause*, depicted teens who questioned these middle-class standards. Alissa understood why the teens played by James Dean and Natalie Wood were acting up. Although she felt her own tragedies were more complicated than those on the screen, she didn't think running a car too close to the edge of the cliff proved anything, Alissa could identify with the misfits in a world that was ordered, prescribed, and with a placid surface while no one was listening to cries for help.

Her world had been anything but placid. But she could identify with Sal Mineo's role of the person in the background who is nurturing, understanding, and protecting while being misunderstood and unappreciated albeit she had no clue that his character depicted a young man struggling with the identity of homosexuality—that subject had not come up in her world.

Alissa always needed to please others. She was the consummate pleaser and appeaser. Her father had directed her to fit his philosophy that women were put on Earth to bring joy to their husbands. That might have worked if all men were honorable and noble. But she had learned the hard way that this wasn't always so. She was frustrated at having to modify her dreams for the sake of compliance and wondered what George had really meant when he said, "Reach for the stars." It seemed incompatible with the fact that he was holding her down.

◆ ◆ ◆

There were practical choices she needed to make. Alissa decided to pursue a career in teaching because it suggested a broad range of things she might teach. She knew that no matter what profession she chose, in her heart she would always be the perennial student in search of knowledge, just as the phrase from Socrates that was inscribed in concrete on the front of Huntington High School said: *The only good is knowledge, and the only evil is ignorance.*

It was also appealing as a goal, since Allisa was of the opinion that teachers don't need to have anything of their own to pass on to the students—they can follow a curriculum set down by others. She was still the obedient follower and if the game of life included calling her to the teaching track, it did not mean she wasn't frustrated. To express her repressed anger, she drew upon the model her mother had taught her. She learned to practice the same kind of sarcastic criticism that allowed Mama to put up with the injustices that had been dealt her from an even more repressed society in the 1930s. Alissa was bringing all this baggage with her as she drove across the country to start over in a different setting, with a modified but achievable goal, and a determination to try to find her own identity along the way.

Attending Swarthmore gave Alissa a unique opportunity to stretch out and spread her wings. She chose Swarthmore College because she believed she would find stimulating ideas at a liberal school started by Quakers. The distinguished liberal arts school was the perfect place to do that. Dr. Solomon Asch had published his studies on conformity, and this was the hot topic among the students. Alissa took from these discussions the importance of dissention in determining the truth. She found opportunities to speak her opinions, but she was able to defend herself only if the greater issue of truth was at risk. She could not yet speak up to promote herself for the purpose of forming a more complete woman.

Alissa didn't slip into the social scene at Swarthmore. She was there to study. She met a friend who was to have a very influential role on the rest of her life. It happened in chemistry class, where Alissa had to confront a great fear: lighting a match.

The fear was the result of a trauma experienced when she was fifteen. She had lit a kitchen match to start the gas stove and was interrupted by a phone call from a girlfriend. When Alissa left the room to answer the phone, she inadvertently left the gas jet open on the stove. So when the conversation was completed, she struck another match at the stove. This ignited the gas, causing an explosion that slammed her to the wall and filled the room with flames. That experience had so traumatized her that, at Swarthmore in 1954, Alissa Barrett could not muster the courage to strike the match to light her Bunsen burner.

Fellow student Jennifer Cohen came to her aid. Jennifer Cohen a senior who had been attending Swarthmore from her freshman year had the campus and environs scoped out...but more important for this day, she happened to be the person who shared the lab table with Alissa. The five-foot-four senior had dark curly hair and wore "cat's-eye" glasses, currently in vogue, that rested on her aquiline nose and complimented her high cheekbones. Her complexion was fair; her voice firm and confident, and her dark-brown eyes sparkled with animation. The two young women began walking to class together allowing a bond to develop.

Jennifer did not seem to be afraid of anything—certainly not matches. "Don't worry about your fear," she said. "It keeps you humble and probably makes you empathetic. That's so not me. I'm one of those altruistic high achievers who are kept out of the best social clubs. But never mind that. I'd bet that your experience has not taught you about discrimination."

"Is it really true?" said Alissa. "I mean, I don't doubt your words, Jennifer, but are you sure that anti-Semitism exists in the United States of America? It shouldn't."

"Let me tell you about being Jewish, darling. Last year, my cousin was having his bar mitzvah at the Kenilworth Hotel in Miami. My family lives in Chicago, and we all made the trip south for the celebration. Dad's first name is Maxwell, but he doesn't like being called Max, so he goes by Mack. When he called the hotel to make the reservations and said he was Mack Cohen, the clerk misunderstood and thought he was Scottish. She gave him the room. She thought he was saying McCollum. All the way to Miami, Dad was saying, 'Please don't let me see any of the No Dogs and Jews Allowed signs.'"

"And did he?"

"No, thank god. This hotel did have one of those signs, but when we got there, the sign had been removed. And he didn't know about the McCollum misunderstanding until we got there and found we were the only Jews staying at the hotel. The rest of the bar mitzvah guests were in the back room of the basement at the celebration, safely out of sight of the other guests. Would you believe it—they had to come in through a back door the hotel employees used?"

"I'm so sorry," said Alissa.

"I'm not looking for sympathy. You asked, so I told you. We later learned that the *no Jews allowed* sign came down when Arthur Godfrey bought the hotel. The sign would have been more honest. Even though the hotel management thought we were Scottish, it was obvious that anti-Semitic feelings still permeated the place. You could feel it. It seemed to ooze out of the walls. It's the way life is, but maybe someday things will change. My father is a wise man. He says *everyone is responsible when there is injustice.* He said *it takes only one person to stand up to start a change."*

"Isn't that similar to the ideas in Dr. Asch's paradigm?" asked Alissa. "Didn't he show that if a position is stated by a dissenter, the group will resist and find the truth? Isn't your dad saying, 'If someone points out an injustice, the larger group will seek justice'?"

"I love your attitude Alissa even if you are a Pollyanna. I wish it was that easy. It takes more than taking down a sign to change an attitude, and Dr. Asch didn't elaborate on what happens to the person who wants a change in society."

"I'm not accustomed to being called optimistic," said Alissa, laughing. "Most people say I worry too much. I really appreciate that you see me differently than my family. I hope we will have many more opportunities to talk."

"No sweat. How would you like to come to a Shabbat dinner tonight?"

"What is that? Is that some kind of Jewish food?"

Jennifer laughed. "No sweetie tonight is Friday and the Sabbath starts at sundown. You do know what the Sabbath is, don't you?"

"I think so," said Alissa, feeling more like a neophyte than an outsider.

"Dr. Goodman is my economics prof. His family invited me for dinner. It's a Jewish tradition to welcome a stranger to the dinner table. If I bring you, that should make them twice as happy. They'll have two invited guests instead of one."

"Are you sure? Won't they feel imposed upon?"

"No, they'll think I have a lot of chutzpah."

"And *chutzpah* means?"

"It means colossal nerve. I was planning on majoring in that in college, but the closest I could get was prelaw."

"Sure, I'll go with you. I like trying new things. But I want to bring them a gift. Do they drink? Can I bring them a bottle of wine?"

"Just be sure it's not Christian Brothers Brandy," said Jennifer enjoying the puzzlement in Alissa expression.

The two women separated to explore different parts of the library. Alissa went to check out the art books searching for a creative way for self-expression. Jennifer went to periodicals to keep up with world events in general and specifically to see if there was more information about the assassination of the dictator Somoza in Nicaragua.

When Alissa and Jennifer arrived at the Goodman house that evening, they found the table set with a white tablecloth. There were flowers in the center, and to the side were candles burning. It was past sunset, so Mrs. Goodman had already said her prayers over the candles and removed the covering from her head. Both the Goodmans were delighted to have the two students as guests and invited them to join them at the dinner table as the tradition continued.

Mr. Goodman placed his hand over a covered loaf of challah and recited a prayer in Hebrew. He turned to Alissa and said, "It means, 'Blessed is God who gives us the wheat of the earth.'"

Then he poured wine, first in his glass and then into the glasses of his wife and guests. Lifting his glass, he recited another prayer in Hebrew with an explanation for Alissa. "This means, 'Blessed is God, king of the universe, who gives us the fruit of the vine.'"

After these moments of reverence, Mrs. Goodman said, "OK, let's eat. Now it's my turn. She went to the kitchen, bringing out a feast of chicken, salad, a green-bean casserole, and mashed potatoes.

The evening was delightful, full of carefree conversation and an abundance of food. Jennifer endeared herself to the Goodmans when she playfully asked someone to "pass over the green beans" when she wanted seconds.

Alissa thought she was catching on to the traditions. "So that's how the holiday Passover got its name?" she asked.

"Not quite," said Mr. Goodman, chuckling at his young gentile guest. "Come back in the spring, and we will show you what Passover is."

"I'm so embarrassed," said Alissa as they were driving back to campus.

"What?"

"About the green beans."

Jennifer laughed. "You mean about not knowing what Passover is?"

"It was a silly mistake."

"You're allowed to make mistakes, Alissa. Don't be so hard on yourself. But, so you won't make that one again, I'll tell you that when the Jews were slaves in Egypt, the Lord sent the angel of death to kill the firstborn males. The Jews painted the lintels of their doorways with sacrificial blood as a marker to the angel so their sons would escape death. Get it? The angel of death *passed over* the homes of the Jews."

"That's awful," said Alissa. "You're celebrating being spared while you know the children of other families will die."

"It's a religious myth. It means it's important to maintain Jewish identity."

"I'm going to have trouble with that concept," said Alissa, staring out the car window as the lights of campus housing came into view. "What good does that do, if it makes you a target for oppression?"

"We're survivors, Alissa. What other culture do you know as ancient as ours?"

"But it's easier to survive if you don't wear your identity on the doorposts," protested Alissa.

The car came to a stop in front of the women's housing, but Jennifer gripped Alissa's hand to keep her friend from leaving before she continued her explanation.

"Listen carefully to me, dear friend. There is strength in maintaining your essence in the face of opposition."

"Forgive me," said Alissa.

"There you go, being hard on yourself again, Alissa. It's okay to be yourself. Take it from a friend with survival instincts in her blood. You're right about my culture making targets of themselves. But after centuries of doing that, we instinctively recognize danger."

"Forgive me again, Jennifer. But if your people are so attuned to recognizing danger, how did they fall for the extermination of the Holocaust?"

Alissa knew her words hurt her friend, and she was sorry she had spoken them.

"We also recognize when we can't win."

"Existentialism?"

"Existentialism."

"I understand."

Jennifer's car became the private office of the two women. There were many opportunities to discuss philosophy as the two friends explored the local areas together on weekends. They had better results in coming to common agreement on issues other than finding the places they wished to explore. Neither of them was good at map reading.

"I don't understand why you can't read a map, Alissa. I have a good reason. It's in my genes."

"Levi Strauss?" asked Alissa.

"I'm the comedian here. My genes—with a *g*, not a *j*. My people never could get to where they wanted to go. Let me tell you the truth about Exodus."

"Never mind. I'll wait for the movie."

"No, it's important for you to understand this. Our oral tradition says that Moses, or as we called him, Big Mo or Moshi or whatever your preference—"

"I don't want to call him at all, unless he has a compass." Alissa was twisting the map to get a better perspective. "I know the top of the map is north, but how do we know what direction we are going?"

"You don't need a compass from Big Mo. A Jewish compass only points east anyway. So, here's the lowdown. Are you listening or not?"

"Do I have a choice?"

Jennifer started to speak as if she was reciting from the Bible. "You have probably heard that Moses did not find the promised land because a generation had to pass before the Jewish people were permitted to enter. It's generally understood that the delay was because they would not be carrying the sins of their forefathers into the land God promised to them.

But that's tradition. That's not what really happened. The truth is that Big Mo did not have a sense of direction. He was wandering around; he was leading the people in circles. This is the origin of the phrase *the wandering Jew*. You must have heard it.

Anyway, this wasn't easy for him. There he was in the hot desert, a hundred degrees, and no shade. The poor man was schlepping those big stones around on his back."

"Stones?"

"Yea, those two tablets with the Ten Commandments on them. Not to be confused with the two the doctor tells you to take and then call him in the morning. All the time, his wife was telling him, 'Moshe, you're walking in circles. I see footprints in the sand, and they are mine.' She told him, 'You have to go east. You know... where the sun comes up.'

"They would have found the promised land in a month or two if Big Mo had listened to his wife. But do men ever listen to their wives? Do they ever ask for directions? They don't now and they didn't then."

"Jennifer, do me a favor," said Alissa. "Don't marry a rabbi. He would never put up with your stories."

"Why not? Rabbis have a sense of humor. These are my *bubbe meises*, and I have a right to say them."

"If you were his wife, he would have to have a sense of humor or no sense at all. What's a *bubbe meises*?"

"What my grandmother calls 'soap operas'. It's literally 'old wives' tales.'"

"Well, if you're telling me a soap opera, can I change the station?"

Eventually the station did need to be changed. Jennifer stayed at Swarthmore three more years for graduate work in economics and a doctorate in philosophy, and Alissa graduated with her bachelor's degree in teaching. Both women pledged to be friends for life, but for now, each went home to family and roots—Jennifer to Chicago, where her arrival would be celebrated by a family gathering, and Alissa to Long Island, hoping that returning home as an adult who had honed an ability to use humor to conceal her anger might help her to cope with her parents.

EIGHT

Whatever I Did to Find Happiness Didn't Work

Alissa was pleased that Mama agreed to join her for lunch at Panetta's. It wasn't Hester's favorite place to eat, but Alissa chose it because Panetta's was the "in" place to be. She assumed nothing would've changed in Huntington and she wanted her friends to know she was back in town. When they placed their order and were waiting for the food to arrive, the waiter came to their booth with an unusual request.

"That gentleman at the table near the window would like to know your preference for wine."

Alissa looked to where the waiter was pointing. A man resembling a young Raymond Massey with a reticent smile was staring at her. She did not recognize him or the woman with him, as she had her back to Alissa.

"Why does he want to know?" Alissa asked the waiter.

"He said I should find out so he can buy both of you ladies a glass of wine."

"That's good," said Mama. "Tell him I like Ruby Red Port."

"Mama, we can't do that. We don't know who he is. We can't accept a gift from a stranger."

Hester looked down her nose and sulked. "I don't care," she said. "I know him from somewhere; I just can't remember where."

Alissa wondered why a man with a female companion would be sending wine to the table of two other women. "Tell the gentleman that my mother and I won't be having wine with our lunch today, and thank him for his gesture."

This conversation could be heard throughout the small dining room, and the Raymond Massey lookalike called out, "Waiter, she can't put one over on me. I'd make a bet that Alissa is a Chablis person. Please serve our friends a glass of Chablis and Port."

The young man rose to his full six-foot-plus height and buttoned his suit coat. He took the hand of his companion, and they both came to Alissa's and Hester's table. "You saw me, Alissa. Don't you recognize me?" asked the man in a warm and kind voice. "You are prettier than ever."

As soon as his words reached her ears, Alissa knew who this was. This was a matured, filled-out, zit-free Fred Walters.

"How could I forget you? You were my first date. I'm so sorry I didn't see you sitting over there. Mama, you remember the Walters boy, don't you?"

Hester nodded her head in guarded agreement and a subdued "yes".

"Mama, Fred was from my class at Huntington High. He played trumpet in the school band and was on the tennis and track teams. If you can't remember Fred, Mama, you surely remember the Walters family, don't you?"

Hester looked as if she was suffering from a serious case of ennui. But her singular raised eyebrow revealed the fact that she was sizing up the situation.

"Please sit down and join us," said Alissa. "Have I met your lady friend?"

Fred's companion stretched out her hand. "Hello, Alissa, I am Dr. Ellen Livingston."

"Oh, Fred, aren't you feeling well?" asked Alissa.

"Ellen is a psychiatrist," said Fred.

"Oh, now I understand," said Hester.

Fred reached out to take Alissa's hand. "No wedding ring," he observed. "Does that mean you haven't found Mr. Right?" he asked in a glib tone.

"Nobody can please Alissa," said Hester. "She keeps changing her mind. She doesn't know what she wants. She is too big for her britches." Mama believed it was incumbent upon her to protect the man who wanted to pay for their wine from becoming interested in her daughter, even if he might be a bit crazy.

"That's not the Alissa I know," said Fred. "Listen, Ellen is on her way to pick up her husband at the train station. He's got this bigwig advertising job in Manhattan. Have you come back to town to stay, Alissa?"

"No, I'm here to visit," said Alissa, watching Ellen as she left the restaurant and wondering what role she was playing in Fred's life. Maybe she was helping him outgrow his teen years, when he was a spoiled brat.

"May I join you ladies?" asked Fred, not waiting for permission before he slid into a chair close to Alissa's.

"No, we're leaving," said Hester. The waiter arrived with their lunch and two glasses of wine. "We don't want them." She turned toward Alissa. "I haven't got time for this. You can take me home now."

"Sorry, Fred. I'll be taking Mama home."

"What a disappointment Mrs. Barrett. I had hoped we could reminisce. I have such fond memories of you."

Hester was defiant. She was not interested in conversation with any of the Walters clan. She stood up, turned her back to him and headed for the door.

"Will you meet me tomorrow? How about Stynko's for pizza?" asked Fred worried that Alissa would leave before he had an opportunity to set up a date.

"Stynko's? Now that brings back high-school memories. Yes, I'd love to meet you tomorrow. Stynko's it is."

Hester was already halfway to the exit without her daughter. Alissa paid the check for the food they had not taken time to eat. She waved 'bye to Fred and hurried to catch up with her mother so that she could help the older woman open the heavy door.

"Six o'clock," called out Fred.

"Stynko's at six," said Alissa.

◆ ◆ ◆

Alissa tossed and turned that night. She thought about the confidence and charm Fred had demonstrated. She considered that the inconsistencies of his offers to be generous and prior evidence that he was a tightwad might be similar to the ambiguities she had not yet been able to work out in her own development. She gave him the same excuse she gave herself—they were both young and had overbearing parents. There was an undeniable physical attraction that could not be rationalized, and she was drawn to that with the same curiosity as the moth is drawn to the flame. She resolved that the next day she would give Fred a second chance to win her heart.

"I'm sorry I didn't recognize you yesterday, Fred. Hope you didn't have to pay for the wine we left on the table," said Alissa starting the date at Stynko's off on the right foot.

"Yeah, but that's okay. I sat down at your table and drank them with the meals you didn't finish."

"You didn't drink both, did you?"

"Both. And I did it the right way. I started with the dry white and moved on to the red."

"That must have tickled you pink," she quipped, proudly revealing the new humorous side developed from her time with Jennifer. "So what have you been up to since you became a wino? Excuse me, I mean since graduation?" she asked.

"I've stayed put. That is, except for the tasting trip to the wine country in Georgia."

"I didn't know they had vineyards in Georgia."

"You missed something, Alissa."

"Perhaps I did. Tell me what I missed."

"Let's see," he said. "You missed Andy Smith, Greg Andrews, Jim Hightower..." Fred was counting names on his fingers as he called off the names of young men in Huntington.

"What are you doing?" she asked.

"I'm telling you the names of the guys whose hearts were broken when you left town for college before you gave them a chance to enter the competition."

"Competition?"

"Don't pretend to be modest, Alissa. It doesn't become you. Surely you knew those guys thought you were cool and would have loved to warm up to you."

"I confess. I knew," she said teasing him along with her most seductive smile.

"Didn't you think twice about any of them?"

"They are all nice guys. Don't forget Hank Taylor. You can add him to the list. What about you, Fred? We dated in high school...if you remember. You were on the list too, weren't you?"

"Very much so," he said meekly. He seemed to be awkward about continuing the conversation. "What about college?" he asked. "Were you popular there, too?"

Alissa was enjoying the game. She pretended to be deep in thought, moving her lips as if she were reciting names while keeping a running count of them by tapping her fingers.

Fred was also counting the movement of her fingers. "You've had nineteen lovers since we were in high school?"

"Nineteen lovers—what do you take me for?" Alissa said with a laugh. "I thought we were counting admirers. I wasn't counting lovers. I had a fan club."

Fred looked as if he had been in a heavyweight boxing match and had heard the countdown before he could get up from the mat.

"It's giving my ego a boost to think that there were other men who admired me. I really hadn't noticed until you brought it up. But I'm not ashamed to say that I'd like to convince myself that I was--and am--popular."

Fred perked up. He ordered a pitcher of beer and a medium pepperoni pizza with extra cheese.

"Not wine?" asked Alissa.

"Excuse me, would you prefer a glass of wine?" he asked.

"How about a bottle instead of a pitcher?" she said.

"I want beer," he said indignantly.

"If god forbade drinking, would he have made wine so good?" But seeing his disappointment with not getting his way, she said, "At least that's what Cardinal Richelieu said."

"Did you want me to buy you a whole bottle of wine?"

"No, a glass of Chianti would be fine," she retorted sarcastically. Now she wanted to change the subject. "It's your turn, Fred. What has happened to you...I mean, besides the trip to Georgia?"

"Well, you remember my father has the investment firm, don't you? I've been working there while I was in college. I can't get past the copy machine. Dad dictates everything I do and then criticizes it."

"If he only gives you clerical work, why did he send you to college?"

"I don't know. He doesn't explain what he has in mind, and he certainly doesn't ask me for any input."

"That sounds like the story I heard about the man who had a trucking business, sent his only son to college, and when the boy came home, the father turned the business over to him. Then he wondered why his son didn't know how to pack a truck and why they didn't teach him that in college."

"It's not that simple. Dad is full of praise for my older brother. He's always talking about how well Bob does in business. It's hard dealing with the old man about this. But I have to be honest. This business is a moneymaker. I'll do anything I have to do to be in Dad's good graces. I want to inherit this someday and live a life as rich as my father's."

"What about a family, Fred? You haven't married, have you?"

"Not yet, Alissa. But I am so pleased to see you again. I still remember you from the way you were in high school. I'm hoping you haven't changed. Maybe we can take up where we left off."

"People are always changing," said Alissa. "Changing is a part of survival. I only hope my changes are improvements."

Fred wasn't interested in discussing anything deep. "Would you like to go dancing tonight? I have a ticket at the office. Harry James is in town this weekend at the Glen Cove Sons of Italy Hall. It's a little out of town, but it is Harry James. One of our vendors left a free ticket at the office. Wouldn't want it to go to waste."

"Sounds good," said Alissa.

The Harry James Band was great, but Alissa had never suspected that she might not have heard him if she hadn't brought her billfold that night. Fred had *one* ticket. He used it for his own admission and waited while she stood in line to purchase her own. When Alissa realized she would have to pay for her own ticket, she wondered why a man who was so interested in making money had none to spend on a date. Perhaps his father was keeping him on a tight budget.

It was two weeks before Hester could find an opportunity to express her criticism of Fred. By then, Alissa and Fred had seen each other thirteen times, and a full-fledged romance was blossoming.

"I want to talk to you about dating the Walters boy. High school was a long time ago. It's not a good idea to try to rekindle something years after the flame goes out. Besides, look at that man, Alissa. He looks like Abraham Lincoln. Do you want your children to look like that?"

Alissa felt Mama's comments were presumptuous. She was now twenty-two years old and had a college education and a teaching contract for a position starting in the fall. She was quite capable of thinking on her own. What business was it of Mama's whom she was dating? It was obvious that Mama resented her dating anyone.

The Barrett and Walters families had lived in the same town for years. George had some opinions of his own to talk about. George warned Alissa that Fred's family was too focused on the almighty dollar. He said there were rumors in town that they were dishonest in business. He told her that Fred's father, Charlie, was reported to be a womanizer. This was more information than Alissa wanted to hear.

"Don't forget to tell her how many children in this town look just like Charlie," said Hester.

Alissa was angry at her mother for saying this. The more Hester put down Fred, the more Alissa wanted him, and the more George had to say against him.

He told Alissa that Fred came from a different culture. "As we have always told you, in our family education is the most important thing. We want you to be as smart as you are capable of being. But in the Walters family, accumulating money is the primary goal. They want to get all they can get."

He explained that he was telling Alissa this because he and Mama loved her and didn't want to see her hurt. "You will never understand them."

Alissa might have considered Daddy's arguments had she not felt that this was another put-down because Daddy was not as successful as Mama wanted him to be, and he would not stand up to Mama's disrespect of him.

Mama had a few things of her own to add. "Joan Walters is pushy. She uses her forty-six triple D bovine chest to push her way into a conversation that is none of her business. She's so top-heavy, that short husband of hers could stand in front of her to keep out of the rain. She parks her car so nobody can get into the parking place next to her. It's impossible to talk to her because she is hard of hearing."

"So, is that it?" asked Alissa, wanting this malicious tirade to stop. Alissa was becoming more and more angry. But her parents continued with their deluge of derogatory accusations against the entire Walters family. This was taking snobbery to the nth degree. If they thought the Walterses lacked culture, what would you call this character assassination? It was catty. It was mean, and it was cruel.

Alissa was fuming. She sat silently, taking their words with a grain of salt—so many grains, in fact, that she almost choked. Who were her parents to talk? When did they get to be so high and mighty? Didn't they realize that if they had been different parents, she might not be in the predicament she was in today? If they had shown her more love and nurtured her through the years, she was certain that she would have been better off and self-fulfilled.

They had no right to look down on Fred's family. She had never heard any of this gossip about them, and Fred's parents seemed to be okay with her. Alissa thought that Joan looked like Jane Russell (albeit on a bad hair day) and Charlie looked like Edmond O'Brien. They couldn't be as bad as her parents portrayed them. She was willing to give them the benefit of the doubt. Fred wanted to marry her.

Fred had money and a business where he could earn a good living. She wanted to raise a family and needed someone to provide for her children in a way that her parents were unable to provide for her. Upton and Sons, the Walterses' family-owned business, would be able to do that. His father was looking into opening a branch in Greenwich, so Fred could work close to where Alissa had her teaching contract. She found Fred charming, and he had charmed her into thinking that if she accepted him, he would be completely hers.

How petty could Mama be? Imagine not liking someone because she didn't park the car properly. Joan Walters seemed to adore Alissa. Fred's mother demonstrated greater love toward her than Mama had ever shown. How disingenuous could Daddy be? He always talked about money not being important to him, but if money wasn't important, why was he putting the Walterses down because they had it?

She wrote off the entire conversation to the narrow-mindedness of her parents and convinced herself that they were probably jealous of the Walterses' financial success.

She kept these thoughts to herself because she did not want to upset her parents by speaking disrespectfully to them. George always taught her to honor her elders, and she had practiced this so long that by now it was second nature. She thanked them for their advice and said she would consider the information they had confided in her.

But while she was ostensibly reconsidering marrying Fred, she went shopping. She bought a Lanz Nantucket Rose nightgown with pink-and-blue flowers. She was preparing for a warm, cozy wedding bed covered with her favorite comforter and a carefully reinvented Fred Walters crafted to her wishful specifications. The Lanz nightgown was the perfect first-night garment. It would initiate a marriage of comfort, warmth, and dependability.

Alissa believed that she had made the decision to marry Fred logically, carefully, and deliberatively. However, she was making it out of protest against her parents, and she made it to her detriment. When all was said and done, her parents were right. Alissa was overlooking Fred's basic behavior. But in time, Alissa would come to understand Fred all too well. She would come to rue the day when she decided to accept the proposal of Fred Walters and become his wife.

◆ ◆ ◆

It was true that George was jealous of the Walterses' money. The Walterses were the richest family in town, and it was important to George that he could impress them by showing that he could afford to pay for a proper wedding for his daughter. When all was said and done, most of the wedding was paid for by Alissa from money she had earned working part-time while in college. George was able to save face only because his father-in-law, Franz Kiraly, had left a small life-insurance policy to Hester, and Hester was willing to spend a portion of it on this charade. But her insurance windfall was limited, as most of the Kiraly fortune was used to keep Aunt Jane out of jail. It galled George that they had to use money from the man the family continued to call "the horse thief," especially when Hester insisted no one had any proof of that, even though her father seemed to be suspiciously lucky in all his business dealings.

The bride's family selected a banquet hall in Sea Cliff, New York, overlooking a harbor on Long Island Sound for the reception. The building had once been a private estate, and Alissa pictured it as her castle where her hero-knight Fred Walters would take her away from all the cares of the world to nirvana.

But Fred was nobody's hero. And she would find that getting any amount of protection, emotional security, financial equity, or tenderness from Fred would be doomed to failure.

Jennifer volunteered to help Alissa find a pretty dress for the wedding. So Alissa and her best friend shopped at Delancey Street, where Jennifer heard that you could buy expensive clothes at reasonable prices. This shopping spree would be an education for them both.

◆◆◆

Alissa was looking at the gowns in a shop window when an old woman came out of the store. "You're going to be a beautiful young bride. Come in. We have your size."

The clerk brought out a dress with yards of billowing white peau de soie dripping from a clothes hanger. "Here, try this on."

Alissa was swimming in a cumulous cloud. She struggled to find the opening for her head and arms. "Help me, Jen, I'm drowning."

"It's a size sixteen," said Jennifer, finding the label in the folds of cloth.

"It's a perfect fit," said the clerk. "It just needs a little tailoring."

"I'm a size four," cried out Alissa, trying to keep her head above the clouds of fabric. "There is room in here for the whole wedding party. I can see the floor from the inside of here. I'm the only one getting married, not the Andrews Sisters."

"Let me show you," said the clerk, taking a fistful of cloth in her hand. "You only need a corselet to give you some shape. It wouldn't hurt if you had some chest."

Alissa and Jennifer decided to look elsewhere. The next stop for wedding-dress selection was a wholesale warehouse. Garment workers labored over their sewing machines while others scurried about, taking the finished products to the display racks and bringing out more material to be sewn into clothing.

"I'm sorry, Jennifer, we can't shop here. There is no dressing room."

"Don't worry," said Jennifer, pushing a five-foot-long rack of clothes in front of her friend. "Stand behind this. No one will see you."

Alissa found a size four dress from the rack that she desperately wanted to try on. It was gorgeous, with a scoop neckline framed with satin roses and sprinkled with seed pearls, simulating dew. It had a tight-fitting waist, long sleeves with buttons on the arm, and a train that could be converted to a bustle for dancing after the ceremony. The dress was made for a queen, and Alissa wanted so much to wear it on her wedding day in the castle at the top of the hill.

She overcame her modesty and slipped out of her street clothes and into the elegant gown while the factory workers assembled at the garment rack to peek over the top to watch her. When Alissa had it on, she was led to a full-length mirror to show it off. Her hazel eyes sparkled, and a ray of light from the factory window shined down, as if it were directed by Hollywood, bringing out the red highlights in her chestnut-brown hair. Her five-foot-one stature was confident and erect. A warm smile showed the elegance she was feeling wearing this beautiful gown. The workers applauded, expressing oohs and aahs in at least three foreign languages.

With the dress selected, the two shoppers would have to carry the gown to the car. It was on a hanger and covered in paper, making it look as if they had picked it up from a dry-cleaning establishment. The shoppers were tired and needed nourishment and Alissa needed quiet time to regain her modesty before heading home. She was still blushing. One of the garment workers advised them of a nearby deli that was known for its specialty, homemade chicken soup with dumplings.

"This chicken soup will give you strength," said the waiter as he escorted the women to a table, "and nourish your soul as well."

"What are you going to give Fred as a present?" asked Jennifer, wondering if there was something else they should be purchasing this day.

"I've been thinking about that, too," responded Alissa, enjoying each mouthful of the warm soup. She was beginning to relax. "This does have medicinal powers, Jen. I'm feeling less hungry already. Don't you feel it?" She laughed.

Jennifer had already finished the soup and was looking over the dessert menu. She decided on the strudel with a cup of tea. "I'm well aware of the medicinal powers of chicken soup."

"I don't want to buy anything from the store for Fred," said Alissa. "I want to make something for him. He was admiring the family crest on the outside of the house where we will have the reception. I have an idea."

That night, after Jennifer left, and while relaxing with a bottle of dark ale, Alissa created what would become Fred's wedding gift from his bride. Onto a twenty-four-inch-square canvas, she copied the Lowenbrau lion from the beer bottle and drew a large silver bowl in its outstretched paws. She then drew cartoonlike wavy lines from the top of the bowl to depict steam. It was meant to represent a bowl of chicken soup. She decided that the motto of her new family should be, *To Power through Chicken Soup.*

The strength-through-soup concept had been inspired by the deli lunch, but using this as a family motto was Alissa's idea thirty-five years before Jack Canfield created an entire personal-development enterprise based on his initial book entitled *Chicken Soup for the Soul.* Alissa felt the motto would be better expressed in Latin. But she couldn't remember the Latin word for soup (if, indeed, they ever had soup in Rome), so using calligraphy lettering, she inscribed the words *A Potens via Pullus Aqua* ("To Power through Chicken Water") on a banner surrounding the replica of the Lowenbrau lion that was bearing a hot bowl of soup. *Chicken water* was close enough.

NINE

Domestic Blitz

Upton and Sons was indeed ready for expansion and growth. As soon as Fred and Alissa were married, the company opened a branch in Greenwich, Connecticut, and Fred was made the manager, precisely as Charlie had promised. This put the young couple on the fast track. Their combined income qualified them to purchase a two-bedroom house on Shady Lane. The neighborhood was charming, but the kitchen of the pre-war home was an eyesore. The floor had large linoleum tiles in a pattern of alternating red and dark green. Over the years, with the buildup of floor wax, the green had become black. Alissa suggested they could play on the floor if they could find chess pieces that were the size of small children.

Joan Walters was not amused. She hated the floor, and one day when she was visiting, she had her fill. "I'll pay for you to remodel this kitchen if you will see to it that you get rid of this awful floor. It makes me sick. I can't eat here anymore."

"We don't have to remodel the whole kitchen only to get rid of the floor," said Fred.

"You mean you are willing to ignore the fact that your wife has to go to the service porch to put food in the refrigerator because the kitchen is so small?"

"We could have bought a smaller refrigerator," said Fred. "Alissa picked out this big one without measuring the space. We can send it back for a different one."

"That's not fair," complained Alissa. "The space in the kitchen was designed for an ice box. They don't sell refrigerators small enough to go into this kitchen. You know that. You were with me when we bought it. The only other option we had would be to move the door that goes into the service porch. You said that we couldn't do that because the roof would fall in."

Joan was determined to get involved in this spat. "I trust Alissa's taste," she said. "I think Alissa could design a kitchen that would work. I will pay for it."

"You aren't serious are you, Mom?" asked Alissa, testing the waters to see how much help Joan was willing to give them. It would be expensive to move the door, plaster up the hole in the wall, and replace the flooring.

"One of the new no-wax linoleums would be nice, but that's expensive," she said, allowing all her ideas for a kitchen makeover to spill out at one time. "We would have to get a professional installer and who knows how much touch-up painting would have to be done after they are finished."

"I don't care," said Joan. "I want you to upgrade this kitchen. I want you to have more cabinets too. I don't see how you have enough room for your wedding gifts. Just let me know how much you are spending, and I'll pay for it. It's my gift to my new daughter-in-law."

What could be a better solution than to have a nice upgraded house at a bargain? There was not a lot of construction going on at this time because of the slow housing market. They would have their pick of contractors to do the work. Fred negotiated some lowball prices and monitored everything that his wife purchased.

Alissa arranged for cabinets, a Formica counter-top, and a double sink to be installed. The door was moved, the linoleum was laid, and the kitchen and service porch were completely painted. The vendors and contractors agreed to take payment at the end of the job. As the work progressed,

Alissa sent copies of all the invoices to Joan, except for the bill for the new kitchen curtains. Alissa wasn't sure her mother-in-law intended to pay for curtains too.

When Joan came over to check on the progress, she complimented Alissa on how bright and cheerful the remodeled kitchen looked. She had been keeping tabs on the expenditures and knew the amount of the entire remodeling job. She pulled her checkbook out of her purse, wrote the check payable to Alissa, and handed it to her.

It was for one-fifth of the amount of the project.

"Thank you, Joan," said Alissa, swallowing hard. "Were you going to give Fred a check for the rest?"

"No," declared Joan with a look so sour it would curdle milk. "You certainly didn't expect me to pay for all this, did you? I just wanted to help you to get what you wanted. Your husband can pay the balance."

How do you express ingratitude to someone who hands you a check for five hundred dollars? Worse yet, how do you pay for two thousand more in bills you would not have incurred in the first place without the promise of reimbursement? The job was finished, and the contractors wanted their money.

It spoiled the kitchen. Every time Alissa put something in the refrigerator (that was now in the kitchen), she was reminded that it had not bothered her so much to take the extra steps to the service porch. The steps weren't as difficult as it would be to pay off a two-thousand-dollar loan from the bank in addition to the mortgage payments. This was especially painful because Fred insisted that because he was making the mortgage payments out of Alissa's paycheck, this should be considered a second mortgage that he would also take from her paycheck. Alissa would not be able to purchase the car she had been saving for and would have to continue to take the bus to her job at the elementary school. It was increasingly difficult to take the bus now that she was pregnant because the fumes from the exhaust contributed to her nausea.

When Charlie Walters heard that Joan had reneged on her promise to Alissa, he came to Alissa's aid. He liked his daughter-in-law, and this would give him an opportunity to undercut his wife. Destabilizing a spouse was the favorite sport of Charlie and Joan. Charlie gave a Fred a sixteen-thousand-dollar bonus at Christmas. That meant the bank loan could be paid off. He also increased Fred's salary comparable to what he would pay someone he hired from outside the family. That would help with the ongoing expenses. It did not mean however, that Alissa would get the promised car. She didn't need it, because she would now be able to stay at home and care for the new baby.

Alissa was overjoyed at not having to work outside of the home when her child arrived. She purchased a copy of Dr. Benjamin Spock's *Baby and Child Care* and read it as if it was the bible. With guidance from the popular book, Alissa was convinced that she could do a better job of raising her children than her parents had done raising her. She knew her decision was right when Mama said, *The best thing you can do with that book is to use it to spank your children.*

Katie was born as soon after the wedding as possible for a full-term pregnancy and as late as needed to not provide a gossip opportunity for those suspicious busybodies who counted the number of months from the date of the marriage to the birth of the first child. Hester could sigh an audible breath of relief when she arrived at the hospital.

"Are you okay?" Mama asked casually.

"Mama, there were women here who screamed and cursed their husbands all night, saying they wanted them castrated. But I want you to know that because of you and your guidance," she said, beating her chest like a sturdy Russian-peasant-woman road worker, "I saved my strength just like you advised me at the age of eight. I'm so thankful to you that you warned me about playing hopscotch."

"I never said that," said Hester, stiffening her back. "Never mind your lies. I got to see the baby. She is in a special room all by herself because she is so beautiful. She resembles my side of the family."

This was when Alissa first realized that Mama could be hitting the bottle. She had wondered about that for years, ever since the time Mama told her about adding water to her husband's vodka. George did not drink.

◆ ◆ ◆

Now that Alissa had passed scrutiny and proved she was an honorable woman, no one cared when the second child arrived except Alissa. She was soon pregnant again, and having a small child to care for when the next one was on the way took a bit of juggling.

It was only a short trip to the Hop and Stop grocery store from their home on Shady Lane. A young mother pushing a stroller with one tot could walk the distance in twenty minutes. When Alissa became pregnant with her second child, and Katie was still in diapers, the busy intersection at Glen Ridge Road presented her with a most challenging problem.

She needed to be prepared to take all three of them across the street safely. The light was fast, and often Alissa did not make it across the street before it changed. At that time, pedestrians didn't have the right-of-way in Connecticut. That allowed the impatient drivers an opportunity to use her and her offspring as a moving target. Alissa had difficulty challenging her child-swelled body to do double time across the intersection while maneuvering a stroller on four little wheels and not losing her balance because of the unequal distribution of weight in those burdensome bags filled with groceries.

She wondered why her doctor was so insistent that children needed to be out in the fresh air every day and why he wanted her to exercise by walking. She was already doing plenty of that at home running after an active toddler who was learning to walk.

Fred wouldn't dream of helping her with her marketing chores. Real men in the early sixties did not do that. Any man caught shopping at the market at that time was suspected of shopping only for himself because he was either a bachelor, divorced, or a gay guy passing as a bachelor. Fred carried this prohibition against helping his wife a bit further than most. When Alissa was pregnant, he was willing to walk with her only when his own needs required it but never when she also had Katie in tow. "I don't want the neighbors to think I'm a sex fiend," he explained.

If Alissa ever thought that explanation was reasonable, she soon learned Fred was not in any way sympathetic to her or her condition. The revelation occurred on the day they had tickets to a hockey game at the local high-school stadium. They reached Hillside Road, where Fred ran across East Putnam Avenue ahead of her. When he got to the other side, he called back over his shoulder, without even looking at her, "Hurry up, Alissa. I don't want to be late."

"I'm sorry, Fred," she called out in distress. "Look at all the traffic."

He didn't look—he just yelled, "Hurry up. You might make it."

His remark knocked her off her feet. Alissa sat her heavy body down on the cement in the median. She sat there, in public, on the curb, amid the smell of brakes, the sound of horns, and the angry gestures from motorists who anticipated her presence might necessitate that they slow down. She was too shaken to care. She cupped her head in her hands and started laughing.

This was real, heartfelt laughing, belly laughing, hysterical laughing, dark-comedy laughing. What did Fred mean, "You might make it?" What manner of man had she married?

She stopped laughing and began to quietly sob when she realized that what she was feeling did not matter anyway. She had no options. She had a child and a second on the way; she had about as much choice about not following her husband through this marriage as she did about not crossing the rest of the street. She was stuck midway and had to proceed—with educated caution, of course. She would never again fully trust that he cared about her well-being or that of their children.

◆ ◆ ◆

When Alissa gave birth to her second child, she needed help from her husband. The night her water broke, she woke Fred and told him it was time to go to the hospital. He had had nine months to plan for this moment.

"Let me sleep," he responded. "You probably wet the bed. Change the sheets. You'll be all right."

Because she was unable to budge Sleeping Beauty, Alissa called her parents to see if Hester would take her to the hospital, and she asked George to stay at the house to take care of Katie. "Fred thinks I need toilet training, Mama. He should know this is my water breaking. It's the way it happened when Katie was born."

Mama asked to speak to Fred.

Whatever she said to Fred, it was said without mincing words. Fred was blushing. It got him out of bed, and he grumbled about Hester's foul language and the indecent hour of the arrival of the baby, and as he got dressed, he warned Alissa that she would be sorry she wasn't giving him time to take a shower.

Hester and George arrived while Fred was still putting on his shoes. "Hurry up, hurry up," said Hester, trying to push him out of the door. Fred was griping about missing sleep, having to work that day, and asking why Alissa couldn't wait. George was astonished that Fred wasn't showing more concern for Alissa. He remembered this and added it to the litany of abuses he noticed from his son-in-law.

But what George didn't know and what Alissa always kept to herself was that Fred had the habit of sulking for weeks at a time. It was common for him to go into his study and lock the door. During those times, he was punishing Alissa by not talking to her, and the result of this isolation was that when he finally emerged, she would go out of her way to find a way to please him so that he would not withdraw again.

But today, rushing to the hospital meant that the baby would not wait for Fred to get over his funk. This time he would act like a man--even if it was only an act.

On the way to the hospital, Fred was fuming about Hester interfering with his domestic life. He reminded Alissa that babies don't come in ten minutes, and there was plenty of time to get to the hospital without having to get her parents involved. When they arrived at the emergency entry, they found that Hester had called ahead to alert the doctor that Alissa would be arriving in the last stage of delivery. The attendants strapped Alissa to the gurney they had waiting. She was only in the labor room long enough for the nurse to take a quick peek. They rolled Alissa immediately into the delivery room, where she gave birth on the gurney without medication to a beautiful, healthy baby boy.

Fred was still in the parking lot, trying to find a parking place closer to the door so he wouldn't have far to walk. Circling the parking lot became tedious, so Fred went to work.

When the baby was born, the hospital called the daytime number listed for Fred. It was at Upton and Sons. The receptionist answered.

"This is the maternity section of North Shore Hospital. Is Mr. Walters in?"

The receptionist routed the call to Charlie. It wasn't the first time someone had called Charlie at the office about paternity accusations, and as far as she was concerned, there was only one Mr. Walters at the firm. No one ever called Fred Mr. Walters. He was just Fred.

"Yeah, what do you want?" asked Charlie.

"We called to let you know you have a healthy, eight-pound-four-ounce baby boy. He was delivered at nine-fifteen. Mother and son are doing well. You can come and see them both at any time."

"OK, thanks."

Charlie really *intended* to tell his son. It slipped his mind.

Later in the lunchroom, Charlie sat down at a table with Fred. "You're not wearing a suitcoat," commented Charlie. "Aren't you on the payroll today?"

"I didn't have time to get dressed. Alissa woke me up early to take her to the hospital. She's probably still in labor."

"Dammit. I forgot. The hospital called. The baby came. They said it's a boy."

"Dad," cried out Fred, rising from the table, "why didn't you tell me?"

"I was working on the Treadmill contract. It slipped my mind. Sue me."

There were tears in Fred's eyes. "This is my first son, Dad. I don't know why it wasn't important enough for you to tell me."

"Get over it. You'll have this kid the rest of his life. Wait a while, and you'll see what a pain in the neck a kid can be."

◆ ◆ ◆

Winter weather in Connecticut meant that small watercraft had to be removed from the ocean and brought onshore. Fred owned a twenty-three-foot sailboat. He took great pride in his boat and had no problem with pulling it onto his property on Shady Lane so he could keep a closer eye on it. Fred must have been nearsighted because he had a distorted impression of what close meant. The boat was moored to the side of the house, under the master bedroom window.

One especially cold night in January, when the overnight temperatures were dipping into the low twenties, Alissa expressed her gratitude to Fred by mentioning how thankful she was for the central heating in their house and especially the matching electric blankets that kept them warm in their twin beds.

Sometime around midnight, a windstorm woke Fred and he worried about the boat. Without waking his wife, Fred slipped over to her bed and cautiously removed her blanket. He quietly opened the window and, folding her blanket, carefully placed it on the windowsill. Then he went outside.

The cold awakened Alissa as Fred was returning to the bedroom. "Where did my blanket go?" she asked, groping in the dark for something to warm her.

"It's outside," he said, crawling back into his own bed and pulling up his blanket to take the chill off his bones.

Alissa sat up in disbelief. "Outside?"

The window was partially opened. Still groggy, she got up and walked over to close it. "Why is this electric cord here? Look, Fred, the cord is going through the window. That's why it's so cold in here."

"I know," he said turning up the thermostat on his blanket.

Alissa turned on the bedroom light. "Fred, don't stay in bed. We have a problem. We've been robbed. My blanket is missing. The window is open. We need to see what else they took. Don't close the window. The police will want to take prints," she said as her teeth started to chatter. "I'm fffffreezzzzzzing. Oh, Fred," she said in dismay, as soon as her mind recovered from the interruption in her sleep. "What have you done? You didn't throw my blanket out the window, did you?"

"Nooo," he said mockingly. "I did not throw it out the window. *I took it out.* Leave me alone, Alissa. Go back to sleep."

"I'm sorry, Fred," she said, trying to calm him as she continued her protest. "But that makes no sense. Why would you take an electric blanket outside? It's still plugged in. You could have been electrocuted."

"It's below freezing outside, and the head in the sailboat could crack."

Alissa knew Fred loved his boat. It had been built by a local man as a hobby. That meant it was carefully crafted with the patience of a man who constructed it only for the creative pride it gave him. The man had hand-sanded the mahogany accessories. The boat was unique. It was a prized possession. Alissa was sympathetic to Fred's fear of having his assets frozen, but surely there was another way to avoid the problem. "Aren't there heating elements you could buy for the boat?"

"I didn't want to waste my money on something I use only once. It will be spring soon."

"Oh, you didn't want to waste the money. I see that spring is right around the corner. The crocuses will pop up out of the snow any day now. But why did you take my blanket? You could have used yours."

"Yours is closer to the window," he said, rolling over to go to sleep.

Alissa took two acrylic blankets and a comforter from the linen closet. She stuffed bath towels in the opening at the bottom of the window and crawled back into bed. She didn't have the nerve to recover her electric blanket that was being used for his beloved boat.

Alissa fell asleep thinking about the wonderful times they'd enjoyed together on the boat. She loved the experience of gliding through the water with Fred at the helm. With the right amount of wind in the sails, a sailboat seems to be floating in the air. It gives the illusion that the boat remains stationary while the shoreline slips by. At night, the saltwater spray becomes a display of phosphorescent sparkles dancing in the moonlight.

She liked boating too, but her electric blanket was being used to keep the toilet from cracking. Her husband had given her a clue how low she was on his list of priorities.

◆ ◆ ◆

Alissa was no sailor. She did what she could to encourage Fred to sail because she loved the experience. She even took swimming lessons to become more comfortable on the water.

At the local YMCA a swimmer's level of expertise is designated by the names of fish. Alissa started out as a Guppy, and she told everyone that her porpoise was to learn enough to keep from drowning. The Guppy group was made up mostly of preschoolers, so the adults in the class learned to avoid the yellow streaks and warm spots in the water.

One day at the Y, the mother of one of the school *of fish* mates came to Alissa and asked if she had seen her son. She had arrived to take him home and didn't see him in the pool. "He's in the fourth level," she said. "He's a Fish."

"No, I've only seen yellow-bellied speckled brook trout," said Alissa.

The woman wasn't amused. "So what level are you?" she asked.

"Somewhere between lobster and caviar," she quipped.

Alissa successfully passed the Guppy level, but she dropped out at the Grouper class because the lessons conflicted with the times Fred wanted to take out the sailboat.

One day George joined them for an afternoon of sailing on the Long Island Sound. "Alissa, show your father how well you can swim. Jump in," barked Fred, trying to hide a sinister smile.

She did. She obediently jumped into the water and started to swim. George was shocked. He knew Alissa couldn't swim. His eyes opened wide in surprise, and his mouth dropped open, unable to utter a word of protest. Alissa had forgotten in the excitement that she wasn't at the indoor pool at the Y, where the sides of the pool could be reached within six strokes.

When she had heard Fred's instruction, she took it as a command. She swam awhile as the boat continued to drift away. But she soon became tired. It was then that she realized her feet did not touch bottom. She panicked and started to sink.

George was watching. He rose to his feet to see his daughter coming up for air the second time. He didn't swim, either. The only swimmer on the boat that day was Fred, and he was too busy laughing and watching his wife struggling in the water. He could almost picture the scene at the mortuary with mourners to comfort him. The role of a grieving husband appealed to him. It was so noble.

There were no life-preserver rings, cushions, or vests to be seen, and the ladder had been removed from the side. If Alissa was to be kept from drowning, she would have to accomplish that on her own.

Her father understood that. "Alissa," he called in his sternest voice. "You get right back in here before you drown."

Alissa heard him. She gathered enough strength to doggie-paddle back to the boat. George reached over the side and pulled his limp, frightened daughter aboard.

"I'm sorry, Daddy."

"What did you expect here today," he asked, "your guardian angel to pull you aboard? He didn't seem to be on duty today, Alissa. You shouldn't press your luck."

Actually, her guardian angel was onboard. This time it was Daddy. After they returned to shore, while Fred was tightly securing the boat to the dock, George pulled Alissa aside to speak to her alone. "Alissa, where did the life preservers go? They were there when we went through the Coast Guard Water Safety Drill. They were not there when you were in the water. He must have disposed of them when we gassed up. That man is trying to kill you, Alissa. I saw it in his eyes."

There were tears in George's eyes. He was worried for the safety of his daughter, but all he was capable of doing was expecting Alissa to fend for herself. He was angry with his son-in-law, but he could not face Fred with his accusations.

"Oh, Daddy," she sobbed, not yet coming to grips with an abusive marriage. "Please don't do this to me. I know you don't like Fred. You are always picking on him."

"I've seen this pattern before," insisted her father. "Remember when we went to the Catskill Mountains, and I was driving Fred's business car and bringing you home from your Aunt Jane's engagement party? Remember when the accelerator stuck, and I had to drive onto the shoulder to stop? That was a close call. I lost control of the car. Remember that the brakes did not work? Even the emergency brake was useless."

"Oh, Daddy, that was an accident. There are always problems with cars."

"But how often do problems develop right after the husband takes the car in to be serviced?"

"Are you suggesting that Fred did something to the car?"

"Yes. Why wasn't he there to drive you home? He expected you to be at the wheel alone."

"That's nonsense," insisted Alissa. "He took the car in to be serviced. You are saying the mechanic did something wrong. Not Fred."

"That's no problem for your husband. He seems to have a lot of connections with people who can be paid to do what he wants."

Alissa wasn't able to believe her husband would intentionally hurt her, but things kept happening that were peculiar. Fred did a lot of things that were neglectful, and Alissa began to suspect there might be more to this than mere coincidence. The question was whether he was neglecting something because he wanted to inflict harm or because he was so self-centered he couldn't care about anyone except himself. All answers were black because, in either case, someone might be hurt. Now that the suspicion was planted, it had penetrated her subconscious and was affecting her dreams.

◆ ◆ ◆

The evening Fred was away on a business trip and called from the hotel to let her know he had arrived safely, he omitted letting Alissa know that the hotel was in New Orleans. This was going to be more than a business trip, but he had reasoned that what she didn't know wouldn't hurt her. He would be heading for the French Quarter as soon as he finished his obligatory call to his wife. He refused to give Alissa a phone number where he could be reached but promised to call again soon. .

She must have sensed his lie. Alissa did not sleep that night. Her suspicion conjured up another of the unending sequence of nightmares. They were all of children in danger with someone trying to protect them. The dream that woke Alissa at four o'clock in the morning and so terrified her that she was no longer able to stay in bed was of her children, Josh and Katie, represented by green stick figures as if they had been fleeing for so long a period that they no longer had body flesh and were now in skeletal form. In the dream, a representation of herself in yellow was furtively running, trying to catch and protect the stick children, who were scattered and incapable of being captured.

But Alissa's nature was to see Fred more as an overgrown child who had not been properly raised. She chalked up the nightmares to being afraid of being alone without him, and she put them out of her mind with determination and effort. She sincerely believed that her husband needed the nurturing that he had not received as a child and tried to compensate for what he lacked.

He wasn't capable of selecting his clothes. All husbands seem to appreciate a wife who shops for them, but this was more than that. Alissa laid out Fred's clothes each day before he went to work. If he got up earlier than she did, god knows what he would wear. He preferred Florsheim shoes and Alissa would buy his sized nine medium for him.

One day as Fred was leaving for the office, he told Alissa to drop off a pair of his shoes at Geppetto's shoe-repair workshop. He had left them for her in a paper bag in the closet.

"Fred needs new heels on these shoes," said Alissa, placing the bag on the counter of the workshop.

"These are two different shoes," remarked Mr. Geppetto. "One is brown, and one is black."

"Fix them anyway," said Alissa. "I'll bring the other pair in later. He must be wearing them right now."

Alissa felt that because she was goal-oriented and was a high achiever, she could guide Fred by showing him the importance of laying out attainable goals and of having backup plans for the times things didn't go as planned. She was taking the logical approach, and because she was trained as an educator, she believed she would be able to teach him how to overcome the deficiency she described as poor planning.

But Fred wasn't anywhere near being taught how to structure his life. He was still stuck in some murky self-confidence issues from minefields that were stuck in the path of success.

◆◆◆

Alissa's place at the family dinner table was across from Fred's. This put her closer to the kitchen appliances so she could better serve her husband and the children. This didn't bother Alissa because it saved her steps. What did bother her was the habit Fred had whenever she served the family meat with the bone intact. Fred's lack of etiquette when eating lamb chops, pork chops, chicken, and spareribs was distasteful and annoying, and it wasn't because he used his fingers.

After Fred had finished gnawing the meat off the bones, he would reach over to place the denuded remnants on Alissa's dinner plate. It did not matter that she hadn't finished her meal and his donation was placed on top of the food she intended to eat. It was useless to tell him that she objected because Fred did not take kindly to criticism, especially when it implied that he was uncouth.

He often brought the newspaper to read at the dinner table, and hiding behind it allowed him to avoid anything he chose to ignore. The bones kept coming from the bottom of the opened paper. He was so practiced in this violation of manners that he didn't have to look for the target. He found her plate by feel, and if he snagged a bit of her mashed potatoes and gravy in the process, he would lick that off his fingers before starting on the next serving of meat.

One day at the evening meal, a worn-down Alissa slowly pushed her glass of milk to Fred's side of the table in a feeble attempt to demonstrate to him that boundaries between people need to be honored. When the glass reached his hand, he put the paper down for a moment to survey the situation.

"What's this glass doing here?" he asked.

"I wanted to show you that we need to respect boundaries, Fred. I'll take my glass back when you stop putting your bones on my plate."

He was angry. He said he wasn't hungry anymore because she had spoiled his dinner. He left the table to retreat to the TV, but not before picking up Alissa's glass of milk, drinking all of it and wiping off the creamy white mustache with her dinner napkin.

Fred's anger caused Alissa to retreat. She thought she would have to modify future menus to avoid having her dinner plate turned into her husband's garbage dump. She considered becoming a vegetarian. The bones-on-the-plate routine was an insult to Alissa's ego and self-respect. Fred's belligerence was often so overwhelming that Alissa wasn't able to coyly protect her dignity by making jokes about it. She pretended his insults did not matter. She was slowly losing the ability to rely on her own perceptions.

But having the diversion of two bright, happy children was a welcome relief from the stress of dealing with Fred.

◆ ◆ ◆

When Katie was selected to play Dorothy in *The Wizard of Oz* for the school play and Josh was going to play Toto, everyone was engaged in the production. Assisting with this event was going to be a major endeavor for the entire family. Alissa took a pair of Katie's old shoes, painted them red, and glued red glitter all over them. Fred donated a bicycle for the witch that one of his message-delivery boys had inadvertently left behind at the office.

Hester bought a bolt end of yard goods for Katie's dress and brought it over to Alissa's house. She was happy to be part of the endeavor, confident that her granddaughter would be even better in the part than Judy Garland.

"Why did you buy material?" asked Alissa. "We should be able to purchase a Dorothy dress for Katie at a costume store. That's where we are going to get the dog costume for Josh."

"I know someone who will sew it," insisted Hester. "My bridge partner told me about Angelica Rizzo; she is a good seamstress. She can make anything without a pattern."

"I've never heard of her," said Alissa.

"Of course not—she's from Italy. She hasn't been in this country long."

Alissa was amused at the thought of a foreign woman making a dress without a pattern and with only the guidance of Mama, who had difficulty reading the menu in an Italian restaurant. "Maybe she doesn't need a pattern to make a dress, but doesn't she have to know how to speak the language?"

"I can speak enough Italian. Don't you remember? When George and I went to Venice on an Italian cruise ship, all the people spoke Italian. I understood them. The people in Venice understood me well enough for me to get some bargains."

"Not to mention your Gucci scarf."

◆ ◆ ◆

Angelica was a thirty-year-old woman whose name described her. "*Buongiorno,*" she said as she opened the door for Hester, Alissa, and Katie.

Hester didn't waste any words. She went right to the heart of the matter. "Angelica," she said, putting both her hands on the chest of the seamstress. "I'ma Mrsa. Barretta," she said, in her very best Italianese, putting her two hands on her own chest.

"Katiea," continued Hester, putting her hands on the chest of the little girl. Katie was squirming. This embarrassed her, and she slipped behind her mother for protection. But she didn't move fast enough for her grandmother.

Hester snatched the picture of Dorothy out of the child's hand to show it to the seamstress. In a loud voice so the woman would understand, Mama said, "Katiea isa Dorothea ina da Wizarda ofa Ozza."

Then Mama turned toward Alissa. "Alissa," she said. But Alissa had anticipated the assault from Mama and not wanting to be her bosom buddy, stepped toward Angelica to shake her hand.

This didn't stop Mama. She moved toward the seamstress, putting her face right up to the young woman, and as she waved the picture in the air, she asked, "Cana youa makea dressa?"

"*Sì, certo,*" said the seamstress, taking the photo.

Alissa placed the material on the table. Angelica took a measuring tape out of her apron pocket and measured Katie.

Mama said, "See? I told you I can speak enough Italian."

Luckily the seamstress was bright. She recognized the picture from *The Wizard of Oz* and could tell from Mama's sign language that the little girl named Katiea was to wear it.

"*Una settimana* [a week])?" asked Angelica.

"*Si, grazie,*" responded Alissa reluctantly having to expose Hester to the reality that her method of communication, learned from a foreign cruise, had proven inadequate for hiring even a bright, acculturated, Italian seamstress to make a dress.

TEN

It's All about Me

Fred and Alissa were very different. Fred's favorite book was the checkbook; Alissa's favorite was the dictionary. She loved the nuances of words and always sought the best word to describe what she wanted to say. Her father prided himself in being a semanticist, so it was easy for Alissa to follow his example and emulate his insistence on being precise. If she made an error, George was willing to assist her. She also developed George's philomathean attitude and emulating his love of learning. For Alissa, getting a degree was secondary to her primary goal of getting an education.

Fred teased her about always finding another class to take and another academic program to enter. He suggested that when Alissa was in the grave, her hand would rise up from the soil proclaiming: *I can't go yet. I'm enrolled in another class.* What he may not have realized was that, one of the things she learned, was that education was a socially acceptable way for a woman to strike out on her own. Taking another class became Alissa's way of building self-confidence to escape Fred.

◆ ◆ ◆

The academic world encourages that people are evaluated by the amount of time they devote to the discipline, with whom they network, and by the prestige of the school that conferred the degree. So, it is not surprising that Alissa met several people who bragged about their academic accomplishments.

One day, when she was attending class for her second master's degree, the man seated next to her bragged about the number of degrees he'd earned.

Alissa tendered this response: "I've been fortunate enough to have an education, but I've tried not to let it go to my head. I am at this institution because it is a seat of learning. That's what makes me such a smartass." She was speaking directly to the Phi Beta Kappa key on his lapel.

When her sassiness did not discourage him from continuing to try to impress her, he told her that he was a member of Mensa. Again, he was surprised that she didn't seem to be awestruck. "You do know what Mensa is, don't you?"

"Yes," she said. "That's a monthly woman's problem."

"No, no. It means I am a genius."

"Ah, shucks, I wish you hadn't told me. I would have liked to guess that for myself."

Frustrated but now more determined than ever to strut his stuff, he explained that his name was printed in *Who's Who*.

Alissa's response was, "I was in *Who's Who* in 1960, but the following year, no one remembered my accomplishments, so that year I was listed in *What Was It?*"

"In the recent book I had published," he went on, showing he had even more in his academic arsenal, "my publisher felt it was important to list all my awards."

"If I ever get published," retorted Alissa, "I think my publisher would want to list disclaimers."

He became exasperated with her, got up, picked up his portable typewriter and headed for the door. "I can see we have nothing in common."

"I would never have guessed that you thought there was anything common about you," said Alissa, enjoying the opportunity to have the last word.

"Bye-bye," she called as he continued to walk away from her in a huff. "Take care, now. It must be lonely up there at the top."

They did actually have a lot in common, but Alissa wasn't about to play this game with him. At the time Alissa had this conversation with Mr. Pretentious, she, too, was eligible for membership in Mensa, her Life Adjustment Program on making the right decisions was published by her school district, and she had been listed in *Who's Who* twice. She didn't brag about what she'd accomplished, and she certainly wasn't impressed by people who did.

This attitude was due to George's insistence on maintaining humility. If anyone in the Barrett family was caught bragging, the family would make it family fun to deflate that person's ego. This applied to all accomplishments, good, small, or average. The target of this Barrett humor would become so frustrated that it would be rare that he would look for accolades from the family again.

◆◆◆

Fred also had a way to deflate egos. He didn't joke with people. He mocked them. This was a major difference in the way the two families operated. Education gave one the ability to state a position with wry humor, while a less-educated person often resorted to curse words developed from emotions of anger and low self-esteem.

When Alissa read Betty Friedan's book, Fred said she was behaving *like a bitch*.

When Jennifer sent her a banner from her trip to Israel with the famous quote from Hillel, "If I am not for myself, who will be for me? If I am only for myself, what am I? And if not now, when?" Fred said the banner gave

Alissa *newfangled ideas* that ruined their marriage. Had he known that it had been written more than two thousand years earlier, he might not have thought it so avant-garde, but he still would have attributed it as ruinous to what he expected their marriage should be.

This came at a time when Alissa was desperately searching for meaning. She had not yet realized her selfhood, although that would eventually change.

◆ ◆ ◆

Alissa enrolled in a sculpting class at a local artist's studio. She could attend only the night class when Fred would be home to watch the children. This meant the class would be comprised mostly of men; because it was more common *at this time* for mothers to take classes during the day when the children were in school. Most of the students were professional—local doctors, lawyers, and businessmen. Alissa was out of place for reasons other than her gender. She was shy and unsophisticated to the ways of the world. As soon as the men realized this, they began teasing her.

One day, the male students took up a collection to hire a live model so they could fine-tune their skills on proportions by practicing their sketching techniques. They told Alissa she did not have to chip in. "Just bring a pad of paper and a drawing pencil," they said.

The next time the class met, Alissa was stunned with what she found. The model was already there, standing nonchalantly *in the buff* in the middle of the room talking to the only other female student--who was enjoying a closer look. All the men were at the corner of the room snickering. All eyes went to Alissa. One of the men greeted her guiding her to a seat in the front of the studio where the model was to pose on the podium.

She sat down and opened her sketchbook, staring at the blank page to avoid looking at the naked man. She could hear chuckles, and although she knew her face was red with embarrassment, she was able to maintain her composure.

The instructor called the class to order introducing the model, Wootsie Dinger, a part-time student at Hofstra University. Everyone took their seats, and Wootsie immediately walked directly to Alissa's table and struck his Hercules pose. This brought hearty laughter from the entire class except for Alissa.

Mr. Dinger mounted the podium strutting his stuff like the professional model he was hired to be. Alissa was sketching his head and shoulders to avoiding looking further. Except for the time she'd spent in labor, this was the longest and most uncomfortable two hours Alissa had ever experienced.

When Wootsie took his break, Alissa considered leaving the classroom too, but she felt it was important to stay. Males were allowed to humiliate women. It was in their power playbook. Alissa understood it was self-preservation not to display the embarrassment she felt in the situation. If the game was not effective, they probably wouldn't try something like this again.

That night, she rushed home after class to tell Fred about the humiliating experience. He didn't care. He wasn't interested in the naked man, the class, the men who teased her, the fact that his wife was in tears, or anything else she had to say about the entire event. He didn't even comment about the fact that since he personally undressed in the closet and never showed his body to his wife, this was the first time she'd actually seen a man's full frame entirely in the nude.

◆ ◆ ◆

Fred had other issues. These were explained in his autobiography, aptly titled *Just Me*. The little booklet had been written in the first grade when he was six years old. He often showed this keepsake of his childhood to

Alissa to point out the extent to which he had gone to try to please his mother.

Joan Walters had wanted a girl, but she got *just me*, Fred explained. He told Alissa that he had tried to give his mother the girl she always wanted. Perhaps he did not realize how big a price he was required to pay. He helped with housework, and he hung around when her lady friends visited rather than doing guy things with his brother or father. His mother loved it, and encouraged him always to be at her beck and call. But living in a woman's world did not make Fred more sensitive or attuned to a woman's needs. It made him clingy and whiny, as he tried to become something he was not. That became a problem with his father.

Fred never felt his father approved of him. If Charlie's constantly berating him in public was any indicator, Fred was probably right. A vicious cycle developed. The more Charlie criticized Fred, the smaller Fred became in his father's eyes, and the more insignificant Fred became, the more his father browbeat him.

Fred was in an untenable position. Nothing he did could please his father or live up to the success of his brother. The only accomplishment Fred derived from his father was when he imitated Charlie's disrespectful treatment of women, especially his wife.

Dinner time at the Walterses' home was not infused with the lively intellectual conversations about the matters of life that Alissa had grown up with. Discussions were exclusively about business and events of the workday and were full of tedious details. The only pleasure the Walterses seemed to enjoy was when they learned of the failure of a business competitor. The Walterses would not have known a creative idea if one had hit them in the head. The only enthusiasm Charlie showed was when he would exercise his impatience by bullying his youngest son, Fred.

Robert, Fred's older brother, escaped his father's criticism by dutifully modeling Charlie, hanging on his every word, and learning all the skills that would one day make him a shrewd businessman in his own right. He and his father would discuss business down to the minutest detail with a goal of accumulating great wealth. Robert was a natural bully who *like his father* demanded that his (and only his) point of view was accepted. Robert believed that people are acquiescent to bullies because accepting a strong, assertive voice telling them what to do is easier than making independent decisions. His modus operandi was to herd his followers into submission. He was everything his father could praise, while Fred was the antithesis of Robert and received nothing from his father except humiliation and denigration.

◆◆◆

Fred's and Alissa's marriage started to erode years before the paperwork for the divorce was submitted to the judge. Seeds were planted while Alissa was attending a four-week-long intensive college workshop in Massachusetts to work toward a master's degree in education. All the women in the class were divorced. She would hear them complaining about their ex-husbands, and although she did not participate in the male bashing, what they described gnawed at Alissa. She was too embarrassed to let anyone know that she was less than happy with her husband. These were competent women, living on their own and thankful that they had rid themselves of husbands who held them back. Each had a different story, but all said they were better off alone. Earning their own salaries had opened new doors and enabled them to close doors that had kept them locked within a system of involuntary servitude where they were denied self-expression and thereby self-esteem.

Alissa came home at the end of the session in tears and voiced her concerns to Fred. "This isn't going to happen to us, is it, Fred?" she sobbed.

"Of course, not," he replied. "We're happy. Don't get so worried. I have a surprise for you." What Alissa was not aware of at the time was that while she was out of town earning her master's degree, Fred had taken steps to position himself financially so that their primary asset would be in his name alone. Surprise!

Prior to the workshop, she and Fred had found a house for sale on the Connecticut shoreline, overlooking Long Island Sound. It was nestled in a grove of old trees. The panoramic view from the property was of sailboats leisurely floating on the water as they sailed past the house. The price was reduced because the Van Heusens, who were selling the property, were getting a divorce. Alissa knew that with her artistic flair, she could improve the property by redesigning the floor plan to take advantage of the fantastic view and make the home fit the lifestyle that was their ultimate dream.

While she was away at the workshop in Massachusetts, Fred completed the deal. He contacted Mr. Van Heusen and proposed a deal that neither man could refuse. They settled upon a price, half of which would be disclosed on sales documents that would go through attorney Ed Bane, and be recorded on the property tax rolls. It was not so incidental that Bane was a business acquaintance of Fred's and on retainer for Upton and Sons. The other half of the price would be cash–between the guys. That way, as seller, Mr. Van Heusen would not have to tell his wife the total sales price, and he would keep some walking-around money while Fred would pay property tax on the under-market transaction.

The seller reasoned that he was justified in structuring the sale this way because he had spent a thousand dollars for his wife's breast augmentation, and she had paid him back by having an affair with the plastic surgeon. This would even things out. She retained custody of the boobs (even though she had always insisted that it was her husband who had urged her to undergo the painful surgery), and he would cagily pocket the cash.

Fred's benefit was that only his name would be on the title. He would own the house exclusively. If Alissa had asked any questions, he consealed the subterfuge by telling her it was not necessary for her to sign any documents except for the loan, since they were married. He reminded her that Connecticut was not a community property state, but they were equally responsible for joint marital debts.

"Remember that new house on Steamboat Road you fell in love with? I purchased it—just for you. Look, honey," he said, showing her the thick file of mortgage papers.

So while Fred was reassuring Alissa that all was well with their marriage, he had already constructed a secret deal that precluded her from ever being able to benefit from the eventual sale of the Steamboat Road house. This did not mean that Fred suspected their marriage, like those of the women Alissa met, might someday end in divorce. To Fred, it was a matter of prudence to structure any business deal to his best advantage. He didn't believe he was cheating his wife. He already had total control of all their business transactions. This was not new behavior. It was an insurance policy, a power trip, and a major coup.

◆ ◆ ◆

The Steamboat Road house was a newly constructed, split-level, three-bedroom home typical of the 1970s. While the property was situated above The Sound, with garden steps descending to the water, the garage faced the view, and all the primary rooms faced the street. It had curb appeal, but for Alissa, it lacked livability appeal. That presented her with a challenge.

For the next two years, using the cash proceeds from the sale of their Shady Lane residence, Alissa, as the designer and prime mover, worked with Art Houser, an accomplished local contractor and architect, to modify the simple structure into a stunning showpiece. Fred arranged to pay the architect's fees by bartering his services or transferring to him the title to parcels of land in the sleeper file of Upton and Sons that had no potential buyers.

What Alissa accomplished with the architect was stunning. They installed large floor-to-ceiling windows on the exterior walls, where there was a view toward the private woods. The rooms downstairs were opened to the view of the sound by removing most of the interior walls. The former living room and dining room were turned into bedrooms for Katie and Josh, with space remaining for a guest room. In the kitchen, cabinets were replaced with custom maple, an island was added, and brightly painted ceramic-tile counters were laid in, framing the newly installed top-of-the-line appliances, including a built-in microwave oven.

Then they added a new structure overlooking the sound. It had a second story across the entire length of the house. This would be the new master suite, complete with Fred's business office, her studio, dual walk-in closets, and a sumptuous bathroom complete with a Jacuzzi, a sauna, and a bidet. The view from her studio overlooking the sound through the glass walls gave her a perfect place to do her sculpting. The house was equipped with a fine stereo sound system. Installation of the indoor pool would be left for the next owner, but they kept the darkroom in the basement for the possibility that one of the kids might one day like to dabble in photography.

◆ ◆ ◆

The remodeling housewarming was a grand event, with both of their extended families attending. Jennifer Cohen and her second husband, Dr. Clark Coleman, who were on their honeymoon, were able to attend and stay for a few days to enjoy the Long Island Sound.

The event had gone swimmingly except for the scene that Charlie Walters instigated when he asked Clark if he was related to Amos Bigley.

"No, I have no Bigley relatives," said the MD graciously.

"Well, you look just like him," said Charlie, laughing.

Clark pretended not to hear any affront.

Both Alissa and Jennifer believed that Charlie was expressing the views of the entire Walters family. "He doesn't look anything at all like Amos," insisted Alissa. "Clark looks like Harry Belafonte, and Amos looks like Sidney Poitier, and I'm sure the Poitier and Belafonte families are not related."

Even that uncouth exchange did not spoil the event for Alissa. She felt she had carved a diamond out of rough stone. She did. What she did not know was that it was *Fred*'s jewel. Thanks to him, her name was not recorded on any of the legal documents showing ownership. Alissa owned only half the mortgage debt and was unaware that there were other documents that had been filed with the county clerk.

Each month, until the mortgage was repaid ten years later, Alissa dutifully signed over her entire check to her husband. While Fred was telling her he was commingling all her money with his because they were "a team," in fact, none of her team participation was being documented. Alissa understood that they needed her salary to satisfy the payments on the mortgage. This was fine with her. She was willing to do her part to build for the future. What she did not know was that by the time the divorce took place and the mortgage was paid in full, Fred would convince the court that during their marriage, Alissa had kept her money for her own personal use.

This is how Alissa was shortchanged ten years later, in 1982, by her husband, with the assistance of Mr. Bane, Esquire, and the approval of the courts, when Fred convinced them all that he was being magnanimous by giving Alissa her "true interest" in the value (i.e., one-fifth of the selling price of their home).

◆◆◆

"There is something wrong with my engagement ring," Alissa cried her alarm to her best friend, Jennifer, whom she had called to convey her latest fears. "Jennifer, I know this is going to sound crazy, but I think Fred had my ring reset."

"Did he tell you he was going to do that?"

"No, but the stone isn't right. It's smaller, and Jennifer, this is not a diamond. It doesn't reflect the sunlight. I think Fred had my diamond replaced with a cubic zirconia."

Jennifer laughed. "Sit down and calm down. Have you been into the cooking sherry?"

"I can't sit down. I can't sit still. I can't stand still."

"Well, you had better stand still before you pull the telephone cord out of the wall. Get hold of yourself. You can't blame Fred every time something goes wrong in your life. Maybe you got soap on the diamond. That can keep it from sparkling. Why in the world would Fred want to deceive you like this?"

"It's a feeling I have, Jennifer. I can't explain it. But I know for sure that the stone is missing. I know it's not mine."

"Well, before you go accusing someone, why don't you go to a jeweler and have the stone checked? But if I were you, I would ask Fred first. You owe it to him, Alissa. There may be a simple explanation."

After she completed the call to Jennifer, Alissa was calm enough to sit down and think more about the ring. She remembered something that might explain the mystery. The prior week when she had taken too much sun during a day of sailing with Fred, Jennifer, and Clark, she'd spent a day in bed with edema. The swelling was so severe that her fingers swelled. She removed the ring because it was cutting off her circulation. She also remembered that when Fred noticed she wasn't wearing it, she told him that it was on the bathroom vanity in a porcelain box where she kept some of her favorite costume jewelry. That explained why and when she'd taken her ring off, but it looked bad for Fred because he was the only other person who knew where she put it.

That night after dinner, when they were in the living room watching an episode of *Star Trek*, Alissa chose her opportunity when the commercial came on. "Honey, would you have any reason to replace the stone in my setting?" she asked, showing Fred her left hand.

"What?"

"I'm sorry, but this isn't my diamond, Fred. I just wondered why."

"You're nuts. That's the same diamond I gave you when I proposed to you. What the hell are you talking about?"

"No, really, honey, it's not the same." She pulled her legs up under her body and rose up on her knees to plead with him. She moved her left hand to give him a better look. "It's hard to tell in this light, but I can't get colors from the facets anymore, and look, honey, it's too small. If you look closely, you can see that someone used an alloy to fill in the space between the old setting and the new stone. That made the area for the prongs smaller. Fred, I think this is a cubic zirconia."

Fred jumped up off the couch.

"Where are you going?" asked Alissa.

"I have to take a crap."

Alissa slumped into the cushions and looked at her ring again. She was still bewildered and argued against her own suspicions. Jennifer was right. Fred had no reason to change her ring. It was her engagement ring.

Fred did not return to watch his favorite TV show. He stopped at the fridge to take out a beer and went upstairs to his office to do some paperwork. Alissa found him there.

"I think I'll take it to the jeweler tomorrow. I may be wrong," she said.

"You will do no such thing."

"Why not? I'll probably fret about this until I know for sure."

"I don't need any more of your bills," he said.

"Bills? The jeweler won't charge me for looking. I'll tell him I want an appraisal."

Fred was furious. He rose up out of his office chair and confronted Alissa. His face was right up against hers, and he was yelling. "You will not. I told you. You will not disobey me again. You are a stupid, suspicious woman, and I won't have you ruining my reputation with your false accusations. I've told you a million times not to exaggerate."

Alissa shivered. She hung her head, taking the verbal tirade against her. Her fingers twisted the ring. She rubbed it, hoping that doing so might make it magically become the beautiful diamond she had worn for so many years and hoping the pain of the confrontation with her husband would stop.

Alissa left while Fred returned to his office work, content that he had again intimidated his wife into compliance. He closed the door and locked it so she would not bother him again that night.

◆ ◆ ◆

Taking unfair advantage of people, not honoring the feelings of others, winning at any cost—these Machiavellian traits were Fred's trademark. He was charming and persuasive. He believed he was cultured and told everyone that he had completed college. Actually, if this was culture, it was yogurt. He had many opportunities to prove this.

Fred took Alissa with him to Paris for a business convention. Before they left for the airport, he weighed their luggage to be sure he would not be charged the excess baggage fee. This wasn't unusual in itself. Many travelers do this. They stand on a bathroom scale to get a reading of their own weight, and then they stand on it again while holding the luggage. It isn't very precise, but it's "close enough for government work" and puts the traveler at ease. When they arrived at the terminal and checked in, the weight on the scales was different from what he had calculated at home. Although the difference in weight didn't result in him being charged an extra fee, Fred wasn't going to let this discrepancy go. He insisted the airport scales were wrong.

"You are violating my Norman Conquest rights," he demanded of the dumbfounded airline employee. "I want these measured correctly before I get on that plane."

The clerk looked at Alissa, searching for someone who might help him deal with Fred's unusual complaint.

"I think he means the Magna Carta," she offered. "Let's not make this an international incident, Fred. Let's go to the gate before the plane leaves without us."

Unfortunately, several of the passengers waiting in line that day were also part of the same business convention the Walterses were going to.

Whenever one of them saw Fred in the hotel, they would laugh and call out, "Lose anything to the Norman Invasion today?"

Fred's response was always to explain that he knew the trick about putting your thumb on the scale, and any prudent businessman would double-check.

Alissa spent days in the hotel while the other wives from the United States were on sight-seeing trips paid for by their husbands. Fred had brought only two hundred dollars to France, and Alissa did not feel worthy to spend any of it on herself. When the convention was over, Fred heard that some of the other men in their travel group were going to purchase gifts in Paris for their wives. When he learned that the wife from Texas was given a Cartier bracelet, the one from Maryland was being fitted for a Dior gown, the wife from Kansas would be taking home a large bottle of Chanel No. 5, and the one from Arizona would be taken on a ski trip to Saint Moritz, he thought of taking Alissa to visit the Louvre.

He would pay to take Alissa to look at pictures but not for cab fare to get there. He completed his gift package by searching the city map at the concierge desk to find out which metro line to take.

Alissa was thrilled at the idea of going to the Louvre. She had been able to practice her French only once, when she asked the maid for *bain mousse* (bath foam). The trip would give her an opportunity to shine for Fred. She could explain the paintings, and he might learn enough about her passion to be able to enjoy this part of her life with her. She accepted graciously and enthusiastically and didn't even embarrass him by pointing out that he had pronounced the name of the museum as *louver*.

When they arrived at the Louvre, Fred directed Alissa past the groups of tourists who were forming for the paid guided tours. He whisked her through the corridors crowded with people viewing the fine art as if he were in a speed-walking marathon. As they whizzed past the French impressionists, Alissa suddenly stopped, tugging on Fred to show him what she saw.

"Do you see it, Fred? This is what I have been trying to explain to you–the use of blues by the impressionists–don't you see? This is what I feel when I paint. These are the moods I try to express."

Fred not only did not see what she was trying to communicate to him, but he was in a hurry to get through the exhibit. He rushed away. Alissa was three steps behind him and whispering to him every time he slowed down long enough for her to catch up.

"Please, Fred; can't we see the Mona Lisa? I'm sorry, but I've wanted to see it all my life."

They found Leonardo's masterpiece surprisingly isolated on the second floor. There were no crowds pressing to view it, and it was not flanked by guards.

"I can't believe this is not protected. This is one of da Vinci's most famous works of art," said Alissa.

Her excitement erupted into a volcano of words telling her husband what this moment meant to her. "It took Leonardo four years to complete this. It's the likeness of the third wife of Francesco del Giacondo. He used other models besides the wife. If Leonardo didn't use Francesco's wife for the entire four years, I wonder if Francesco's marriage lasted the entire four years. Maybe this was the doing-in for Mr. and Mrs. del Giacondo," she said with a laugh.

"You have to see this, Fred. Come closer. Look at her hands. They are reputed to be the most perfectly drawn hands in Italian art. Leonardo thought her face was perfect, an ideal type to paint. You are looking at da Vinci, right now, Fred. Don't you feel it, Fred? It comes off the canvas to reach out to you and yet..."

Alissa paused as she suddenly realized Fred was not by her side. Other visitors to the museum were listening to her explanation, and they crowded around her and began asking her questions. She continued with her description of the masterpiece, but she kept looking into the crowd, straining to find her husband. She was getting worried.

An organized tour group arrived to view the Mona Lisa, and lo and behold, there was Fred at the edge of the group, where he had slipped in without paying. He was listening to the guide's explanation. He had missed most of Alissa's. The tour group moved on, leaving the wayward husband in its wake. His explanation for his leaving her was pure Fred. He wanted to find someone "who knew what they were talking about."

Alissa was crushed and could not utter another word. She was suddenly fatigued and lost her interest in the museum. "Fred, couldn't we take a cab back to the hotel? I'm sorry, but I'm too tired to walk."

She understood that Fred did not share her passion for art. But couldn't he be a little more sympathetic? A dispute went with them onto the streets of Paris. They weren't arguing because of her request to leave the museum but because of her extravagant suggestion that they take a cab to get back to the hotel.

"You don't know how to hire a cab. How are you going to tell them where to go?" Fred asked.

She faintly defended her plan. "Fred, I've studied French for five years. I can direct the driver to Avenue Opera and the Hotel Edouard VII."

When the cab arrived, a fatigued Alissa—with a reluctant Fred following behind and worrying about how much this would cost—entered for the short trip.

"Hotel Edouard VII Opera, please," she said.

The driver shrugged his shoulders.

"Rue Opera et Champs," said Alissa, remembering her father's instruction to always put the correct inflection on foreign words when traveling in the country where it is the native tongue.

Once again the driver shrugged his shoulders.

Fred was ready to jump out of the cab. "I thought you said you could speak enough French to give this man directions." His hand went for the door handle.

The cab driver turned to stop him. "Thank god someone speaks English. I'm Portuguese, and I don't understand French. Where would you two like to go?

ELEVEN

You Have to Know the History

Something new was going on with Alissa. She sat at the kitchen table without speaking through the happy chatter of the children eating pizza and talking about their Christmas presents. After Josh and Katie went to bed, Fred reminded Alissa that it was time for her to retire as well. She didn't move even when he yelled at her; the best she could do was to make her way into the bedroom, where she stood and stared at the wall. Fred selected a pair of pajamas for her and guided her into bed. He was worried, but he didn't have a clue what would be needed to help her, and he wasn't going to tell anyone about this because they might blame him.

Alissa stayed in bed for more than a week. When the school called to see why she wasn't back in her classroom after the holiday break, Fred told them that Alissa *was depressed again*. This was totally unfair on Fred's part. She had never before missed work due to depression. His remarks were meant to discredit Alissa.

Ever since they had returned from the trip to Paris, Alissa was distant and unanimated. She wasn't taking care of herself. Fred or the children brought food in to her. They tried to engage her in conversation, but she responded only with a *yes* or *no*. They brought her new books and saw them remain unopened on the nightstand. They turned on music for her, and she got out of bed to turn it off. They opened the drapes to let the sunlight in, and she closed them. She refused telephone calls, and when Hester came over, at Fred's urging, to admonish her for not taking care of her family, she fell into an uncontrollable period of crying. When George left a message asking if she was okay, she said *no.* All efforts her family made were ignored. She remained in a black hole of her own creation.

Alissa was reverting to a tried-and-true pattern of escape taken when things were beyond her ability to cope. As a child, her favorite withdrawal had been to hide out on the island near her parents' home. This time she fled with her pain, by car, to Webb Island.

It was night. It was raining. Alissa did not feel the rain. She was not bothered by the darkness. She backed the car out of the garage and had traveled five miles before an oncoming motorist caught her attention by flashing his headlights on and off, signaling her to turn hers on.

The flashing of his headlights interrupted her spell. Alissa reached to the dashboard to turn on her headlights. By accident, she turned on the windshield wipers as well. She rolled down the window for air. She was more alert now but intent on continuing whatever drive was causing her strange behavior.

She approached the bridge to the island. Her headlights picked up the weathered wooden railing that was in such poor repair it no longer served as a guardrail. It was only a boundary marker. She was determined to go forward.

Beyond the rail was the sound of the slapping of the waves against the pilings under the bridge. The moon caused the surf to shimmer. The tide had submerged the rocks--concealing their danger. The smell of the water was inviting. The cadence of the waves was mesmerizing--Alissa was captured in their call.

She feared the water, and she did not want to die. She only wanted to fill her emptiness, and she knew the water could do that. The cold water would take away the heat of anger she felt burning inside her. She made her decision. She pressed on the accelerator and turned the steering wheel toward the railing.

She was focused.

She was determined.

But there was something greater at hand.

From the corner of her eye, she could make out a faint image behind her. There was an essence in the back seat. The presence restrained Alissa just as the wheels of the car were about to ram into the railing.

As the force from the presence overcame her need to move forward, she heard a voice clearer than anyone she had ever heard say, "Alissa…it is not your time."

Alissa steered the car away from the railing. It was traveling at fifty miles per hour. She lost her ability to control it. It careened down a narrow, winding utility road, stopping at water's edge. With her wits intact, she suddenly became aware of her predicament. She didn't know where she was. The sky was black, she heard distinct sounds of life from as far as the city, and she was able to see particles of air floating past her face showing that the world had expanded--she would have just enough time to stop the car before it plunged into the sea.

She sat silently, hearing her heart pounding with a sound so great it superimposed the splashing, ominous sound of the surf crashing against the rocks.

She shivered. She felt fear of the unknown, but when that passed, she slowly became acclimated to her surroundings.

Her brain felt like jelly and she feared she could not rely upon her reasoning. She was afraid she would not be able to get the car back to the main road. The engine had stopped and she was afraid she would not be able to start it again. She turned for help to the backseat--to identify the presence in the backseat that had called out to her.

Moonlight filled the car. There was no one there with her. But the moonlight was soft, the sea air felt warm, and Alissa was slowly being released from her depression. Replacing the blackness was a consuming feeling of awe.

◆ ◆ ◆

When Alissa returned to the classroom late from the winter break, she had a message that Dr. Dudley, the principal, wanted to see her. Dudley was concerned because Fred had told him that Alissa had been too depressed to come to work. This was not the Alissa he knew. He wanted to check out this information himself. He knew Fred, and he did not trust what he said.

Dr. Dudley knew the couple's marriage was strained, and he had previously advised Alissa to leave her husband. Dudley felt that Alissa had outgrown Fred. He recalled Alissa's comments at the time. Alissa said that she might have grown apart from her husband but had not outgrown him. Dudley understood this comment to be evidence of her modesty. He understood Alissa better than she understood herself. This was the woman who had come to him stating that she did not want to teach the children how to answer multiple choice and true-or-false questions; she wanted to teach them how to think for themselves.

Dr. Dudley also knew that for years Fred had been having an affair with his married psychiatrist Ellen Livingston. It was common knowledge in professional circles, and he knew that the affair had been going on long before Fred married Alissa. He was not going to divulge this secret to Alissa, but if she was depressed, Dr. Dudley looked to Fred as the underlying cause.

When she arrived for the meeting, she was in pain from a dislocated shoulder.

"Alissa, you seem to be uncomfortable in that chair. Can I get you another?"

"It's not the chair. I think my shoulder is dislocated. It's causing me a great deal of pain."

"How did that happen?"

"It happened this morning. Fred was trying to be good to me. I've been complaining that he doesn't show me enough affection. So he came to the bed to kiss me good-bye before he went to work. He sat on my shoulder. I heard it pop."

"What did Fred say when it popped?"

"He didn't say anything, but I think he heard it because he got up before I got my kiss."

"Did you tell him what he did?"

"I didn't want to discourage him. He was finally going to give me affection."

"So you are going to get affection even if it cripples you? Promise me that you will see a doctor about your shoulder."

Alissa didn't want to promise the principal anything. She didn't see that she needed help. She was quick to explain how much better she felt since her encounter with the spirit on the bridge. But Dudley surmised that this woman needed more help than his encouragement could provide. He wasn't impressed with her spiritual encounter, but he was impressed with her optimism to continue her life. What also impressed him was her trusting honesty that caused her to admit that she had tried to commit suicide.

This presented a conundrum for him. According to state law, he was obliged to report this, and if she was found to be unstable, she would lose her job. Dr. Dudley had difficulty with the black and white of this rule, and he observed that Alissa did not appear to be suicidal. He noted that the incident had taken place during school break, and her absence would not affect her class. In spite of the pain from her dislocated shoulder, she radiated serenity as if she had been touched by an angel. He came up with a compromise—one that would keep a valued teacher in the classroom and allow him to meet the requirements of the intention of the law, if not the letter.

He offered that if Alissa were to get a consultation from a psychiatrist, he would treat this as a medical condition, approve some sick leave if needed, and put off filing the report with the state of Connecticut, *at least until he had additional time to observe her.*

◆ ◆ ◆

Alissa selected her psychiatrist carefully. She called the New York University School of Medicine for a list of graduates practicing in Connecticut.

She thought a woman would understand her better, but there were only a few women listed, and none had a practice near her home. She chose three male names and called the office of each to interview the staff and see if they would be a good fit.

Dr. Silvano Lovato, with a second degree in theology from Georgetown University, was her choice. She knew of the emphasis the Jesuits had on education, and she felt comfortable that Dr. Lovato would have high moral standards and respect for the sanctity of marriage.

She was reluctant to seek professional help because she didn't want anyone in the community to know that she was in therapy. It would have threatened her job if anyone in the school district discovered her. Dr. Lovato's office was in a large professional building that housed a variety of medical offices. Anyone seeing her going into the building would not know which doctor she was seeing. The exit to the parking lot was in the rear, so no one would see her leaving.

◆◆◆

The session began as she told Dr. Lovato of the episode that she thought was the issue she needed to resolve, her unsuccessful attempt at suicide. Alissa explained that she felt it was because of problems she was having with her marriage.

True to professional form, Lovato showed no sign of disapproval or shock except to set some guidelines. "You must realize that I can in no way encourage you toward a decision to get a divorce. It's an ethical standard of our group. But let me ask you this. Are either you or your husband having an extramarital affair?"

"Not me, but I believe he's had several affairs. Do you want to know about the latest one or the ones he has had before?"

"Let's start with the latest, but before we go there, let me ask you, how would you rate your sexual life?"

"Nonexistent. Fred is impotent with me."

"When did that start?"

"About a year ago. At first I thought he was only tired because he was working so hard. He had to keep late hours. It was at a time when his business was not successful. The harder he worked, the angrier he became with me."

"And you think that he expressed his anger toward you by withholding sex from you?"

"I suppose so."

"Often anger arouses men to be more sexually active."

"He is. But it's not with me. I think I'm not attractive enough for him any longer. I've been running to keep my body in tone. He used to compliment me on my legs, so I bought a really cute pair of short shorts. They are very provocative. Last week after a run, I dropped in at his office to surprise him. It wasn't the proper attire for the office, but I knew I would turn heads, and I wanted him to see that other men would find me attractive."

"What kind of reaction did you get?"

"The guys in the office loved it. They whistled. Fred came out of his private office to see what the commotion was about, and he scolded me. I was expecting both of those reactions, but what I wasn't expecting was to be told in a confidential whisper from one of the company employees that my husband was having an affair with Roberta Jones."

"Do you know who Roberta Jones is?"

"Yes, she is the wife of one of the real estate salesmen."

"Do you think Mrs. Jones is more attractive than you?"

"No. I think she is sleazy. She wears low-cut blouses and rubs up against the men whenever she has the opportunity."

"Is that why you are modifying your behavior?"

"Yes. I'm trying not to be as conservative as I have been in the past. I've been reading *Cosmopolitan* magazine to get hints about how to please my husband."

"And did you see any change in your husband because of this?"

"Yes, he kept a record of which issues of *Cosmo* I was reading and accused me of being wicked."

"We might consider having your husband in therapy, too."

"He would never consent to that. He has been in therapy for years, and he doesn't talk about it."

◆ ◆ ◆

This was the beginning of weekly sessions that lasted for one year. At Dr. Lovato's direction, she talked about her parents, her children, her job, her dreams, and her disappointments. In fact, they talked about everything she could think of, and since they weren't finding a cause sufficient to explain her attempted suicide, the only relief she had from her continuing unhappiness was that her mood swings could be regulated with medication. Alissa was beginning to wonder if perhaps her potty training might be at the bottom of all this.

She continued the sessions based on questions Lovato posed at each session, and after a period of time, she learned it was indeed the potty training, or as Dr. Lovato explained, "It started when you were too young to control anything in your life. Your parents trapped you. You were the weapon they used to fight each other. It was their battle, and you were the way they fought."

"I think I understand that," said Alissa, "and they made me feel it was my fault they argued. Maybe that's why I kept saying *I'm sorry*. That annoyed Fred. He said that he counted me saying *I'm sorry* thirteen times one day."

"It annoyed him because it reminded him that saying *I'm sorry* was his behavior too."

◆ ◆ ◆

Alissa told Dr. Lovato about the time when Fred beat her. She was physically shuddering as she related the event. "Fred and his friend had just come off the golf course, and Fred wanted to go to the Gay Paris

Ballroom. They invited me and his friend's wife to join them. The guys traded us on the dance floor, and my partner was sweating. The aroma of his aftershave turned into the musty odor of a locker room. He held me so closely, the only way I could distance myself was to pull my head back. My body was stuck against his. It was more like vertical sex than ballroom dancing."

"Yes," Dr. Lovato said, believing he might be observing a frigid wife. "Please go on."

"Fred's friend said, 'What would you do if I started blowing into your ear?' And I said, 'What would you do if I raised my knee into your crotch?'"

Dr. Lovato slumped back into his chair, trying to hide a smile.

"When we got to our house, I ran inside. Fred stayed outside awhile talking to them. He was probably apologizing for my rude behavior."

"Is that what you think he was talking about?"

Alissa started to sob. "No, I think he was telling his friend's wife that he was sorry that I had spoiled the evening for them. He obviously was captivated by her. She had told us during the dinner conversation about a time she had sex with her gynecologist on his examining table. She's a beautiful woman. She's pert, small, busty, has good legs, and thick black hair that cascades down her shoulders. She has an absolutely radiant smile, and her natural, provocative personality enchanted us all as she talked."

"Did she make you jealous?"

"I didn't admire her actions. She is also crude. She told us she pulled in front of a cement truck, cutting him off. And when the driver rolled down the window to yell at her, she gave him the finger and drove away laughing. I didn't know how crude she would be with us or how far she would have gone that night."

"You did know how far she would go, Alissa; you do not want to admit it."

Alissa started to cry. "When Fred came in the house, he was raging mad. I was already in the bedroom and getting ready for bed. He slammed the door shut and pushed me onto the bed. He knocked me down. He tore off my clothes. He was so angry," she sobbed, unable to control her shivering.

Alissa could not tell the psychiatrist the entire story. She paused to collect her thoughts. *She had not been in the bedroom getting reading for bed when Fred found her. She had hidden from him. She was instinctively frightened. While he was putting the car into the garage, she had run down into the basement, turned off the lights, and was cowering in a fetal position in the darkened room. She could hear his footsteps as he searched the house. He was calling her name. She put her hands over her ears to try to block the sound. She closed her eyes.*

He searched the basement last, and turning on the lights, he screamed profanities at her as he ran down the steps. When he found her, he slammed his fist into her face. Her head hit the concrete wall, and she lost consciousness for a brief moment. When she revived, Fred was gone. She dragged herself up the steps, went to the bedroom, washed the blood from her face, and crawled into the bed next to her husband.

She was still sobbing and shivering when Dr. Lovato interrupted her thoughts. "Alissa, you don't have to continue if you don't want to. I get the picture. Did he tell you he blamed you for ruining his evening?"

"Yes," she cried out in anguish. "He had wanted me to have an affair with his sweaty friend so he could have one with his friend's beautiful wife. He was bartering me as if I was a slave at the auction block."

"Did he rape you that night?"

"No, Fred doesn't have sex with me. But he lit into me, really hitting me hard. Thankfully, his fists hit only my stomach."

"Why are you thankful about blows to your stomach?"

"The bruises didn't show. No one would have to know."

Alissa had convinced herself that she was the reason her husband was not able to perform sexually. Her father had told her that it was a woman's place to "bring her husband joy." She had failed to do that. Although she didn't believe she deserved to be beaten up, she concluded that she must have made some poor choices and that these were at the bottom of the feelings of guilt that dominated her moods. Alissa felt that she had sabotaged herself and that she was punishing herself, and she was not living up to her father's expectations to be intelligent and able to solve any problem.

But Dr. Lovato said she might look at this a different way. He explained that she was allowing Fred to project his guilt on to her, and Lovato assured her that sexual impotence is very complicated. "You can't be as bad as you say you are, Alissa. When you tell me that one day you counted that you had apologized thirteen times to your husband, I think you are overdoing it. No one makes thirteen offensive errors in one day. Are you that incompetent? I think not. Are you protecting your husband? I think you are. Alissa, consider this. You have already emotionally left him. He has physically abused you. That behavior will continue and get worse. The only person you need to protect is yourself. If you want me to help you save your marriage, I need to meet him."

That request from Dr. Lovato went nowhere. Fred refused to attend sessions with Alissa or private sessions with her psychiatrist. He stopped paying the medical bills.

Dr. Lovato could offer her medication and talk therapy as needed. He had no answers except to tell her that there was nothing wrong with her or the feelings she had; in fact, he complimented her on her strength. *No one could have put up with this unless that person was strong.*

"I don't like to stop therapy unless there is someone in your life that you can talk to. Is there someone else with whom you can confide?"

"Yes. There is Jennifer Coleman. I've known her since Swarthmore, but she doesn't live in Connecticut."

"You have a phone, don't you? Use it. Use it often, Alissa."

TWELVE

The Shell-Out Game

The Walters brothers made their fortune when they discovered a boarded-up building for sale on Tuckahoe Road in the Bronx. They purchased it with all its contents. It had been standing vacant and came loaded with a hidden treasure. The basement was filled with rusty old farm equipment, automobiles, and vehicle parts. For years, the old, two-story brick-masonry dinosaur had been a dumping ground for local car-repair establishments whose owners were reluctant to pay fees required for hauling away their heavy rusting relics. The collection began during the Depression from vehicles that had been held for collateral. Out of financial necessity, these were often relinquished when the owners could not make the payments to regain their property secured by the chattel mortgages.

The junk would be so expensive to move that Fred's father, Charlie, and Fred's uncle Larry were able to negotiate a lower-than-market price when they purchased the building in 1933, lock, stock, and barrel. They found a real bargain, but the building could not be used except for the street-level corner office they cleaned up for a real estate office. The brothers allowed the whole mess to continue to deteriorate while they blamed each other for tying up all their funds in an investment that generated no income. It was well-known that the Walters brothers were the fastest persons in town to put a deal together, because in 1942, when railroads were tearing up unused rail lines, cities were removing ornamental fences from around parks, housewives were saving cooking grease, and children were collecting the silver linings in cigarette packaging, Charlie and Larry made some big bucks. They sold all that junk from their building as scrap metal for the war effort.

The result of this serendipitous windfall was twofold. First, the feuding brothers mistook themselves for savvy businessmen, and second, they kept trying to repeat this once-in-a-lifetime lucky jackpot. The brothers were never again content with the ordinary profits of tried-and-true business procedures. Beginning as the masters of angle iron, the brothers broadened their horizons and became the masters of angles in general. Their newly acquired fortune changed them both for the worse. Larry dropped any pretext of ethics, and Charlie just dropped his pants.

◆ ◆ ◆

Charlie wasn't the only one dropping his pants; his son Fred had also learned to disrespect women in this way. One fall, when Charlie and Joan were leaving for their annual winter escape to Florida, Charlie arranged for Fred to winterize the house for them. This meant Fred promised to periodically show up at their estate to check to see that everything was in working order and the heat was keeping the house adequately warm as the temperature dropped. Charlie didn't want the thermostat operating all winter when his son could be required to monitor the heat inside the house.

This was a bonanza for Fred, because he would have a place to entertain the ladies in beautiful surroundings where no one would interrupt them, and he would save money on motel bills. One of the ladies who engaged in these escapades with Fred was Cynthia Lucci, the young woman he had recently hired to be his office clerk. Cynthia was a quiet, devout woman who had been educated in a strict parochial boarding school. But under the spell of Fred's charm, an illicit relationship developed. It began with his playfully calling her Cyn and progressed with touchy-feely teasing to "Lucci, Lucci, Lucci, you're my Lucci Poochie Coo." The relationship soon became lascivious. Fred admired her legs, especially when they were wrapped around him.

Each afternoon, the couple served each other a decadent dessert at the Walterses' estate. It was a perfect business ploy for Fred. Unwilling to pick up the tab for his lover's lunch, he would stop by one of the nearby restaurants where the manager saved lunch receipts for him that other customers left behind. Fred collected these for his tax return. He could screw another one of his girlfriends while he was screwing the IRS.

Cynthia was awed by the magnificence of the Walterses' property. She had never been in a home so opulent. She imagined herself as the lady of the manor as they drove onto the gated property to the portico, where Fred would park the company car, assured that the dense landscaping would shelter it from public view.

For Fred, a man who never sweated the details, this was always a rush to gratification. He knew nothing of foreplay. On their way back to the office one Friday afternoon, a threatening storm was making its way onshore. Had Fred noticed this before they left the house, he might have paid more attention to this ominous threat and raised the temperature on the thermostat. But he didn't. He had other things on his mind. He had to get Cynthia back to the office before her husband arrived to pick her up for the long Christmas holiday weekend.

Meanwhile, back at the manor, as the storm came in, snow started to fall, covering the grounds to a depth of three feet. It looked like a winter wonderland the following morning as Fred arrived, intending to check on the property. It was useless to enter the house with all that snow on the driveway. *His customary method of snow removal was to wait for spring.* But he didn't have to wait that long. He had to wait only until the night he got the call that jarred him out of his sleep.

Charlie was calling from Florida. He was screaming into the phone. "The police are at the house. What the hell is going on? They said the neighbors called because the alarm is ringing. You have to get your butt down there and let them into the house."

"I was just there Saturday," said Fred, whining. He hoped his father would believe that he was doing his duty. But the excuse was useless; Charlie had already slammed down the receiver. He did not trust Fred to solve this. He anticipated that the house had been broken into. He drove immediately to the airport with a panicked Joan muttering, "They had better not have taken my Waterford crystal," as they booked the first flight back home.

Fred moved as fast as he knew how. That meant he would first have to call Amos Bigly, the ever-patient handyman who could always be relied upon to get him out of a jam. This time, Amos really was going to bail him out.

All the commotion woke Alissa. "What's happening?" she asked.

"It doesn't concern you, Alissa. I'll take care of it," yelled Fred, imitating the same angry tones his father had used on him. "Go back to sleep."

When Fred arrived at the manor, three police officers were on the property, one at each entrance. They had already cleared the snow off the main driveway and areas under the windows so they could look inside. The alarm was still ringing, and the cops were cold, wet, and unhappy. The vapor from their breath hung in the air.

"What the f—— went wrong this time, Fred?" demanded the cop at the front door, who had sheltered himself where the roof of the portico kept the snow from accumulating.

Fred had the key to the front door. He and the officer were met by a flood of water rushing out as the door opened. Sprays of water were shooting out of the walls.

"Your pipes broke. How did that happen, Fred? Trying to save some money by not heating the place?" The policeman laughed. The two other officers arrived to see what was so funny.

"Charlie's not going to like that, Little Freddie Boy," chided one of the officers.

The other officer gave Fred a mocking slap on the back. "There go the Walterses' frozen assets. You're gonna make Pop really proud again this time. What I would like to see is how the hell you are gonna turn off that damn alarm before it wakes up the rest of the neighbors." All three burst into laughter.

There was nothing more for the police officers to do, so they returned to their squad cars and drove away, leaving poor, hapless Fred standing alone with his head bowed in self-pity and nothing more to protect him from the bitter cold than a winter coat over his pajamas. It was Fred's responsibility to turn off the alarm, but first he needed to get the water shut off.

Amos arrived in the nick of time. He found Fred standing alone, shivering at the front door.

"Wow, that's a big mess you got there, Fred."

That was all Fred needed to hear. This time it came from someone he could dominate. "You have to get this damn place cleaned up."

Amos always carried emergency tools in his truck, including a turn-off key for the water main. He didn't wait for instructions from Fred. That would have been a waste of time. Amos was the one who had installed the alarm system, and he would know how to turn it off. After the water to the house was shut off, Amos explained that the intrusion alarm must have been activated by the water accumulating on the floor and refracting the beam of light used in the sensor. He would need to turn off the electricity at the circuit breaker box and disconnect the wires that fed the alarm.

"What kind of alarm system is that?" asked Fred.

"It's the same system we have at the office."

This was a bigger job than Amos could do by himself. It didn't help that the neighbors were up in arms because his turning off the water at the main meant half the block was now without water. Amos worked diligently, but at the end of the day, when he closed up the house and called Fred, he reported that they would need more than a handyman to get the house back in order.

When Charlie and Joan arrived at their estate before dawn, nothing seemed out of order. There were no police. The alarm was silent. The doors were locked, and the snow had been cleared off the driveway. The shocker came when they opened the front door.

"The lights won't go on," exclaimed Charlie. "Keep back, Joan; I think the rug is soggy. You might damage something. Don't come in until we can see something."

Charlie struck a match and held it high to peer inside. It was lucky for Charlie that god watches over fools and children, and Amos had already turned off the gas. If this weren't so, it would have been more than Charlie's temper that exploded that night.

The light from one match wasn't adequate to survey the damage, so he used it to ignite an entire book of matches. The effect was spectacular.

With the room lit up, Joan could see inside too. "My wallpaper, my wallpaper, my beautiful flocked wallpaper. I paid ten ninety-eight a roll for that designer wallpaper. It's flocked."

"It's not flocked any more. It's flucked. Shut up about it. I never liked that wallpaper, anyway."

Joan was weeping, Charlie was cussing, and the couple headed for Fred's house on the other side of town so Charlie could read his son the riot act. Luckily for Fred, he had already left for the office when his parents showed up at his house.

Alissa had no idea what was going on. Fred had left early to avoid having to talk to her and would be waiting anxiously at the office for Cynthia to arrive for work so he could cry on her shoulder and enlist her sympathy for his misfortune.

"Alissa, I need to use your phone," said Charlie.

"What's wrong?" asked Alissa.

"I need to call the police."

"Police? Is someone hurt?"

"Not yet, but Fred soon will be. Why don't you girls go have a cup of coffee in the kitchen? I'll take care of this."

The police department dispatched one of the officers who had responded to the call the prior day to Fred's house to give Charlie the report. He told Charlie they went to the house because the neighbors had reported an alarm going off. They waited there until Fred arrived to let them in. They determined that there was no burglary because the house was flooded. They left Fred in charge to turn off the alarm. They had no reason to stay any longer.

Meanwhile, back at the office, Fred had only a brief moment to speak with Cynthia alone. Barely able to speak and with eyes glazed over, Cynthia asked him, "Did you dispose of the condoms, Fred? Was the bed made?"

"What difference does that make?" asked Fred.

Charlie arrived, fuming. He yelled obscenities at Fred.

Cynthia did not want to be seen. She cowered behind Fred, thoroughly frightened by Charlie's ranting and the exposure of her *mortal sin*. Fred was crossing his fingers, and Cyn was hiding her face.

"How did you let this happen? You were supposed to be taking care of my house. What were you thinking?" Charlie suddenly became aware of Cynthia hiding behind Fred. "Oh, I get it. You were busy bopping her instead of taking care of my house. You were thinking, all right. You were thinking with that little head."

He turned his attention to Cynthia. "Did you use my bed? That would be a waste. I wasn't there. You would have been much happier with me rather than wimpy Junior here."

Cynthia was trembling. She was ready to collapse. Her face was red. She ran out of the office, sobbing audibly.

As the rest of the employees were arriving for work, some caught the tail-end of the monstrous encounter that had taken place in Fred's not-so-private office. Charlie did not miss this opportunity to publicly mock his son. He was still yelling profanities and using Fred's name so that everyone within earshot would know of his contempt for his "lazy, stupid, ineffective" son.

◆◆◆

He was still fuming as he arrived at Alissa's house to pick up his wife. Joan had been taking a short nap to settle her nerves, but she didn't mind Charlie waking her to take her to breakfast at Tippy-ease.

She had an inspiration to discuss with him, and she didn't waste any time getting to the point. "Listen, Charlie, I have an idea. We will get insurance money for this. I was getting bored with that wallpaper anyway. Natalie has redone her house. She found a good interior decorator. He's expensive, but he does good work."

Charlie almost choked on his coffee. *Expensive* was not a word he wanted to hear from his wife. "Interior decorator? What the hell do you need an interior decorator for?"

"He will tell me what goes well together."

"You have to pay someone to tell you that? I can tell you that. You got a wall, you put pictures on it. You got a window, you put up curtains. You got a ceiling, you hang a lamp. You got a hallway, you screw on a coat rack or better yet, a moose head so I can remember what your mother looks like. You got a toilet, you put paper in it. What's so hard? Here's your interior decorator, and you don't even have to pay me."

"You know, Charlie, you are so low class. I want to fix up my house. I want to hire a decorator again to help me. We will have the insurance money, and it won't cost you anything. We are going to do this, and Natalie Snout is going to eat her heart out because I am going to do my house better."

She had a point—there was the insurance, so Charlie conceded begrudgingly and allowed her to completely make over the house for a second time. What choice did he have? He couldn't live in it the way it was, and he could barely live with Joan the way she was.

◆◆◆

Alissa was uncomfortable attending the funeral of Cynthia Lucci with Fred. Fred asked her to go, and the only reason she was there was as Mrs. Fred Walters, the boss's wife. Attending important events with her husband was part of the job description. But this time it was different. No one likes to go to funerals.

Alissa wasn't fond of Cynthia; in fact, Cynthia had been rude to her. Once she was downright crass. Alissa had come into the office to see Fred. This usually brought friendly greetings from the employees–but Cynthia did not respond to Alissa's hello. She stepped into Alissa's path, obviously turning her back on the boss's wife. And then she wiggled her right hip in a manner that looked as if she was pushing out her rear-end at Alissa. This was more than a cold shoulder.

Cynthia recently had a nervous breakdown and was no longer working for the family business, but Fred was particularly upset when he heard that Cynthia had taken her life. At the cemetery, Alissa overheard gossip that would change her life forever. The people at the office were mingling together and expressing their sympathy for the grieving widower.

Mr. Lucci was standing at the casket with family members and crying uncontrollably.

Fred and Alissa tried to join the group from the office, but people kept drifting away from them and whispering among themselves. This conversation was loud enough for Alissa to hear.

"Boy, Fred had a lot of a nerve coming here today."

"And Alissa, why is she supporting him?"

"Surely she doesn't approve of the affair."

Alissa was stunned. *Affair? What affair? Had she heard correctly? Oh my god. What have you done, Fred? No wonder Cynthia behaved so rudely toward me,* Alissa thought. If she had known at the time that Cynthia was having an affair with her husband, there might have been a way to stop this before the poor woman became so despondent that she took her own life.

Alissa had some serious thinking to do. This was the final straw. Fred had had many affairs during their marriage, and one way or another, Alissa had usually found out about them. In the past she had ignored them, hoping they would go away. But this time it was different. This time the woman had died. That night she called Jennifer, explaining the tragedy and asking for her advice.

"You must have been humiliated," said Jennifer. "I know exactly how you feel. I had to file for divorce from Clark on grounds of adultery."

"I won't file on grounds of adultery. I don't want to make this ugly, and I don't want the children to know about it. I only want the pain to go away."

"Fred was using you, Alissa. He believed he could do anything he wished and still have you standing beside him. If you stay with him, you will have to accept the fact that it is the way he will always be. He doesn't respect you. Can you live with that? The next suicide may be you."

The following morning, after calling a divorce attorney, Alissa booked a flight to Europe for Hester and herself.

◆ ◆ ◆

Bopping was monkey business as usual in the Walterses' household. The first-time Joan caught Charlie in the house with his pants down, *a family secret that was only whispered about when the lady at the bottom of this social outrage wasn't within earshot*, Joan used the scandal to blackmail Charlie into redecorating the manner house. You have to understand Joan's position, which was never on the bottom if she could help it. Image was important to her. Joan was a pillar of the community. The only question was whether her style was Corinthian or Ionic...or perhaps ironic.

She had hired Pierre and Philippe Bellecour, the most "in" interior decorators in town. Pictures of the elegant do-overs of the Bellecour brothers that hung in the showroom of their studio had been selected by Joan for her house. She was never one to buy something without squeezing it first, so she would never have consented to hire them to create something new. She'd chosen some photos she liked. But if her house differed from the posted photographs, it was only because, to the chagrin of the decorators, Joan's personal taste was to be incorporated into the endeavor. The newly decorated house gave her more prestige than she had ever before known. Everyone was talking about it.

So it was absolutely humiliating when Charlie's transgressions continued and the next one was consummated under the Bellecour sixty-by-twenty-inch gilded mirror that hung on the living room wall over her expensive paisley, red-and-gold, brocade, overstuffed Italian Renaissance sofa with the eagle's feet. It was a good thing Joan had covered the sofa in plastic; otherwise, it would have been more than her reputation that would have been stained. The angry, scorned wife wanted to get her husband out of town. She came up with a plan to liquidate their assets, or at a minimum, the *assettes* of the other women. This time she demanded a penthouse in Florida.

Joan was not a woman to be pushed around. She drove her 1980 Cadillac Brougham with tail fins as if it was her personal Abrams Tank and armed with bazooka missiles. She was always dressed to the nines and loaded down with a collection of expensive baubles acquired over her lifetime from her husband, who enjoyed showing off that he was a man of means. Meeting Joan in public, surrounded in her armor, was the equivalent of encountering a direct frontal attack. Her voice was loud. She did not mince words. Joan did not have to have the facts right; in her own simple way, that only complicated matters. She was obsessed with the ideas she had composed to her own liking, and she lied as much about what she had as her husband lied about whom he had.

◆ ◆ ◆

Charlie had no problem with Joan wanting them to move. There were lots more pretty young girls in Florida. He would make new friends. He would, however, have problems cashing out of the business arrangements he had with his brother. The brothers had expanded into many businesses over the years, always operating as partners under the fictitious name of Upton and Sons.

They chose the name because it sounded high class. There never was a business associate named Upton, *with or without sons*. There were only the two Walters brothers, their wives, and their sons bound together by verbal agreements that were constantly in a state of flux. The business of Upton and Sons for IRS purposes was listed as an investment firm; the brothers believed this gave them a blanket so large that under it they could venture into any kind of business arrangement for any product and purpose and construe the deal as part of their investment empire.

The brothers' major asset was that loosely connected ton of bricks they called a building. The books showed they had spent over a million dollars to renovate it and bring it up to code. In reality, however, they had only removed the boards from the windows and doors to let in a little light.

Larry was not willing to buy out Charlie's half ownership of the building. Nor was Larry willing to purchase Charlie's interest in the thriving investment enterprise. That was what had made them all their money. Upton and Sons had provided both families the wherewithal to acquire spacious homes with the right addresses that put them in the proper social circles, Joan in jewels and furs, the brothers in expensive cars, and top-notch educations for Robert and Fred.

Larry wasn't willing to pay a dime to Charlie for anything. He had already raided the bank accounts and had used the business collateral to run up more debt than the going enterprise could cover. Larry had already rented out suites from the building and was pocketing the rental income. He had branched out into other lines of business by trading off some of his partnership interest. He was a flexible man who was intent on having Charlie believe they still had a fifty-fifty business arrangement so that none of his subterfuge would surface.

If Larry were to let Charlie know that Charlie's actual interest in Upton and Sons was 50.1 percent interest, making him the principal partner with several people other than Larry, Charlie would find out that he was in control and could make the decisions on his own. Why tell him? Why kill the goose that laid the golden egg? It was better for Larry if Charlie thought Larry had a say in how things were to be run. Larry was better with the technical details than Charlie, and he liked being asked for permission.

Larry was concerned that Joan wanted to sell out and move. The Bronx building was now filled with homeless people, and he was collecting rents from them by claiming it was HUD housing. They would have to be cleared out and the property rehabbed. He worried that other information would surface if she and Charlie pursued that direction. There wasn't much left for Charlie to sell in an arm's-length transaction, and Larry certainly wasn't going to put in any of his own money for their buyout. He would have to wait and see how this played out.

What Larry was not aware of was that Charlie had not been totally aboveboard with him either. Sometimes ownership of the building was in Joan's name. It had changed ownership so frequently that he would have to go through all that paperwork in his desk at the office and see what deed had the most current date. Most were recorded in the wrong county. This was a dilemma that would have to be worked out.

THIRTEEN

Attitude Adjustment

Alissa's decision to file for divorce was a monumental event. Although the Lucci affair was the proverbial straw that broke the camel's back, it was not the only thing that led to her making this decision. There were too many wounds to count, too much pain to examine, and too many conflicting emotions to sort out. If a mirror could examine her psyche, the glass would shatter, and the broken fragments would distort the image of the woman who deserved to be reflected.

She couldn't stop beating up on herself. How dare she be so presumptuous as to break up a marriage that had been the cradle for her children and had given her the opportunity to develop her professional life? How could she walk away from the dreams and goals that had been the focus of her life's plans and expectations? Who would she be after the role of wife and mother that had given her purpose and meaning was gone?

In an attempt to keep her from leaving, Fred had threatened her. His words were still ringing in her ears. "You won't have a dime to live on. I'll see to that. If you stay with me, I'll give you half of what I own."

But who would know what half was? She never found out how much he was worth financially. That was the world he kept to himself. It was how he exercised control.

The divorce did not bring Alissa freedom. It brought a new burden she had not anticipated. This difficulty had nothing to do with her ability to support herself. She was competent and could continue teaching. It had nothing to do with receiving approval and affirmation. The people whose opinion she valued and who knew what she had experienced during the Walterses' marriage supported her decision to file for divorce, and she knew intellectually that divorce was necessary for her survival. Even Katie, at only sixteen years old, understood this and observed, "Mom, you are dead behind the eyes. You have to leave Dad. There is no life in you anymore."

Her burden had to do with replacement value. She felt that she had been cut loose and discarded in the same way one might take out the trash. She did not understand the new emotions she was feeling. Hers was as hollow a feeling as the anguish true believers experience when they come to grips with the fact that something they had accepted as truth can evaporate into meaninglessness. There is nothing to replace it, because there is nothing that fits the hole that was cut into the fabric. The myth is gone. The disciple is not.

The sun still comes up the next day, but the former devotee learns to hate it for doing so because the world has collapsed and the sun does not have the self-respect to know it. It also should set a new course. Doesn't it know that the cycle of life has changed?

◆ ◆ ◆

Alissa was entering this new phase of her life: wounded by the relationship with Fred, and stripped of the time she had invested in him. Her mind was conflicted. She was constantly challenging her own thoughts with doubt, so something as common as marketing became a major dilemma. She felt beaten up and not deserving of having her needs met. She would choose the smallest size of an item and hold on to it with the desperation of doubt, wondering if she could afford it, if she deserved it--far away from the question that asked *if she wanted to purchase it.*

Alyssa had married Fred to escape what she perceived as imprisonment, and she fell for Hollywood's mantra, *to live and love happily ever after.* The marriage was doomed right from the start as it merely substituted a prison with new problems but one that would continue her servitude. She was property in the eyes of her husband, and that was something she had no ability to change. By marrying Fred, she would not hear the constant cacophony of her parents' yelling, arguing, and nagging. But with Fred, the trade-off was to live with silence when he punished her by turning away, or without intellectual stimulation when she wished to engage him in conversation. Ideas and thoughts were not spoken to enrich the mind as they had been at her father's dinner table. With Fred, plans for material enrichment were considered the highest form of conversation.

For a time, even that was better than nothing. It was the periods of silence that were killing Alissa. It wasn't until the death of her spirit was so inevitable that even the love of her children *which had nurtured deep and powerful emotions within her and made her decision to divorce their father seem to betray her commitment to them* was no longer enough--if she was to breathe.

But as her children grew she realized they weren't providing them adequate support. There was little fun or joy in their family. To believe that Fred was wonderful was a lie that she tried to make real. She gave him the gifts to bring to their children on birthdays and other occasions while praising him for his thoughtfulness. Fred didn't recall any of their birthdays, not even hers. They weren't that important to him. He brought no compassion into the relationship..

Fred would continue to complain. Living with him brought a never-ending pattern of problems to solve. She would listen to one problem and try to help him solve it, only to have another take its place. It was as though she was living in the children's story of *Bartholomew and his Many Hats.* (The child, Bartholomew, would take one hat off, only to have another one appear.) For Alissa, the constant repetition of predicaments and the impossibility of finding any permanently solutions was a nightmare. Without realizing that this was wearing away her love for him, the repetition became unbearable as she was beginning to be able to move on. Alissa had lost respect for him.

◆ ◆ ◆

A woman without a man in the 1980s was still vulnerable. Sexual liberation may have brought more freedom for women, but it came at a price. It was now anticipated that a single woman would be sexually active. Divorced women were easy prey for the sexual advances from men and women who hoped the divorcee would be open to casual sexual liaisons.

In the past, these people would have been viewed as vultures who knew all too well the loneliness a divorcee feels and how she longs for and needs to be comforted. They would have been considered predators capable of deluding the unsuspecting wounded into believing they would offer compassion and that they were capable of being nurturing and supportive.

But now, in the times of sexual liberation, casual sex was a game to be played, enjoyed, and shared. Many sharks in the sea of life surfaced who did not share the *old-fashioned* dream of a lifelong commitment to a spouse. Alissa would soon learn about the change in social mores for herself, but she would not understand all the implications until she was ready to look life boldly in the face. For now, it was enough to function on a day-to-day basis and restrain herself from betraying her personal standards. Her desire to satisfy her sexual needs was powerfully frightening. Although she had lived in a sexless marriage for years, she was still a healthy, attractive woman. Some days, looking out the window at life passing her by, she felt the urge to run out of the house and have a sexual encounter with the first man she met. She had the fortitude to restrain herself, but there were different ways she would injure herself.

Her first bad decision was to rent a small, run-down apartment in a seedy part of town. She could afford something better, but she could not picture herself in anything other than this bleak little hovel into which she crowded a few pieces of borrowed furniture. Two days after she moved in, she learned that a woman in the complex had been raped in the laundry room and had been left bleeding on the floor until someone found her dead body the next morning.

It was not surprising that Alissa developed agoraphobia. For the next two months, she was afraid to leave the ugly prison she tried to make her home. Her dilemma was that if she left the apartment, she might have to make a decision, and it might be another bad decision. There was no point in asking anyone for help. Because she had been emotionally abused, it was impossible to take advice from anyone because she couldn't make the decision as to whether or not she should accept the advice. So Alissa sat in her shack alone, silently waiting for something to change.

There was no change until the day her guardian angel brought hope back to her. An ethereal presence caught her attention by showing her what she was doing to herself. She didn't see the angel. It did not speak to her. She felt it. And that reality was as trustworthy as anything Alissa could touch or see or smell. The angel presence was with her the day she looked into a mirror and saw herself accurately. It wasn't a pretty picture. Her face appeared hollow, her hair was dirty and uncombed, and she looked old and tired. Alissa felt the angel had nudged her back on course, made her face reality, and given her twenty-twenty insight. The angel had a helper.

◆ ◆ ◆

One day, as Alissa was taking a good look at her surroundings in roach haven and feeling the first urge to do something to change them, Jennifer arrived at her door.

"I would have called you, but you don't have a phone. What's going on, Alissa? It's a good thing I was passing through town on my way home. Got your address from Katie," said her college chum. "When I saw the neighborhood, I thought I had the wrong address. Did you look for this apartment, or did public housing force it on you? How in the world did you ever decide to live in this place?"

"I haven't lived in an apartment since college. I couldn't remember how to find one."

"What were you thinking? How long have you been here? Please tell me you don't have a lease on this dump."

"I didn't know if this was a good place or not."

Her friend could hardly believe this. "Well, I have a car parked in the street, and I don't want to keep it there. Alissa, I'm afraid someone will break into it even as we stand here talking. You can't stay here. This is insane. I don't believe you are thinking. Tell me you will come with me to find a decent place for you to live. Please let me help you."

"I'm okay."

"Yes, I see you are okay. That's why you look like a *shmata*. That's a rag, in case you don't know it. Well, baby doll, if you are not going to do this for yourself, do it for me. I don't like spending any more time in this neighborhood than I have to."

"I'm okay here. I don't need to move. I just need to straighten the place up a bit."

"Look, honey, I've got the weekend free. I was looking for some entertainment. Apartment hunting will do. Want to come along? I have a newspaper in the car. Let's check out the real estate section for apartments."

"I'm tired today. Can't you just stay and visit with me?"

Jennifer sensed the emptiness in her friend and agreed to take the time to accommodate her needs. The next morning began with Jennifer arising at daybreak and opening the drapes to the new day. She found some generic tea bags in the back of the cupboard and boiled water in a small saucepan, anticipating that the caffeine would be good for Alissa when she awoke. There was nothing to eat in the house, so Jennifer took a quick trip to a nearby twenty-four-hour market. The homeless people sleeping on boxes near the entrance had not begun their day, and Jennifer parked near the entrance so she could keep her eye on the car as she ran in for some sweet rolls.

Alissa had awoken by the time Jennifer returned and was thankful for the hot tea. She smiled reservedly as Jennifer sat down at the table to share breakfast with her. "It's nice to have you here with me, Jennifer. I wish it was at the Steamboat Road house where I could treat you as a proper guest."

"It's not the place we are gathering that's important; it's where your head is that matters."

Alissa began to sob. "What has happened to me? I don't know how I got here."

"You know, Alissa. I don't have any answers for you, but I have two ears for your words, and my heart is as full for you as it ever was. Let's try to find your way out of this together."

"I can't," said Alissa. "I just want you to stay here and visit with me. I need to rest. I'm too tired to take on any projects."

"Projects?" said Jennifer. "You're not a project. You need another woman to help you."

Alissa began to sob. "I didn't know if I was doing the right thing. Fred told me I failed, and I thought I had. I couldn't decide what size box of salt to buy at the store that was the right size for only me. I didn't know how to shop for myself. I've always shopped for a family, and now I don't have anyone. Mama said I didn't deserve to be happy."

"Humor me, Alissa. Tell me you don't listen to Mommy Dearest anymore. Come on—get yourself out of this place. There have been enough Christian martyrs. They don't need any more. Put on some lipstick and comb your hair. You don't have to do any thinking. I'll drive. I'll do the research. All you have to do is sit in the front seat beside me. I brought in this map from the car," she said, handing it to Alissa. "You're capable of reading one of these, aren't you?"

"I suppose so."

"I suppose so too. If not I'll give you a *zets in di kishke*."

Alissa stared at the map. "Can you spell that? I can't find it."

"Oh, my poor baby, it's Yiddish. It means a 'punch in the gut.' If you're looking for it on the map, it's to the right of Tel Aviv. Come on, sweetheart. I only have two days."

"Okay," said Alissa, giving her friend a weak, unenthusiastic hug. "I'll just be a minute," she said as she walked toward the bathroom.

"Great, honey, and Alissa, sweetheart, while you're at it, maybe you should brush your teeth too."

Jennifer was not certain she could help her friend. While they were driving, Alissa was staring ahead blankly as though she was keeping herself from making another mistake by not being part of the present.

"Why didn't you call me before you got into this state?"

"Huh?" asked Alissa. Her thoughts were of her mother, who would have criticized her for not calling.

"Call me. Call me. Why didn't you let me know you were in trouble?"

"I don't know."

"I need a cup of coffee," said Jennifer, pulling into the parking lot of a diner with a blinking Open sign.

The two friends found a booth in the corner where they could talk. Alissa was deep in regret, believing that she had once again failed. She thought that Jennifer wanted to blame her for allowing her life to disintegrate. She was convinced that once again her mother was right. She was worthless and did not deserve even a nice place to live.

"Why isn't my apartment okay? It's good enough for me. Fred took away the house I loved. I had a beautiful home when I was married."

"Why didn't you stay there and make Fred move out?"

"I didn't own any part of the house anymore."

"How did you let that happen?"

"I truly didn't know, Jennifer. I think he may have tricked me."

"What did you do when you found out?"

"I took the steps to divorce him. No, I didn't divorce him for the house. I was humiliated. There was a funeral. His lover died. Oh, Jennifer, I can't believe everything that has gone wrong. All I wanted was..."

"Okay, darling. But you didn't fight for your rights, Alissa. You ran away."

"What rights does a loser have?"

Jennifer was outraged. She loved Alissa and respected her, and the woman in the diner with her didn't even have the pride to love and respect herself. She looked again at her friend and saw her more accurately. Alissa was wearing a stained shirt, her hair was unkempt, and her eyes were swollen from too many tears.

"How did this happen to you?" she asked.

"Slowly. I allowed it. Little by little, I compromised." Alissa looked directly into Jennifer's eyes. Her mouth was trembling, and tears rolled down her cheeks as she bared her soul. "It was Mama. Mama was right. I'm worthless. It's always my fault when something bad happens to me. Mama told me that when I was born, Daddy called me a 'gift from God,' and Mama told him, 'She is a gift all right; she is a gift of poison. I wanted to give you sons. A man deserves to have sons.'"

Jennifer was furious. "Get over it, Alissa. We are not living under sharia law. The woman is not the only one to blame. It wasn't only Eve in that garden. Adam was there too. Your mother wasn't a sexist. She was a mean and hateful woman who didn't know how to treat you. That's her problem. Don't let it be yours. I want to know what led up to this point where you are so demoralized."

Alissa sighed a sigh that came from deep, deep, inside of her psyche. "You know I married Fred to get away from her."

"So, how'd that work out for you?"

"My psychiatrist said women sometimes pick husbands who have traits that are familiar. If they grow up in an abusive family, this is their comfort zone. They know how to cope with it. They marry someone they are familiar with. They learn how to be a successful victim."

"Is this the legacy you wish to pass on to your daughter?"

"Stop this, Jennifer. I don't want to talk about this anymore. How can you say that when I love my daughter so much?"

◆ ◆ ◆

The quest for the new apartment was successful. By the end of the day, Jennifer had not only located a lovely furnished garden apartment in a new development in an upscale part of town, but she had negotiated a price with the landlord that was less than Alissa was paying for the dump she would be escaping. Jennifer left Alissa in the new apartment, sitting in front of the TV and scrolling the remote control through the channels, but she was incapable of focusing on any program in particular.

Jennifer tended to some loose ends. She drove back to the old apartment and carried out what junk she could stuff into the dumpster. Then she packed Alissa's personal items into her car and, after locking up the apartment, returned the key to the landlord and asked if Alissa had given him a refundable deposit.

As Alissa continued to wait in her new apartment compulsively changing channels, Jennifer used the cash from the deposit to stock Alissa's new refrigerator, and before returning to Alissa, she picked up an eight-piece chicken meal at Colonel Flanders to share with her that night.

"Alissa, tell me what put you into such a state. What went wrong?" asked Jennifer.

"I filed for divorce," said Alissa.

"And?" prompted Jennifer.

"And I'm alone now." Alissa started to cry.

"You call that a problem?"

"Well, what would you call it? I've failed at my marriage. Being a wife in a loving marriage is important to me. I wanted so much for my marriage to work out. I don't understand what I am doing wrong," Alissa said in a whisper, unable to hold her head high to look into the eyes of her friend.

"Okay, if you want to call this a failure, fine. But you didn't have a pickle."

"Pickle?"

"Alissa, let me explain to you how to evaluate things. Last summer, when I was roaming around southeast New York to check out the local ambiance, I made a discovery about life that may help you. There was this huge pickle barrel in the front of Weiss's Deli. The pickles looked great, all plump and juicy, and I was ready to reach into the brine and take one out.

"Then this older man came by. He reached into the barrel, pulled out a pickle, and took a bite out of it without offering to buy it. He pursed his lips, spit out the piece of pickle, and said to Mr. Weiss, 'You call this a pickle?'

"Mr. Weiss didn't object. He took the man to the back of the deli. I followed as much as I could. I stepped into the store where I was within earshot. I didn't want to miss this. Next thing I know, I hear Mr. Weiss tell his customer that the best pickles are in the barrel in the back of the store. Weiss urges the customer to pull up his sleeve and reach down to the bottom to find the best ones."

"I don't know what you are talking about, Jennifer," said Alissa.

"I'm saying that to get the best from life, sometimes we have to go to the place where the best is stored and be willing to reach down to find the best. We have to work for it. Sometimes the good stuff is hidden, Alissa, but it's available if you look for it. The best in life is not the easy stuff in the front of the store that everyone has access to. It's worth checking out the back rooms to see what's there. Maybe you weren't reaching deep enough when you settled on a life with Fred."

"That's cruel, Jennifer. I wasn't buying a pickle; I was looking for a man who would be the father of my children."

"You have a right to have something better, pet. How hard did you have to work to make something of yourself? You know what you want from life. You got a degree from Swarthmore; in fact, you have received several degrees by now, haven't you?"

"Three," said Alissa.

"Okay, look at who you are. You have three degrees, a teaching credential, and you authored a substance-abuse program that was so successful you made the press and recognition in *Who's Who*. You have two great kids, good looks, and you are still young. The pickle barrel that everyone has access to isn't good enough for you. You learned that the hard way. You bit into the ordinary pickle and spit out the piece. You got that part right, Alissa. That pickle may have been sour, but don't let it sour you. I'm here to tell you, sugar, there is a pickle barrel in the back of the store. It has really good pickles in it, but you have to roll up your sleeve and go down after it."

"I don't think you should compare Fred to a pickle," said Alissa.

"I'm not. Your life is messed up because of the pickle. Spit it out and go after the better one at the back of the deli."

"What's wrong with my life?"

"Bingo—you got it. You asked the right question. Now, you work on the answer. Your life didn't work out the way you expected it to, but sweetie, I know you. You can handle this and more. You're not a puppy anymore, but you can learn some new tricks. There is more in life in store for you. It can be exciting, and it can be the best pickle in the store. Get it?"

"I think so," said Alissa. "You don't think I am going crazy, do you?"

"Crazy? No. You're needy and vulnerable. I think they call that being human. You are as neurotic as I am." Jennifer laughed. "But if you ever get as bad as my Uncle Irving call me, we'll see about putting you away. 'Cause that's what my Aunt Sophie had to do."

"I know what you mean. We have people like your Uncle Irving in my family too."

"Every family does," said Jennifer. "It gives us something to talk about when we get together during the holidays. But Alissa, don't complain about your choices in life to me again, because if you do, I'm just going to say, 'You call that a pickle?'"

After dinner and a bath to settle her frayed nerves and relax her tense muscles, Jennifer slept soundly on the sofa in the living room. But this was only after urging Alissa away from the TV and encouraging her to retire to her bedroom for much-needed rest. The two women spent the entire next day talking things through, and Jennifer saw to it that Alissa was eating properly. By the time Jennifer left that evening, Alissa had lost all evidence of her agoraphobia. Jennifer called Katie and Josh at their respective colleges to give them their mother's new address. Without describing any of the personal details of their mother's condition, Jennifer instructed the kids that it was imperative that they visit Alissa soon and to call her within the next twenty-four hours. They both promised.

◆ ◆ ◆

It's probably difficult for anyone who has not personally suffered from bouts of depression to appreciate what a difference the new apartment made in Alissa's life. The building was surrounded with fragrant, colorful flowers. Alissa loved living there so much that she named her new digs the Sunshine Suite. Katie brought her potted plants and baskets of hanging vines for the balcony. Josh delivered Alissa's painting and sculpting materials and other personal items she had put into storage when she'd moved into "the dump." Both children visited Alissa often that summer when they were home from college but not as frequently as the migratory hummingbirds that played outside the kitchen window, sampling the lavender flowers blooming in the garden.

During this quiet time surrounded with beauty, comfort, and warmth, Alissa swept the ghosts out of the corners of her psyche. Being on her own, with no one to care for except herself, she had the opportunity to seek out each of her tormentors, face them, and chase them so far away that they never again returned to disrupt her beautiful soul.

She learned to identify the abuse she had experienced from Fred and to understand how and why it happened. It helped with her self-analysis to work on a sculpture of a bust of Fred while she allowed her mind and emotions to direct her hands. With each piece of clay, Alissa shaped the features of his face. She started by sculpting an expression of joy and contentment like the face he had worn when they were newlyweds on their honeymoon in the Bahamas.

With each discovery, there was a reshaping of the bust and an exorcise of another part of her descent into hell with the man she had at one time loved so passionately, she thought her life would be meaningless without him at her side.

She eradicated the times she'd asked for Fred to back her up when she was raising their children singlehandedly because he was spending every evening locked in his private office upstairs. In so doing, the face of his bust changed from contentment to rigid obstinacy.

> *"Fred, you need to show them that they should respect me. I'm their mother. They won't respect me unless they learn that example from you."*
>
> *"You have to earn their respect."*
>
> *"Fred, when I ask the children to do something, you tell them they don't need to obey."*
>
> *"The children have two parents, and if they both ganged up on the child, it would be two to one, and the child would have no one to take his or her side."*
>
> *"But that makes no sense, Fred. We are not ganging up on our children when we agree to a philosophy of discipline. We are giving them guidance."*

She eradicated each of the times she would not speak out to take a position in opposition to his. In so doing, the face of his bust changed from pride to arrogance and from obstinacy to aloofness.

> *With the passage of time, it no longer occurred to Alissa that she could oppose Fred's opinions. Their marriage started out with patterns of behavior that she thought were fine. She believed that everything would continue to go well. But changes are often subtle and are not always noticeable. By the time the changes in the Walterses' marriage were so noticeable that Alissa wanted to express her protest, there was no opportunity to speak another opinion because she had changed, too.*

She no longer believed any of her opinions had value. She didn't notice her change, either, until it was too late. She had become passive, and changes in the marriage relationship no longer mattered as much as they might have if they had been challenged earlier—so when they became so large that she could not help but notice them, she didn't know how to be anything other than an ineffective observer.

She eradicated the fact that she went from being passive to being compliant. In so doing, the face of Fred's bust changed from an expression of questioning to one with a sinister snarl.

Alissa's pattern was to become the mirror reflection of the man she married. For example, when Fred asked her what movie she would like to see, she would either respond by saying she didn't know, or she would search her mind to pick a movie that she knew he would prefer. By the time her marriage ended, Alissa didn't know what she preferred. So one of the joys of living alone at the Sunshine Suite was to read the entertainment section and choose a movie to go to for the experience of determining if she liked it.

Alissa could no longer blame this relinquishing of identity on the social mores of the fifties. Although women from that era were taught to subordinate their will to that of their husbands, decades had passed since then, and every red-blooded American woman in the 1980s knew how to determine and pursue her personal preferences. Alissa had simply not kept up with the enlightenment of the times. The damage to her identity was something for which she needed to take responsibility.

She eradicated the fact that she didn't know how to handle her anger. In so doing, the face of Fred's bust changed from an expression of anger to one of total rage.

Psychologists tell their patients that repressed anger is dangerous because it often ends up with one or both people "blowing their top." That may be true more often than not, but it didn't work out that way for Alissa.

Alissa gave up when she became angry. She walked away. When her limit was reached and she had taken all she was capable of standing, she separated herself from the problem. She didn't actually raise the white flag of surrender, because in her act of fleeing the scene, she wasn't conceding that the other party had won. She hoped the opponent would follow her, engage her again in conversation, and maybe (if dreams could be dared to be dreamed) he might, if only once, agree with her position and want to make up and call a truce to the conflict.

But she might as well have surrendered because her leaving the scene of the turmoil was a surrender of her position, abdication of her ideals, and ultimately destruction of her personhood. Fred never followed her to ask her to return. Her behavior was ineffective for wining an argument. But her flight was useful to keep her anger at bay. She didn't become the irrational, raving wife that men like to point to while blaming the behavior on raging hormones. She didn't rant or rave; she retreated. Alissa was not capable of any other option.

When Fred's positions were challenged, he punished her by taking away his affection. Alissa believed there was no way to challenge Fred because fear gripped her about what might happen if they were to really get mad.

Alissa eradicated the physical attraction she'd felt when she had become Fred's wife. In so doing, a peace came over her, but the face of his bust changed from the warmth of love to one of anguish.

Dr. Lovato had explained love to Alissa this way. Lovato said, "You know you are in love when it doesn't matter to you that your mate's socks smell." This could not have been a more fitting description of her marriage to Fred than if Alissa herself had said it.

Fred's socks did indeed smell. They were smelly because his feet were smelly. The odor was so strong that it was only because Fred was so tall and his feet extended off the edge of the bed and were far away from Alissa's nose that she was able to tolerate the offensive odor. It helped that they had a king-size bed, and she could crawl into the opposite corner and sleep in the fetal position.

One day when her mother was visiting, Fred took off his shoes while he was watching TV. Hester went through the whole house looking for a dead animal before she traced the smell back to his feet. Alissa tried to make light of feet that stank by making jokes about it.

"I'm handing down a gag order, Fred. Wash your feet before you go to bed, but this time, don't do it in the bidet."

"Don't take your shoes off when you come into the house; it will frighten the children. They will think I'm preparing garbage for their dinner."

"I know your favorite sport is fishing, but do you have to fish with your shoes on?"

But there was something else about the attraction of love that Dr. Lovato did not discuss. This was something Alissa had noticed on her own. She believed Fred was the right man to be the father of her children. She believed the imminent need created the physical desire she felt for him. It wasn't that she was an opportunist, swapping sexual favors for the things she needed in life. It was that her primary emotional needs caused her hormones to fire up when she found a potential mate she believed would satisfy those needs. And building a nest with him was her need.

Alissa was proud of her theory and had tried to explain it to Fred, but he misunderstood what she was trying to say. He interpreted her description as her telling him that she married him only to help her produce children, as if he were a stud service. Because of that misunderstanding, Alissa believed she had been unable to communicate to Fred that her love was sincere, her attraction was genuine, and her need for him to be a good father was noble.

When Fred started having extramarital affairs, Alissa started looking for a reason to excuse him. It would be easier if *she* were to blame instead of him; then she could do something to change her behavior, hoping that it would take care of the problem. Alissa had to be pretty creative to come up with a reason that Fred's infidelity was her fault, but she worked diligently, and she came up with a hypothesis. Alissa believed that Fred became anguished because he never understood her love for him to be real. So the bust she was creating of Fred remained in its final form, that of a man screaming out in an expression of anguish. He never understood love, and that was incredibly sad.

Fred continued to have his lady friends, and Alissa had continued to be pained by his infidelity. But she created a scenario in which she could continue to believe that Fred loved her. She construed that if he had the capacity for higher intellect, he would have been capable of understanding that she loved him too. But it wasn't a matter of intelligence. It was a matter of being a whole, complete person, capable of empathy and love. Love should grow because of the respect, caring, and intimacy that should be part of the marriage.

Fred's moral compass wasn't set for the same course that Alissa was taught to follow. There was nothing in his background that would have persuaded him to think that extramarital relationships are immoral. He knew how to charm the ladies. He was capable of sizing them up and saying what they wanted to hear. He was at his best when he was using the right words to sell himself. It was a game with him. Fred was a great conversationalist. But he used his words to bait rather than debate. He loved the challenge of seduction as much as he loved the excitement of the business world, where a man's prowess is evaluated with the same standards as economic success.

Alissa correctly concluded that Fred wasn't deep. He would have fallen asleep while she was presenting her hypothesis. Fred understood sexual attraction as love, but he lacked an appreciation of the poetry of life. Fred believed it was the woman who should do the listening, not him. He thought women were to listen for the purpose of knowing what they needed to do in order to be in compliance with their husband's wishes. It was part of the *obey* clause that they accepted at the altar when they got the wedding ring. He would often check to see if Alissa was in compliance. He did this with one of his favorite questions: "Didn't you hear me when I told you not to..."

Alissa could also have made a bust of *her* face with an expression of anguish. But why should she remind herself of the pain? It was behind her now, and she was thankful that with the help of those who cared for her, she had found a safe port during the storm.

◆ ◆ ◆

Katie wanted to take her postgraduate work in California. She had always been good at argumentation and debate and was looking at Pepperdine University, where she would study law. Alissa was glad that Katie had found a school that met her needs, but Katie would be too far for Alissa to visit from Connecticut, and she wanted to keep her daughter close. Alissa considered moving to Los Angeles with her. This would be a major decision and one that had no clearly defined benefits versus detriments. Josh would be staying in Connecticut to continue working on what was left of the Walterses' family businesses. If Alissa moved away, it would mean she would not see Josh and his wife, Rachel, as often, and since the newlyweds were talking about starting a family, Alissa might be moving away from an opportunity to enjoy being a grandmother.

Any move might mean that Alissa would not immediately find employment and would have to live off her retirement. California would not recognize her out-of-state teaching credentials. That would mean she could either go back to college in California to qualify for a credential there, teach in a private school for less money, or move into another field altogether.

Alissa wasn't running away from home this time. She was strong. She was emotionally well and wanted to enjoy her life. This was the time to begin to explore what more she was capable of achieving. The thought of moving to California presented challenges, but these were choices she cheerfully made.

That night, Alissa was visited by a recurring nightmare that had plagued her for years. It was always the same, and it always caused her to wake up terrified and in a cold sweat.

In her dream, she was driving the car and talking to Fred, who was in the front seat. The car became stuck on the railroad tracks. Alissa could see the train coming down the tracks toward them. Its bright light blinded her.

"Fred, help me! We're going to be struck by the train. Help me!"

He did not respond. He did not move. His face was expressionless. Fred had become a mannequin, with no blood, warmth, or emotion. She would always awaken at this time—before the impact of the oncoming train but in the depth of her terror.

This time, however, she was not immobilized by the oncoming train. She was able, on her own, to drive the car off the tracks. When she awoke, there were no cold chills. They were replaced by a feeling of empowerment. She understood now what the dream had been trying to tell her all these years. The dream showed her that Fred could not help her. But it didn't matter any longer. He could remain the mannequin. Alissa had regained her strength. She had known this logically, but now she understood it emotionally as well. It was her catharsis toward self-actualization.

Fred had always been a mannequin. He was a facade of a man who was incapable of helping anyone because he wasn't capable of helping himself. Like the mannequin indifferent to the danger on the tracks, he had created a persona without an inner core of existential meaning. He was the opposite of the example Jean-Paul Sartre had used of the man who saw danger in an approaching tiger and knew he was doomed, so he capitulated. Fred wouldn't look at the face of the danger; if he had, he would have known there was a solution. So he had given up because he did not look.

None of that mattered to Alissa any longer. It did not matter who Fred was or what he had done, because he was no longer a part of her life. She had moved on. She was going to make a life for herself. She knew she had the love and encouragement of her children. She was moving to California to live it to the limit of her ability, and perhaps, to find that pickle at the bottom of the barrel.

◆ ◆ ◆

In the meantime, Josh would soon be making important life-changing decisions, too. He finished college at an opportune time. His grandmother, Joan Walters, was pressing her husband to move ahead with selling the business with Larry.

"What are we worth?" Joan asked Charlie.

"It's a good business. It makes us two million gross a year," he said.

"How much do we take out?" she asked, calculating their options.

"Maybe sixteen thousand a month."

"Okay, that makes about two hundred thousand each for Larry and for us, and we have medical, business cars, expense accounts. What do you think? Maybe it pays us each three hundred thousand dollars a year. That should be easy to sell. Why are you so worried that Larry won't buy us out?"

"I don't know. And you shouldn't want to know, either. This is not a subject for me to discuss with you," snapped Charlie. "What don't you have, anyway? Haven't I been a good provider? Look at you. What are you lacking?"

Joan was no dummy. She had never totally understood the books she had been asked to keep, but she was certain they didn't reflect what was going on at the business. She had signed a lot of papers over the years, and she understood that the building was currently not in her name only because it was needed as collateral for a business loan. She also understood that Charlie had borrowed from the business whenever a vacation was indicated. He had taken loans on the building to purchase their home when it was in her name. Most important, she knew her husband and his brother well enough to know they wouldn't stay with a deal that was not lucrative.

What Joan did not know was that the savings and loan held by the partnership they had set up to finance their real estate developments was shaky. The amount of interest they could pay their depositors was regulated. But the public could get higher rates of interest elsewhere, and their S&L was experiencing a drain of capital they could not control.

Joan was emphatic. "I don't care how you do it. I want you out. Just do it. We are not spring chickens. We should live better before we die. I still have some things I want to do, and you are going to see to it that we have enough money to make that happen."

To work out a deal, Charlie was going to have to talk to his brother. He expected Larry to be displeased about his wanting to sell out his business interest. Larry already thought Charlie was a wimp, allowing his wife to make such a fuss over his exploits. Wasn't that what men do? Why should a wife complain if it had nothing to do with her? Why didn't he buy her another piece of expensive jewelry like he had in the past?

But that wasn't the subject today. Today Charlie needed to know only what Larry would think about being a fifty-fifty partner with Josh, and if Larry was willing for Charlie to sell his partnership share to Josh, what would Larry think was a good price?

"Sell him the whole thing if you want. I'm not going to go into business with that greenhorn," said an argumentative Larry.

"You want to sell, too? Why?" asked Charlie.

"Because you are not going to be here with me. You are really making this a problem for me, Charlie. When you leave, the value goes down."

"How far down?" asked Charlie, thinking he might be able to pull off a deal for his grandson.

"Sell it to him for half a million. I won't take anything for my half," suggested Larry, not explaining that he didn't have a half interest anymore because he had already sold out. "I only want to stay on the payroll. I want to continue receiving a salary of sixteen thousand per month and have my medical paid. Just so he continues to furnish me with a new car each year—he can put me down as a consultant. Don't forget the car insurance and maintenance."

"It's a deal," said Charlie, smiling and shaking his brother's hand. "Josh can keep me on the payroll too. We'll both make the same agreement with him. But I'm going to need cash for my interest. I'll call Josh tomorrow and let him know what a lucky boy he is. It's very nice of you to be so kind to my grandson and give him your half for free."

◆ ◆ ◆

By now Josh was making Upton and Sons operate efficiently on a day-by-day basis. He saw no reason to purchase the Bronx building. What would he use it for? Wasn't Uncle Bob the only one who cared about the monster anyway? Bob was still in the building with some kind of chemist he had hired. All the family knew was that they were working on some secret formula that he thought would make him rich.

Fred wasn't surprised that Josh wanted to talk to him about the possibility of purchasing the family business. Charlie had already called him with the details.

"You know, son, I need to get out of these cold winters, too. Tasha wants to move to San Francisco."

"Tasha? Who's she?"

"She's my girlfriend. I met her last week."

Josh shook his head in disbelief as his father continued about the business arrangements. "It makes good sense for you to take this all over now. Our attorney, Ed Bane, can help you with the legal documents."

"Will the business be able to support Grandpa Walters and Uncle Larry?"

"You're not going to be supporting them. They are retiring. Just like me. The business will support them."

"Now, wait a minute," said Josh. "There's something fishy here. Why is everyone bailing out at once? Are you leaving me holding the bag?"

"Josh, you should be ashamed, talking to me like that. My father and my uncle are old men. They don't have long to live. They have worked hard to build up this business. I know how hard they worked. I did it, too. And you know, too. You saw how many hours the business took me from the family. Now that we want to retire, I think we should have something to live on. Do you want us to die in the poorhouse?"

"Don't get angry, Dad. You need to understand. I have other things I can do with my education. I have other job prospects. Why should I take on the burden of running the family business? I don't know if I want to work as many hours as you did. Maybe Rachel and I want more for our lives than slaving over a business."

"Who is going to do it if you don't?" Fred looked sad and empty.

"You mean to tell me that in all the years that Upton and Sons flourished, you didn't train someone to run the place?"

"Yes," replied Fred. "That was me. We've had lots of people employed over the years, but they were only clerks. You are looking at the business manager."

Josh was in a spot. He had only a cursory knowledge of how Upton and Sons operated. He knew that the family owned this big dilapidated building in the Bronx and that the investment company generated enough money to make his grandfather and uncle wealthy. If it worked for them, he surmised it would continue to be a money-maker with him running the business.

"How do you suggest I get my feet wet, Dad?"

"I hate that expression. Last time I got my feet wet, I got pneumonia and was in the hospital for three days. I don't know what more you need to know, Josh. If you think you can't generate enough money, then operate the business from the Tuckahoe Road building. That will cut down on overhead. You don't need the branch offices, now that Grandpa and Uncle Larry are moving away."

"And?"

"And what?"

"And what else? Isn't there anything else I need to know? Really, Dad. I'm a greenhorn with this. Help me out. Shouldn't I be getting on-the-job training or something? Aren't there tax returns to look at and accountants to talk to?"

"Your high-priced education isn't good enough for you to run a little family business? What's the matter, Josh," he said mockingly, "didn't they teach you how to load a truck?"

"Load a truck?"

"Forget it. It's a joke your mother told me once about a son who went to college to learn how to run the family trucking business but didn't learn how to drive a truck. Don't worry about it. Ed Bane will help you. He's been the family attorney for years. Everything you need will be provided by him."

"And the accountant?"

"You'll need to find a new one. The last one we had is still in federal prison on embezzlement charges. Take my advice—find someone who can add better than he can subtract. Black is better than red."

"Level with me, Dad. Am I going to make enough money to provide retirement income for all my ancestors? I would prefer to support my descendants. I'd like to start raising a family of my own, too."

"Nobody is going to give you a handout, Josh. Work hard, and the rest will come. It won't be my fault if you don't make a success of this. Just remember, if you fail, I won't have any income, either."

"I'm sorry, Dad. I wasn't thinking clearly. It wouldn't make sense for you to entrust your entire income source to the continuation of the business unless you were reasonably sure the business could support you. I'm a little nervous about the responsibility I'm taking on and wish you could give me more guidance. Are there any employees working there now I can rely on? Will you have time to show me the ropes before you move away?"

"You are really starting to annoy me, Josh. Grow up. Be a man. Get in there and roll up your sleeves and work. We all did. That's how I learned the business. If you need to borrow money for the purchase, take it out of the Savings and Loan. If you need help in the office, put that wife of yours to work. I've done my part in raising you. Now, can I leave?" he said, glancing at his watch. He rose from his chair and walked to the door. "Tasha is waiting for me. You know where I am. Call if you have any questions. I would like to enjoy my retirement while I'm still young."

"Sorry, Dad, I'll do the best I can. I'll make you proud of me. Tell Gramps and Uncle Larry I really appreciate this opportunity."

"That should wrap it up, son," he said, opening the door to leave. "I really have to go now. We have dinner reservations at Manero's tonight. A nice, thick steak will hit the spot."

"Dad—please, just one more question. What is Uncle Bob doing at the Bronx building?"

FOURTEEN

Dated and Outdated

Becoming a *California Girl* in the early 1980s looked as if it would show promise. This was going to be Alissa's personal crossing of the Rubicon. She eagerly set forth to start a new life away from the despair of the past. Alissa began by immediately locating the LA Library; she joined the Los Angeles Historic Society and Museum of Art and had several places in Los Angeles in mind for potential employment, even though the experts cautioned that the country was experiencing an economic downturn.

She brought seven suitcases of clothing and personal items on her move from the East Coast. The closets and storage cubbies in La Chateau, the newly constructed, furnished condo on Wilshire Boulevard in Century City, were adequate for her treasures. Unpacking was fun, especially with her daughter Katie there to help her plan for a new life.

"This place is awesome. It will be great for entertaining," said Katie, enthralled with the view from Alissa's sixteenth-floor garden patio. "Do you have a boyfriend you haven't told me about?"

Alissa slumped into the comfortable, oversized stuffed chair. "I wouldn't know where to start."

"I heard there is a 'choice' singles bar on Hope Street called the Meet Market. I haven't checked it out myself yet, but several girls at my office go there on Friday night after work. They have met some really cute yuppie guys."

"Katie, don't forget, I'm a woman with two grown children. I don't think I would find someone my age in a bar on a Friday night, even in LA."

"You're being old-fashioned, Mom. There are a lot of single professional men here who are your age. Besides, you can pass for being younger. We could go together if you'd like. Don't be uncool."

"No, it doesn't seem right. Especially at a place called the Meet Market."

"Mom, let me explain something to you about the LA scene. This is not Kansas, Dorothy. No one knows anyone here. Everyone has come from somewhere else. I thought you came to LA to start a new life."

"I did."

"Well, join the club. So has everyone else. You are not out of place here unless you want it to be that way."

"I'm ready to meet someone new, sweetie. But I can't walk up to a stranger in a bar who knows I am there because I am looking to be picked up. It's not seemly. It seems so crude. There must be another way."

"I think you have the wrong idea, Mom. This is a perfectly respectable restaurant. It's near the LA Central Library. It has another name; I just can't remember what it is. People started calling it the Meet Market—that's m-e-e-t—because single people meet there on Fridays after work. It's become a play on words, and now everyone calls it the Meat Market meaning m-e-a-t. Like I said, it's LA."

"LA? Is that a play on words, too? What does LA stand for—loose asses?"

"Mom, when did you get to be so gross?"

"*Loose asses* is more vulgar than *Meat Market*? Let me explain something to you. It's not about jumping into bed. For women my age, it's about building relationships that might lead to bed. I realize the Pill has changed sexual activity for women, but it hasn't changed anything for me. I would prefer just living my life and finding someone along the way who is embarked on the same journey. Then if a sexual relationship develops, I'd be happy to participate and enjoy it."

"You make dating sound so clinical, Mom. So you meet someone who just happens to enter your life. So what? How would you know if he is interested in getting horizontal with you? He might not even be attracted to you."

"Women have always known when a man is thinking about sex, and that's eighty percent of the time. Men flirt and suggest, and some are downright vulgar, and in polite society, women were taught not to notice. It doesn't mean that we didn't understand what was going on behind the scenes. Women have to know enough to be able to protect themselves. 'A dame who knows the ropes isn't likely to get tied up.'"

"You're being a dweeb, Mom."

"I have no idea what that means, Katie." But she knew the word was not intended to be flattering. "If you are trying to emphasize our generational gap by using your slang, so be it. But realize women from all ages have things in common. That was a quote from Mae West. She delighted her entire generation with her double entendres."

"Mae West? Who's she? Is she from your mother's generation? What do you care about her ideas? You are more hip than that, Mom."

"That's right. I learned about her from my mother, but that doesn't mean what she said does not apply today. I'm old enough to remember Tennessee Ernie Ford. I'm telling you that when he said, 'I've been ridden hard and put away wet,' do you think he was talking about his horse or horsing around?"

"Okay, you win. You know what you are doing. Just remember that in today's world, bad is good. I don't know what's holding you back. I know you're not a wallflower."

"No, I'm not a wallflower. Maybe it's because I would like a relationship to be romantic. I'd like to be asked out for a date. I'd like to be wined and dined, and most important of all, I would like the man to respect me."

"Oh god, Mom, I didn't realize you were so hopelessly out of date. And you probably will be out of dates, too. Why would you want to be held on a pedestal, when we've worked so hard to give women equal rights? You have a career. You should understand this. Don't have a cow over this. Women have the right to sexual expression just like men have. There is no difference in our needs."

"I agree, Katie. We have similar needs, but I want to reserve the right to express my needs differently than the men express theirs."

"I don't know what you are talking about. You aren't going to get far by being a couch potato, waiting for someone to call you for a date."

"I have a right to opt out of the new social rules if I wish. If women don't reserve their right to say no, how far will these new freedoms go?"

"'For sure, you can just say no. Rape is against the law. But how do you expect to be desirable unless you are out in the world, strutting your stuff? Your body is totally bodacious, Mom. There is nothing wrong with that. Don't you feel liberated?"

"You are making me feel like a bimbo, Katie. Maybe I don't fit into this brave new world. I don't know how to begin."

"Have you thought about trying one of those new dating services?"

"Dating services? You don't mean an arrangement where someone I don't know sets me up with a man neither of us knows? No!"

"I think they take a video of you and ask you questions. They try to match you with compatible people. It's all very scientific. You always said you wanted to be a scientist rather than a schoolteacher. Here's your chance to be part of the new science of dating."

Alissa was a realist. A video-dating arrangement did not sound as scary as the Meat Market. Sitting with her daughter in her new apartment with a view of the city lights highlighted her feeling of aloneness. The setting was romantic, and she had no one with whom to share it.

"Scientific," she said contemplatively. "I suppose that if I knew someone was compatible with me and had the same values and interests as me, it could work theoretically, unless both of us are lying."

"There is always a chance of that, Mom. You might run into some 1980s-type sex fiend who will lie to you to get you to do the nasty. What a shame that would be. I don't know if history would recover from your disgrace."

"You don't have to be so cruel. Let me think about this a while," Alissa said. "Now, would you help me move some of this furniture around? I don't like that table where it is. Let's put the brass lamp on this one and move it closer to the window. I like the warmth of the feeling it gives, showing that someone is home."

"While I'm waiting to hear your answer, shall I put a red bulb in the lamp? It might help get you started," said Katie. "You really need to chill, Mom."

◆◆◆

When Katie provided her mother with the address of the dating service, Alissa still wasn't committed to the idea. She was tolerating Katie when she accepted the address, but she was intrigued with the idea and already imagining what kind of man would respond. She ordered the forms to set up the appointment to make her video and completed the enrollment application honestly and conscientiously, wondering if her potential date would be as forthright. With the wheels in motion, Alissa searched for a hairstylist who could help her look as young as possible, and she went on a quickie diet so she would be able to wear her slinkiest skirts.

Alissa was out of her element in Los Angeles, and the more time it took to make these arrangements, the more misgivings she had about this method of meeting a man. It seemed too artificial to work out well. But Dr. Laura Schema, a local talk-radio psychologist, strongly recommended dating services for professional people who did not have an opportunity to meet anyone outside of work. *Maybe Katie was right, and a nice professional man might be looking for someone like her.*

Weeks later, when she was informed by the service that they had a match for her, she almost withdrew her application. She had reconsidered. She wished she had not participated in this foolishness. But the video arrived before she officially backed out of the program, and when Alissa viewed it, she was pleasantly relieved. Alissa liked what she saw. With candidates like Harry I., Alissa understood why this system could really work.

But she hadn't learned all the ropes yet, and Mae West wasn't around to explain them to her. Alissa misunderstood the reason why the service recommended that the first meeting be in a public place and that everyone be on a first-name basis. She was opposed to the idea of meeting someone at a public "meat market" (even if it was near the library). She thought that, initially, it would be better to meet the video man on her own turf so he could see who she really was. Her apartment was a romantic setting. He would get the whole picture at once, and if things worked out as Alissa imagined, he could also have the whole package at once.

Alissa spent hours preparing a sumptuous meal from her *McCall's Illustrated Dinner Party Cookbook*. She would begin the evening with port wine and honeydew melon balls wrapped in prosciutto. The entree would be veal scaloppini, noodles with pesto, and artichokes with lemon sauce. And if the meal conversation turned amorous too soon, she thought she would keep control of the situation by delaying him with the promise of spumoni for dessert. This strategy would only have worked if the maxim "The way to a man's heart is through his stomach" was true.

Poor Alissa had been out of the dating scene so long, she didn't know she was playing with fire and might not be able to control things by skimping on the spumoni. The table was elegantly set, and the food was on the table in serving dishes covered with silver steamer domes to retain the heat for the proper moment. This way she could concentrate on her guest without needing to hire a server. The moment of truth had come at last. He would arrive any moment.

Alissa did not remember being this nervous since she'd walked down the aisle to marry Fred. Pacing the floor, she stopped each time she passed the table to rearrange something, a fork not lined up properly, a leaf in the bouquet of flowers that obstructed one of the flowers, or a napkin whose seam was folded next to the plate, not away from it. She checked her appearance in the mirror at least ten times. Every hair was in place; her gold lame belt accessorized her forest-green jumpsuit beautifully, allowing the fabric to stretch provocatively as it tucked in under her hips.

She waited for the doorbell to ring while torturing herself with presumed insufficiency and self-doubt. *I don't know if it was such a good idea to meet him here,* she thought, reconsidering. *Who knows—this could turn out ugly. Maybe I shouldn't be dressed so provocatively. Maybe I look cheap. He may think I'm too obvious.*

Assumptions she had heard from girlfriends surfaced like bullets into new words from her own inner, insecure voice:

This man could be a sex fiend, and you want to meet him there alone?

When he finds out how well off you are, he will want to marry you just to take your money away from you.

You will be left with nothing if you don't learn how to protect yourself.

This is how you want to spend your old age—with a sex-fiend gold digger?

At the same time, her daughter's youthful energy enticed her with the possibility of a new life where she would not only set the theme but choose the characters and write the script. The stage was set. She could approach a prospective companion and not wait around to be selected by a man with whom she would have to develop an interest. Alissa felt she was competent to determine who was right for her. *Hadn't she seen his video? Hadn't she read his resume? She was intelligent and perceptive.*

All the people who had told her she was strong should see her now. This wasn't strength. Her head was spinning with conflicting ideas:

If I don't want him and can't get away from him, what should I do? If he finds out my last name, I may have to get an unlisted number. I might have to move. Maybe I should use my maiden name when I apply for work, so he can't stalk me. If I don't reach out, maybe I will miss out on someone special. If I don't meet someone in Los Angeles, I may have to spend the rest of my life here, among strangers, all alone.

She slumped into the big easy chair and regained her composure. *Oh, hell,* she thought to herself. *This isn't so bad. I can handle it. It might even be fun. At a minimum, I will have a nice meal at home with a handsome, eligible man.*

The buzzer rang, announcing that someone in the lobby at the Wilshire entrance had selected her apartment to call.

"Yes?" she said with a quiver in her voice as she pressed the reply button on the intercom.

"This is Harry Illingsworth. I have an appointment with a lovely lady, and I hope I have not inconvenienced her by arriving a tad late. Is this Alissa Walters?"

"Oh my god," she cried out loud. She turned off the intercom but not until after she had broadcast her call of alarm. She realized how he had learned her last name. She had been careless. He matched the unit number of her apartment to her name on the directory in the lobby. She promised herself she would learn from this mistake, and if and when she ever video dated again, she would not be this careless.

"Sorry about that," she said. "I stubbed my toe. Yes, it's me, Harry. I'll buzz you into the elevator lobby. There are two elevator banks down there. Be sure to take the elevator that goes to the top floors. See you soon."

◆ ◆ ◆

Harry Illingsworth looked even more professional in person than he did on the video. In his dark-blue suit with the red power tie, he looked as if he had been cut from the pages of *Fortune* magazine. He was tall, dark, and handsome and as smooth as someone created by central casting. But there was something alarming about him. He looked furtively around as if he was casing the apartment. However, Harry's voice seemed gentle, and if his video could be believed, he was a banker in Santa Barbara at US First Bank of California, a divorced father of two.

First impressions are the most lasting, and there were many ways Harry might have enhanced his impression on Alissa. He might have joked about the two elevators and asked if one was the express and one the local. Everyone in the building made those kinds of jokes. He might have commented about her appearance; all women like that. He might have commented on his finding her building, which was brand new. Or he might have mentioned the fact that the rain had stopped and the stars were especially bright that night. But unfortunately for Harry, he did not continue the advantage of the first impression.

"I must warn you," he said, taking her hand as she opened the door to her home, "I must not suffer any rejection, Alissa."

He pushed his way into the room. "I am deeply bruised by a wife who left me for another man. I found her in bed boinking my best friend. I go into depression if I sense any kind of rejection. It's happened many times, and I get deeper into my grief each time." He delivered these words with a wistful smile. "I'm sure we won't have any problem," he said, glancing at the dining room table already set with table service and food. "It looks as if you are planning to dine in."

His assumptions astonished Alissa. He had observed correctly. She was planning to entertain him at home. But he didn't have to say it out loud. It made her efforts for seduction too obvious and uncouth. Who did he think he was to notice that she wanted this date to turn into a romantic private evening?

Yes, she was planning an intimate dinner for two but not under the press of his threats. If he thought he was going to whine his way into her bed, he would have to do it with Dom Perignon and not by demanding sympathy. She held the key to the bedroom, not him. His hands were empty, and she was not persuaded by pathos. When she raised her children and they whined, she would tell them, "A whine is half a cry. If you want the other half, just keep it up." This was not a child, so other methods might be warranted tonight unless he changed his tune.

Alissa decided to skip the Campari cocktail aperitif she had planned to serve before dining. He did not appear to need appetite stimulation. She moved to the table and scooted the floral centerpiece to hide the bottle of Graham's ten-year-old Tawny Port. She wasn't going to give him wine with his whine. It would give him more encouragement. Alissa did not like Harry Illingsworth's presumptions and had already decided she needed to concentrate on how to get rid of him without having him feel rejected. The last thing she wanted was a basket case. It didn't go with the décor. She realized he must leave, but he must leave on his own accord.

"Oh yes," she said, reaching for her chair at the table. "But I didn't prepare this meal. I don't cook. I had this delivered by the Italian restaurant on the corner."

Harry had not noticed an Italian restaurant on the Century City part of Wilshire. He politely pushed her chair in. "Shall I remove the heat covers in the kitchen?"

Oh Lord, there's the double entendre again, thought Alissa. The last thing she wanted was for him to think he could remove anything related to heat.

"Whatever," she commented shrugging her shoulders, using the word the Valley Girls used when they wanted to sound blasé. At least he would think she was hip.

When Harry saw no Styrofoam cartons in the kitchen, he rightly concluded that his date had prepared the gourmet meal to impress him. He sized Alissa up as an easy lay and returned to the dining area, bearing that same wistful smile he'd worn when he pushed into the room. He took his place at the table and began the obligatory first-date small talk, believing that this conquest was going to be easier than most.

"So tell me, Melissa, your résumé said you recently moved to LA. You didn't mention a job. Are you looking for something?" he asked as he placed food onto her plate. "Is this the correct portion, Melissa?"

"Yes, that is the right amount of food, and yes, I am looking for work. But I have several interesting leads."

He served himself and used this opportunity to continue playing his "poor me" card. "Did I tell you that my wife took everything?" he asked, not waiting for a response. He was piling on the food and the garbage in equal portions. "We had a home in Marina Del Rey, right on the marina. I had a new, sleek thirty-foot Sonic Prowler that was docked within sight of our living room. My wife got everything, but that's okay. She had breast cancer, and I'm glad I was able to provide her with a nice life while she was still alive. My biggest loss was the kids." He said, continuing to eat and dabbing a would-be tear from his face with his dinner napkin. He did not notice that she had not been speaking.

He hardly changed the inflection in his voice. "Berkeley is twelve, and Bronson is only three. Poor baby, Bronie will grow up without ever knowing who his father is. My ex-wife won't let me see them because she didn't understand that when Berkeley was arrested for using drugs, I would not agree to have him sent to live with her parents. They are such peasants; I couldn't bear to have him grow up that way. It's all so sad and meaningless." He started to sob and reached across the table to take her hand for comfort. He brushed away a tear.

Alissa allowed him to touch her hand for a moment, and then she pulled it away. She stiffened her back and curtly offered to remove his plate. But Harry wasn't finished eating. He took another helping and switched from his self-absorbed monologue to probing for information about her. "What is your line of work?"

Somebody should have warned Harry not to ask that question. Alissa was annoyed and armed and ready to answer that one.

"I'm a research analyst," she said.

"Research?"

"Yes, I have very interesting work. I do field work."

"Field work in LA?" he asked, noticing the empty wineglasses and looking around for something to put in them.

"Oh, you can do field work in LA. I send the specimens to the lab by mail."

Harry wasn't going to be put off. He concluded that there was no wine to be had, but he continued with the questions as eagerly as he was consuming the meal.

"Lab specimens?"

"Yes, lab specimens. I'm in the field of scatology. I go into the field and gather specimens, and I send the interesting ones to the lab."

"I don't understand. What does *interesting* mean for you?" he asked, to encourage her.

"My research has shown that animals that are herbivorous make round feces, while animals that are omnivorous and carnivorous make feces that are very oddly shaped. The most interesting specimens are the ones that have lumps in them and are not too dry. I find them mostly in cow pastures, but horse corrals will do as well. I have special equipment that picks them up." She raised both her hands and wiggled her fingers. "Can I give you some more Harry pesto; I mean pesto, Harry? It's an interesting green color, don't you think?"

Harry was astonished, and it looked as if he might be turning a slight shade of pesto. In any event, he stopped eating.

She continued. "Someday I want to branch out to work on fossilized specimens, but for that I will need a research grant. In the meantime, I'm looking into getting a dog to help me sniff out and find the examples of the predatory animals."

"You're thinking about getting a dog?'

"Yes, perhaps a Belgian Malinois or maybe a Doberman Pinscher." She noticed the thought of a guard dog was threatening to him. "My current research, combined with what we are learning about DNA, is already very important for humanity. Someday, who knows, we may be able, through the study of scatology, to trace the migration of humans into our continent, and just think, I am part of it. But for now, I am content with doing the groundwork. For my thesis, I am specializing on categorizing the odors and establishing what diet causes them and what use they may have for further identification and classification. When I find some that aren't too fragrant, I roll them into balls, dry them in the freezer, and rub them until they shine."

"Thesis?"

"Yes, my feces thesis...and when I find the right man to do this research with me, I will name the feces theory after him. What about you? Harry I. Feces Thesis has a nice ring to it, don't you think so, Mr. Illingsworth? Surely you have heard of polishing shit."

Harry Illingsworth stood up, almost turning the table over. "This is not funny, Clarissa," he said. "You have ruined what I expected to be a really promising evening."

Alissa knew she had frightened him. It was to be her carpe diem moment. "This is great," Alissa exclaimed, dancing around him, pirouetting, and giving him a tap again and again as he tried to move away from her. "Clarissa Walters and Harry Lickingsworth—has a nice ring to it, doesn't it?"

"I'm not in the mood anymore. I'm leaving, and I don't think we should see each other again."

"I understand, Mr. Ickingsworth. I'm so happy that I did not reject you," she said, opening the door for him. "Will you need help getting out of the building, or can you find your way out on your own? Take the express elevator," she called as he fled down the hallway. "It's faster."

When he was out of the apartment, Alissa realized her heart was pounding. She took a deep breath and let it out slowly. Her fear slowly subsided. She walked to the kitchen and poured herself a tall glass of cold Chardonnay from the wine box in the refrigerator. *I wish I could be at the bank when he tells the story to his coworkers,* she thought. *I'm glad I wasn't planning on getting a loan from US First Bank of California.*

◆ ◆ ◆

Katie was not having a good night. She loved her mother, but the anger Katie felt from the divorce of her parents burned with a fire that would not be extinguished. Like most young women, she would have preferred her parents to stay married. They hadn't, and Katie was confused about why. She never had the courage to ask her mother the intimate questions to learn what caused it to fail.

Now tonight, her anger had prompted her to encourage her mother to enter the dating scene. Worry set in. It was now eight o'clock, it was dark, and her mother was with a total stranger. Who knew what kind of man this might be? Katie had not discussed danger with her mother and how the mood of women in Los Angeles was clouded by the Hillside Strangler, whose dead and mutilated female victims had been found strewn along the freeways of LA in the late seventies. Now that the trial was in progress, horrible details were coming out about the deeds of the two killers. Without another thought, Katie picked up the phone and starting dialing.

"Mom, are you okay? Is this a good time to talk?"

"Well, that was an experience," said Alissa, moaning. "You know, Katie, I have never been good around people who are negative. This man did nothing but complain. I am totally drained."

"Did he take off?"

"Yes, thank God, and I'm sure he will not show up again."

Katie's anger was coming back. Her mother was nitpicking. This would be the same kind of behavior Katie believed Alissa had shown when married to her father.

"Oh, Mom, you didn't dump him just for being negative, did you? Maybe he was having a bad day. You have to learn not to be so major critical."

"His values and attitudes are from before the Dark Ages, Katie. This man is a perfect specimen of coprolite."

"Oh, Mom, I'm so sorry he was a scumbag."

"No, not *coprology*. He didn't have a preoccupation for obscenity. He didn't say anything that indicated he was fond of pornography. I mean a coprolite. Harry Illingsworth is a piece of fossilized dinosaur shit, and he isn't interesting enough to leave lumps. How's that for 1980s slang, Katie? Is your mother fresh enough to suit you? I tried and I failed. I can't handle negative people, Katie. I really mean it. It takes me where I don't want to go. Negative people put the brakes on creativity. I need to go to the light, not live in the Dark Ages."

"So what are you, a monk? I have no idea what you want out of life. You are the one who is doing the complaining, and I'm tired of hearing it. You are the one living in the Dark Ages. You are the one who can't be pleased. You could have worked things out. You can handle anything you put your mind to, Mom."

Alissa's voice started to quiver. The evening had drained her emotionally. She had hoped it would have worked out, but it hadn't. That wasn't as bad as now having to discuss it with a daughter who thought she should have stayed to work it out. She pleaded with her daughter to understand.

"You see me as a strong woman who can handle anything, but you don't know how the hurtful things that have happened to me affect my personality. I need to be around people who don't push me and who don't pull me down. I become too anxious when I'm forced into something I don't want."

"Oh, please spare me," said Katie. "You had a beautiful home, everything you wanted. You shopped at the finest stores, had recognition in the community. You even had your own career, and Mom, you had accomplishments of your own. You were able to pursue your own interests. Who was pushing you down?"

Katie was not able to continue expressing her disappointment because she began to cry, too. "Everyone loved you, Mom, and you threw us all away."

"I didn't throw everyone away. I still have you and Josh; at least I hope and pray I do, Katie. Are you still with me, darling? I'm finally listening to myself. All my life, I've been held down. It's time you learned a little bit about your mother. I was drowning."

"Stop it, Mom. You don't need to be the drama queen. What you were drowning in was your own self-pity."

"God, Katie, I'm so sorry you feel that way. You should have been here tonight. I kicked out an expert in self-pity. He could have shown you how people use self-pity to get what they want. It was an art form with him. He was full of hot air. That's not me, Katie. If you think it is, you really don't know me at all."

"What do you mean, I don't know you? I've known you all my life, Mom. What other life do I have except the one with you?"

"Please listen to me, Katie. Let's talk about this. I want to start by telling you I love you with all my heart."

Katie was sobbing uncontrollably. She was trapped in a triad of competing personal needs. She sobbed for her mother, who she felt had been in free fall since the divorce. Katie sobbed for her lonely father. But most of all, Katie sobbed for herself. From Katie's point of view, Alissa had not only divorced Fred, but she had broken the entire family. Now Katie felt she had to choose to stand by her mother and the Barrett side of the family or to side with her father and keep the Walters relatives.

Katie's choice was easier now that the dating scene wasn't working out for her mother. And yet Katie knew in her heart that her mother's need to assert herself was necessary for self-preservation, and Katie had not yet understood the difference between quitting a relationship because of a character weakness and escaping because of abuse.

"Mom, I can't talk now. This is gagging me out the door." She hung up the phone.

FIFTEEN

On Tap

It troubled Alissa that Katie had cut off their conversation before she was able to fully explain the reasons it was necessary for her to leave Fred. Hanging up the phone on conversations that had the potential of exploring the intricacies of her mother's truth was becoming an annoying habit of Katie's. Alissa vowed not to try communicating with her daughter on this delicate issue until conditions were right. She wasn't looking forward to it, because she didn't want her daughter's love for her father to be diminished. Alissa convinced herself that she was waiting for the opportunity to arise when they could discuss this quietly in person without interruption. But what she was really waiting for was for her daughter to learn the truth on her own, to accept both her parents for who they were, and after she had learned why the marriage failed, put it away and get on with enjoying her own life.

Katie focused on how badly she personally was injured when her parents' marriage ended in divorce, and it would be natural for her to be looking for someone to blame. Katie's conclusion, judgment, and anger were keeping them from developing the kind of mother-daughter bond that Alissa longed for and both women needed. While Katie was always kind and compassionate with her mother, her resistance to exploring the reason for the divorce was not going to make matters easy. If Alissa was to be the bearer of the information, it would have to wait for a time when Katie would not be able to escape until she was made, once and for all, to understand her mother's position. They were probably going to have to go to the mat with this one, and Katie was a black belt while Alissa felt she would be showing up on wimp wheels.

◆◆◆

In the meantime, as soon as Alissa found a job she liked and could see that she had opportunities in Los Angeles she would not have in Greenwich, she began to feel more confident. She soon grew tired of only working and longed for some extracurricular pleasure and fun. She thought her best opportunity to do that would be with her second video-dating selection.

This eligible man, Samuel, was equal to Henry Illingsworth in appearance and his suave, well-dressed video presentation. His stats disclosed him to be a little taller than Henry, and his video showed he was suntanned, muscular, and had a full head of healthy gray hair. Samuel was semiretired from BowLink Inc., a company that manufactured airplanes at their large facility in the California desert. He listed watching comedy movies and surfing at Malibu as his favorite activities. Samuel said he was looking for a long-term relationship leading to marriage with a woman who liked moonlight walks on the beach and intimate candlelit dinners at home.

Alissa was concerned that walks on the beach and dining in might indicate Samuel was a tightwad, but he might just be a romantic. That would be nice for a change. As long as he could take care of his own expenses, she anticipated no problem. Although she had a generous heart, she did not want to support a man. Alissa wanted lighthearted adventure that would lead to a carefree and warm marriage, and Samuel looked and sounded like he would fit the bill. She made the phone call, and at his suggestion, they agreed to meet for a dinner date at the revolving bar at the top of the Bonaventure Hotel. This would be on his tab.

Maybe Samuel wasn't a tightwad, but housing was expensive in LA, and Alissa had put herself on a budget. Appalled at the price the Bonaventure was charging for their underground parking, she took advantage of another option. Kitty-corner from the Bonaventure was an empty lot where several cars were parked. Alissa had heard that the lot had previously been the site of a service station, and the land was in the process of being prepared for new high-rise construction. The delay had something to do with clearing the toxicity from the gasoline tanks. The cars parked on the vacant lot were newer models, did not appear abandoned, and were easily accessible because the property was not fenced. The city streetlights illuminated the property, and she perceived no danger with parking her car there. Why not? This was the upscale financial district that was patrolled by the LAPD, and parking was free. So what if there might be latent toxic fumes? She wasn't going to light up a cigarette.

◆ ◆ ◆

"So you are new to LA," began Samuel as Alissa found him at one of the intimate tables in the windowed section. "My name is Samuel A Woods and I've laid out our town for you to see," he said, rising from the table to greet her and sweeping his arm at the sparkling city lights twenty floors below them.

Alissa was star struck. The bar on the very top of the hotel continued the cylindrical shape of the hotel. Glass windows at the periphery dramatically displayed the city lights in the surrounding skyscrapers.

"Yes, Mr. Woods," she said, "LA is a totally new experience for me, and I am learning to enjoy it."

"Please start by calling me Sam," he said, immediately focusing his eyes on her bosom as he reached for her hand to pull her closer to him.

"We don't need to be formal. Won't you sit down?" he asked after kissing her hand.

"I'm not comfortable with formality, either," she said, carefully choosing her words as well as her seat across the table from his, so she could retain her distance. She chose not to say she was casual because that might imply she was easy. "I suppose you might call me ordinary. But my real name is Alissa Walters."

"Well, I'm not ordinary," he retorted emphatically, moving to the seat closer to hers. "Actually, my mother is an Adams. I don't like boasting about our Adams connection. But it's interesting. It's me to the core. I'm drinking a Manhattan in honor of the lady born in New York I've just met. Would you like to join me? Waiter, please."

"That is a very sweet thought," said Alissa, appreciating his way with words. "That's a little strong. I'd prefer Dubonnet on the rocks. Thank you."

Sam did not miss a beat with the interruption to place her order. "You do know who the Adams family is, don't you?"

Alissa was amused at his pretentiousness. "Just don't call me Morticia."

"Morticia? I thought your name was Alissa. I'm sorry. So, Morticia, how do you like LA so far?"

"My name is Alissa. I was making a joke. You know, *The Addams Family*—Morticia, Uncle Fester, Pugsley..."

"Why would you say that?" Sam was looking very confused. "Would you rather be called Morticia? I'll call you anything you wish."

Alissa was relieved he had not suggested calling her Creep. "Let's rewind this conversation. I am Alissa, and you are Sam. You were telling me about your mother's family name. Were you asking me if I knew that Adams was an important name historically?"

"Why, yes," he said. "Didn't you know that?"

"Yes, I do know that. Are you telling me that you are related to the Adams family who gave us the father-and-son presidents?"

"Yes. That's it. That's who we are. See, you got it. I am a member of Sons of the American Revolution. We have a family crest. I don't like boasting, but bloodlines are very important to us patriot types. My first wife was a daughter of a patriot as well but not as famous as mine. And no one in my family thus far has broken with tradition by marrying anyone who does not also have patriot lines. I am a direct bloodline descendant of John Adams."

Alissa was annoyed. "With or without the Q?"

"The Q?"

"Yes, the Q, like in John Quincy Adams. If you don't like Qs, perhaps you can have an *S* for Sam or maybe an *S*, like in General Ulysses S. Adams. Forget it, Sam. You have caught me off balance. You say you don't like boasting, but don't you think it's a teeny bit pretentious of you to bring up pedigree during the lead-commercial announcement on a first date? I thought the patriots in this country were trying to get away from all that royal-family stuff. The only pedigree in my family is my dog, Clipper, who is a full-blooded terrier. You might say she is a real terror. Sam, you invited me for drinks. This is a lot to swallow."

She paused to catch her breath and her composure. "I'm sorry. Forgive me. I interrupted. You were telling me about yourself. I'd like to learn more. Please go on."

"I'm not trying to put you down, Alissa. Don't be hostile. If you don't also have an important family name, it's not going to be an issue for us. I've never heard of a patriot named Walters. I'm not interested in having more children. I've done my part for posterity. Four is enough." He leaned toward her for a closer inspection. "You are probably past the child-bearing age, anyway, Alissa, so there is nothing lost on my side. Don't feel badly. You are fine as you are."

"I'm not feeling put down, Sam. I have no problem with the fact that my people came into the country after the immigration laws were more restrictive. I'm just a little lost in the maze of Sam, son of John. I might have understood better if you were John the thirteenth and if your last name was Adams. But tell me, how does the Adams's duo get you qualified for the SAR? They didn't actually pick up arms to fight, did they? I don't see how your ancestor John Q. could have been in the revolution; he was too young. And John the father was an attorney during the Boston Massacre, wasn't he?"

"My mother has the certificate."

Alissa could not resist showing her smarts by interrogating him further. "Does she have the family crest? Who earned it? Those aren't hereditary, are they? I thought they belonged only to the person who earned them in Europe. I thought the only thing the family inherited was the land grant. Did your crest come with a grant? I've heard about Grant's Pass but not Grant's Crest. Where is that, anyway? Just outside of Crescent City? That's it—you inherited Crescent City from your family. But tell me—was it the one in California, Florida, or Illinois?"

Sam sat in stony silence. Alissa went on. "Are you sure it's the Johns in your lineage? If you were a descendant of their cousin, Samuel Adams, perhaps the contribution he made by throwing the tea into Boston Harbor would qualify as service in the revolution. What do you think, Sam? That might work. Was it Sam or John? Maybe that's why your mother named you Sam. What's in a name, anyway? What's it all worth in 1983 Los Angeles? Probably not even a free ride on the airport shuttle."

Sam was still looking stunned, but he did not look injured, so she went on annihilating him. "So what's with *Sam Woods the fourth*? Is *Woods* an important family name too? Was your great-great-grandfather a president, too? Or maybe it's a place name. Perhaps that ancestor was from Vienna. Strauss was inspired by their woods."

Sam did not understand these to be insults. The sarcasm was over his head, and Viennese waltzes were beyond his cultural experiences. The only Strauss Sam knew was the tailor who made his expensive suits.

"I don't think so. I should ask my father about that. He was from Austria. Anglicized the name at Ellis Island, you know. It was W-a-l-d something or other. It's very interesting. Funny that you should suggest that. I hadn't thought about the German part being in the revolution. I wonder if my fraternal ancestor may have been a Hessian soldier. Thank you, Alissa. You may really be on to something."

"Well, Hessians as patriots—now that would be really something. While you are looking into that, you should thank your lucky stars that we take our names from our fathers. You could have been named Samuel Adams. Sounds more like a beer to me, maybe a light beer."

"What did you mean by light beer?"

"Never mind," said Alissa, wanting to change the subject after achieving her coup de grace. "Is it time to go down to the restaurant? I think you said that you made reservations at eight. Does the restaurant rotate too?"

"No, only the bar rotates," he said. "But I've arranged for a western view. It's a clear night. You'll be able to see all the way to Century City."

"That would be nice. I'm bored with going in circles. I'd like to get my bearings so I can find my way home."

◆ ◆ ◆

The dinner was elegant. Sam knew how to spend money (so long as he could charge it on the company credit card). He had preordered chateaubriand with bearnaise sauce, asparagus vinaigrette, and salade nicoise. They would begin with champagne and escargots for appetizers. Alissa did not mind that he had not consulted her for her preferences because his generosity and good taste were a pleasant surprise. The service was impeccable but subtle, allowing the twosome to focus exclusively on each other. Alissa chose to disarm her arsenal of sarcasm and allow her tenderness to surface.

With time, she learned how tenderly to tease out Sam's humorous side. He did have one, and she found it. This evening was more fun than she'd had in years. Her cares were melting away. He could imitate famous sports personalities, and when telling anecdotes about them, he mimicked their voices so accurately that other guests in the restaurant looked toward their table, expecting to find a celebrity. Sam was at his best when talking about movies he had seen and even had some of the dialogue memorized. Sam was a ham. By the time the waiter brought the delicious *anna torte* and espresso for dessert, Alissa was boldly laughing out loud and enjoying the attention they were both receiving.

While Sam was in the process of telling her about another of the movies he had seen recently, Alissa was feeling the need to connect with this man. She remained restrained because the honor of intimacy with her would be given to him only after she had the opportunity to tell him more about herself. That would keep her in control of what she wanted to share with him.

Alissa knew that men want to be the center of attention. They brag about themselves to impress a woman. A woman should understand a man's bragging rights are designed for a quick and easy relationship. It's not too different from the mating habits of some of our distant cousins in the larger animal kingdom. But for Alissa, the way to establish a long-term relationship required that the woman disclose selected information about herself and that he buy into her standards. The more he knew about her, the better were her chances that she would get into his head and heart and stay there. She must control what she wanted to divulge, and the method of disclosure could be very seductive if she chose the right time and place to bare her soul. If she did this carefully, he would want to learn how to adapt to her. But most important when meeting someone new was that her information must be interwoven with the task of further evaluation of him. This was what she did that evening at the Bonaventure.

The movie Sam described was the new Burt Reynolds comedy, *Starting Over*. Sam described Candice Bergen's role as a wife who pursues a singing and songwriting career and disposes of husband, Burt Reynolds, to do so.

"I can relate to Candice Bergen wanting to be a singer. That requires a lot of training. Was she any good?"

"I guess so."

"If I had been Candice Bergen, I think I would also have liked to be a painter. But she's not at all like me. My life is more like the lead in Ingmar Bergman's *Scenes from a Marriage,* when the wife learns her husband is cheating on her."

"A painter," replied Sam. "Do you mean, like, an artist? Do they make any money?"

This hurt Alissa more than he could possibly know. Her eyes filled with tears, but she remained dignified, and no tears dropped down her reddened cheeks to give away the pain she was feeling. He was more interested in talking of money than being willing to allow her to speak of her *Bergman-esque* pain. This remark was uncalled for. Her primary focus in life had not been making money. Painting was something she yearned to do. For Alissa, who was so intent on expressing herself, heaven would be having a lifestyle that would allow her to pursue her creativity with a man who loved and respected her.

She had lost her chances for the Met. She needed to see if she had any talent as an artist. She worked well with clay, and she sketched whenever she could, but she had not yet found her style. She was still a novice, and she was reluctant to push her needs because she wasn't sure if her talent was worth encouragement. He would not be expected to know of these stifled needs because she had given him no hint of them. They were a long way from her allowing those needs to be communicated. She tried another approach.

"You were telling me about the movie, and I interrupted. I'm sorry again," she said, putting her needs aside and deferring again to what interested Sam. "Please go on."

He didn't miss a beat. "Then Burt Reynolds joins a therapy group. His brother sends him there. It's full of guys who are having problems with women. There's this old geezer who thinks all women want to marry him so when he dies they can get all his money. And there's this other guy who keeps going back to his ex-wife. What a bore that would be."

"What problems did Burt Reynolds have to talk about?" asked Alissa.

"He didn't have any problems. He was really cool. This part was so funny. He meets this new girlfriend, goes over to her house, and when she is taking a shower, he climbs in with her, clothes and all."

"What was the new girlfriend like?" Alissa was putting the brakes on talking about showering-together intimacy. "Was she more suited to his personality than Candice Bergen?"

"I don't know. They didn't say. She was a blind date. He bumped into her on the street, and he didn't like her, but he went through with the date even though his sister-in-law warned him that this gal didn't have large breasts," he said, allowing his eyes to focus again on Alissa's.

"She must have had a name," responded Alissa, feeling more than a little uncomfortable. On one hand, Alissa was pleased that he was sexually attracted to her, but she didn't want to encourage this until she first had the opportunity to let him understand who she was. So far this was not happening. She wanted the total Alissa to be there when they would become lovers. As much as she longed for a sexual relationship with this healthy, handsome man, she was beginning to understand that it would be best if that did not happen tonight.

"Marilyn. She was a neurotic preschool teacher."

Oh no, not a Marilyn, thought Alissa. She didn't want the conversation to go down the route of talking about sex goddess Marilyn Monroe. Sam's eyes were already glued to her breasts. This was not going to work out until Sam saw how lucky he was to have found her, she reasoned. There was a head and a heart attached to her body, and she hoped the same could be said about him. She continued to slow down the path to intimacy.

"What was Burt Reynolds's occupation?"

"He must have been out of work because he took this part-time job as a schoolteacher."

Alissa continued to hang on to every word he said to see how she could take another example from the movie that would give her an opportunity to direct the conversation to her personality. After his disdainful remark about schoolteachers, she certainly wasn't going to remind him that she had taught elementary school for fourteen years. Maybe he had forgotten that bit of information from her video résumé. She wanted to connect with Samuel Adams Woods IV, even if he was a light beer. At this point in her life, she wasn't looking for the intellectual type. But at the minimum, she wanted a long-term lease with an exclusive right to occupancy.

"I can relate more to Marilyn than Candice. I'm a bit neurotic, too. But tell me, Sam, what did Marilyn see in Burt?"

"He was good looking and made her laugh."

"I can relate to that too."

The roving photographer came by. When the photographer asked Alissa to pose closer to Sam, she jumped up and stood next to the photographer. "No pictures, please! He's married. The senator can't be seen with me in a hotel."

Sam did look like a senator. "You're my cup of tea." he said. "When can we meet again?"

"Well, first tell me more about yourself. I know you're not a senator."

"I would describe myself as a self-made man."

The adult in Alissa rose to the occasion. She allowed Sam to keep his pride.

"Is that wide street Wilshire?" she asked, pointing into the Los Angeles lights below.

"Yes."

"My place is on Wilshire. Would you like to see it?"

"Waiter, the check, please."

Sam wanted to be sure they would be leaving together. He didn't want her to back out of the invitation to visit her apartment. He intended to follow her car. He quickly formulated a plan that would make that happen. He would pay her parking fees to be sure they would leave at the same time.

"I'll walk you to your car," he said. "Let me pay for your parking."

"I can't," said Alissa, observing the disappointment register on Sam's face. "I didn't park in this building. I'm in the vacant lot across the street."

"No problem." Sam was thankful that this was an easier arrangement to work out. "Come with me to my car, and I'll give you a lift to yours."

Sam signed the credit-card receipt for the meal. Had Alissa known that this sumptuous meal was a sham, as the credit card belonged to his employer and not to him, she might have had a hint that Sam was all show and no substance. But it would have only been one clue, and tonight she was looking for reasons to connect, not for reasons to reject him. So perhaps she would have created an excuse for him.

◆ ◆ ◆

When they arrived at the vacant lot, Alissa's car was the only one remaining. She took her keys out of her purse to open the door.

"What's this?" called out Sam in alarm. "You have a flat tire." He walked around the car and bent down for a closer examination. "All your tires are flat. They look as if they have been slashed. Why did you park here, anyway?"

The tires weren't the only thing that went flat that night. The magic of the moment was interrupted. There was the call to the police department to file a vandalism report. The officer was familiar with the problem and asked Alissa why she was willing to risk parking on the street after business hours. Then there was the call to the only nearby twenty-four-hour garage on Figueroa Street near the freeway. The cost of the tires went on Alissa's credit card.

With the sun coming up to start a new day, the unfulfilled pair bid each other good night. Sam would be heading home to get ready for his part-time job. Alissa would be heading home to call her insurance company to file the claim under the comprehensive coverage of her policy. Slashed tires seemed like a bad omen, and they weren't sure they would continue to see each other. Sam thought it was taking too much effort to get Alissa into bed. There were other women he could pursue. Alissa felt she had spent the entire evening and had failed to get into his head and heart.

She was surprised when Sam did call her again about a month later. He returned to try again when the thought stuck him that some other man was bedding her down. She thought it was because he had reevaluated the evening and had recognized the value of a relationship with her.

Many dates followed. They saw every new movie, and they spent each weekend at the beach. Alissa wished Sam was more interested in hiking, biking, or even sailing, so that she could go with him, but that was not to be. Sam was competitive, and the sports in which he participated were ones where he could show his prowess. If this relationship was to continue, Alissa realized, she would have to content herself by staying on the sidelines. That was incredibly boring for her, but by now she was hooked, and as long as they were together, she was willing to go along with the printed program. She knew how to retreat into her books for companionship and intellectual stimulation.

Alissa had to overlook the jibes Sam made at what he considered her deficiencies. Sometimes the jibes weren't so small. The fiasco of the slashed tires in downtown LA came up a lot, with the story evolving each time Sam applied his rendition of revisionist history. The latest version of the story had him driving over to the garage, picking up the tires, paying for them, and personally getting down on his hands and knees in the dirt in the dark to put them on Alissa's car. No mention was made of the man from the garage, the policeman, or the fact that her insurance company had reimbursed the whole tab on Alissa's credit card *and* her insurance rates had increased.

Josh was the first to point out the pyramid of cruel insults that Alissa was enduring. Josh didn't mince words. He warned her months before she married Sam.

"Mom, you are giving up your values and playing down your intelligence just to have a relationship with him. You are free, Mom. This is not the time for you to bury your head in the sand. Ostrich feathers are not in vogue. You're not getting anything out of this relationship. What do you talk about—movies and how great he thinks he is? He doesn't get it. He doesn't even understand a plot line. He mimics life. He's a wannabe. There is no depth to him. You two are different. He doesn't understand you, and he puts down whatever he doesn't understand."

"No, he's not as unreasonable as you think. He didn't graduate high school with his class because he wanted to stay back and continue to play basketball. He was a star. He was very popular. He looks like Glen Campbell."

"Oh, Mom, get real. Okay, he's good looking. He's probably even good in bed. But he failed high school, Mom. He's an airhead. You are not making good decisions. This man is not for the long haul. Mark my words, Mom, in five years he won't even remember your name. Is it true that he is younger than you?"

"Only eight years."

"Eight years? Since when is that 'only'?"

"Eight years makes sense, Josh. Women usually live eight years longer than men."

"So you die together. That's thinking ahead, isn't it? What are you aiming for—a twofer casket? What do you have while you are waiting to die? Remember at Christmas, when he wanted you to give him a Gucci watch? What was that all about?"

"He offered to give one to me, too."

"I didn't know that. Did you get one?"

"No. He wanted me to have one because it was a status symbol. I told him it was a lot of money to spend to wear someone else's name on your wrist."

"That's fine, Mom. He thinks status can be bought, and you bought him some. He's schmoozing you. Maybe you should think about this some more before you make any serious commitments. Does he have any money?"

"He's semiretired."

"What does that mean? He doesn't have a full-time job."

"His company allows him to work part-time."

"Allows? What company?"

"BowLink."

"Oh, really, that's interesting. He's an engineer?"

"He is their purchasing agent."

"There you have it. It's all bogus. He's not smart enough to be an engineer, but he's smart enough to spend other people's money at a job they don't need a full-time employee for. I rest my case, Mom. You have bought yourself a boy toy."

Josh was right, but Alissa brushed off his advice. It did not make her proud to have a son who spelled out her blunders so clearly. Isn't the parent supposed to advise the child? Josh had the street smarts that women in Alissa's generation were too sheltered to learn. This was a more sophisticated and skeptical era. Alissa needed to change with the times. At this crucial time, when she should have been truthful with herself, she refused to accept Josh's wisdom.

"He's not putting me down, Josh. He knows my accomplishments. I'm an improvement over everything he's ever had. He needs me. We are living the life he always wanted. He would never be able to have accomplished that with his ex-wife. She works as a motel maid."

"Does she ride any of those brooms in her housekeeping cart?" asked Josh. "From what you've told me, she sounds pretty devious. Why is she always calling him to come over and help her with his kids? Aren't they grown up enough by now to not need their daddy?"

Alissa didn't feel threatened by Sam's ex, so she did not consider things from Josh's perspective. But if the truth were known, Sam did believe that Alissa was inferior to him. In his mind, everyone was, and he liked things that way. He had not learned to appreciate her except for what she could give him. When he proposed to her, he promised, "I will provide for you by assigning the widow's benefits to you on my pension plan."

She needed to have him express this statement to take care of her. Her intention was never to be a financial victim again. Sam's commitment was the antithesis of Fred's attitude, and Fred's words still resonated in the back of her mind: "If you divorce me, you will never have a dime." In reality, Sam needed Alissa's money to live the style he wanted to become accustomed to, and Alissa needed verbal expression that he would take care of her financially even when she knew in her head this was not true. Her fear dominated her intelligence.

Alissa's need for money throughout her life was not to have power as Fred had described it, but having grown up poor, she was yearning for comfort and security. The green money monster was not her god. No, she longed for the day she would have security, peace, and quiet. How grand, to never be dependent again. She would not have to fear the other shoe falling or the screaming threats of bill collectors falling on her with such terror that it made the guillotine seem kind and gentle.

Sam was full of himself and his simple world, where he was important because of the accomplishments of ancestors who died two hundred years ago, his high-school popularity, and his applause-generating showmanship. She was in love because she was attracted to him. That attraction was greater than any she had experienced heretofore. Surely this was an indication of love. She helped him financially because she was a generous soul whose need for love and acceptance was greater than her need to accumulate wealth.

Alissa was making this relationship work as best she could. It never occurred to her that the fact that she had to work on it meant there was something wrong—drastically wrong. She convinced herself that she was happy tagging along behind him. When Sam wanted her to always be at his side, she saw this as *her* devotion, not as *his* control. She reasoned that it must mean he was as physically attracted to her as she was to him.

SIXTEEN

Rag Mop

Alissa had never been the athletic type, so she was relieved to discover that spending a day with Sam at his family's vacation home on Highway 1 north of Malibu did not mean she was expected to ride the waves with him. While he surfed, she would sunbathe and read, or she would swim, carefully avoiding the kelp beds and strong currents. She quickly learned that brushing up against the California kelp would stain her swimsuit, and that stain was impossible to remove. But the more dangerous obstacles in the California waters were jellyfish that stung anyone who came close to their poisonous tentacles.

On occasion, when the day was extremely hot, she enjoyed being refreshed in the sea. But that was only when she used the rubberized beach shoes that had an elastic strap to hold them on her feet when she was swimming. The beach shoes protected the bottoms of her feet from the hot sand and the hard beach stones. These had been purchased during a business trip to Europe with Fred, but Alissa hadn't used them after she discovered France had nude bathing beaches.

One day in the summer of 1983, while they were at the Malibu house, Sam brought his surfboard to shore as the sun was setting. He did not find Alissa waiting for him. Her beach towel, beach robe, the portable radio, and the book she had been reading were all where she had left them on the sand. Her beach shoes were missing, and she was nowhere to be seen.

Sam panicked. This had never happened before. It wasn't like Alissa. She always waited for him to finish surfing. She had never gone somewhere without him. He gathered up her belongings, clutching them in his arms, while he fretted about what he was going to do without her being there for him as the primary member of his personal fan club. When he turned off the radio, he heard a voice in the distance. It was so faint he could barely hear it, but he was certain that it was Alissa, and she sounded distressed. He detected that her call was coming from the water, along the shoreline to the south. He hurried down the beach, still clutching her beach towel and robe as he ran.

There, near some rock outcroppings about ten feet offshore, was Alissa, struggling to keep her head above water. She was flailing her arms and calling for help. Sam dropped her clothes at the shoreline and dove into the water to swim toward her. He was concerned that the waves would crush her against the rocks before she could be rescued. Alissa was so panicked she resisted his help. Sam put his arm under her head and was able to turn her over on her back despite her flailing. He swam toward shore with Alissa's thrashing body in tow.

When he reached dry land with her, Sam rolled Alissa onto the beach blanket, wrapped her in her robe, and lying on the sand beside her he rubbed her body warm and comforted her with his words "You're okay, baby. You're fine. I have you."

"I was drowning."

Sam laughed. He rolled over on his side and laughed at the sight of his wet catch beached during a night with the full moon. "You look like a female grunion come to lay her eggs in the sand. I am so relieved that I found you."

"The current was taking me under," she cried, still choking on the water she had swallowed.

"You weren't going under," said Sam. "The current was taking you toward the Malibu Pier."

"But I wasn't strong enough to swim anymore."

"You only think you were in danger," said Sam, trying to assure her. "You just got a mouthful of water. That's because you couldn't keep your mouth shut, Alissa. If you'd missed being rescued at Malibu, someone at the Santa Monica Pier would have spotted you. Thousands of people would have seen you and could have picked you up out of the water. There is no way to drown with everyone watching. You were making too much noise."

"But I was frightened."

"I was frightened too," he said, rolling closer to her. "I was afraid I would lose you, Alissa. When I didn't see your ugly, old-fashioned beach shoes, I thought you had left me. You always wear them."

"Here they are," she said, raising her leg into the air and wiggling her foot.

"Alissa, I don't want to ever feel like this again. I want to bind you to me forever. Will you marry me?"

It was so easy for Alissa to say yes. There was the rescue, the feeling of safety in his strong arms, the full moon to lure them, and her desperate need to be loved and protected. She vowed that they would be insepa-rable. She believed this would mitigate all their other differences. She ignored many signs of discord because Alissa took togetherness to mean permanence.

That closeness was consummated that night on the beach south of Malibu, when the two lovers expressed their undying love under the watchful eye of the California moon, while Alissa wondered where she could purchase a new Lanz nightgown.

The next morning, Alissa received a call from Katie. "Mom, I have to go to San Diego."

"Fine, Katie, I'm glad you called. I have some news for you."

"Can it wait? I'm really in a hurry. I just wanted you to know that I will be out of town for a while."

"Yes, dear, my news can wait, but why are you in such a hurry?"

"It's difficult to explain, Mom. Remember when Josh and I were kids, and you and Dad took us to California for a vacation?"

"Yes."

"Remember that we went whale watching?"

"Yes."

"Mom," said Katie with a shiver in her voice, "I had a dream last night. It was a nightmare. It was so real. There was a whale beached on the shoreline. It totally needs me, Mom. I have to go to San Diego to help that whale."

"Katie, relax. Take a deep breath."

Katie began to cry. "You don't believe me. But it was so real, Mom. I don't understand it. First I thought it was déjà vu because it was so real, as if I had been there before. But when we were whale watching, I didn't see any whales in distress."

"I'm not surprised, Katie. I've always felt you had psychic powers because of your affinity for nature. Katie, I was the beached whale. Last night I was stranded on a rock outcropping here at Malibu. Sam had to rescue me."

"Mom. You don't swim. What were you doing in the water?"

"Don't scold me, Katie. I'll tell you all about it another time. I'm all right. I just wanted you to know that your dream might have been you sensing my distress."

"You mean god was sending me a message?" asked Katie.

"Well, if he was, it wasn't very clear, was it? I don't know how these things happen. They just do. I think you can save yourself a trip to San Diego. I don't think there are any whales there that need you. Save your money for a wedding present. Sam and I will be getting married."

There was a pause.

"You are getting married again?"

"Yes."

"When?"

"I don't know. Sam proposed last night."

"Are you sure you want to marry him? Isn't he a lot younger than you are? I can see how you might be having fun spending your time with him. But marriage?"

"Weren't you the one to tell me that I look younger than my age? Sam doesn't seem to care that I am older than he is."

"I'm not going to argue this with you, Mom. It sounds kind of cheesy for a forty-eight-year-old woman to marry a younger man. But do me a big favor, will you?"

"Sure, Katie. What is it?"

"Ken and I will be getting married, too. How about letting me get married before you do? Is that too much to ask?"

"I don't know. That will depend on Sam. Not everything in life is in my control. Who is Ken? I don't remember you telling me anything about him."

"I didn't want to jinx the relationship by talking about him. Don't worry. You will like him. He's smart."

As Alissa finished her conversation with her daughter, Sam came into the bedroom, carrying the morning paper and a cup of coffee for Alissa. He dropped the paper onto the bed. The headline read "Whale Beached off San Diego."

◆ ◆ ◆

In the early autumn of 1984, Alissa was again the nervous bride. This time the bride's dress was rosy beige with black accessories. She was so tipsy at the wedding reception that she could not remember how many drinks she had had. This was not because she'd had too many; it was because she couldn't remember where she'd put them down.

Alissa wanted to talk to everyone. She personally visited with the guests at each table with a mixed drink in hand. She would place the glass down at the table and forget it. Then, before she went to the next table of guests, she returned to the bar and got another beverage. The socializing developed a pattern of getting a drink, chatting with guests, putting an unfinished drink down on the table, getting another drink, and moving on to the next table of strangers at her wedding.

The semi-sobering event happened when she was mingling at the table where Sam's boss and his wife were seated. The boss's wife had already decided she wouldn't like Alissa. Why should she? They had nothing in common. Alissa was a liberal Democrat, and Mrs. Boss was a Reagan Republican. Alissa's education at Swarthmore had prepared her to be a political activist, and she was currently working as a volunteer for Walter Mondale's campaign. This election offered women like Alissa the opportunity to support a candidate who advanced women's rights by taking Geraldine Ferraro as a vice-presidential candidate. Ferraro was a former second-grade teacher who was only one year older than Alissa. Her accomplishments as a successful attorney and member of the House of Representatives were an inspiration to Alissa. She identified with Geraldine and wanted her to win.

The boss's wife and the bride had words...lots of them. The more Alissa defended a woman on the ticket, the more the boss's wife pushed the platform of the Hollywood movie star turned politician. Alissa loved the excitement and challenge of presenting her opinions and debating new ideas, whereas the boss's wife was threatened whenever her myopic conclusions were challenged. The argument was not going well. It grew louder and louder. When Alissa observed that Mrs. Boss was (as in *Macbeth*) "full of sound and fury and signifying nothing," the boss's wife rose to her full six feet to settle the debate by saying that she would "beat the shit out of" Alissa. Alissa threatened to return the compliment by punching her in her ample midsection.

Sam wasn't going to get involved. He was at the bar with his back toward the commotion, pretending that he did not hear the argument that was becoming a great source of amusement for the other guests. The best man, Katie's husband, Ken Streeter, and two groomsmen from BowLink came to the assistance of the ladies. The groomsmen stood behind Alissa, each lifting the inebriated bride into the air by her elbows.

"Say good-night, Alissa. It's time to go," said Ken as he stood between the two women and kept the boss's wife from making a move against his mother-in-law, the bride.

"Not before I consult with my shrink, the bartender," slurred Alissa.

"Not tonight, Alissa. You have said enough." The men carried Alissa across the room by her elbows and put her down in front of Sam. "Doesn't look she'll be in any condition to consummate the wedding tonight," said Ken.

"I did that already," slurred Alissa, not too drunk to know where she had been.

◆ ◆ ◆

The adjustment to blend their lives was easy, as long as Alissa was willing to work on it with good humor. She sublet her Wilshire condo to an Asian businessman who was in the country to look for real estate to purchase. This was the period when the economy was experiencing stagflation, and because of the low value of the US dollar, investors were coming into the country to purchase property. Alissa also had some serious financial planning to do, and she took her cue from the foreign investors. If they were investing in the US real estate market, perhaps she should too, but she wasn't ready to make any decisions on what to do with the money from the sale of the condo.

With the remaining money from her divorce settlement from Fred, she made a down payment on a house she and Sam had found at Solana Beach in northern San Diego County. The town's center, with the midcentury buildings along Cedros Avenue, had a slightly Bohemian character (or "boho," to put it in the New York vernacular of the eighties) that beckoned to Alissa. It wasn't an area that looked like it had been planned by the people constructing shopping malls. It was scattered, as if the weathered buildings had popped up like colorful flowers. Solana seemed like an ideal place to set up an art studio for her sculpting and the oil painting she was experimenting with. She wanted to put down her roots and blend into the town in the same manner she wanted her relationship with her husband to grow.

Surfing was different on the southern beaches, but that was fine with Sam. He wasn't so interested in surfing now that he was working on getting his tennis arm in shape for a nationwide tournament that was coming up. Alissa convinced herself that he'd changed to tennis so he'd have more time to spend with her on dry land. And she interpreted an increase of attention as a sign of his deepening love. She was incorrect on both counts. Sam was on the golf course every morning, the tennis court during the coolness of the late afternoons, and when he could put together a team of his male buddies, he was on the basketball court after the evening meal with the guys at the local gym, trying to imitate the players on his favorite team, the Boston Celtics. Naturally, Alissa could not do any of these sports with him. When he was at home, his favorite activity was to watch sports on TV with his wife beside him doing crossword puzzles.

Meanwhile, Alissa was still working. She found a position in Long Beach that shaved a half hour per day and thirty miles from her prior commute to Los Angeles. But this trip still required three hours per day commute time. Although this was not unusual in the metropolitan LA area, it was stressful. She listened to books on tape, but she had no one to discuss them with, even when some were made into movies that Sam was no longer interested in seeing. She wondered who had written the stupid script she was living.

One Saturday, while she was home mopping the kitchen floor, Hester called to see how the newlyweds were doing. "We're doing fine, Mama. How are you?"

"My arthritis is bothering me, but that's what everybody gets when we grow old. Remember, life is a terminal illness."

"Mama, that's so depressing. Are you sick?"

"I didn't say I was sick. I said I had arthritis. I'm getting old. I'm going to be a great-grandmother soon."

"You should be pleased that Katie is pregnant. I'm going to be a grandmother, and I'm proud as punch."

"You can't fool me. It's just another sign of aging."

"You wait until this baby is born. You'll see. It's a reincarnation of us, Mama. All our dreams and expectations might come true with this new gift of life."

"I would rather be a cow in India. At least they get respect."

"Is it respect you want, Mama, or sympathy?"

"I am entitled to respect because I'm your mother. I expect sympathy from you because you are my daughter. I'm not well, and you should not mock me. Remember when your father was sick with Parkinson's disease and had the flu and everything was going right through him? It can be serious. He died from that. That's how I feel."

"I thought you said it was your arthritis, Mama."

"Yes, my arthritis. But it's killing me."

"What did the doctor say, Mama?"

"What does he know? I know how I feel. I am just another patient to the doctor."

"Sounds like you've lost your patience, Mama."

"Yes, and when I stop paying his bills, he's going to lose his patient too. I called so I could talk to Samuel. I want to welcome him to the family and tell him why I didn't make it to California for the wedding. I hope you got the money I sent."

"Yes, we did, Mama. We bought some beautiful patio furniture with the money. Thank you. When you come to visit, we can have a meal outside on the deck. Mama, they just opened a cute European café here in town. It has a market too. We can pick up some food and bring it home. I've wanted to check out the Zinc Cafe, and you can be our excuse to go. How about it, Mama? You would like California. The weather here is beautiful. It's nice and dry. It would be good for your arthritis."

"If California is such a good place to be, why didn't you go there when you were married to Fred? Maybe he would have liked the sunshine too. I don't know why you had to go all the way to California to get married. It's so far away. And I don't know why you have to live on the beach, where the sharks are. How can you expect me to want to visit you?"

"Mama, there hasn't been a shark attack in California since 1959. You can stay inside. I don't think you have to worry; they rarely attack houses. I think you will be safe. Sam said he knew the man who was killed in that attack. You won't believe what Sam said, Mama. He told me that the man died from 'eternal bleeding.' Are you sure you want to talk to Sam? The conversation won't be very deep. If there is something in particular you want to talk to him about, I can tell him when he comes home for dinner."

"Is he at work?"

"Sam's on the golf course, Mama."

"What are you doing home while he is on the golf course?"

"The floor was dirty. I spilled some flour this morning when I was preparing pancakes for breakfast. You always told me I was messy. Guess you were right after all."

"Sam is playing golf while you stay home and mop the floor? Is that something wives do in California? Listen to me, Alissa. When your husband comes home, he does not want to see a clean floor; he wants to see a happy face. You stop that right now. Comb your hair and change your clothes, and you go right out there to that golf course, and you surprise him by taking golf lessons. Then you put a smile on your face when you tell him you can play golf too."

"I don't think he wants me to learn to play golf, Mama. I'm afraid my husband likes to have time for his own interests."

"You married him. A promise is a promise," declared Mama. "But don't think I don't know why you can't keep a husband."

Alissa was suspicious of her mother's advice to put the mop down and go out to play golf with her husband. Perhaps she had mellowed since George died. Hester had certainly never been sympathetic about women needing relief from household chores.

Alissa began remembering some things that had happened long ago. The time when the principal of the Huntington High School called the house to tell her parents that she had tested high on the Stanford-Binet IQ test came to mind.

Mama's response was consistent with Mama's personality: "It doesn't matter if she is a genius or not. She still needs to help with the dishes if she expects to be fed in this house."

George had no accolades for Alissa, either. His response was philosophical. "People have no right to brag about a high IQ. They have done nothing to deserve it. It is a gift, and it is their obligation to use it to make life better for humanity. It is what you do with your intelligence to make a difference in life that is commendable."

So what had she done with her life that was commendable? She was mopping the floor while her gorgeous husband was away playing golf.

Her parents meant this. Alissa was never allowed to boast about her academic achievements. That wasn't done in the Barrett household. She continued to be the scullery maid who washed dishes even when she was a full-grown, accomplished woman and there were younger and fitter members of the family who could have filled that role. Alissa was punished by Hester for being a cut above her intellectually, and George did nothing to help. His philosophy was a sham. Alissa had put her intelligence to several good causes, but they still gave her no respect for her accomplishments. Alissa wondered if her father had a problem with women excelling, and this was his extension of his battle for authority with Hester.

But trying again to make excuses for her father wasn't going to work if Alissa was ever to be all that she was capable of being. She had to put the responsibility where it belonged. Daddy's failures belonged on his shoulders, not hers. It was not a matter of blaming him. He was gone now, and if there had ever been a time to work this out with him, it was gone.

But it was also not her responsibility to forgive him. She did not have the powers of the priest who could have heard the penitent say, "Bless me, Father, for I have sinned." The forgiveness would require a higher power than Alissa had been given. She was only a humble mortal desperately wanting to live her own life. It was time for Alissa to take ownership of that and abort the programming that had been designed for her by her parents.

She had to learn to question her own motives. She had to ask, "Is this what I want, or am I merely continuing something someone convinced me to want?" She needed to touch her creativity, to be a risk taker, and to not worry about having to explain what her art was about any more than she needed to account to anyone but herself what life she would choose. She wondered if she was strong enough to do this or if she would spend the rest of her life boxing with shadows.

The kitchen floors were not the only thing Alissa was polishing to put a good face on her unhappy marriage. She had glossed over the fact that Sam had no money to invest in their Solana Beach house. If she had thought about it with her head instead of her heart, she should have questioned him more about that before she sunk her cash into the cottage. It wasn't as though she hadn't been put on notice.

Sam was fond of telling her of the woman with money he had been seeing before he met Alissa. That woman had purchased a townhouse in the suburbs in the San Fernando Valley for their love nest. It was where he could live and a place for her to meet him when they wanted a private rendezvous away from her husband. Sam had a pattern of living off women. Alissa was beginning to realize that it was her turn to finance his lifestyle. This was a huge disappointment. She did not enjoy being the major wage earner.

She persuaded herself that she was different from the paramours in his past. After all, by now Samuel Adams Woods IV had learned everything there was to know about Alissa Woods. To know her was to love her. She convinced herself that he must have fallen in love with the total woman. That's what she wanted the relationship to be. Alissa wasn't calculating how much this marriage was costing her. She was working on ways to make Sam happy, and it wasn't working out. The more she gave, the more he took, and the less she got out of their relationship.

Alissa was writing the alimony checks to Sam's ex, and Meg was taunting Alissa in turn. Meg would write "received" in the memo section of Alissa's check. Then she added to the insult by initialing the memo and coloring in a star over the *i* in *received*. This was meant to show Alissa that Meg wanted Alissa to believe that Meg was still the star in the relationship. When the check cleared Alissa's bank account and Alissa saw the insult Meg sent, Alissa was hurt but could think of no way to express this hurt except to imagine a time when she would have the courage to stand up to the ex-wife who was flaunting the fact that she was still a player in this game of lost love.

Then there was the issue of the tributes Sam made to his former wife. Alissa did not understand why she was beginning to feel competitive with a woman she previously thought did not measure up to her toenail clippings. There was also the issue of the four sons Sam and Meg had fashioned together. The boys were lazy, rude, dull, uncultured, and antisocial. The only thing to commend them was that they did not live in Alissa's home and could more or less be ignored. Alissa made more excuses for Sam's behavior. Perhaps Sam was honoring Meg only because of her status as the mother of his children. This delusion was less painful than the truth she was avoiding—the only reason Sam was not living with Meg was that he was better suited for the life of a gigolo.

The more Sam showed his stripes, the more she looked for reasons to excuse his actions and the more vigilantly she looked for some indication of his approval and acceptance and love. Alissa was reliving the basic patterns she had developed in her odd relationship with her mother. Alissa could never please Hester, but she didn't stop trying. She learned to be accommodating and adapting. She learned to search out ways to try to receive love by earning it. Children often do that for the love of a parent, but this was a husband. And this man was a user and loser, and she should have found a way to lose him. But first, there was ironing to do.

◆ ◆ ◆

Her deep reflection was interrupted by Sam returning from his golf game and wanting to shower before he set out again for the tennis court. He separated her from her thoughts when he announced, "I need to jump into the shower," as he whisked past her.

"Don't jump too hard," she said. "You may break something."

"I wasn't jumping. I was golfing."

"Golfing or goofing?"

"Why did you say that?"

"I was goofing around."

"What can I break? Did you put something in the shower I might break?"

"No, I was just goofing around."

"Sometimes I don't understand you, Alissa," he said, stripping down to his birthday suit. He went to the kitchen, returned with a bowl of corn flakes in one hand and *Sports Illustrated* in the other and headed for the toilet.

"Sam, I didn't know you were into multitasking," said Alissa.

"You don't make sense," he said as he walked past her while she continued ironing. "By the way, I want to remind you that my first wife ironed my underwear."

"Why did she do that? Who is going to see your underwear?"

"It doesn't matter who sees them. I like to look my best, and that means my clothes should look good—all my clothes, Alissa. That includes my underwear. If you really cared about me, you would do what pleases me."

To which Alissa, in a commanding, projected, theatrical tone that would make Sarah Bernhardt proud, said, "Well, put them on, jump up on the board, and I'll iron them for you."

◆ ◆ ◆

Alissa got more doses of reality on a weekend golfing trip at a resort in Florida. Sam had made these plans with his buddies and charged everything to the American Express Gold Card that he had opened in Alissa's name because his credit rating wasn't up to par. The trip got off to a bad start.

When they boarded the plane at LAX, they discovered that someone else had taken their seats at 17A and B. There was no opportunity to evict the occupants, but Sam pointed out the confusion to a flight attendant. He told them to take a place wherever they could until the plane had been fully boarded. Alissa found an empty seat at 19C, and Sam found one at 22D, next to one of his golf buddies.

As soon as the Fasten Seat Belt sign was turned off after takeoff, the flight attendant informed Alissa that there were two empty seats together at 14A and B.

"Do you want me to tell your father, so he can sit with you?" he asked.

Sam overheard this, and so did his buddy, who teased him about it for the rest of the trip. So Sam didn't want to be seen with his daughter, Alissa. He played the links with his friends while she stayed poolside at the hotel, hoping the sun would remove the chill she felt at being left alone again in another strange town. Alissa suspected that Sam's snit was because of the flight attendant's remark, but knowing the cause did not help her discomfort. It made matters worse when the Seligmans, another couple with their group, expressed their sympathy at seeing her alone, reading a mystery novel.

"I don't participate in these events unless my wife can join me," said Mr. Seligman, thinking he was helping Alissa by expressing an understanding of her predicament.

"It's not like Sam to do this, either," she fibbed to keep up appearances. Alissa hated pity. "He wouldn't bring me here only to leave me alone. I just can't put this novel down, and I told him I would wait for him here. He'll find me when he's finished playing and is ready to go to dinner."

Protecting herself with a tall story was better than allowing them to feel sorry for her. The Seligmans believed her explanation. Alissa stared at the pages of the mystery novel that lay open on her lap. She was remembering a time when she wished she had challenged Sam's immature behavior at a prior outing.

◆ ◆ ◆

That evening, Sam got a phone call at the hotel. When he heard who was calling, his spirits lifted, and a big smile came over his face. He did everything but rub his palms together with voracious anticipation.

"Rodney, I can't wait for you to meet my wife, Alissa."

Rodney Goodbar was Sam's nephew, a stockbroker in Florida. They arranged to meet the next day at his office.

Rodney had some investment ideas for Alissa's funds from the Wilshire condo. He suggested a waste-management company, Arab investments in the United States, and several public utilities, but he was really pushing a startup company because he personally knew the man founding it. She relied upon his advice, and for a major part of her portfolio, she purchased five thousand shares of Enron Corporation, recently formed from the merger of a natural gas company in Houston and InterNorth–companies Alissa had never heard of. The entire portfolio was to be held in a limited-liability company that Rodney managed. She also agreed to purchase an apartment complex Rodney was having built in Memphis with Sam as her partner.

Rodney's fees were steep. Not only did he charge her a management fee on the LLC, but he received a percentage of her profits. The result was that the investments never earned more than the amount Rodney was keeping as commission.

◆ ◆ ◆

By the time the fateful day arrived when Sam asked for a divorce, Alissa's ego had been eroded so often by him mopping the floor with her emotions that she felt like a rag. When he explained that he wanted the divorce so he could remarry his first wife, Alissa felt the anger this deserved. It was as if the next thing Sam would ask for would be for her to go along with him and Meg so they could use her in Meg's motel-cleaning business.

"Josh suggested that he could give you and Meg a flying mop for your wedding present," she said, unable to respond to Sam with anything more than a joke.

"You haven't been telling your family about our marital problems?" asked Sam. "How do you like that? All this time, you have been looking me in the eye and talking behind my back."

"Forget what Josh said. I have a better idea. Your wedding gift from me will be an iron that has a setting for underwear."

Alissa knew that facing a second marriage on the rocks was not something she should be making jokes about. Still, this was serious but not fatal. Telling jokes was how she coped with anger, insecurity, disappointment, fear, and anything else that had the power to take her to the depths of depression. The healthy thing about her sarcasm was that she realized the more jokes she came up with, the less depression she went down with. Alissa realized she had better give up on wedding bells and take care of herself first. The termination of their marriage was the only meeting of the minds she and Sam had had in years. She hired an attorney.

Sam had to reimburse Alissa for $35,000 he had charged to her credit cards for clothing and a clandestine meeting with Meg in Florida. Sam had moved out of town and gave her no forwarding address. He had borrowed the $35,000 settlement money from his sister. The attorney held the funds in his trust account for months while Alissa paid only interest to the credit-card companies or she would be unable to meet her current bills. But the attorney was no help on the Rodney Goodbar investments. When the apartments were completed, there should have been income belonging to Alissa and Sam, but Alissa never saw any of it.

Alissa eventually put this all behind her. It was easier to run away from the conflict. The past was being swept under the carpet. She told herself, "Bon voyage, Alissa. You think you are ready to set sail for a new life. You believe you can live up to Daddy's philosophies, and you even think they are beautiful. But you are not capable of doing that. No one is."

When her father said, "Look to the stars," and Mama said, "Watch your step, or you'll fall," Alissa thrashed around in a sea of turmoil. It was not within her power to aim for any stars. Daddy had given her a goal for which she had no model. He couldn't reach for this goal himself. Mama's caution that she would fail became a path she could follow. Mama had taught her well—that she should fail and that she would be rejected because she "wasn't good enough to deserve to win."

SEVENTEEN

Knight in Ill-Fitted, Corroded Armor

Alissa's life was a void—missing love and needing an anchor in the storm. She had only enough resources within herself to realize that something was missing, but she had no clue how to correct the problem. She felt a need to explore a more spiritual and peaceful path–a search that drew her to drastically change her life. She also wanted to have more time to paint. These goals would require leaving Los Angeles and moving to a location where there was less competitive tension and where housing was more affordable.

Until now, her best financial decision had been her investment in the Solana Beach house. The town turned into a trendy tourist spot featuring stylish boutiques, design firms, and a prosperous art gallery that, had things turned out differently with her marriage to Sam Woods, might have been the ideal locale for her art. The town boasted a train station that was designed after one of the military Quonset huts that had been the community's hallmark when Alissa first discovered it. Cedros Avenue and Highway 101 were now dotted with restaurants and bars with good food and featuring reggae music for their patrons. The town still had its bohemian quality and had not been spoiled by overdevelopment. She sold the Solana Beach house for a handsome profit and headed north, to find a place where an investment in a home with land would launch her to a new lifestyle.

During her quest, Alissa discovered Sharon Fuller, an artist whose technique and use of vivid colors were exciting. The artist had a studio in Mariposa, where she was teaching watercolor painting. Alissa sought her out in the same way she would have chosen the best school for a master's degree. Hers would become a classical form of education where the student takes apprenticeship with the master. She wanted to go to the best and to learn directly from that teacher. That's what she did.

Mariposa is a unique community off Highway 49, described as the gateway to Yosemite Valley. This was where the original forty-niners had come to California and where modern-day searchers are still panning for gold. Alissa wasn't interested in panning in the traditional manner. She felt her gold was within her, and she was ready to travel the path of personal knowledge to develop it. She found a motel in town to use as a base of operations while she eagerly expanded her painting style at the Fuller Art Studio and learned the artist's tricky techniques.

The studio was next to a real estate office, where pictures of properties currently on the market were displayed in the window. Alissa would stop to scan the window for new listings whenever she passed on the way to the studio. The first to catch her eye was a photo of a property that included a gold mine described as being in a remote area. In this part of California, *remote* meant no access to water, electricity, gas, or paved roads. Because Alissa was a big-city girl driving a late-model convertible with no access to the donkey of Don Quixote de la Mancha, she passed over this listing for a more suitable quest. The gold-mine property was too much of an impossible dream.

Another property did fit her profile, however, and when the agent took her to see it, she knew it was the right place for her. The property was forested with majestic Jeffrey Pines that reached 60 to 120 feet toward the sky. There was a stream on whose banks she could sit and draw inspiration from its babbling. The cozy house had a view of the mountains of Yosemite, and in the spring, the melting snow produced a waterfall that was framed by a profusion of mariposa lilies. All these attributes taken together caused Alissa to understand why people commonly referred to the area as "god's country." Alissa experienced an unusual sense of peace there and believed that on this land, she had found her own personal cathedral to the heavens.

At the south end of the property, Caltrans had constructed a turnout designated as a vista point along the state highway. She made an offer to purchase the property, in spite of the fact that the natural quiet of the location was broken by a large stray pig with trailing, squealing children that greeted her and the real estate agent when they arrived to inspect the vacant house.

The property turned out to be more isolated than Alissa had anticipated. For several months after she moved in, the only visitors Alissa received were the children of the Miwoc Native Americans who lived adjacent to her property. The nearest shopping was thirteen miles away, where the inconvenient convenience store sold groceries as well as live bait for fishermen coming for the rainbow trout. There was no TV reception, and the radio station wasn't interesting. Her daily routine was to content herself with painting while listening to her collection of Mozart CDs.

The paintings Alissa created while living at her Mariposa property were exquisite depictions of the area. Sharon Fuller, her artist mentor, allowed Alissa to sell her paintings on consignment at the studio. Many tourists from all over the world visit Yosemite, and Mariposa was on the way for travelers coming from the south. Alissa sold enough paintings of this awesome area to support herself in a simple and modest lifestyle. She was happy. She was developing an inner contentment, and she was earning a reputation as an accomplished local painter.

Alissa felt she needed all the help she could get. She would often stand in her private cathedral of jeffrey pines and evoke the assistance of the spirits of the north, the south, the east, and the west. For Alissa, this supplication was not as easy as it sounds. She had no sense of direction and was concerned that she might be evoking the wrong spirits. In the beginning, she oriented herself by finding the moss on the base of the trees. That would get her started toward the north. But if it was midday, she was never sure about which direction was east and west. It's easier to do this in a church, where you know the address, and the altar is in the front.

One day while she was doing a plein air (outdoor daylight) work of a nearby waterfall, a tourist became intrigued with watching her. The woman came closer, either to get a whiff of the paint for a high or because she was captivated by Alissa's technique. Whatever the reason, Alissa was annoyed with the intrusion into her space. She wanted the stranger to back off. It was distracting.

The woman came closer, hovering over Alissa and breathing down her neck as she scrutinized each stroke. Alissa put down the brush, turned to the woman, and said, "Please stand back. I'm afraid you will see the numbers."

The most loyal supporter of Alissa's watercolors was a middle-aged single woman named Marie Michaels, who shared Alissa's love of the local scenery. Marie was suffering from cancer. It had metastasized, and she knew she did not have much more time to live. Marie told Alissa she was purchasing the paintings as gifts for each of her four brothers and three sisters and their children. These paintings would be the only estate of value that Marie would leave behind, and she wanted her family to share in the peace and beauty the pictures represented. The paintings were to remind them of the beauty of creation. Marie believed Alissa's art would help her communicate to her family that, in spite of her constant pain and suffering, she was leaving the world with an acceptance inspired by her understanding that everything in life was an undeserved blessing from God.

But even with her health deteriorating, Marie kept a sense of humor. One morning she called Alissa to tell her she had read the art advertisement in the local paper.

"Alissa, darling," she said with a bubble in her voice, "it says here that you are hanging in the post office. I was wondering, is it your art or a mug shot?"

"Oh, Marie," replied Alissa. "There you go again with your flummery. It will get you nowhere."

The pig belonging to the Miwoc children wasn't the only lively visitor that frequented Alissa's property. There was the arrival of the mule deer with their distinctive black tails, the scruffy gray California ground squirrels, the bushy-tailed western gray squirrels that visited during the winter when the ground squirrels were hibernating, and the marmots who loved to sunbathe when the creek was full. She learned to respect but not be frightened by the coyotes that serenaded the moon and the rattlesnakes that she trusted would warn anyone approaching with the ominous rattle at the end of their tails. The scorpions she found in the kitchen sink were another matter, as their deadly sting was unexpected from an insect so small. On the other hand, the tarantula was not as deadly, but one day she saw one so large she was convinced it was capable of carrying away the stray kitten that came with the house. It was understandable that people might become hysterical when seeing the ugly, black, hairy-legged spider that inspired the whirling Italian dance, the tarantella.

◆ ◆ ◆

Once at daybreak, a herd of wild mustangs thundered across her property, churning up dust and confusion. Alissa was awestruck and delighted. She had a close-up view of the horses from her kitchen window. They were proud and strong. It was an uplifting experience to watch them, and Alissa was disappointed when they chose to move on. She wasn't aware of the inherent danger posed by the presence of the wild herd. It was good that she did not go outside when they passed. These horses were as capable of destruction as the cattle stampedes in movie Westerns.

Alissa was breathless with excitement when she reached the studio to relate the news of her encounter with the horses. Her mentor was suitably surprised, but the reaction from a stranger in the studio that day was much more than Alissa expected.

"May I look at your palm, dear?" asked the customer. "I'm a psychic. Wild mustangs don't come into populated areas. They are too afraid of people to do that. There is something going on here that we should take a look at."

"I guess so," said Alissa, wondering what the woman had in mind. For Alissa, it was as unusual to have a visit from wild horses as a visit from a clairvoyant, but she was adapting to the nuances of her new home and was willing to listen to what the woman had to say.

She extended her hand. "How did you get to be a psychic?"

"I didn't 'get to be.' I am. I was born a psychic."

The spiritualist introduced herself as Ursula Swanson. She said she had discovered her psychic abilities while she was an adjunct biology professor at UC Berkeley. When her gift grew so strong that it interfered with her teaching position, she resigned and relocated to Mariposa to focus on practicing her spiritual skills among clients who spread her reputation by word of mouth. Ursula had a reading room in town but was willing to do an impromptu reading today for Alissa for a fee.

"How will I know what you tell me is true?" asked Alissa, hoping the spiritualist would explain her gift in pragmatic terms.

"The essence of the truth does not depend on what words are used to express it," said the ex–biology instructor.

"Okay," said Alissa, shrugging her shoulders and understanding that she would have to figure it out for herself later.

The psychic examined both of Alissa's palms carefully, and after several moments of contemplation she spoke. "You are going to lose a close friend soon. Someone who has become very important to you spiritually is dying. Her first initial is *M*. Her death will bring you much grief. The horses were sent to you today from Tashunka Witko."

"I know Marie is dying," said Alissa, "but who is Tashunka Witko?"

"You would know him as Crazy Horse. I used his Lakota name. I see his life-force standing next to you right now. Tashunka Witko is your spiritual guide. You must understand that this is a great honor. Crazy Horse was told by his people, the Lakotas, that he would be the protector of his tribe. That position is his alone for as long as any of his people walk the face of the Earth. He must have felt that you could help him with his mission, or he would not have wanted to communicate with you."

"Why would he choose me?" asked Alissa.

"You have a nature that his spirit is comfortable with," said Ursula. "He can teach you a lot. You have only to listen to him."

Sharon Fuller was witness to this reading, and she could no longer restrain herself. She wanted to help the psychic. "Do you ride, Alissa?" she asked.

"No. I have never even been on a horse," said Alissa.

"Do you have empathy for Native Americans?"

"I saw one once doing a dance, but I wouldn't even know if it was for rain or fertility. I'm not good with dance interpretation, but since it didn't rain, I guess the crops will have to grow on their own." Alissa was annoyed with Sharon's interruptions and wanted to learn more from the reader. She leaned toward her to show her interest.

"You are divorced," said Ursula, oblivious to Sharon's comments.

"Well, yes, but who isn't these days? As a matter of fact, I have been divorced twice." She laughed, enjoying the reaction she saw in her mentor's face.

"Twice is not unusual. But I see in your palm that you soon will meet your soulmate, and that marriage will last for life. He is tall and handsome. You were lovers in a past existence. I see his family crest. It's blue and yellow. You are interlinked for all times. Your spirits will be together in death."

"Death? Whose death, mine or his?" said Alissa. "I'm not ready to die. How will I know it's him when I meet him?"

"You'll have Crazy Horse to help you find him. He'll know the importance of having the correct mate. Crazy Horse must have found your spirit compatible with his tribe's. Are you aware of the Lakota divorce customs?" asked the psychic rhetorically.

She continued without a reply from Alissa. "Lakotas allow the women to divorce their husbands. All a Lakota squaw needs to do is to take her belongings and move in with her family or with a different man of her choice. If she doesn't want to move out, she can evict her husband by placing his personal belongings outside their lodge. The rejected husband is expected to accept his wife's decision for the good of the tribe. But sometimes, if the husband is especially hurt by this, the wife might compensate him with a personal item that belonged to her. Don't take this as a 'blame game,' but if you have been divorced twice already, chances are that at least one of your life transitions must have been your own decision. It's so Lakota-esque," she concluded.

"It was a necessity," said Alissa, wondering if *Lakota-esque* was a word.

"Taking action in the light of necessity would be understood by the Lakota Tribe. It shows leadership traits. No wonder Tashunka Witko believes you are a strong enough woman to help him protect his people."

Sharon Fuller wasn't willing to accept this analysis of Alissa's encounter with the wild horses. She had a simpler explanation.

"I have some information that may be important for you to know, Alissa. The realtor should have informed you. Part of the property you purchased is an Indian burial ground. The property has been on the market before, but no one was willing to buy it. I'm surprised that the Miwocs have accepted your living there. Your presence has probably disturbed the spirits of their ancestors, and it's likely the horses are accustomed to returning to the property."

"I tried not to be too noisy," Alissa said, laughing. She was delighted with the stories she had learned and wondered if it could possibly be true that people had spirit guides. She wondered if it was something like having a guardian angel. She was intrigued with the information that she would soon meet her soul mate, and if he had a family crest, she dreamed of him being her knight in shining armor.

Alissa returned to her personal cathedral of trees. Her new home was away from everything she had previously known. She was a lost soul, looking for guidance and desperately wanting this to be her home. Hoping for a sign from Crazy Horse, Alissa even purchased tobacco on the advice of a local who said it would attract the spirits of the Native Americans.

As time passed, she became discouraged, and even her beautiful trees offered no encouragement. This was a period of drought in the mountains, and the bark beetles were attacking the trees and killing them. Dry branches fell to the ground. The sharp, dead needles crackled beneath her feet, sticking to her socks and painfully pricking her legs. Alissa recognized this lack of nourishment was doing to the trees what her life was doing to her. They were dying from lack of moisture, as her strength had been sucked out of her.

Every day at sunset, Alissa communed with the spirits. Her favorite place was on the rock-bed of the seasonal stream coming from Yosemite. Having the setting sun establish the direction of the west gave her the confidence to define her position. Standing with her hands outstretched overhead, she repeated her daily incantation while turning first to the position of the setting sun.

"Spirit of the west, let me call upon you." She turned her back to the setting sun. "Spirit of the east, hear me." She turned to the right. "Spirit of the north, guide me." She turned her back on the north. "Spirit of the south, I stand humbled before you." Then she called upon the spirit of Crazy Horse. "Guide me. Give me your strength. Teach me your ways. Allow me to be your messenger. Open my heart and soul to the truth."

One day when several locals arrived to look at Alissa's paintings on display in the Fuller Art Studio, a man approached her and politely introduced himself.

"I heard via the grapevine that you have a teaching credential," he said. "I'm on the school board in Happy Valley. We may be looking for some new teachers as soon as we find a replacement for our principal at Lupine High."

"I have administrative certification," offered Alissa. "In fact, some folks might say I'm clearly certifiable."

"Interesting," he said, responding favorably to her humor. "We need someone at the high school who is independent and a strong leader. You may have read in the press that our former principal had some issues with her personal life. What are these certifiable credentials you claim to have?"

Alissa sighed. She had felt that going back into teaching was her insurance policy if she couldn't support herself in any other way, but she was doing so well as an artist, she wasn't sure if she should break her run of good luck. Maybe a principal's position was more than she should bite off. She was already aware of the problems they were having in this remote area of the state with people who took advantage of the isolated areas that were inaccessible to law enforcement. She knew that teaching kids here would be a challenge, and supervising a staff of teachers was a huge responsibility in a state where the academic-performance ratings were sliding downhill. But she was willing to try. It would give her a platform to implement the ideas she was eager to develop. At her core, Alissa believed she was up to the challenge.

"I have a baccalaureate in education from Swarthmore College, a master's in education, and a second master's in administration," she proudly announced.

"From California?"

"No, but I did well on the CBEST (California Basic Educational Skills Test) exam. I was considering going back into teaching, but I want to teach in secondary schools. I've recently been employed in business, and I'm aware of what skills employers are looking for these days. I think our kids should be prepared to enter the workforce, and I don't see that we are providing them with the skills they need to compete in the world market so they can maximize their potential," she said, explaining her new business approach to education and showing that she was still an educator at heart.

Alissa's background offered much more than the other candidates who were applying for the principal's slot. Her personality was captivating, and her appearance was impeccable. She got the job but had to hit the ground running. Within a month after her September hire date, she was interviewing candidates for new staff members to replace the teachers who had left because of the previous scandals. Her most pressing need was to get someone into the math classroom, which had been vacated because the prior teacher was terminated when he showed up in his classroom drunk so often that he became the laughingstock of the school. Students would hiccup when they passed him in the hallway, and when they showed up wearing T-shirts that read "One tequila, two tequila, three tequila, floor," the administration could no longer procrastinate in finding a replacement for him.

Interviewing for a math teacher was how she met the man who would become her next husband. Roland Michaels was one of five teachers who had applied for the position. Alissa was impressed with his credentials and the fact that he had returned to school as an adult to complete his education after a more lucrative career as a carpenter and welder. His letters of recommendation described a man who was loved by his students and always gave more to his teaching job than was required. Roland had already passed the interviews with the personnel office and head of the math department and had cleared the background security screening required for anyone working with children in California. He would be the first of three candidates Alissa would interview for the position. This meant no decision could be cast in concrete until she had met with the other two applicants.

Roland exuded confidence as he walked into her office. He planted his feet firmly as if each step anchored him precisely to the place he had chosen to be, while his body rhythm produced a jaunty swing typical of a man comfortable with a life on the sea. He had been a handsome man–a blond, blue-eyed Nick Nolte lookalike in his younger days–but with his strong presence, crowned with hair that had turned to white silk, he was still physically when Alissa met him the day of the interview.

His strong concern for children set him apart from the other candidates. He had retired from teaching and spent many happy hours in his favorite hobby, sailing his sloop *The Unsinkable Molly Bea*. As the interview progressed, Alissa was impressed that this was an unusually good man with a zest for life and adventure whose values were not monetary.

She moved from the chair behind her desk and walked toward the chair where he was sitting while she pondered what question to ask him first.

"Why have you come back to teaching? Weren't you happy in retirement?" she asked, leaning back against her desk for support.

"To be perfectly honest, it is a financial necessity. I ran up my credit cards, and now they are out of reach. I'll be returning to sailing again soon enough. I figure I need only a year teaching to be solvent."

Alissa hoisted herself up to sit on the top of her desk. She leaned forward and looked directly into his eyes. "Our pay scale is not up to what you have earned in the past, Mr. Michaels. Are you sure you will be back on your feet in a year?"

"Well, Mrs. Woods, I am a math teacher. I've worked with numbers all my life."

Alissa leaned back, contemplating this situation. She had no problem with a new hire who would stay for only a year if the new hire had as many qualifications and attributes as Mr. Michaels. But she would be happier if he stayed longer.

Inadvertently, her right foot began move. It moved back and forth, and then it rocked side to side, and without her being aware of it, it was forming a circle. She was contemplating how she was going to persuade Mr. Michaels to stay on. It was as if her moving leg was keeping pace with the wheels turning in her brain. Her foot stopped.

She reached her decision. She would hire Mr. Michaels. The other applicants would receive a perfunctory interview. As soon as her decision was made, Alissa realized the position she had taken when sitting on her desk and the inexplicable behavior of her right foot was all happening as this nice man was seated a few inches lower than her perch.

Feeling embarrassed, she quickly stood up and resumed a businesslike demeanor. She thanked him for the interview and walked with him all the way to the front door of the high school.

"Thank you for coming in, Mr. Michaels. I'll be sending my recommendation back to the personnel department. You will be hearing from them soon. If it takes more than a week, please feel free to call me," she said, handing him her business card and wishing she could tell him not to fret about getting the job; he was a shoo-in. Her foot had recognized this.

"Thank you," he said.

"Do you have family here?" she asked, wishing to learn more about him.

"Yes. I have a sister in Mariposa," he said.

Roland had moved in with his sister when she was diagnosed with cancer, but he would never talk about her health to anyone outside of the family. It was a private matter. He was too modest to boast about moving in to help her. In Roland Michaels' world, people helped each other, even when to do so meant personal sacrifice.

"A sister?" asked Alissa, perking up. "Her name wouldn't be Marie, would it?"

"Why, yes. It is Marie. But how would you know that?"

"The Michaels surname isn't so common. I think your sister bought some paintings from me," said Alissa, smiling.

"You must be A. Barrett, then. Those are the only original paintings Marie has. I know your paintings. They are nice. But I thought your name was Woods."

"I use my maiden name when I paint."

"I'll be damned. Excuse me. You're really good. What are you doing in a high school with talent like that?"

"Thank you, Mr. Michaels. I'm not too different from you. You told me during the interview that you have always had a desire to help kids keep on the right track. I have those kinds of ambitions as well. I think there is a lot more the schools can do for our students before we cut them loose."

The Native American children at the high school were often the object of discrimination, and Alissa made it her new mission to try to understand their culture better so that she could help teach the students mutual respect. She used her insight as an artist to explain the differences in culture to the students.

"Human needs are identical," she would begin whenever she had the opportunity. "While needs are the same, they are expressed in different ways, depending upon the culture of the combined group. Think of these needs as differences in colors. Each distinct culture has a pattern. Colors do not clash; they are compatible. When an outside force threatens the culture, the colors become submerged. When the culture lives peacefully, the individual colors can shine, and they are like a rainbow when they blend. If the blending does not happen, no new colors are formed in the rainbow, and much of the beauty of life is missed. Let's find what each of us has to create that beauty. Let's find your own personal hues. Perhaps we'll find some nuggets of gold."

Alissa had not fully recovered from the emotional accumulation of the stress she had been exposed to during her life. Because of the long drive needed for committing to her job as principal, it was becoming more and more difficult to retreat from tension by painting.

The ideas bouncing around in her head kept her from sleeping soundly, and she frequently experienced feelings of anxiety that took her breath away. When this happened, she would pause, take a deep breath, and try to focus on only one thought, although many emotions swamped her conscious mind with conflicting ideas for appropriate action. When she identified the specific fear that was the culprit causing the current panic attack, the dizziness would stop, and she would be able to control her emotions and move toward problem-solving mode.

But the anxiety took its toll. She was more forgetful than usual and often omitted important elements of planning. This was making her look foolish. An example was when she invited all the teachers from Lupine High to her home in March for a Saint Patty's Day dinner.

The invitations were mailed, and the telephoned RSVP responses indicated many people at the school were curious about their new principal and would be attending her party. Fifteen minutes before the party was scheduled to start, Alissa's phone started to ring with urgent requests for directions. The teachers had reported to the address Alissa had put on the invitation and discovered that it was incorrect. Some gave up the quest and went home in disgust. Only eight tenacious teachers called for help and found their way to Alissa's home that night. One by one, they dribbled in while the corned beef and cabbage dinner in the pot was stewing as much as the hostess who had temporarily forgotten where she lived.

When Roland Michaels arrived, he saw her distress and offered to help her salvage the party. His cheerfulness was a blessing. "It's not such a big deal that you wrote east when your house is west."

"Thanks, Roland. I have always had a problem with directions. The staff will think I am losing my compass."

"I figured out the mistake, they can as well. Your teachers should know that your home wouldn't have a confederate flag on the outhouse. Is there something I can help with?"

"I need someone to take out the corned beef and slice it when it is cool enough. Would you see to that and let me know when it's ready to serve?"

Roland went to the kitchen where he immediately removed the corned beef from the hot water and held it under the cold water so he could handle it. Then he placed it on the cutting board Alissa had set out. He selected her sharpest knife and proceeded to cut the six-pound slab of meat into eight equal pieces for the eight guests who had arrived.

Roland wasn't Irish. He was French Canadian with a drop of Native Canadian blood and had never been to a Saint Patrick's Day event. He didn't know the beer that night would be colored green and the guests would be persuaded to wear silly hats, and he certainly did not know that corned beef was to be served in thin slices, not in large chunks. Even the most dedicated Irishman could not eat one-eighth of a six-pound portion of meat with his cabbage. A math teacher should know that much corned beef would cause a wee bit of discomfort.

From that day on, Alissa called Roland her hunk, and everyone from the party knew it was inspired by the corned beef. Roland, however, hoped it was because she was attracted to him. She was.

Roland found his way back to Alissa's house often. One day he brought his clothing with him and asked if she had room in the closet for them. She did. From that day on, theirs was a committed relationship that had all the attributes of marriage except the legal documents and the customary acknowledgment from the community.

In the springtime, when the property was covered with California golden poppies and the regal color of blue lupine, Roland said this was the place his heart belonged. Alissa insisted on keeping their living arrangement a secret. This was not the kind of example she wanted to set for the children in their charge. Neither Alissa nor Roland was seeking marriage at this point in their lives. They both knew that marriage was no guarantee of happiness or of permanence. But they enjoyed being together, and Alissa and Roland made an awesome duo both in and out of the classroom. But their personal life could not be spoken of in public, as she would be in jeopardy of losing her job as principal for nepotism.

Alissa said, "Think of it as being in the CIA. This is top secret. My reputation is at stake."

Roland said, "But think of what divulging it would do to improve mine."

Roland was there to protect her, to shelter her, and to allow her to grow and mature into the person who was at the core of her being. This didn't mean they agreed on everything. They had many provocative discussions.

When Alissa would say, "The student should maximize his or her potential," Roland's eyes would roll. "How would you know what the student's maximum potential is? Those words are liberal BS for permitting nothing to get done. Give the student the needed skills to perform a job well, and he or she will maximize his or her own potential."

Alissa said, "I know what maximum potential is because I've had the benefit of a wonderful education and intelligent conversation with some well-known professionals."

Roland said, "Well, that must make you some sort of god, and if that's so, this French Catholic has just become an atheist. And I'll say to you what every teenager says: 'Gee, Mom, I'd rather do it myself.'"

"That's neither acceptable nor appropriate."

"Well, Alissa, you have your *A*s covered, but you are flunking out on reality. You liberals put up all kinds of programs under this category of maximizing potential. There is no way to analyze these programs to see if they work. What's your control group? Show me some definitive analysis of what is being accomplished."

Roland rose from his chair and paced the floor as the ideas poured out. "You can't get away with a statement like 'maximizing your potential.' No one can maximize his or her potential except the student. It's the student's goal and potential, not yours."

"But we want the student to feel the sky is the limit and not have him or her restricted by norms."

"You can't get away with that. Haven't you heard? The sky is no longer the limit. We are in outer space, Alissa, and this is a good example of having the teacher's goals being too restrictive. You can't consider all the options. What is this—a lab test like the rat running in circles? You are avoiding conclusions. That's fine if you don't want to be held accountable for the outcomes. Is this a teachable moment or an exercise in futility for the value of the feel-good sound of it? The results of not having an accurate way of measuring these programs are devastating costs and poorly educated youth who are not equipped to do anything."

Alissa had turned pale. She had never been confronted with a challenge to her philosophy. "What about the dreamers who want to be artists, writers, or even philosophers? What skills would your idea of education provide them?"

"Of course they are still there. They are the *creme de la creme*. It doesn't matter if you have a program to teach them. You never really have. You just create an environment of daydreamers who are bored. They grow up to live in la-la land, just as you have."

Alissa gasped. His words stunned and frightened her. "What is that, Roland's rules?"

"It's not my rules. Tests measure what is accurate. When tests are given to ascertain whether the student understands specific skills, they also provide data to judge whether the teacher has fulfilled his or her obligation. When students in a particular class fail to score well, this reflects equally on the performance of their teacher. I believe this is why poor teachers don't want their students tested."

"You are being unfair, Roland, and what you are saying is unsubstantiated. I worked very hard to maximize my students' potential, and they scored well on their tests. Oh, Roland, I wish you weren't so cynical. You may be a math teacher, but what you are saying doesn't add up."

Frowning and with a tired voice, Roland attempted to justify his thinking and softly replied, "Yes, Alissa, I am a math teacher, and I taught my students that one plus one equals two. I do not value the premise that one plus fairy dust equals education."

One day, the daily debate was interrupted by the doorbell. When Alissa opened the door, Roland was still spouting off. "No wonder this country is going to hell in a handbasket; it's the outcome of a mindless society."

"It's Phyllis Diamond, Alissa."

"Come in, dear. Roland is leaving," said Alissa. "Wouldn't this be a good time for you to run down to Nick's Bar and cool off, Roland?"

Roland had always been a little hard on Phyllis Diamond, the third-grade teacher who lived down the road from Alissa. He thought she was an inept teacher, but more importantly, he felt she was a poor role model. She dressed for teaching as if she were going to work in the back yard. Phyllis thought her appearance was unpretentious to better reach her students, and Roland thought it was lazy and sloppy and that she should dress in a way to inspire her students to rise above their current level.

The young teacher was flushed with excitement as she rushed in to share her news with Alissa. But seeing Roland, she said, "I never did understand that phrase, Roland. What does it mean to say 'Go to hell in a handbasket'?"

"Do you really want to know?" said Roland.

"I'm just curious," said Phyllis.

"Don't worry, it's not complicated. It's another way to say losing your head."

"Now I'm confused."

"And I'm not surprised," said Roland, in a scoffing tone. "You had to see the movie."

"Never mind him, Phyllis. It came from a movie about the French Revolution. Roland has seen them all. But what brings you here to see me today?" asked Alissa.

"Alissa, I'm so excited. The superintendent gave me the Happy Valley Teacher of the Year award. It comes with a check for five hundred dollars. Would you believe it? It was largely based on my outline for the school year," she said, grabbing a chair and placing it next to Roland to show off her certificate. "I wrote that back in September. I never did get around to implementing the plan, and I can't even remember what I wrote. What a wonderful surprise this award is. I could use the five hundred dollars for my next vacation. I've always wanted to go to Hawaii."

Roland wondered about the wisdom of the superintendent, if this was his choice of best teacher in the district. "That's great. You should work on writing a plan you don't implement again for next year and who knows, next year you might be able to afford a five-star hotel in Tahiti."

He felt the heat of Alissa's glare on his back and decided not to say any more. *I'll save this discussion for the next round,* thought Roland as he tucked it into his memory bank, wondering if he had learned all the stories that had given the district its bad reputation.

"Well, I can't stay and visit. I want to stop by to see the rest of the neighbors to tell them about my good fortune. I didn't see your car outside, Roland. Can I give you a lift home?"

"Never mind, Phyllis, his friends dropped him off, and I'll be taking him to Nick's Bar," said Alissa.

As Phyllis left, her bracelet slipped off her arm and dropped to the tile floor. "Damn, will you throw this thing in the trash for me, Roland?"

"Would you like me to fix it for you?"

"No, don't bother. I'll get another," she said as she floated out the door on her cloud.

As soon as Phyllis drove off, Roland took Alissa in his arms, looked into her eyes, and said, "Are you really going to take me to Nick's Bar, or did you just think of that in the nick of time?"

"No and yes. I have more to offer you here than at Nick's."

Alissa went to the bedroom to slip into something more comfortable. Roland dropped the discarded bracelet into the trash can. He could have fixed it but the bracelet had no value for Phyllis, so what was the point in suggesting a mend. *The only things recycled these days were empty soda cans.* He looked down at his hard, gnarled hands. These hands had provided him wages from the time he was a child when every penny mattered. He sighed, walked to the liquor cabinet, and poured himself a double scotch.

"I'll be there in a minute," he called out in response to Alissa's invitation to join her.

Roland was suffering from former-marriage shell shock. Although he seldom mentioned anything about his second wife, he did tell one story about his hot-headed first wife. She had been irrationally jealous of imagined competition. The slightest attention any woman gave him would set her off. Once, when a waitress smiled at him, his ex-wife threw her dinner in his face and stormed out of the restaurant, raging. Roland was relieved that Alissa trusted him and was not irrationally suspicious, but he understood she wanted and expected his entire devotion.

Roland's hobby, carpentry, gave him a great deal of satisfaction. He was a gifted and skilled handyman. However, their personal choice of artistic expression differed. One day Roland came home with two electrical shadow boxes he had purchased. In these, one of his creations was a waterfall scene that could have been inspired by Mariposa, except that it was more complicated than the natural scene. His had trees that moved in the wind, the sound of running water to match the falls, and the background light could be controlled to show the brightness of a sunrise, the warmth of high noon, or a sky colored with a golden-and-amber sunset. He wanted the waterfall scene over the bathtub. The other was made into an image of a wolf, teeth bared and stretching menacingly forward. This was the one he wanted to hang over the couch in the living room.

Alissa was dismayed, but she didn't want to hurt his feelings. "Have you considered it might be a hazard to have it over the bathtub?" she suggested. "Or is there something you aren't telling me?"

Roland got huffy. "Okay, I didn't think about that danger. But the wolf is definitely going in the living room, facing the front door."

Alissa thought for a moment and then offered her compromise. "Let's put the wolf over the commode. That way, when it scares the crap out of our guests, they will be in the right place."

The deck Roland built around the perimeter of Alissa's house was probably the best-constructed structure in the entire valley. He was a passionate and intense man, and during the time cancer was slowing stealing the life of his sister, Marie, he had expressed his anguish by working at such an intense pace that he'd developed carpal tunnel syndrome. With each swing of the hammer, Roland cursed god for allowing his sister to suffer. He discharged his rage at the injustice of his loving sister having to die a painful death when other people who were evil, mean, and deserving of punishment were well and whole.

Roland had spent his childhood taking the blows intended for his mother and siblings. As a result of this, Roland developed impatience with anyone who was unfair, inconsiderate, or rude. In fact, Roland would deliberately provoke people to anger who reminded him of his pigheaded, obstinate father. What he did not notice, however, was that as he grew older, he was also becoming pigheaded and obstinate.

The coarse psychological armor he wore so obviously protected a warm, giving, and loving heart. Women felt safe near Roland, because they believed he would protect them. On the other hand, Roland said the women would be well advised to have a man to protect them against him. In today's vernacular, Roland was a womanizer because of his numerous relationships that were only physical and in which he was not willing to commit to anything except the amour of the evening. In fact, Roland said of himself, if a woman was alive and moving, she was adequate to be the target of his advances. But his *bon vivant* sexual tastes were practiced only when he was a single man. He never disclosed the relationships of his flamboyant escapades, as many men enjoyed doing, and when a conversation in mixed company became *risqué*, Roland would turn away from it and lower his head.

Roland showed his guardianship of others by taking on the responsibility for numerous foster children. He was one of those rare, gifted people who were born to teach. He used these skills with the children in his care. But more important, he was a father figure to them all. This was especially important, as most of the foster children were runaway girls who needed his firmness as much as his kindness. He was strong without being cruel and was consistent, dependable, and constant.

This meant Alissa finally had a relationship with a man who helped her appreciate who she was. Roland had the insight and was willing to take the effort to understand her. If she spent too much time putting more final brushstrokes on her painting, he would encourage her to accept that it was perfect. "You can't go past genius, Alissa. Step back and see how good it is."

She noticed a change not only in her attitude but in her language. With Roland, she was witty without being cruel, and when she teased, he responded by raising one eyebrow, lowering his head to the side, and giving her a look that said, "Oh, brother."

EIGHTEEN

Death of the Mother

Roland suggested they take a summer vacation on *Little Bertha*, a houseboat he and Alissa had purchased. Because he wanted this trip to be extra special, he spent days on the computer arranging the details. He also called his sister Catherine and brother Henri to join them for a combined family reunion and boat-christening party. Alissa had never been on a houseboat, but she encouraged the adventure by helping in the only way she could think of—she sewed cushions and curtains made of canvas material with sailboats floating across a field of royal blue. She edged them in white rope piping. They were nautical but nice, something you might find in a magazine advertising how to decorate a little boy's bedroom. Roland, after all, was just an overgrown kid.

Alissa was always up for an adventurous thing to do with Roland. It was reasonable to believe that houseboating was going to be a good experience. Alissa had loved the sailing excursions with Roland along the California coastline on *The Unsinkable Molly Bea*, especially since he had never suggested she jump off the boat to swim. A houseboat might be something she could enjoy with her grandchild.

Her thoughts drifted to a particular moment on the *Molly Bea* with Roland. She had been sitting in the cockpit of the sailboat, surrounded by several of their friends from the school. The boat was moving effortlessly through the water, and Alissa had been enjoying every moment. As the boat glided through the water, it left a small wake. Her perspective was as unique as was that of the others around her. It changed moment to moment. *We will all go home this day with our own personal images,* she thought.

A sailboat moved past. Its smiling occupants waved an unspoken moment of aloofness. There was the undeniable contrast with the cost of their boat and the easy manner of people quite comfortable with wealth. A strand of hair had blown across Alissa's face, disturbing her reverie. She had guests to host. She had cleared her throat and asked, "Does anyone need a refill?"

◆ ◆ ◆

The houseboat was moored at Lake Mead on the Colorado River, but Roland wanted to take a trip down the Mississippi. His arrangements included having a boat-transport company meet them at Lake Mead to pick up the boat at a launch ramp at Callville Bay. All Roland had to do was pilot the houseboat to the ramp. The plan was to have Roland's bachelor brother, Henri, meet them so Alissa would not have to do any heavy sailor-type work. That should have tipped Alissa off that this was not going to be like a luxury cruise on the *QE2*.

Little Bertha was a little worse for wear. She listed to the left, she needed paint, and she smelled of wet dog and cigarette butts, but worst of all, she was little. Actually, she was more like a premature birth. There was barely room for two adults to stretch out in the house part of the boat, and the deck around the cabin was only navigable by the brave soul who was willing to press against the cabin and inch his or her way sideways, holding on to the chain that served as the sides of the boat. They planned to be on the houseboat for an entire month.

"Where is Henri supposed to sleep?" asked Alissa, trying hard not to show her disappointment as she climbed onboard.

"He can sleep here," said Roland, pointing to a space between the engine housing and toilet. "There's plenty of room."

Just then, the houseboat in the next berth started its engine, spitting water into the lake and nearly inundating *Little Bertha*.

"Oh, I see," said Alissa. "You mean here in the puddle of water."

"It wasn't there a minute ago," said Roland.

"No, but it's here now. You can't expect your brother to sleep in the head and swab the deck every time another boat goes past or we hit a patch of rough water. Are you sure this thing is seaworthy?"

"OK, smarty-pants. So you know some nautical talk. Stop talking naughty and get those pillows of yours into the cabin."

"They are wet now, Roland. Why would I want wet cushions inside the cabin?"

"Because they match the deck?" said Roland, laughing as he gave Alissa a big hug. "I know it's not fancy, Alissa, but give the old girl a try. You will love it once you get used to it. I'll gas her up now so we'll be ready to go as soon as Henri catches up with us."

Alissa braced herself for her first trip – to the gas pump ten feet away. Roland started the engine. The houseboat jerked. The engine sputtered and spit a bit, and then, because he had it in the wrong gear, the houseboat lurched. It attacked the deck, bounced off into the fifty-foot beauty in the next berth, and promptly stopped without a mutter because the gearbox had frozen up.

Luckily, they were still near the deck. Roland jumped off *Little Bertha* and ran to the car, returning with a box of tools. He was a handyman par excellence, and that's what accounted for the lack of care he had given to *Little Bertha*. When you are a "he man" who can fix anything, it doesn't mean everything is fixed. You pick and choose what you want to work on. And since *Little Bertha* wasn't needed for a while, there was no sense in having her fixed up and ready to go until Roland wanted to get up and be ready to go.

Three pints of axle grease later, a tall, thin man arrived at the dock. He peeked into the window of the cabin at Alissa. "Hi. I'm Henri. Is my brother on board?"

"You will find him in the engine room," said Alissa. "But you will have to swim to get there. It's that thing over there in pieces. Roland is taking it apart. You can't miss him; he's the only thing that's working."

Alissa was glad to have Henri around to help Roland. It meant that she could hide out in the cabin so no one would see her, and Henri would be the one to shout directions at Roland in a vain attempt to keep the captain at the helm from crashing into everything that came within twenty feet of the *Little Bertha*. It meant that Henri would be the one to jump onto the deck when the houseboat needed to be tied to the moorings, and it meant that a relative stranger was present, and thus she did not fall prey to her urge to scream, shout, and cry her eyes out every time Roland crashed the boat or ran it aground onto a sandbar.

Henri had the patience of Job, although he probably would have identified more with the circumstances of Jonah in the belly of the whale when he saw where he was expected to sleep that night. The temperature on Lake Mead that night was forty degrees, and no matter how he positioned himself, he was not able to force his sleeping bag with him into the space between the head and the head gasket. The days were all the same. When Roland awoke, he would find Henri stretched out on the roof of the cabin, drying out and catching some sleep. By midday, when the temperature rose to ninety degrees, Roland would wake him for another day of adventure. Groggy but dry, Henri would always comply.

But the day they ran out of gas in the middle of the lake and the crew realized they had no radio or red flag to signal for assistance or fishing poles for something to do with their time, Henri found the limits of his patience. He didn't suggest where Roland should park his houseboat, but he did suggest that although he was invited to join them for a trip down the Mississippi, he didn't want to start from where they were. Henri wanted to get out of Lake Mead as fast as possible. He would go by plane and meet Roland and Alissa in Iowa.

It took three days to drift back to shore, where Roland and Henri could trek back to the marina for gasoline. When the day arrived when they were to meet the boat-transport crew, Alissa and Henri decided to walk to the launch ramp to watch *Little Bertha*'s voyage from a distance. Roland was full of excitement because his plans were shaping up, but he still had to navigate the boat into the bay.

Roland was having a tough time. The winds were blowing, the small motor was straining, and the current tugging on Bertha was restraining her. The bottom of the lake was rising, or, you might say, the level of the lake was lowering. In either event, Roland didn't see the rocks.

With Henri, Alissa, and two impatient men from the boat-transport company watching, Roland was doing his best. He ran from one end of the houseboat to the other, alternately turning the wheel and monitoring the sides of *Little Bertha*. There were no mirrors to guide him; there were no sails to help him. The only thing that proved him to be the old salt that he was his salty language that rippled across the top of the water, reaching the crowd who had gathered onshore to observe. An audience of water skiers, fishermen, and house-boaters watched with amazement as *Little Bertha* approached the dock. From Roland's perspective, the dock was getting higher and higher, and the boat was in danger of sinking–had it not been for the unexcepted opportunity of running aground on an outcropping of rocks. *Little Bertha* didn't move. The propeller was broken. Alissa was sailing midway between humiliation and prayers.

The houseboat was adrift but floating within reach of the crane. Henri helped his brother and the men from the transport company hoist the houseboat onto the truck, and then Henri made his escape. He was scratching his head and muttering, "*Mon dieu, mon dieu*. God help you, Alissa. I'll connect with Catherine, and we'll catch up with you in Davenport."

A blustering, cursing Roland joined Alissa at the parking lot. He didn't wish to stay at Callville to have the propeller repaired with everyone watching. He had called ahead to be sure the repair could be done in Davenport on the arrival of *Little Bertha*. As they started the drive to Iowa, they passed the truck on the highway carrying *Little Bertha*.

"That's the fastest that little boat has ever moved," said Alissa as she removed the life jacket she had been wearing since first boarding the houseboat.

Henri was over his frustration when he arrived in Davenport. He and his sister coordinated a meeting at the Midwestern Motel. That evening at dinner, Catherine arrived with a large box decorated in white paper and white satin ribbon. "I have a christening gift for your new houseboat. Please open it now. I regret I won't be joining you on your adventure."

Alissa knew by observing the size of the box that this gift would take up more space than Henri was using for sleeping. She opened the gift cautiously, wondering what she needed for the houseboat that would be so large. It wasn't heavy enough to be an anchor. Maybe it was a propeller, if Henri had told her about the one that they left on the rocks at Lake Mead. To Alissa's dismay, the box contained a complete table setting for six of California pottery. She realized that Catherine was emphasizing the *house* part of *houseboat*.

"I hope you like them." Catherine smiled. "I couldn't resist getting them for you when I saw those cute little dolphins painted on them. They are hand painted, you know. Don't you just love the darling way they are flying through the air?"

Henri was trying to cover up the smile that curled the sides of his mouth.

Roland was staring blankly at his sister. "Is it all right to get them wet?" he asked.

"Thank you, dear," said Alissa to Roland's sister. "What a sweet thought. It will remind us of you every time we use them."

◆◆◆

The Mississippi presented new challenges. Most notable were the horseflies. Seasonal flooding on the river had generated flies resistant to chemical control. The most effective spray against them was available only from a veterinarian. The flies were particularly attracted to Alissa, and before the trip was over, she could count two dozen bites on each leg.

It did not help her mood when Ronald remarked, "I don't know how good she paints, but she sure knows how to draw flies."

The Mississippi was a different experience for the novice houseboaters. Within ten minutes after entering the river, Roland ran *Little Bertha* into the side of a lock.

"Have you ever piloted a houseboat before?" shouted the man operating the gears to control the water level.

"You bet I have," called back Roland, confident that he could fake his way down the course of the river. The water in the lock was rising, and *Little Bertha* was providing them a joyride. Roland pulled an oar out of the cabin to steady her. He pushed the oar against the wall of the dock to move *Little Bertha* away from it.

"Grab the other oar," he shouted to Henri. "Catch her on the other side in case I push too hard." So much for piloting. Roland's lack of experience to navigate the river was obvious.

The would-be mariners stood out for other reasons. Private boats on the Mississippi are elegant, huge, expensive party boats used by their well-heeled owners for entertaining business clients. And now, traveling among the best of them was *Little Bertha*, chugging along like *Little Toot*, the reluctant harbor tug. Alissa was feeling very uncomfortable. While the ladies were drinking cocktails and looking down from the decks of the boats that passed them, Alissa was again eating humble pie, and it wasn't compatible with the incessant itching from the attack of the killer horseflies.

Henri noticed Alissa was uncomfortable. "I think you have a fever. Your cheeks are all flushed," he said as he reached over and felt her head. He was right; she did have a fever. It was her body's reaction to the fly bites and to the spray from the vet. Everything seemed to be attacking Alissa at once. The flies, the spray, and the feelings of inadequacy were intruding on her psyche.

It worried Roland that there were no landmarks on the Mississippi that he could rely on to establish his position. This wasn't like the California shoreline, where the mix of mountain ranges, harbors, and rolling, open ranchland helped the sailor navigate. The land along the Mississippi is flat everywhere, except where it is underwater.

"Go the other way," he would holler out to Henri. "Maybe there is something on the other shore we can identify."

For all they knew, they might be floating the boat past New Orleans and into the gulf before they realized where they were. This fact did not get past Alissa or Henri, who was fed up again with the houseboat adventure. He disembarked at the next town with an airport, and Alissa and Roland had to continue down the river without his assistance.

Roland abruptly gave up the Mississippi misadventure. They had traveled only fifty miles, but that was far enough. He brought the tipping *Little Bertha* up on a sandbar, and when some local citizens came out to complain, he insisted he was going to leave her right there.

"You can't leave that leaky old barge here. This is private property," insisted a man in uniform.

"Does this place have a Sea Scout troop?" asked Roland.

"Yes, sir. What's that got to do with anything?"

"Well, I've brought this fine houseboat all the way down from Davenport to donate it to my favorite charity. I've got the papers on board. Whom do I make the title out to?"

"That would be the Riverview Sea Scout Troop, sir. I'll call into town and have the scoutmaster come out to meet you."

"The only scoutmaster I ever heard about was Tonto," said Alissa as they waited on the sandbar for his arrival.

"By the looks of the amount of smoke coming out of that old Ford, that may be your Indian coming now," said Roland.

"I hope this means we can finally surrender the fort to the natives and go home to dry sheets and sleep in a bed that does not move."

"As soon as I find out where the car-rental agency is," said Roland as the scoutmaster was approaching from the Ford.

"None within an hour's drive," offered the scoutmaster. "You have to go to Davenport, mister, but my cousin Jeff has a clunker to sell. It'll make the trip. He wants five hundred dollars for it."

"Sold," said Roland.

With the Mark Twain excursion behind them, Roland and Alissa settled down for a relatively uneventful life back at her house in Mariposa. When Henri came for a visit the following year, it was only because of his good nature that he did not mention the *Little Bertha* misadventure. There were more important things to talk about now. Their sister Marie was failing.

◆ ◆ ◆

Although the grim reaper had been waiting in the shadows of her life for years, Marie's death came too suddenly for them to absorb. No family is willing to believe that a vital, loving person is really going to leave them. Roland's pain was especially evident. During a particularly severe thunderstorm, Roland voiced his despair to the heavens.

"Cool it, *grand dieu,* enough of this thunderbolts-and-lightning stuff. You are scaring people to death. It's only us little people down here. Why is Marie punished for living in this miserable world you created?"

Alissa also had family concerns. Mama wasn't calling as often as she had in the past, and when she did call, Alissa detected signs of dementia. Alissa's uncle Bill and aunt Holly had been keeping a close eye on the old woman ever since they encouraged Alissa to move away and leave her mother's care in their hands.

When George had passed on, Mama Barrett had turned away from her social activities, and she'd developed a suspicious and gloomy attitude. She no longer wanted visitors and was cranky whenever they called to check up on her.

One day when Aunt Holly stopped by Mama's house, she made it her business to see if the old woman was keeping up with her daily needs.

When Holly found a fur stole in the closet with the tags still attached, she told Alissa not removing tags might be signs of senility.

"What about the stole, Alissa?" asked Holly. "Should I set it aside for you?"

"No, the stole is Mama's," said Alissa. "She bought it many years ago when she and Daddy were fighting over who had control of the money. Leave it there. She will notice if it is missing."

"But it's never been worn."

◆◆◆

The decision to have Mama put into a nursing home probably had more to do with the story Katie related to Josh about the chocolates than anything else.

"You won't believe what happened," said Katie, calling her brother to warn him to stop by their grandmother's house to see how she was doing.

"You're right, Sis. I won't believe it. I might believe it if you gave me a chance. Do I have to guess what this call is about?"

"Well, I sent Grandma a large box of assorted chocolates from Trader Juan's."

"Stunning. Amazing. I'm dazzled," he quipped.

"Oh, stop it, Josh. Just because you never send Grandma gifts."

"I hate to tell you this, Katie. It's not her birthday, it's not Christmas, it's not even her anniversary, and it would really be tacky to send her an anniversary gift now that Gramps is gone."

"Mother's Day, Josh. I sent her a gift for Mother's Day."

"She's not your mother," chided Josh.

"Okay, let's get real. Grandmothers are mothers too. She didn't call to thank me, and I wanted to be sure the store sent it. So I called her."

"It's still not very amazing, Katie. Is there a punchline here somewhere?"

"She had it blown up, Josh. Can you believe it? She called the police. She told them she had gotten a package from someone she didn't know, and they sent over a bomb squad."

"I can believe that, and it is funny. I can see it all now. The headlines read: Huntington Police Find Unabomber. Sources say she had been hiding in California under the assumed name of Katie Streeter, using the guise of Mother's Day to take advantage of a local woman. Or was that a loco woman? Her weapon was chocolate pellets."

"This is too unreal," said Katie. "Grandma said that when the police came, they took the package to her driveway and detonated it. Grandma never even opened it. It never occurred to her it would be a Mother's Day gift, and she had never heard of Trader Juan's. She thought it was from a terrorist group from the Philippines."

"Well, at least she still reads the papers," said Josh, laughing. "Got to admit, Katie, if you sent me a gift, I would think it was a devious plot too. So why are the terrorists out to get our grandmother? Was it something she said?"

◆ ◆ ◆

One day Alissa heard a faint meow coming from the back of the house. Investigating, she found a small, straggly, wide-eyed kitten. The stray kitten was hungry but would not allow her to come near. She went to the house, returning with a bowl of milk for the stray. That act of kindness was the equivalent of giving the kitten a lease on the house. The kitten remained and eventually grew large enough to live on the mice she caught. When it was obvious the cat was going to stay, Roland and Alissa decided to name it. Gender-specific names were out, as neither of them could get close enough to establish its sex.

"Any ideas for a name?" asked Roland, and just as one popped into his head, they both blurted out "Orphan" in unison.

Several months later, a little girl from the nearby Miwoc tribe saw Orphan and said, "I had a kitten that looked like that one." This was the closest the Michaelses had to identify Orphan's original ownership, but when Alissa asked if this might be her kitten, the child said, "No, my cat was much smaller."

Roland felt sorry for the stray kitten that had to remain outside because Alissa was allergic to cat dander. So he built a cat house for it, with running water. It was constructed near a stream by the tunnel under the highway where the bats had their home. Alissa named this the *chat-eau* (cat-water). Whenever Alissa went to the highway to get the mail, she stopped to deliver cat food to their Orphan.

◆ ◆ ◆

Alissa noticed something was very wrong with her eyesight. There were a large number of black floaters in her vision, and she knew they were not bats. When she reported this to Roland, he insisted that she get to the ophthalmologist as quickly as possible. Problem was, the nearest specialists were seventy-five miles away in Fresno. That required traveling on curvy mountain roads and an overnight stay in town.

This was an emergency. The doctor operated on Alissa the next morning for a detached retina. Roland had been by her side as much as was permitted. But after the surgery when Alissa was dismissed from the hospital, he left her alone for a moment to bring the car to pick her up. Alissa was highly medicated, and she miss-stepped. Roland saw her fall, but he was not close enough to help. He ran to her side. He was crying.

"I should never have left you," he said, bending down to help her to her feet. "I should have walked you to the car and stayed with you. I'm so sorry."

Alissa was not injured. But seeing her lover exhibit such care and tenderness, her heart was moved. "You may be sorry now, but not as sorry as you are going to be. Roland, I want you to marry me."

"I thought you'd never ask," said Roland, holding her in his arms.

The Mariposa city clerk performed the civil ceremony that made the awesome twosome, Alissa Barrett-Walters-Woods and Roland Michaels, a legal deal. Alissa had already purchased her replacement Nantucket Rose nightgown via a phone order to the Rhode Island County Store. The package would be waiting for her when they returned home from the city clerk's office.

"I knew what you were up to that day in your office," commented Roland to his bride as they were leaving the clerk's office.

"What day in my office?"

"You know what I'm talking about. When you were wiggling your foot."

"Oh, that day." Alissa laughed. "Did you like it?"

"I had a hard time keeping my concentration."

"Just so it was hard for you."

No one had anything negative to say about the marriage except Mama, who asked Alissa, "What do you need to marry him for? You haven't had any luck with marriages. Everything was going fine for you. Now you are going to ruin it like you did with all those other men."

"Because I'm tired of calling him Honey Bunny. I want to call him husband."

"Every woman should have a Honey Bunny. It's preferable. But it doesn't have to be your husband," said Mama.

Only three months later, Roland and Alissa were RVing through Wyoming on their way back to Mariposa on one of their many casino holidays. They had traveled the entire country, stopping at each gambling casino along the way. It was a beautiful evening with not a cloud in sight. The air was still, and the drive along the back roads through the open expanse of cattle country was serene. They were both enjoying a relaxed mood.

"Alissa look out your window—to the east," exclaimed Roland, pointing. His voice was excited and animated.

Alissa was awestruck. There, stretched in the sky, as if it were drawn to protect them, was the most beautiful rainbow she had ever seen. It was bursting with vivid color, each taking its rightful place before blending into the next.

"How can there be a rainbow? There has been no rain. Do you think it's an omen?" asked Alissa.

Roland, always the skeptic, said, "And you think this portends...?"

"I don't know. I just have a peculiar feeling about this, Roland. Something is happening that is important." Alissa slumped into the seat of the car and became silent. Her thoughts were racing she knew not where. But her body was shivering as she realized an emotional excitement was surrounding her.

At the same time, her mind was remembering photos of Gothic cathedrals with gargoyles on the edges of the roof, whose mouths were designed to pour out the rainwater gushing down from a heavy storm. But there was no rain.

Instead the feeling she was experiencing was as if a Gothic iron gate somewhere in the deep recesses of her mind was pushing back hell. The gate sometimes swerved open, allowing her to see the nightmares that had plagued her as a child. She shuddered. Her teeth clenched; her eyes were shut tight. She wanted the gate to close. In her mind, not part of real existence, was a sound like thunder. Everything darkened, and opening her eyes, she knew the gate was finally shut. No longer did she dwell in the childhood darkness that shrouded her meager grasp of life. She was surrounded in warmth and sunlight. She had indeed become a survivor of the nightmare.

Hours later when they had pulled into an RV park, Alissa's cell phone rang. She was gripped with fear. Who would be calling her in the middle of her vacation? It must mean trouble.

"Mom, I have something to tell you," said Josh.

"Is something wrong?"

"I hate to break it to you this way. Uncle Bill called. He has bad news. Grandma has passed away."

"When?"

"Two hours ago."

Alissa sat down on the stair of the RV. She was shivering. Her mind was racing so fast she could not put her thoughts together. She handed the phone to Roland. "It's Josh. My mother died."

"Josh, this is Roland. Your mother wants me to talk to you to get the details. I'm sorry about your grandmother."

"And I'm sorry to interrupt your vacation with bad news."

"Don't worry about that. We're close to Salt Lake City. They have an airport. How much time do we have to get your mother back to Long Island?"

"The funeral is day after tomorrow. Won't you be coming, too?"

"We have the RV here. I'll need to drive it home. But don't worry. I'll see to it that Alissa makes it back in time."

"Tell Mom she can stay with Rachel and me. I'll pick her up at the airport."

Alissa was still unable to put two thoughts together. She was in shock. It wasn't grief. She felt as if a weight had been taken off her shoulders. She didn't understand why she was feeling this way. She felt lighthearted, as if a burden was gone.

She looked up at Roland as he was putting the cell phone away.

"Do you think the rainbow was your mother saying good-bye?" he asked.

"No. Please don't talk about it now." Alissa didn't understand the rainbow. She didn't understand why she was feeling relieved. If it was an omen, she didn't understand the message.

"Maybe it's a coincidence," said Roland.

"No. Josh said she died two hours ago. That's exactly when we saw the rainbow. It was too spectacular. It stretched to the east. I felt it was pointing directly at me. The rainbow was intended to give me a message. I just don't understand yet what it is."

Roland took over the details of getting Alissa back to Long Island. They stayed the night in a campground, and the next morning they drove into town and found a travel agent. Alissa purchased luggage for her flight, and they drove the RV to Salt Lake City, where Roland put her on the flight to La Guardia.

"I wish you were going with me," said Alissa as she prepared to board the plane.

Roland smiled and held up a slip of paper where he had written a confirmation number. "I'll be picking you up at McCarran Airport when you come home. Be sure you have your ticket for the trip back."

"McCarran. Where is that?"

"Vegas. This confirmation is for Sam's Town, your favorite casino. The RV and I will be there, waiting for you to come home," he said as he gave her a quick kiss on the cheek. "See you in a week. It's my duty for the green ecology to recycle some of those greenbacks."

Alissa waved at Roland as the airport tug pushed the plane into the takeoff position. She suddenly stiffened and sat up straight, straining against the seat belt. "I know now," she burst out aloud over the roar of the engines as the plane reached toward the sky. "The rainbow was telling me Mama can't hurt me anymore." Her voice dropped to a whisper as tears welled in her eyes.

Alissa had lived for years in subrogation to her mother. Her decisions came only after long bouts of wondering what Mama would want her to do. Each item of conflict that she had been collecting in her Pandora's box of unhappy events could now be revisited with no danger of nullification of her spirit. She vowed never to open that box again, or at least until the moment she could deal with the unhappiness.

A few days after they met at Sam's Town, Roland asked if Alissa would like to see the Metropolitan, the newly opened casino on the strip. This required leaving the RV and taking a public bus. During the trip, Roland convinced Alissa that she would enjoy the art display at the Metropolitan, and he would go to the low-stakes poker game, where whales did not play. It was not only the thinness of Roland's wallet that prompted his choice; he never could read the thoughts of the big-time, wealthy high rollers.

While Alissa was considering if she was being pushed off by Roland or if she would rather be alone on her own doing her thing while he was off doing his own, something happened on the bus that caused her to panic.

She grabbed Roland's arm. "Look over there."

A visibly drunk man was seated next to a woman dressed in a hotel uniform and obviously on her way to or from work.

"Alissa, what's wrong?"

"He's out of control, and he's going to hurt her."

"No, she's fine. She is getting up to move her seat."

Alissa was sobbing. "My mother is looking away; she doesn't want to help me. She's looking away. Mama, help me."

"Are you remembering something, darling?"

Alissa broke into tears and fell on Roland's strong cheek for support. "A man was going to hurt me on the trolley. Mama left me alone to sit with him, and she didn't look at what he was doing," she sobbed. Alissa regained her composure. "Maybe Mama didn't realize she had placed me next to a drunk."

Roland took her hand and held it tightly. "A loving mother would not place her child in danger. A decent mother would not let her child out of her sight on a public bus. Any woman who would do what she did to you is cunning and cruel. A mother protects a child. She does not place her child in harm's way and walk away. I think you can add this to your list of cruel and unusual punishments."

"The psychiatrist told me she hated me and was very deliberate in hurting me."

"He may be right."

◆ ◆ ◆

December 31, 1999, closed the millennium and ushered in a new beginning. Phone calls to family and friends that evening were especially important.

"Happy New Year, Mom. Have you and Roland cracked open the champagne?" asked Katie.

"Happy New Year, darling. We have enough champagne here for you, too. Want to fly over from New York and join us?"

"I could fly over without a plane. I'm on cloud nine, Mom. I have such wonderful news to tell you."

Alissa motioned to Roland to pick up the extension phone so he could hear Katie's news, too.

"We just heard from Juilliard. Daniel has been accepted for high school. They want him to start classes right after spring break; they are excited about his voice. Mom, this is so terrific. We all felt he had talent, but the school was waiting to see what would happen when his voice changed. Now they are offering him a full scholarship. Mom, your grandson might someday be famous. I wish Grandma was still living so she could share in our happiness."

"Don't worry. She won't miss anything. She is a cow now in India, claiming her right to reverence."

"What are you talking about, Mom? Have you have had too much champagne?"

"There is no such thing as too much champagne, Katie. Just as there is no such thing as too much joy. I'm truly happy for you. 'Bye, darling. Happy new millennium." She hung up the phone and slumped into the nearest chair as she started to sob. The color drained from her face, and Roland rushed to her side.

"You look like you've seen a ghost," he said. "What's the matter, Alissa?"

"I have seen a ghost. I saw myself standing next to Daniel on the stage of the Met." She began to cry. "I've never told anyone about the disappointment I've had all these years at not being able to fulfill my first, deepest, and strongest dream."

"Cheer up. I thought Katie's news was wonderful. Hasn't she invested a lot of time and money into that boy? Looks like it's paying off."

"Katie has prepared Daniel well. She gave him voice and piano lessons. He has traveled to Italy and Germany for music consortiums. He has been nurtured by two dedicated parents. Daniel has natural ability. He has drive and dedication. I'm proud of him, but I'm even more proud of my daughter, because she believed in him and gave him the love and support to accomplish this. Katie was completely unselfish. She even helped finance his lessons by taking extra clients in her law practice. Look what my daughter has managed to do, Roland. By becoming an attorney and fulfilling her dream, she not only helped herself, she has helped Daniel."

"So what is the secret you have been keeping to yourself all these years, Alissa?"

"I didn't want my family to be burdened with my resentment and regret. It's kind of like my own personal R&R program," she smiled nervously, uncomfortable with touching a subject that had been buried for so many years.

"You are not a burden to me, Alissa. I think you need to get this off your chest."

"It's complicated, Roland. During my freshman year at Huntington High School in Long Island, I believed I had the talent to be a coloratura soprano. The choirmaster at Huntington High School was the first to encourage me. He showed me how to apply for a professional evaluation. I used my babysitting money and purchased an audition with the famous vocal coaches Roberta Peters and Robert Merrill."

"And it didn't work out?"

"No. The audition was great. They said with my voice I could one day sing on the stage of the Met. I knew this would require a great deal of professional training, and Mama and Daddy were not warm to the idea. They didn't see how voice lessons would help me earn a living. Since I was their only child, perhaps they thought they might need me to help them financially in their retirement years. I really don't know why they were opposed. They didn't give a reason; they just ridiculed the idea. But I didn't let them dissuade me. I paid for another audition, this time at the Second Street Music School, and I won a partial scholarship. I thought they had to take me seriously. I promised to pay the three dollars per lesson reduced fee with babysitting money. For three years from my freshman through junior years, I performed with all my heart for my vocal coach, Madam Hiltz."

"I take it that Madam Hiltz was a reputable coach."

"Yes, she had trained several people who went on to perform at the Met. Madam Hiltz had been a diva with the State Opera, the resident company performing at the Vienna Opera House. When she retired from the stage, she moved to New York.

"Daddy was present the day Madam Hiltz recommended that I audition for the Crane School of Music in Potsdam in upstate New York. Attending boarding school brought another ugly family discussion of who would pay. At Crane, the administration offered to arrange that I could work on campus to pay my tuition. I still got no encouragement at home. Daddy minimized the prestige of the school by calling it the 'Damned Pot.' True to his habit of imposing his will by mocking ideas he did not like, he would chant, 'Pots, pots, pots, dam, dam, dam; do you want to go to a school with that kind of a cheer?' Daddy was mistaken to assume the Crane School of Music would have cheerleaders for a football team."

"Oh, I'm sure he knew better. It's the way he used criticism. He didn't want you to go."

"But it was Mama who was responsible for putting the final nail in the Potsdam coffin by pointing out that ours was not a family of financial means (just in case I had missed this point)," said Alissa, wanting to defend her father. "Mama told me that if I was to be given a job at the school, it would probably be to pick up the cashmere sweaters that the other girls dropped on the floor."

"You knew she was trying to discourage you, didn't you?"

"She was successful. I felt humiliated and insignificant. The humiliation caused me to become intimidated. I gave up trying to persuade them. In my heart, I could not allow myself to believe that Mama had been cruel. In order to hold on to the trust I had in my mother, I convinced myself that Mama was saying this only to protect me. I allowed myself to feel unworthy of attending the school so I would find acceptance at home. Had I gone to Crane Music School, I would have learned that none of the girls there wore cashmere sweaters, and the job they were offering me was to work in the library. I would have fit in beautifully with the other artistic students, who couldn't care less about economic status. But I didn't find this out until I was in Huntington for Mama's funeral and went through her paperwork. When I was in high school, I preserved the authority of my parents in order to avoid the feeling of deep regret I had for abandoning my dream.

"I've thought about this for a long time. In retrospect, I think it was Daddy's attitude that most disappointed me. He brushed away all my dreams by quoting Goethe in *Erlkonig*. I tried to tell him I was hearing things Daddy did not. He dismissed me, and by not allowing me to pursue my dreams he allowed me to die," she sobbed.

"Are you saying it was entirely the fault of your parents? After all, you still wanted to go. Why didn't you?"

"I wasn't twenty-one yet. I had no legal authority to sign the contract. I'll admit I bought in to their proposition that I had to earn their love. In that way I played a part in my own defeat. I convinced myself that when the people at the audition told me, 'You must marry music if you want music for a career,' they were setting the bar higher than I wanted to reach. I persuaded myself that everything in my life would have to be sacrificed for the sake of the great dramatic love of the arts. I had another scenario that influenced me—the movies. I didn't want to become the obsessive Nicky in the movie depicting the life of Rimsky-Korsakov. In *The Song of Scheherazade*, Nicky's passion for music trumped even his attraction to the dancer Cara de Talavera, played by the beautiful Yvonne De Carlo. I chose to travel on a less fanatical path. I didn't want to marry music. I wanted to marry a husband. One who would love and adore me."

"You gave up a dream that was important to you."

"More than that. I gave up the potential of success. But I didn't give up the effort I was making to prove I had talent. I continued with my vocal coach, but I allowed my path to be turned away from the Crane School of Music. I consoled myself by concluding that I was probably better suited for the musical-comedy stage and not the New York Metropolitan Opera. But after I could no longer look to classical opera to help me fulfill my dreams, conditions at home became more and more unbearable."

"Mama was increasingly critical. It was as if she knew that she had made a mistake by keeping me from attending the music school, and to keep from acknowledging her error, she worked instead on trying to prove I was a hopeless failure who was not capable of achieving anything worthwhile. That way, Mama would prove that I was unworthy, and Mama's role would be a noble one. She would be protecting her child from being hurt by others. She was keeping me from endeavors that, in her mind, would ultimately fail. So you see, Roland, it was not just giving up the chance for a possible career on the operatic stage. It was giving up on believing I was capable of any path I would choose."

"Sorry, love. I don't see you as someone who gives up easily."

"But as a child, I didn't have the power to do it on my own."

"You are not a child anymore, Alissa. Live in the joy of the moment. Stop dwelling on the past. Don't take your pleasure from tragedy. Live now. You have so much to be happy for."

"I'm not hedonistic either."

"Where did that one come from?" Roland pulled her gently out of the chair to enfold her in his strong arms.

"Mama said I was."

Let go, Alissa. We are entering a new age together. Let's leave the grief and sadness behind in this one. Tomorrow will bring 2000. Happy birthday."

NINETEEN

The Power of Arrogance Squared

At the beginning of the millennium, Alissa was looking for a place to live where she could enjoy her retirement years with a circle of close friends. She wanted to be surrounded by people with whom she could share common interests and depend upon in a mutual support system. She also wanted to be away from Mariposa, where junked cars were parked on front yards and fishing worms were for sale at the grocery store. Riverview Estates, the retirement community she Googled, appeared to fit the bill.

This new development in the desert was comprised of hundreds of houses planned for people with similar tastes and demographics. The Riverview website advertised a relaxed lifestyle within a gated community, away from the congestion and crime of large cities. The photos of evening sunsets spilling over vast expanses of open, undeveloped desert pictured on the website inspired her to imagine relaxing with a glass of California wine and drinking in the joys of life with the congenial friends she hoped to meet with the move. Her friends thought she was crazy to move to the desert and suggested she get help. But Alissa said she would "rather have a bottle in front of me than a frontal lobotomy."

Riverview was laid out around a well-manicured golf course and was advertised as an ideal place for people looking for an "active adult lifestyle." The developer didn't spell out what was meant by "active adults," and Roland and Alissa suggested that since an inactive adult might be one of their compatriots who suffered from irregularity, they would qualify as active due to their ready supply of prunes. They decided to check out the area to see if this housing development and the nearby town of Trickle Creek Valley would meet the needs of their senior years.

Roland wasn't sure if this move would suit him. He was at the wheel, insisting there would be no side trips to slow them down. Alissa was getting cold feet.

"Riverview might be out in the sticks somewhere. I don't want to be in another community where it is a full-day commitment to go shopping. If we have to go all the way into Los Angeles for stores, I'm going to be really disappointed."

"What do you need to buy?" asked Roland.

"Nothing right now, but what will happen when I run out of things? I like clothes that have some style. What if there is no place to buy my favorite line of cosmetics? What if they don't have a decent place to buy shoes?"

"Do the same thing you did in Mariposa. Buy your stuff online."

"I know, honey. But I'm tired of shopping online, and I'm tired of having my hair cut in a barber shop. I would be happy to shop in decent stores. It's not shopping if you can't try things on. I would love to have a makeover once in a while."

"How important is that to you, Alissa? You say you don't want to live in a big city. You'd better decide if you can make do with living away from shopping malls."

"You're right," she said, sliding down into the seat to make herself comfortable for the long motor trip. "I'm not sure I like this makeup anyway. I was reading an article in *Health* magazine that said the brand of cosmetics I use has uric acid as one of the ingredients. The FDA should require a listing of all ingredients on the label so we know what we are buying."

"FDA? You're not supposed to eat it. You're supposed to put it on your face."

All traffic came to a stop. A cattle rancher was moving his stock across the highway to graze on federal land. "Well, some government agency should tell us," said Alissa.

"Why, Alissa? The acid removes a layer of dead skin. Isn't that what you ladies say keeps your skin soft?" At that moment, Roland observed that one of the cows had stopped to urinate on the side of the road. "There you go, babe. As long as we are waiting anyway, you might as well run over and get a facial for free."

When traffic started up again, Roland turned on the engine. Alissa wasn't ready to turn on a smile. Roland drove south on Highway 99, through the Tehachapi Mountains and onto the Mojave Desert floor. It was difficult for the couple to leave the green-and-gold majesty of Mariposa, but the exploratory trip to check out Riverview in spring was a good decision. The desert is best in spring, when the native wildflowers are in bloom.

As they were leaving the Central Valley and were no longer within range of the Santa Barbara radio stations, Roland was pleasantly surprised to discover that stations from Barstow and beyond featured the old tunes from the sixties he most enjoyed. The farther they traveled into the desert, the closer he felt to the prime of his youth.

"I haven't heard that one in years," he said, listening to the Carpenters singing "We've Only Just Begun." "It's like being a kid again," he commented as his thoughts drifted to happy times. "Will you miss your waterfall?"

"Yes," she said. "But I can wait for water if these flowers can."

◆◆◆

The town of Trickle Creek Valley had been constructed to look like a set for a Western movie. During the time Alissa was growing up in New York, TCV had been a quaint destination for Hollywood big names looking for relaxation away from the big city. Its guest ranches, adobe buildings on dirt roads, hitching posts, and a saloon on Main Street with authentic swinging double doors could have been situated on the Melody Ranch Motion Picture Studio back lot. But that was a generation ago, when film star Troy Hodges had his ranch on old Highway 66 and might have been spotted on his way to town to mingle with the local fans. TCV was proud of that heritage and used it to promote its present pseudo-western, semi-relaxed, partially healthful lifestyle.

Troy died, Main Street was paved, and the saloon was turned into a bowling alley. The Troy era was alive only in the memories of the people who remained after the show was over. As Roland and Alissa drove into town at the beginning of the twenty-first century, they discovered a town like all others on the desert that were still a little conflicted about what they wanted to be when they grew up. For decades, the economy of desert towns had been sustained by a scattering of family medical clinics, drugstores, thrift shops, and the cash-advance facilities that provided services to folks who didn't have bank accounts and might be in urgent need of the local bail bondsman.

TCV discovered a new cash cow and was still thriving. The western-looking frontages on Main Street were attracting the newest guests to ride into town—the senior citizens who were escaping the high cost of living in the big cities. TCV restaurants featured large-print senior menus with more selections than the regular menus, including stewed prunes smothered in fat-free whipped cream as the senior-friendly featured dessert. Dinner specials started at 2:30 p.m. so that the senior diners could be home in time for a stimulating evening of *Oprah* at 3:00 p.m., *Dr. Phil* at 4:00 p.m., *O'Reilly* at 5:00 p.m., *Larry King* at 6:00 p.m., *Jeopardy* at 7:00 p.m., and bedtime at 8:00 p.m. without having to rush through their meal. Servers were certified in CPR and automatically delivered water glasses when they saw the meds being lined up on the table. They provided placemat-sized table napkins for spillage and drippage without insulting the patrons by personally scraping the spilled food off their chins or chests.

The one-and-only department store in town catered to fashion statements of the retirement community by hiring buyers who selected clothing lines in the style of the 1948 Sears and Roebuck catalog. Cowboy boots with hard-rubber golf cleats were available for those who wished to amble the links in the spirit of the Wild West. Senior-preferred practical walking shoes with dual-purpose air cushions were a popular item in the sporting-goods store. The air-cushion insoles afforded the walker comfort even when limping or slouched over, and because the soles expanded with friction, they also provided warmth to weary feet. Thick white socks recommended for sleeping were popular, and when worn with the shoes, the senior citizen could purchase the image of the agile athletic type until he or she looked into the mirror and faced reality.

There were plenty of activities in town to keep the seniors connected with the larger world. Both the Republican and Democratic parties had local headquarters and welcomed volunteers, especially at election time. All major service clubs had branches that met weekly in the local restaurants, and retired businesspeople were welcome at the TCV Chamber of Commerce as auxiliary members. The one and only hospital recruited seniors as volunteers until they showed up as patients. For the women, there was the Assistance League, the Women's Club, and the American Association of University Women. There were garden clubs for those who were willing to make the effort necessary to grow flowers in the harsh desert climate. For the overly active men who still could give a hoot, there was the Gentlemen's Club. All this was available locally, and it was only a morning drive to Las Vegas, Primm, or Lake Havasu for those who planned ahead by saving their quarters.

Several novelty stores featured a large selection of decorations and joke gifts to accommodate the proliferation of over-the-hill parties, and some one-stop shops also had a pharmacist on duty and carried mobility products such as walkers, canes, and body alarms. For those seniors who were beyond the point of independent living, TVC also had a large selection of nursing homes and funeral parlors, including one that would allow adjacent placement of their favorite pets or seeing-eye dog.

◆ ◆ ◆

But before anyone was ready to buy the farm or move back in with the kids, there was certainly much more within Riverview Estates to keep those active adults active without having to leave the confines of the security gates to enter the community at large. These were probably the features of community living that attracted the residents to move there in the first place. At least, this is what they were paying their association dues for. There was golf, tennis, squash, a gym, bocce ball, billiards, a swimming pool and sauna, bike lanes on the streets inside the development, card games, potlucks, movies, a choir, an Internet cafe, a travel agent, bingo, bunko, poker, bridge, the thespian society, dancing, martial arts, a community thrift shop, archery, church services, cooking lessons, scrapbooking classes, needlepoint classes, and a clubhouse that could be rented out for private parties. Many of these accoutrements were actually used. There was always the opportunity to participate in the management of the retirement community, to plan activities and enforce social regulations.

Whenever a Riverview resident was away on vacation, the neighbors picked up the newspapers that were delivered when the subscriber forgot to put delivery on vacation hold. Neighbors set out the traveler's trash can on Fridays, even though it would remain empty until the tourist returned home to put something in it. The ever-watchful eye of the fellow citizens assured that anyone who breached the gate security and made it to someone's front door was routed out of the community, even when these might be family members collecting mail or checking to see if houseplants needed watering.

All good systems have backup, and at Riverview, backup was in the form of the paid security guard who roamed the streets armed with the Official Residents and Guests List. It was security that assured that only residents and preapproved guests were in and everyone else was out. Some errors may have occurred because no vision test or English-language skills were required for the position.

The security guard also served as traffic cop, making certain that no motorist drove more than the speed limit of twenty miles per hour or parked on the street after dark. For too many senior residents, the speed limit was racing, and the myopic drivers hunching over their steering wheels for balance never broke five. If all residents drove the speed limit, stragglers would not be wasting what was left of everyone's precious time. If someone was behind the slower driver, it was tempting to want to pass. But the narrow streets didn't permit circumnavigating a traffic jam even if the rules might. Caution is the better part of valor, and because there is no law in nature that says, "If you can't see something, you can't hit it," it was probably best not to rush a driver who may not have passed his or her last eye exam. One would hope that when the drivers were going slowly, they might be able to notice someone with a cane or wheelchair who was inching their way across the street.

The worst traffic nightmares occurred when a motorist saw someone who needed assistance crossing the street and stopped to help. If the next car tapped the bumper of the Good Samaritan, neighbors flooded out of their homes for the excitement. They bunched up in the street to express opposing views of the accident and offered to testify for the anticipated lawsuit. When this happened, drivers were held up for hours without knowing what was happening on the road ahead of them. They would wait patiently for traffic to move and pined for the "good ole days" and the All Clear announcements of the LA SigAlerts.

Flagpoles with Old Glory waving in the breeze were proudly displayed on most Riverview Estates front yards. These were not so much an indicator of patriotism as an announcement that the resident could still keep track of holidays or the man of the house was alive and had the strength to hoist the colors (if nothing else). But this didn't mean the flags were always removed at sundown. Much of the time, the eager flag-waver would forget and was already settled in for the night by the time the sun went down.

What might appear to be contentiousness or arguing to anyone who is not old was often only the exchange of information and opinions. Those who still had their hearing might complain that the decibel level of a conversation was far too high, while those who believed they had to shout to be heard complained that others were mumbling. It all worked out with good-natured grace, because when a real insult or unkind word was expressed, the target of the complaint probably wouldn't remember it anyway.

At Riverview, people shared the same core values and choice of HMOs. This was especially important in an age when grandchildren, instead of threatening to run away from home as their grandparents did when they were kids, were selecting what part of their body to pierce or tattoo. The retirement community offered an escape from a world that was changing too fast. It was the place where people offered suggestions for the word you couldn't recall that was needed to complete your sentence. It was a place where you could judge the accomplishments of people by their possessions because the best cooks had the oldest edition of the *Betty Crocker Cookbook*. The golfers who were addicted to the game had the newest shoes, the jazziest carts, and the latest clubs, and those couples with the most young guests coming to visit were probably the ones who had married a much-younger spouse.

Conflicts happened. When those older members who couldn't put away their memories of the past regurgitated them to anyone who would listen and had worn out the listening audience, a common suggestion might be, "Get a scrapbook and put all those old ideas in it."

This was countered by the old-timer, who might emphatically state, "That's what I miss most today. Civility is no longer practiced."

So, an impasse was made, understood, and remained unsolved for as long as more than one generation resided in the retirement community. It was no different from the times when more generations lived under the same roof. The fast pace of current society is always a thorn in the side of generational relationships. If they could hang around long enough to observe cyclical change of the greater society, maybe there would be more tolerance and understanding. The generation that resented the use of plastics and saved the glass to be reused was followed by the generation that disposed of everything, but they were followed by the recyclers and green generation, which didn't even want plastics in the dumps.

◆◆◆

Roland and Alissa considered all the ups and downs of retirement-community living before they decided to purchase a home in Riverview

Estates. It wasn't just purchasing a house. It was a commitment to a lifestyle. Riverview would become the paradigm shaping their lives. They looked at several of the cookie-cutter houses, but when Roland found one with the address 11188 City Lights Drive, he was convinced this place was meant to be his regardless of the fact that there was no city to view and the only lights visible were on the golf carts of the residents who could not book a tee time during the day. Roland called the house his "Aces over Eights" and knew it would be lucky for him even though it hadn't been for Wild Bill Hickok.

The house was charming and the setting serene. The view from their bedroom and family room was of the green rolling expanse of the golf fairway that touched their backyard, and beyond that, a segment of the Mojave River flowing underground through Trickle Creek Valley.

The Michaelses were treated to the typical Riverview Estates hospitality welcome wagon when three sets of neighbors came over with pizza and drinks just as their moving van was leaving. The neighbor women invited Alissa to join them when they exercised at the gym, although this would mean they would have to change the name of their group from the Three Musketeers to the Awesome Foursome. Roland was invited to join their husbands, Buzz, Sid, and Al, for a round of golf the next morning.

"But we need time to unpack," said Roland.

"We can help Alissa get moved in," said Betty, getting assurance from the other Awesomes that they would help.

The Awesome Foursome developed into a tightly knit group of close friends confiding in each other and sharing joys with laughter and sorrows with compassionate tears. Meanwhile, the newly expanded group of golf guys developed a unique reputation throughout Riverview. Roland was soon identified for his colorful language on the links that came to be known as his morning prayers. Buzz was the bag man, not for the clubs, but for holding the bets for this group of guys whose genial wagers were no threat to the economy of Las Vegas.

Holidays were a time for all the Riverview residents to gather for planned activities in the clubhouse. It was an opportunity to display culinary skills, and those who didn't have any were encouraged to bring deviled eggs or bring the same dish as the prior year and hope that no one remembered…or swing by the market to pick up some takeout. When the Easter potluck was announced, the Awesome Foursome thought it would be fun to wear colorful, flowery blouses instead of the traditional Easter bonnets. The idea caught on and spread like wildfire, probably due to the gossip-line expert, Sid Revere. Sid knew the power of his words. All he had to do was to ask any lady at Riverview, "Are you wearing a flowered blouse to the potluck?" and the rest was history, as all women would show up dressed according to the latest gossip.

Betty was best at using the velvet-glove treatment. She claimed to have learned how to do this by listening to politicians. During the Easter potluck, she found a way to use the treatment on one of the ladies in Riverview who was easy to intimidate. Ida was shy, modest, and frugal. But for the Easter potluck, she had gone out of her way to look good. She was sporting a new hairstyle and was wearing a flattering tunic patterned with soft flowers in impressionist mood on the order of Monet. Betty couldn't let Ida take all the attention.

"I love those colors. They are so much prettier than the drab browns you usually wear," said Betty, softening Ida up before placing the knife in her back. Ida's smile faded into humiliation. When Betty moved away, Ida whispered to her husband to take her home.

Roland had observed the entire scene, and he was outraged. When they returned home Roland asked, "I'd like to know what Betty is trying to prove, Alissa—how clever she is or how cruel she can be."

Alissa hadn't seen the exchange between Betty and Ida, and Betty was her best friend. "Why are you so upset with Betty?" she asked.

"She doesn't deserve to be your girlfriend. She took all the energy out of Ida. She says something nice, and as soon as the defenses are down, she comes in with a knockout punch. That's not the way you treat people."

"Look who's talking about the proper way to treat people. You went to finishing school?"

"Look, Alissa. If I have something critical to say, I say it. I don't pretend to be something I'm not."

"That's your problem, Roland. It's not what you say; it's how you say it. You intimidate people. Betty does not."

"No, but she leaves them a bloody mess. She sets traps, snares them in, and eats them alive."

"So it's better to come into a situation with a hostile, confrontational mood?"

"I don't do that."

"You do it to me."

"I tell you how I feel. I don't have your polish, but my mind is not deteriorated, and my words are true."

"Roland, you need to learn finesse. Be more selective in your choice of words, watch your tone, and lay off the beer. If you don't, you will lose your audience."

"I don't need an audience," he said, heading to the fridge for another bottle.

◆ ◆ ◆

Estelle Reynolds, one of the women in the development, was known for writing letters to the editor of the local newspaper. Her latest complaint was with the Valley Estates Water Company. The whole town had received flyers from the water company in their monthly bills. The flyers said: "We are having drought conditions. Water is getting scarcer. It's up to each and every resident to help us conserve water. Valley Estates Water Company will pay up to fifty cents per square foot for all grass removed. Call today for an estimate of what our Cash for Grass program will provide you and for ideas on how to beautify your landscaping with drought-resistant plants and decorative rocks."

Homeowners who were encouraged by the idea of saving money spent a fortune on this suggestion. They were quick to participate in the Cash for Grass program, and within months the residents of Trickle Creek Development watched their lawns fade from lush green to tans and browns natural to the native desert. An entire new industry arose as another fell.

There was no longer a demand for bug spray, lawn mowers, seed, fertilizer, and flowering plants. In their place, hardware stores set up displays of resin statuary, artificial boulders featuring a standard secret place to hide the house key, and whimsical garden lights powered by short-lived solar batteries or tripping hazards from the electric cords.

The new industries that were finding their way into town hired clerks whose only skill was to read the bar code on the product. The nursery worker who had been knowledgeable about the care and selection of plants was no longer needed and faded out of view just like the old soldiers who do not die (or perhaps they joined the welfare rolls to survive).

An abundance of replicas of Greek and Roman statuary sprouted up on places that once held grass, trees, and flowers. Dogs in the neighborhood were psychosocially challenged, looking for a place to pee. Fountains appeared on the yards of people who were convinced that the water was recycled and therefore not wasted. No one warned them that the hot desert climate, made even hotter with the loss of growing plants, would evaporate the water so quickly. The new look in fountains was white calcification where water used to be.

Within six months of this major makeover that turned an inviting, restful garden spot into a pile of rocks, a new flyer came with the water bill.

Those who had worked hard to make sure they consumed less water than they had used at this time last year were surprised to discover that they were fined a low-usage fee. When the fee was compared with others, they found that it matched the increase in the bills for those who consumed more water than they used at this time last year, and they were now in tier three and paying more per gallon.

It was at this point that Estelle had had enough of the water-conservation scheme. She composed a sign to place on her newly acquired statuette of *Venus De Milo*. It read: "Victim of the Valley Estates Water Company. Her arms were lost to pay the low-usage fee. Another year of this, and she will lose her legs as well."

◆ ◆ ◆

Every village has an idiot. At Riverview, it was Pete Cox. Pete's gift was to say things that made folks uncomfortable. No matter what the occasion, Pete would find a way to make suggestive remarks in a manner that, if the person objected, Pete would point out that any smut was only in their mind and not what he intended. The day of the Easter potluck, Pete complimented the Awesome Foursome on their colorful shirts.

"Well, ladies, I want you know I'm wearing flowers, too," he said, raising his shirt so they would see the top of his underwear.

Alissa fanned her face as if she was cooling herself. "Be still my heart," she said quietly as the rest of the ladies at the table burst into laughter.

Pete had met his match. He didn't know if flashing his underwear was igniting her passion or if Alissa was having a hot flash. Either way, his face turned red, and he retreated to the safety of the table where his wife was patiently waiting.

◆ ◆ ◆

There is more to golf than a group of guys getting together to play. It's a culture. At Riverview, it was celebrated with a golf-cart parade on July 4th and Christmas. All neighbors along the parade route placed folding chairs on their miniature front lawns and settled in for a morning of fun, food, and camaraderie. One Christmas, when Roland was asked to lead the parade as Santa Claus, Sid's granddaughter from his first marriage was also on the lead cart as Santa's helper. She was dressed as an elf and handed out candy canes from a colorful basket created by Sid's wife, Donna.

When the parade was over, Santa's elf ran to Alissa to tell her a secret. "That's not the real Santa Claus, Alissa. That's your Roland."

"Oh, so it is. I'm glad you are keeping this secret. We wouldn't want to spoil it for the other children."

"I'm good at keeping secrets," she said proudly.

The wealthiest couples in Riverview, according to Alissa, were the ones whose children stayed overnight so that young grandchildren were in the community long enough for the neighbors to enjoy their antics and laughter.

Riverview didn't change the people who came into it; it allowed new groups of people to form and rearrange themselves to find other people whose quirks were compatible with their own or at least interesting to explore. Retirement communities are a mosaic of people. It would be nice to think that when they encountered and observed the anomalies of their new companions, they might do so with love, acceptance, and understanding. The idea of Riverview was a good one. But it was, after all, only a setting. Whether it served the needs of all its residents or whether it served the needs of any of its residents was ultimately dependent upon the interaction of the people who chose to live there. And the Michaelses hoped their idiosyncrasies would fit into the mix. Having the Beignets next door proved a major hurdle.

◆ ◆ ◆

"I can't find any of the 'what's-this-here' sauce," said Roland, sitting down to his first dinner in their new home.

"Would that be Worcestershire, dear?" asked Alissa.

"Yeah, there is none in the pantry or the fridge. The meat needs to be kicked up a notch."

"I'll run to the store and get some."

"Make it fast."

Alissa grabbed her purse and made a beeline for the garage. No sooner had the garage door opened than the Beignet's four-year-old lavender-blue Cadillac appeared in Alissa's rearview mirror. Coco was at the wheel.

Alissa started the engine, waiting for Coco to pass before setting the car in reverse gear. Coco decided it was time to chat. Oblivious to the obvious, Coco stopped her car, blocking the Michaelses' driveway, rolled down the window, and started yelling to Alissa.

"Boy, you won't believe what happened in church. Remember Elizabeth? She wore the most ***stupid-looking*** hat. She must have taken it off a lamp. I couldn't see past it. She was sitting there in front of me for the whole service. Sometimes she talked to her husband, and I couldn't hear a word she was saying. How rude. She should have sat in the back."

"Hi, Coco. I'm in a hurry. See you later, dear. You can tell me all about it then."

Coco didn't miss a beat. "So now I couldn't see anything, and she was talking so softly I couldn't hear anything. She's not very considerate."

Alissa got out of her car to walk over to Coco. "I need to go to Mirage Market to pick up something for Roland."

"I never go to Mirage; I only go to major chains for groceries. You never know how long produce can be sitting around in these little markets. I like everything fresh. You're spending way too much money, Alissa, and they don't always take coupons. I don't have all the money you have. I have to live on a tight budget. I do the best I can. When I come home from church, I clip coupons and go shopping the next day. Not everyone is as extravagant as you are."

"I only need one item, and I'm in a hurry."

"Well, why didn't you say something, instead of just standing here talking? I'll give you a lift to the market. You know I like to help neighbors. It's the Christian thing to do."

Alissa bit her tongue. The tiresome mechanics of her neighbor's droning on and on felt to Alissa as if she was stuck in the dentist's chair waiting for the pain to stop. "Please, oh please," thought Alissa, "let my Novocain work. I'm not into self-flagellation."

Coco was still talking. Alissa walked back to her car and turned off the engine. She pressed the remote to lower the garage door and made a dash toward the lavender limo before the door closed.

At the end of the block, Coco announced that she didn't know the way.

"Continue straight down this road, and make a left when you get to Oasis Avenue."

Coco was going too fast to turn at Oasis.

Alissa said, "It's coming up now, Coco. You'll need to make a left."

Coco slammed on the brakes and jerked the wheel to the left, screeching into the busy intersection. She regained control, but was now facing oncoming traffic as she pressed on the accelerator.

Alissa screamed, "You're on the wrong side of the road." The car came to a full stop, but only after Coco had completely lost control. They were sitting in a vehicle perpendicular to two lanes of traffic. Brakes were squealing, and luckily all oncoming automobiles were able to screech to a halt.

"Don't yell, Alissa. That's what causes accidents."

◆ ◆ ◆

Roland had agreed to leave the three acres in god's country for the close community of rules and regulations that he neither admired nor desired. He had been the captain of his own ship, where he often had as his kingdom the expanse of ocean as far as he could see. When landlocked, he moved to Mariposa, where he loved the freedom and nonconformity it offered. Now he had moved to Riverview for Alissa's sake, so she could have the benefit of the social interaction she desired. She was very happy at Riverview, but the move didn't work out as well for the independent, opinionated, rough-around-the-edges Roland. He felt cramped and hemmed in.

The garage was too small for his woodworking equipment, so he solved the problem with his typical pragmatism. He worked with the garage door open. The infraction was reported to the board of directors. It was clear from the written word of the Covenants, Codes, and Restrictions (CC&Rs) that residents were not allowed to leave garage doors open unless they were in the process of moving a car, an approved pickup truck, or a golf cart in or out of the garage. This was written in chapter 79, page 322, in the subsection titled "Violations."

The committee graciously brought the matter informally to Roland before they threatened to bring out the big guns and impose the hefty fees should he not comply. Roland agreed to heed their warning, but he was a big man, and the garage was full of the boxes they had not yet unpacked. There are three kinds of garbage people collect: the kind you throw away when you move, the kind you move with you, and the kind you throw away ten years later when you realize you didn't need it after all. These boxes contained garbage that was waiting on the ten-year plan from Alissa's move to Mariposa. Having the garage door closed as he worked meant he would have difficulty moving around the table saw, and he would not benefit from the illumination of the sunlight.

One day after the Michaelses had been living in their new home only for three weeks, while Roland was busy in the closed garage making a magazine rack for the bathroom, he slipped. He caught his fall by grabbing the saw, but in so doing, the end of his middle finger was severed.

Roland walked into the house, holding his hand tightly to try to stem the profusion of blood. "Call 911," he calmly said to Alissa.

When the ambulance arrived, several neighbors rushed over to see if they could be of assistance. A medevac helicopter landed at the far end of the development, where open land had been cleared for the next section of houses to be constructed to sell to the next batch of seniors, the baby boomers. The paramedics assisted Roland into the ambulance for his ride to the helicopter while one of the neighbors diligently searched for the digit Roland had removed from his body, hoping he would find it in time for it to be sewn back on.

Roland and the amputated piece of finger were evacuated to the nearest trauma hospital sixty miles away over the west range of the San Bernardino Mountains. When Alissa caught up with Roland at the hospital, he was sitting up in bed, holding up his hand with half the middle finger missing.

"I've been emasculated," he said. "Now I will only be able to flip people off halfway when I give them the finger."

Had they still been living in Mariposa when Roland had had his emergency, there would not have been the support of the neighbors to help, the paramedics would not have arrived so quickly, and it's probable that Roland would have lost a lot more blood before he received medical assistance. Perhaps he would have lost too much. On the other hand, the paradox was that in Mariposa, Roland would not have had an accident in the dark, crowded confines of a garage with a door that could not be opened because the rules did not allow it. He would have the entire property to set up a saw anywhere his network of extension cords could reach.

From that day forward, whenever Roland entered a restaurant with Alissa and was asked how many people were in the party, Roland would hold up his index and middle finger and say, "One and a half, please."

Losing half of one of his fingers did not diminish Roland's verbal capability to curse. These colorful expressions were especially offensive to Coco Beignet, whose moral standards did not include tolerating profanity from a next-door neighbor. The accident also did not diminish Roland's natural ability to look life directly in the face and laugh.

◆ ◆ ◆

Alissa tried very hard to make friends with the Beignets. It was prudent to be cordial with them. In Mariposa, the only neighbors who had stopped in to visit were the Native American kids who enjoyed watching her paint. Alissa needed more than that. Even though it did not appear that she and Roland had anything in common with the Beignets, she wanted to try to make friends. Russ Beignet played golf, but he was much better at it than Roland, so Alissa was concerned that Russ would not be tolerant of Roland's amateurishness on the golf course or his lack of social finesse. But guys tend to be able to work out those kinds of things, so she felt that if she could make friends with Coco, everything would be just fine.

The Beignets were the flip side of the Michaelses. Russ was soft-spoken and seemed shy. His conversation was trite and without wit or animation. He was rather like an old basset hound, looking as if he was full of self-pity. He had long ago stopped trying to please Coco and had resigned himself to the role of chauffeur, obediently taking her to the next place of embarrassing encounter. He survived by mentally blocking out entire parts of her conversation. It had become too arduous to listen, and as a result, he could barely participate in any socializing requiring a give-and-take conversation. It was the autumn of his life, and the last of the brown, withered leaves hung tenuously onto the skeletal remains of what had once been a fine, manly oak.

Coco was taller than her husband, and with her ponderous size, she outweighed him twice over. Where most women had cleavage, Coco had spillage. Her cups *runneth over*, and not with love. Although Russ appeared to be totally devoted to her, she was intolerant, bossy, loud, opinionated, critical, and domineering. Other than that, she meant well and probably had been nice at some point in her life. For now, her personality was like an overly carbonated diet drink that left her companions with a slight sour aftertaste. Somehow, she always managed to dominate the conversation and showed herself to be the epitome of social anthrax–the woman with her foot in her mouth.

Alissa's first impression of their neighbors was to connect them visually with Rosanne Barr and Art Carney. Roland didn't like Alissa's habit of describing people as movie stars, but he had his own preconceived ideas that also needed more objective evaluation. He thought Russ was sneaky rather than shy. He had seen Russ slip into their backyard to take a package of cigarettes that had been left on the patio by one of their houseguests.

Alissa invited the Beignets over for a barbecue on their patio. It was an unusually warm day, and rotund Coco was dabbing her makeup with a handkerchief. "You know the climate has a lot to do with the temperature," she said, making an excuse for her discomfort.

"That was one of your more profound thoughts, Coco," said Roland, covering the smirk he wanted to hide.

No sooner had the Beignets entered the living room when Roland upset Coco.

"That's an interesting picture," said Coco, spotting the newest of Alissa's paintings on the wall. She stared at it, trying very hard to make meaning out of the double helix painted against the turquoise background.

"I call it the family tree," said Alissa.

"But it's not a tree," remarked Coco. "It looks like the pearls on a necklace I own."

"You're right," said Roland. "Let's just call it the family jewels."

Coco turned red. Roland moved to the backyard, leaving Coco hiding behind her husband, expecting protection. She gathered her composure reemerging as an art critic.

"Do you find your paintings have similar themes, Alissa?" asked Coco, glancing at several. "I find them rather *rediddit.*"

Alissa looked confused.

"I think she means *redundant,*" said Russ, nodding his head in agreement.

Coco was annoyed. "Don't bother to explain anything to these people. I can speak for myself. I meant what I said. I know what I like in art, and this isn't it."

Roland returned to invite them outside to eat and arrived in the middle of the insults. His dander was up. He would not allow anyone to be critical of Alissa.

"Perhaps in Coco's case, the painting would be redundant," he said as he smiled. "That is, if they all look the same to her. Dinner is served. We will gather in the patio, as we have no gallery level."

Alissa escorted the Beignets to the patio, where Coco made a beeline to do a munch attack at the potato chips and dip on the table. She plopped down before she was invited to take a seat, and while she was seated, with the excess bulges of her *overstated* body, she looked as if her head was stacked on three inner tubes tucked away under her triple-plus-size muumuu. The bottom tube parked on the chair was her abdomen filling out her size-ten panties while oozing over her thighs. The center was the fat roll at her tummy line finding space to squeeze in between her abdomen and boobs. And the top tube, was her bust line, which almost matched in girth the two lower tubby-tube rolls.

Coco leaned forward for another handful of chips, looking like a roly-poly clown toy with a magnet to keep it upright. Unfortunately, there was no magnet to keep Coco from toppling over. She lost her center of gravity, upsetting the table, and the bowl of condiments fell to the ground.

"I'll get them," she said as soon as she had stuffed the handful of chips she was still clutching into her mouth. But when she leaned to the side to pick up the bowl of condiments, the leg of the patio chair creaked and then snapped in two.

Roland was quick. He lunged to help Coco, luckily avoiding the rolling olives on the floor. He reached her as the chair totally abdicated its supporting role and she smashed onto the wooden deck in an unfortunately ugly heap.

Alissa watched in freeze-frame, her mouth open in astonishment, staring at a mishap that looked as if it would result in a sprained back for Roland or a broken arm or twisted ankle for Coco.

"Are you all right?" she called out in alarm.

Coco was a limp lump of lard sprawled on the patio deck, stuffed between the legs of the table and resting in the arms of Roland, who had successfully broken her fall. Roland's face was red from exertion. He was puffing. He looked as if he was in pain, but he did not complain. He rose to his knees and grabbed Coco under her arms, hoping he could leverage her weight so that he could help her to her feet. He was successful.

"Allow me to weigh-in on this," said Alissa. She helped by pushing, and in a matter of moments, the two of them had Coco standing upright, although she didn't seem seaworthy. Her knees quivered as if they might buckle at any time. Coco must not have been hurt because she seemed oblivious to the disaster she caused. She was soon stuffing her face again; this time it was the carrot sticks and cream-cheese dip that still remained on the tabletop.

She munched, strolled the patio to check out the decor, and then went back for more to eat. Then she strolled some more, perusing the layout of the Michaelses' patio as if she were measuring it for drapes. She wasn't talking, not even to thank Roland for breaking her fall or Alissa for collecting the olives that had dispersed.

◆ ◆ ◆

Russ had not seen any of this. At least, it appeared that he had not seen it. Actually, he was so accustomed to Coco breaking furniture that he was past noticing. He was standing at the end of the patio nearest his house with his back to the others, totally absorbed in watching the beautiful sunset. He moved slightly onto the golf course, inadvertently triggering the security lights that were installed to warn the residents of someone approaching their property. It was hard to believe he had not heard his wife grunt or the chair crack when she fell, but he was elderly and perhaps a little hard of hearing...although not so hard of hearing that he missed the call from the golf course.

"Hey, turn off that goddamn light. You're blinding my shot," said one of the passing golfers.

"Don't tell me, Roland, that those lights are part of the community development? I'll bet you put those lights up yourself," said Coco.

"Russ, if you will join us again on the patio, they will go out so the golfers can play," said Alissa.

"Well, we don't have security lights, so you must have installed them on your own," said Coco.

"I can explain that, dearie," said Russ, hoping his wife would let him get a word into the conversation. "It was the prior owners who put in the extra lighting, not the Michaelses."

"Well, how come we can't have any?" asked Coco.

"Why would you want them?" asked Roland. "I can see all kinds of problems with these lights. You can see how they blind the golfers. So what's next? They miss a shot because of the light and the ball goes through your window. Now you expect me to pay for it because it was my light that caused the accident. I don't like them. The golfers don't like them. You are the only one who wants to have them. I'll tell you what, Coco. Tomorrow morning, I will take down my lights and bring them over to your house. You can have them."

"Thank you. I would like that," said Coco. "Russ can put them up for me."

"Is that all right with you, Russ?" asked Alissa.

Coco was outraged. *How dare Alissa question what she had just arranged?* She was determined to put this woman in her place. "You should mind your own business. I know how to keep a husband. I've heard that's more than can be said about you. Your theory of domestic bliss must be 'out with the old and in with the new.'"

"What you describe sounds more like domestic blitz if you ask me," said Alissa wondering what other gossip about her was being circulated in the community. She refused to be defensive. "More than that, Coco, I've learned how to save attorneys' fees. I use the Erasermate pen on marriage licenses to substitute the name of my next spouse."

Russ was avoiding the women's cattiness. He was still feeling the effects of being henpecked, barely able to hold up his head. There he was again, being ordered by his wife to do something that he didn't want to do. He momentarily forgot his position and spoke impulsively. A pent-up flow of words came tumbling out of his mouth.

"Do you like living here on the desert, Alissa? Some people think it's too dry. I kind of like the Joshua trees, but some people don't like them. Do you like them? A lot of people are afraid of the snakes, but I've never seen one, have you? Pete was bitten by a black widow spider once, but he got to the hospital in time. Are you afraid of spiders? Some people think the medical care isn't good here, but we've never had any problems. Do you have a doctor? We did have trouble..."

Alissa lost track of his questions and thought she had better stop his file dump. "I do like the desert," she said. "I just wish it weren't so windy. Roland says I won't need a face peel living here. The wind and the sun will take care of that for me. But I do like the Joshua trees. Did you know they grow both here and in Israel?"

"We can't afford to go to Europe," said Coco.

"Since when is Israel in Europe?" asked Roland.

"You know, honey, Israel Moskowitz. I think he moved to Europe after the Six-Day War," said Alissa enjoying her pun.

"Honey, we did go to France once. Don't you remember?" asked Russ.

"Remember? Yes, I remember. I remember how the neighbors treated us when we came back and I tried to give the neighborhood a little culture."

"Culture, is that what you call it?" said Roland. "You haven't heard about this one, Alissa. The architectural committee was called in when Coco's neighbors complained about the statue on her front lawn."

"You're not going to tell me it was a nude, are you?" asked Alissa.

Coco was miffed. "You haven't got any culture, either. It was a one-fifth size replica of Rodin's *The Thinker*. I'm still angry about what the Smiths' grandchildren did. I still haven't spoken to them."

"What did the Smiths' grandchildren do?" asked Alissa.

"They TPed it, of course. What do you think a couple of teenagers would do to a life-size statue of a man sitting in that position on a stool?" said Roland.

"I thought the statue was very nice," replied Russ. Russ was desperate to save face. He couldn't let Alissa and Roland know how little value his opinions had in his marriage and how much Coco henpecked him for not being a better provider. The only way he could think of to show strength was to find something else about his new neighbors to criticize.

◆◆◆

"How did you get away with that?" he asked, pointing at the half wall between their houses.

Roland had returned to the barbecue, where the steaks were starting to smoke. He was as fuming hot as the charcoal. Although he hated the light with the motion detector, he hated the wall between their properties, but most of all, he was annoyed that Russ was being *picky*.

"I didn't get away with a dammed thing," said Roland, slapping a steak onto a plate and motioning for Russ to sit down and eat it. "That wall was here when we bought the house."

"We never noticed it before. You must be mistaken," whined Coco, stepping up to the wall to estimate its height. "It's more than three feet tall. That's not allowed."

"How could you not notice it?" asked Alissa, astonished at their continuing rudeness. "You must be able to see that wall from your patio."

"Whoa," said Russ, "take it easy. You're not calling my wife a liar, are you?"

Alissa was stunned. Now they were both picking on her. Alissa had inadvertently walked into a hornets' nest. She didn't know what to say. She sank into the chaise longue and stared at the couple who were living so close to their house she could reach out and touch them if they both had their windows open. She wondered how she could be on neighborly terms with them or why she had ever thought she wanted to be.

Coco made another assault on the food. She had long ago lost the Battle of the Bulge and stood next to Roland, extending her plate for some of the sweet corn that was roasting on the grill. Her expression said it all. She could get away with anything. She was allowed to be pushy. She could create an uproar and make inciting comments, and her husband would condone all her rude behavior with a complicit smile. Coco took her plate of sweet corn to the table and sat down next to Russ.

"You forgot to pray," she said, directing her condemnation to the man of the house.

"But you've already started eating," said Alissa. "We didn't know that you wanted us to say a table prayer."

Roland had deep spiritual convictions, but he was private about expressing them. He saw through Coco's self-righteous facade and baited her. "I don't know any prayers."

"That's okay," said Coco. "I'll pray for you." Coco mumbled something inaudible while Alissa, Russ, and Roland remained silent in respect for the moment. But when Coco raised her voice as if this was an appeal to the Almighty from a prophet of old and ended her supplication with "and please, God, help our new neighbors to fit in to our little community. Help them to understand the rules so that they may learn to live in harmony with us," Roland became infuriated.

"Get Coco a drink, Alissa," said Roland as soon as the "amen" provided him an opportunity to speak. He wanted Coco to stop trying to manipulate God into doing her will. God didn't need any directions from Coco Beignet. If she thought she was practicing the will of God, she was doing it without a license.

"I don't drink," said Coco, smiling.

"I would never have guessed," replied Roland, placing a steak on her plate and smiling with a knowing expression that said, "You just drive others to..."

Alissa went into the kitchen, placed the six-pack of Heck's Beer in the refrigerator, and made a pitcher of iced tea. While she was gone, Roland joined his guests at the table.

Being new to the community, Roland and Alissa did not know that eating corn on the cob was a problem for some members. This was the land of bridgework—but not the kind that came with federal infrastructure funding. Coco was having trouble eating hers. She didn't really want to put her teeth into the corn, but it smelled so delicious, especially after she had slathered it with gobs of butter. The butter had smeared off her lipstick and was dripping down her chin, running over the folds in her neck and landing on her ample bosom.

Alissa had returned to the three on the patio in time to see Coco hiding her mouth behind a napkin to remove her dentures so she could clear the kernels from her mouth. Roland was watching with eyebrows raised. He motioned to Alissa that he wanted to say something to her. "Don't try to butter her up," he said, whispering. "She's doing a good enough job on her own."

Coco was still fixated on the offending wall. "It isn't fair to the others. None of the rest of us has a wall on our patio," she mumbled. "Your wall keeps your cushions from being carried away by the wind. The rest of us have things that might blow away, too." She stuffed her hand into the pocket of her muumuu and, with considerable effort and fidgeting, pulled out a tape measure that she happened to have brought with her.

She waddled to the wall, calling for Russ to come over and help her measure it. Russ obediently held the end of the tape at the bottom of the wall while Coco stretched it to the top.

"See?" she announced with glee. "I was right. It's three feet and five inches. That's not allowed in our CC&Rs."

"Do you realize how stupid that is?" replied Roland.

Coco gasped. Russ did not come to her defense this time. He meekly returned to his meal, holding his head so low that the steak sauce was in danger of being painted onto the tip of his nose. He knew in his heart that Roland was right, but he would not be able to admit that, especially in front of Coco. He was hiding out in a plate of barbequed steak rather than be skewered by his wife. The only thing Russ added to this confrontation was the blush of embarrassment on his face.

Roland went into the kitchen to cool his temper.

"Roland, are you feeling poorly?" called Coco. "I've heard from your friends that you often have an upset stomach. You know, these episodes might be messages from the Lord."

He returned with the six-pack of Heck's. "That's interesting, Coco. I didn't realize the Lord was communing with me through my belly.

"I realize that both of you are newcomers and haven't learned our ways," said Coco. But I feel it I incumbent upon me to tell you that we don't drink beer here. We have wine-tasting parties."

I don't drink wine –not even at communion. I don't care about wine-tasting parties and if I'm in a good mood, perhaps he might even put up with your whine. I like beer, and that's what we're serving."

Roland opened two cans, one for Alissa and one for himself.

"I'll take one, too," suggested Russ, trying to keep on good terms with what might become a future golf partner. But he couldn't leave the gesture there with Coco watching. To impress her by displaying a level of snobbery almost equal to hers, he added, "But it would be nicer if I could have it in a frosted pilsner glass. I've been taught that it is not proper manners to drink from a can."

Alissa was giggling. He must like the foam on his face, she thought. If he thinks I am going to pour it for him without a head, he has another think coming. She quickly left the patio before she burst into laughter in front of them. Alissa was amused by a man who would not drink beer from a can because he thought it was low class but ignored the offensiveness of his wife that was completely boorish. Alissa wished she had a wide-mouthed beer mug that she could give Russ so he could really froth at the mouth, but they had gotten rid of their collection when they moved from Mariposa. She would have loved to walk back to the patio with a tray laden with sloshing beer mugs the way the Bavarian barmaids serve guests at the Oktoberfest. That thought amused her, but she wasn't able to play it out. She returned to the patio with two water glasses and another can of beer.

"I've used all my glasses for milk, and they are spoiled for serving beer. That won't give you a good head. Sorry. And this beer wasn't put back into the fridge, so it's not as cold as it should be, but maybe you would like your beer on the rocks," she said, setting down two glasses, one with ice cubes. "That way, you'll know I'm serving it to you cold."

Coco had a prissy look on her fat face. She didn't catch the insult and thought Alissa was stupid. Coco might be a teetotaler, but she knew enough about beer to know that no one drinks it over ice.

Roland wanted to pick up his wife and give her a bear hug. He was as fast as Alissa. Roland assisted with his wife's advantage by continuing with the issue of the wall. They were enjoying going head on against the Beignets.

"Let's ignore the fact that my privacy wall serves your interests as well as mine. Your privacy will not be disturbed by the guests Alissa and I plan to invite to our home, and we will be relieved that because of this wall, you two won't have the distasteful experience of peering at us through your window to see us drinking beer out of cans."

Coco got up from her chair. "We'll be leaving now."

"But you haven't had dessert," pleaded Alissa, not wanting the fun to stop. "I have some sorbet churning in the electric ice-cream maker. You must stay a little longer."

"Yeah, no need to rush. We have some coffee brewing. Stay a little longer. Russ. Let me get an ashtray for you," said Roland, carefully watching Russ's reaction. "You might like to light up a cigarette with your coffee."

Russ laughed. "Not me. I don't smoke. Coco is allergic to smoke. She can smell it a mile away. She has such a nose for cigarettes. Last week I had to—"

"You were saying?" said Roland, smiling.

"Nothing," said Russ. "Coco, you wanted to leave. Let's go."

It was futile for Alissa to negotiate with the red-haired hothead who died her roots black. Coco had written the Michaelses off her list of desirable contacts, and now she would be leaving with only a partially successful turf war. She had not convinced the Michaelses to remove a wall just because she and Russ did not have one at their house. However, she was looking forward to the delivery of the lights to her house the following day. Roland's language and drinking beer from a can was too uncouth for Coco. She would have a plethora of gossip to disseminate. She would surely be omitting the parts about her falling on her derrière, breaking the furniture, stuffing her mouth with food, and insulting her hosts.

"We really do need to leave," said Russ, looking at his watch. "I'm expecting an important call from Pete Cox at seven thirty."

"Are you going to be on the links tomorrow?" asked Roland, thankful that his guests were leaving and hoping he would not be running into Russ on the golf course.

"Russ has to help me tomorrow," said Coco. "Our windows need to be washed now that we will have a light on the patio."

◆ ◆ ◆

"What's her problem?" asked Alissa as she and Roland returned to the patio for a double-sized bowl of sorbet. "Do you think she needs to wash her windows so she can spy on us better?"

"I think she needs to have her windows washed so she can have something to keep her husband under her thumb with. She is a fanatic," said Roland. "Can't you hear the drums in the marching band? Everyone has to keep in step. She is scary. Don't try to placate her, Alissa. It will come to no good. She will dominate you and twist everything to her advantage if you give her the opportunity."

"I know I won't serve corn on the cob to her again," said Alissa. "Poor Russ—did you notice how she intimidates him?"

"Yeah, makes you wonder what she has on him. But don't feel sorry for him. He's as much a part of the problem as she is. Alissa, do you remember when the package of cigarettes disappeared from the patio? I saw Russ take it that day. I thought it was because he needed a smoke. But guess what? Now we know he wanted to stop smoking. He was only being Coco's errand boy that day because she could smell the smoke from our patio."

"Do you still want him for a golf partner?"

"Are you kidding? If he can steal cigarettes from his neighbor's property, he can fudge his golf score. There are lots of other guys here to play golf with. I won't miss anything by not playing with him. So anyway, it's still early, Alissa, and we no longer have plans for the evening. What do you think? Should we take in a movie tonight?"

"Hope they are showing a comedy," said Alissa, knowing that Roland's invitation would apply to only the free single-feature movie showing at the clubhouse.

TWENTY

Washington Slept Here

It wasn't that Roland was what you would call a cheap date. It was just that he came from a poor, large Catholic family and grew up with only the bare necessities of life. He wasn't accustomed to spending money. That was many years ago, and he had ultimately overcome poverty and become a professional adult—he would even wear a suit if the occasion required it. But he never carried more than a twenty in his billfold.

Let's rephrase that. Roland was a cheap date. In fact, Roland was such a tightwad that he would not consider dining out if the total tab was expected to be more than fifteen dollars. In most towns, that would be a problem. But it worked in Joshua Heights, where the desert's top-of-the-line restaurants were the chain of clones lined up along Ranch Road, a twenty-minute drive from the retirement community. Joshua Heights had Gigi's, Applewhite's, Chippie's, South of the Mason-Dixon Line, Johnny Caruso's, The Olive Pit, Road Rage, and Baja Hash. A careful scan of the right side of the menu could get dinner for two for under fifteen dollars, but only if you remembered to bring the coupon.

A slight distance was developing in their marriage, and Alissa was concerned. She used Valentine's Day as an excuse to persuade Roland to try out Maison Chan-Cheng, the dinner house secluded in the parking lot behind Mocca's. The Maison touted fine French-Chinese cuisine. It was an acculturated Chinese restaurant known to have knives in the place settings without special request. With Roland being French Canadian, Alissa thought she would deemphasize the Chinese part and get him into the place at midday, when they could order from the less-expensive luncheon menu. He was willing to try her suggestion because he knew Alissa would not ask him to take her to a restaurant where he would be embarrassed by having to walk out without being served. This was going to be a Valentine's Day date, and Roland agreed to meet her there.

Alissa dressed with care, choosing a snugly fitting white sweater that buttoned at the neck and powder-pink, loosely flowing, shantung slacks. Posing in front of her full-length mirror, she carefully evaluated her appearance and considered how many of the pearl buttons on the sweater she should leave open. She wanted a look that would encourage cupid.

It wouldn't do to leave all five buttoned up, because it made her look top-heavy. She leaned over to slip on silver high-heeled sandals. That twisting caused all the buttons to pop open. It was an interesting look. Perhaps they should stay open. She evaluated this change.

It wasn't quite right; too much cleavage showed. It was too risqué for a luncheon date with her husband. She experimented with various button options and settled on leaving four open and the bottom one closed. That was the right amount of provocation. She was in a teasing mood today and wanted Roland to notice how nice she looked. Perhaps he would be inspired to take her away on a romantic weekend. She backed her car out of the driveway to meet Roland, who had taken his car in for a tune-up that morning.

Maison Chan-Cheng sent out mixed signals. On one hand, the windows, covered with dark, translucent shades, gave an aura of secrecy and intrigue. It wasn't as dark as those opium dens from 1930s Charlie Chan movies; it was more suggestive of a place you would go to have a secret rendezvous. That's how Alissa had described it to him. Roland was intrigued with the idea of a rendezvous. That was a French word he was very familiar with. Roland was one sexy hunk of a healthy Frenchman and easy to arouse. Prospects for the weekend were going to be good.

On the other hand, Maison Chan-Cheng was one of those places where the clatter from yuppies and boomers with cell phones interrupted the ambiance. In that respect, it was like a Starbucks but with white tablecloths and a tropical fish tank. Young couples dining at the same table were conducting business by phone with someone at a distance. One wondered if they were enjoying the fine food or the company of the person dining with them. No one seemed to mind the noise distraction, except for Alissa on that particular Friday afternoon.

When Roland arrived, he found her seated in the restaurant waiting area on the bench adjacent to the cobalt-blue Chinese lion.

"Did you need protection?" he asked. He put his hand into the gaping mouth of the ceramic lion. "It's a little tame, isn't it?"

Alissa rose to enter the restaurant, smiling at the scene of Roland with his hand in the lion's mouth. Roland made a sound like a ferocious lion's roar.

Alissa jumped. Roland laughed.

Alissa laughed too. "You remind me of *Roman Holiday*," she said.

"Did you see that movie, too? Gregory Peck, 1953."

"I loved that movie," replied Alissa, following the maître d' to a table in a darkened corner.

Alissa never in a million years expected Roland to pick up his cell phone. It happened quite suddenly, between the time they ordered and the time when the food was presented. He picked up his phone even though his date was showing a hint of breast. He did it when the waitress was removing one course to make room for the next, during the moment when Alissa wiggled in the way she knew would make the fifth pearl button pop open. Roland blew it. This was the moment when she wanted to initiate a romantic encounter. That was when he picked up his phone.

He totally missed the cues she gave him, and Alissa was ever so clever in delivering her offer. She would never be crude or obvious. But if he would put the phone down and look at her, he surely would notice how voluptuous her body was in that tight white sweater.

She wasn't getting his attention, so she stage-whispered to the lady dining at the next table. Alissa wanted Roland to hear what she said and act on the suggestion. He was still on the phone waiting for someone to answer.

The lady was dining with a gentleman who did not seem to care that his companion had had too many facelifts. She was the only other woman in the place over fifty, and she was wearing a dress. It wasn't one of those tailored, dress-for-success numbers designed for business. The dress was very flattering and feminine with ruffles hiding her throat. Alissa sensed that this woman was someone who would empathize with her dilemma. Winking at the lady and glancing at Roland to let him know she wanted him to hear, Alissa said, "This would be a nice place to have a clandestine meeting."

The lady raised her head ever so slightly, showing the creases in her neck. Her tight skin shined in the reflected glow of the candlelight. The tightness of her facelift produced lines from the edge of her mouth to her ears, creating the appearance of a new jawline above the natural one. For a moment Alissa believed the woman had a double chin. Without the ability to register any emotion on her face but with her best Tallulah Bankhead impression, the tried-and-taut woman said, "I know. I have."

Alissa smiled coyly, tilting her head to the side as she looked up at Roland and coquettishly said, "See. Did you hear that?"

He hadn't.

She wiggled again, but that was useless; there were no more buttons she could pop open.

He missed it all. He missed the entire magical moment. He ignored Alissa when she was inspired and putting on her best performance. He didn't care that she was feeling romantic and had revealed her disappointment to a woman she felt unequal to her own nonstretched age lines. Roland totally destroyed all her romantic feelings, and Alissa knew she would not likely be able to rekindle any urges for him again for at least the next day or two.

He hadn't heard a word. He was preoccupied with calling his mechanic to see when his car would be ready. Alissa couldn't believe it. He thought more about that clunky, old, run-down car than he did about the woman who staged the optimum opportunity for romance. Saint Valentine's Day would be just another ordinary day without the least hint of romance. It was ruined when Roland appeared to care more about his possessions than he did about her.

So Alissa did the best thing she could think of to show him the deepness of her hurt. First, she buttoned up the sweater—all five buttons, all the way up to the top. All this went unnoticed by Roland, who remained inert to the possibility of romance.

Alissa then walked proudly out of the restaurant without taking the check, as she had promised to do. She moved slowly, taking her time so as not to cause a public scene. Her head was held high. She was satisfied, knowing how unhappy he would be to have to pay for the meal she did not eat.

Roland finished his meal leisurely and glanced at hers as if briefly considering eating that one as well. The tight-lipped lady was watching. He decided against eating the second lunch but asked to have it boxed up to go. No point in wasting money. He reached for his cell phone a second time and hit the redial button. "This is about that 2000 Mercury again. I've had a change of plans. Can you send someone to pick me up at Maison Chan-Cheng when it's ready? I'll be waiting in the lobby."

◆◆◆

Roland was beginning to feel tired all the time. His five-foot-eight frame was carrying a weight of 220 pounds. Alissa persuaded him to see the doctor. The results identified a major problem with cholesterol, but he was unwilling to give up his ice cream and gallon of milk each week. And the more serious problem was the diagnosis of an irregular heartbeat, which caused him to gasp for breath whenever he bent over.

Instead of resigning himself to medication and a change of lifestyle, Roland was determined to do battle with fate. He chose his path right from Dylan Thomas—"Do not go gentle into that good night." He had finally reached the point in his life when he no longer had to do for other people, and now that he could afford to live the kind of life he wanted, he was determined to do so. He wanted to travel.

During the preceding year, he and Alissa had visited every continent. If Roland wanted to see ice, he needed more than the amount in the Seven and Seven, which he called Fourteen. They went first to Alaska and next to Antarctica. He had given up cigarettes years ago, but when it came to camels, he had to ride one in Egypt, even though the camel driver so frightened Alissa by hoisting her up on the teetering camel and placing his sweaty turban on her head that she screamed loud enough to wake the mummies.

They took the Silk Route to China, although the route they chose was circuitous because Roland, inspired by the film *Laurence of Arabia*, wanted first to go to Jordan, Turkey, India, and Greece via the Suez Canal before arriving in Italy. By this time, the trip to Europe and the British Islands was tame by comparison. And Roland had such a wonderful time and was in such good spirits, he was able to kiss the Blarney Stone.

They returned from the trip, vowing that this Christmas was going to be special. Roland invited all his family members to celebrate at their home at Riverview Estates. He wanted to tell them in person about the next trip he and Alissa were planning. Catherine and Henri Michaels, Roland's sister and brother, and Ted and Simone Montaigne, the son and daughter of another of their sisters, were happy to accept the invitation. Roland was planning a trip to the Languedoc Region in France to explore their family history. The Michaels family originated in that area. He had researched the meaning of the crest of their ancestry. Alissa was excited by the adventure because it would mean that they would be visiting Toulouse, the home of Henri de Toulouse-Lautrec, and Roland was looking forward to ending the trip in Paris with a visit to the Moulin Rouge, where he would enjoy seeing the legs of the cancan dancers.

Roland was especially warm and gentle and loving that Christmas. There was no sharpness in his language, and he wasn't looking for an argument. But he seemed tired and spent much of the time on the couch, observing the others in their carefree joy. Roland's melting into the background wasn't his nature, and the family noted this.

"This is a different Uncle Roland from what I remember as a kid," said Ted.

"You're right. I haven't heard him curse all evening," said Simone, laughing.

"Or pick a fight," said Henri.

"Is there a problem? Does he have a headache?" asked his sister, Catherine.

"No, it's not a headache, Catherine; he's tired."

Ted was suspicious that it was something more serious, but he didn't want to admit it. "People in our family are very healthy. Mother and Marie may have died too soon, but that was cancer. Roland looks okay to me."

"Yeah," said Henri. "My grandmother lived to be a hundred, and Grandpa lived to be one hundred and one."

Alissa said, "He's not sick. He's mellow because it is important to him to have you here. He's so happy about the trip we are planning. It's an opportunity for him to get in touch with his roots, and he has been so excited while we were planning it. I've never seen him this content before. I find this absolutely wonderful. I'm enjoying the peace and quiet."

But Roland was ill, and Alissa knew it. Neither of them wanted his family to know how sick he was. So the family left after the holidays without anyone being told.

One week later, Roland started feeling really ill, and Alissa insisted he go back to the doctor. He was sick enough to know she was right. The doctor sent him home with recommendations for a diet and an order to have a stress test the following week.

The next day Alissa asked Roland if there was anything extra he wanted her to pick up at the market. "Does that mean you're going to buy me ice cream?" he asked.

"No, darling, no ice cream. I'm getting fresh fruits and veggies for you."

"The French eat rabbits, not eat like them," he quipped, giving her a hug and a kiss. She choked up and told him how much she loved him and turned away so he did not see her tears.

Roland started having chest pains while Alissa was marketing. He called the paramedics and waited for them to arrive to help him. But when they got to the house, Roland no longer had the strength to open the front door, and the paramedics had to break a window to get inside.

When Alissa arrived home, it was to the scene of a paramedic truck in front of her house, loading her husband into the ambulance. Neighbors had gathered. Alissa begged the driver to take her with them, but she wasn't allowed to go.

Al and his wife, Betty, came to help Alissa. Al was doing crowd control, and Betty was comforting Alissa. Al assigned the job of contacting the family to Sid and Donna and asked Buzz to notify Jennifer. As the group disbursed with their assignments, Al and Betty drove Alissa to the hospital. Alissa was in shock. The drive seemed to take forever. It was only two miles away, but to Alissa in the car following the paramedic truck carrying Roland, it seemed more like a funeral procession than a medical-emergency response. Alissa had an overwhelming feeling that Roland was leaving her. She felt helpless and angry. Why couldn't she be with him? He needed her now.

"I need to take him to the doctor for a stress test next week," she blurted out to Betty. "Why is Al going so slowly? Roland needs me."

"That's okay, Alissa. Al is driving as fast as the ambulance. We'll get you there in time."

"No, you are not," screamed Alissa. "He can't wait." She sobbed hysterically. But in her heart, she was beginning to understand that Roland would no longer need her. "It's taking longer to get to the hospital than it's taking Roland to get to heaven," she said, crying uncontrollably.

When Al, Betty, and Alissa arrived at the hospital, the couple was told to wait in the waiting room while Alissa was escorted by one of the nurses to a private room to wait for the doctor.

It took an eternity, but when the doctor arrived, his only words were, "Your husband has passed away."

"I want to see him."

The trip to the hospital was Roland's last trip. He was indeed of nobility. He was as brave as the knights of old who had earned the family crest. He died, still in charge of his life to the end. No one was to make a fuss over Roland. No one was to be troubled by caring for him. He was again the captain of his ship and the master of his life, even though the ship was only an ambulance.

A nurse took Alissa to a room where Roland was lying on a bed. She pulled up a chair and touched him, wanting so much for him to say something funny so they could laugh again. She stroked his arm, still warm from recent life. Alissa was unable to fully take in the reality that he had been physically taken from her. He was still as real as when they'd first met on the day in Mariposa when she'd interviewed him for a position as math teacher. She wished the desk were there in the hospital; she wanted to climb onto it and wiggle her leg to attract him. It had worked to capture his interest before.

Many of the neighbors from Riverview drifted into the hospital. No one could believe that vital, energetic Roland was gone so quickly. Notably missing were Russ and Coco, their next-door neighbors. But because of the strong chain of friendship among their friends, a pastor was called to minister to Alissa. When he arrived, he put his arms around Alissa and tried to comfort her. A merciless quiet filled the room as Alissa tried to be brave. But the depths of her utter loss overcame her. Why couldn't the doctor have saved him? Anger engulfed her. Aching cries rose from her as a confusion of doubts swirled around.

She had several offers to stay overnight at various homes, but Alissa preferred to be alone with whatever she could keep to herself of Roland's essence. The required task of filling out forms at the hospital was numbing, and finally, a shell of the vivacious Alissa finally was able to retreat home. Several close friends stayed to comfort Alissa at her home that night. At dusk, a majestic sunset more beautiful than any of them had seen lighted the entire western sky. Buzz took photographs. Alissa said the sunset was the Lord welcoming Roland home.

That night, she slept clutching his pillow.

Alissa was in shock for months and adrift in her despair. But when she had an opportunity to break that mood and return to normal life, she was grateful.

◆ ◆ ◆

Alissa received an engraved invitation to the wedding and reception of Elizabeth Andrews and Gustav Oleson on June 30, 2006, at the Swedish Embassy in Washington, DC. The groom was a member of the diplomatic corps. Jennifer, the proud grandmother of the bride, wanted her best friend, Alissa, to share in this joyful occasion. This gathering would be Alissa's opportunity to meet Jennifer's third husband, Greg Madison, a retired air force colonel. Jennifer was coming again to help Alissa during a difficult period.

The wedding was simple and tastefully understated. The bride was dressed in an off-the-shoulder white cocktail dress, and the groom wore a dark-blue suit with a navy-and-gold satin cummerbund. They each had one attendant. The service was held in the embassy drawing room, and the guests remained standing while a military chaplain, Mark Grant, officiated in the simple ceremony. A trio chamber ensemble composed of violin, viola, and cello played selections from Haydn for the guests. The room was filled with white-and-blue flowers. The flowers, the gentle classical music, and the loveliness of the young couple carried Alissa away from her feelings of emptiness to joyfulness inspired by the lovely occasion.

When the service was finished, the wedding party and guests were served finger sandwiches and hors d'oeuvres in the embassy garden. An elegant table held the wedding cake. A few small tables were provided, but the setting was intended to encourage the guests to mingle. Alissa was deemed to be the guest of honor because Jennifer introduced her to the guests as her best and dearest friend.

Being with Jennifer again brought a warm smile to Alissa and a bounce to her step. Alissa was beginning to feel whole again. "I haven't felt this warm and accepted since the Shabbat dinner at the Goodmans'," she said to Jennifer.

"You remember that word, my dear little gentile friend. You even pronounced it properly."

In the west end of the garden, a round table held a large silver punch bowl with a silver fountain in the center. The punch bowl was embossed with the blue and yellow Swedish national crest. As the crowd was thinning, Alissa wandered over to get a closer look at the fountain in the middle of the punch bowl. It was an unusual presentation, surrounded by a colorful arrangement of fruit. The punch was an effervescent mixture of champagne and ginger ale, cascading from the fountain over a block of vanilla ice cream. This caused creamy white foam on the surface that remained when the beverage was captured into crystal punch cups. The sweet combination overlaid colorful fruit cocktail that also could be captured – by silver ladle. Alissa had never tasted a champagne punch quite like this before and was trying to figure out how she would get some of that fruit cocktail out of her cup without a spoon when she heard a pleasant male voice that sounded like the actor Sam Elliott.

"It's a clever centerpiece. But I really prefer a glass of Dewar's."

She turned to see a gentle-looking, distinguished man in uniform, but there was no horseshoe moustache. He stepped toward her. "Excuse me Ma'am, may I take that white-foam moustache off for you? It seems out of place on your lovely face."

He took a cocktail napkin from the table, folded it, and gently wiped her upper lip. The colonel suspected this was a lady who needed a man like him.

Greg found the two of them standing awkwardly at the punch bowl. Alissa's face was as red as her lipstick, and for once in her life, she did not know what to say. She had expected Sam Elliott, the actor, with a distinguished moustache, but what she found was a distinguished colonel who was removing hers.

"Have you two met?" asked Greg. "Please allow me. Alissa, this is my old buddy Calvin Zach. Cal, Alissa went to Swarthmore with Jennifer. You two have something in common," he said with a laugh. "You're both from the same neck of the woods."

"DC is such a microcosm of the world," said Alissa, accepting the handshake Cal extended to her. "You're from out of town, too?"

"I'll leave you two alone to figure that one out," said Greg. "You will be coming back to the house with us tonight, won't you, Alissa? I know that Jennifer has lots to talk to you about before we let you rush off to the West Coast."

"You live on the West Coast?" asked Cal.

"I'm a sunny southern girl."

"I'm from the south too. I was raised in South Carolina."

"I'm sorry; I meant I was from southern California. South Carolina explains your accent, but why did Greg make a point of telling us that we are from the same place?"

"I don't know what he had in mind," replied Cal. "I live here in DC, but I did just get back from some special training at Glynco. Maybe that's what he meant."

Alissa was having difficulty with his accent and was getting annoyed. *Where in Glen Cove, New York, could a colonel in the air force receive any training? Could it be at the naval academy? The Webb Institute, designed ships.* She knew people from the institute and she had been there to visit. "Was your training at Glen Cove, Long Island?"

"No, ma'am. I was referring to Glynco, Georgia. But I've been to Glen Cove, Long Island. I attended a meeting at the Webb Institute."

Alissa didn't know how much of this was true or if the colonel was only trying to impress her. She didn't know what Greg had in mind, but she was *back on her feet*, so she took the conversation in a direction she wanted it to go.

"Tell me more about how you know Greg. Were you both in the same unit?"

"Actually no. When Greg was busy flying the planes, I was flying a desk. I am in the Air Force Office of Special Investigations," replied Calvin.

"That sounds complicated," said Alissa. "What are special investigations? Is this something I can ask you about? Or is this another puzzle we are supposed to work out? Is this the enigma for the day?"

Calvin laughed. "You can ask me if you wish. But as the corny old line goes, if I tell you, I will have to kill you."

Colonel Calvin Zach (Ret.) had been in the OSI almost since its beginning. He had changed duties several times, but for most of his air force career, he was assigned to the criminal investigations unit, where he investigated fraud. His talents in photography were needed, so after 9/11, he was called back as a retired officer in the OSI and had been retrained at the Federal Training Center at Glynco, Georgia, in specialized antiterrorism techniques. Alissa got the whole explanation from Greg that night when she was visiting with him and Jennifer.

"Did you like him?" asked Jennifer. "We were hoping you would. Cal is top-drawer. Or should I say he's one of those special pickles in the bottom of the barrel in the back room of the deli–that I told you about."

"What do you mean, 'like him'? I am still trying to figure out what we have in common. What about that, Greg? What was it all about?"

Greg laughed again. "That's a pickup line, Alissa. Anybody who has been to an officer's club would know that."

Alissa was annoyed. "Do I look like a pickup?"

"Don't be angry with us, sweetie. Didn't you notice, Alissa? Cal's not wearing a wedding ring."

"Oh, that kind of 'like him.' Jennifer, I don't want to disappoint you. I'm sure Greg's friend is a very nice man, but Roland just died. I'm still hurting. It hasn't been that long. How would you expect me to be ready to get involved this soon? I loved Roland very much. Thanks for the introduction to your friend, but I can't think about another relationship."

"That's exactly why you and Cal need each other, Alissa. Cal's wife of twenty-six years died after a long and painful illness. He lost his wife six months before you lost Roland."

"I'm so sorry," said Alissa. "The whole idea of dating a man from the OSI is too intense for me. It reminds me of Mata Hari. You've met Mama.

That was enough spying to last me for my whole life. Mama made me feel like she would turn me in to the enemy forces for torture if I wasn't careful about what I told her."

"He likes you, Alissa. He told us you were very charming, and he said you looked too young for him. I told him that he wasn't much older than you, and he didn't want to believe me. He asked what you did to keep your youthful looks. Isn't that sweet?" said Jennifer.

"You actually told him my age? You really didn't have to do that, Jennifer. If he's such a good special investigator, he should be able to figure that out for himself."

"You're being overly dramatic, Alissa. I think you should give Cal a chance. He's not a spy. He's a negotiator. I don't think there is a subversive bone in his body. Greg first met him when they were both involved in bringing Somoza's body out of Nicaragua to be buried in Miami."

"I hope General Somoza rests in peace," snapped Alissa. "Please allow me to have some space. I need peace, too."

Greg saw that he would need to assist Jennifer. "Cal's talent is in diplomacy. There is an art in diplomacy. Both sides carry overt prejudice and latent feelings that keep old attitudes alive. It takes a skilled diplomat to bring about compromises and agreements that will really work—one who is strong enough to stay focused on the goals and compassionate enough to understand both points of view."

◆ ◆ ◆

Two weeks later, when Alissa was back at home in Riverview Estates, the phone rang.

"Hello, Alissa. I don't know if you remember me. This is Cal Zach. We met at Liz and Gus's wedding in DC. I'm Greg's friend."

"I certainly remember you, Colonel. How are you?"

"I'm fine. I'm in Los Angeles on an assignment, and I'll have a little spare time for the rest of this weekend. I was wondering if we could meet for dinner."

"That's great. If you have time this evening, why don't you come here? I'll fix something for you."

Alissa didn't fix dinner for Cal. She did, however, plan to start to fix dinner, and she perused some of her cookbooks for ideas. After changing into green slacks with a beige sweater and sandals to shop at Don's Market on Wisteria Road, she purchased fresh shrimp, wild rice, and an assortment of salad greens. She was in the process of unpacking the packages when Cal arrived from LA. Alissa brought him into the kitchen so she could continue with the meal preparation.

"Is there something I can help you with?"

"It will only take me a minute," she said.

"That's okay," he said, looking over the food items. "Let me do it. I like to cook. This looks like all the ingredients we need for a really fine meal. I brought the wine."

While they were dining, Cal tried to amuse Alissa by telling her about some of the latest unclassified events in the Pentagon. "Military budgets are being discussed. They are still flying the F-15s and F-16s. We need some better birds."

Alissa was bored to tears. This didn't sound unclassified. To her point of view, it didn't have any class at all. "This is new jargon for me, Cal. But I did see the movie *Top Gun*. Is the plane Tom Cruise flew the kind of plane you are talking about? The only thing I know about planes is which gate number I have to find to board one."

"Yes. These birds are more than twenty years old. General Selva gave a very interesting presentation about the needs of the air force. But this is probably boring to you."

"It's not boring. I'm just not informed. But I'd prefer if you told me about something you personally are doing."

"Well, let's see," replied Cal, searching for something he could tell her about. "It would have to be something from my past. Okay, I have it. Have you ever heard of the A-10 Thunderbolt?"

"No," replied Alissa, wondering if this man had nothing but war stories. "Unless that is the thunderbolt they used to jump-start Dr. Frankenstein's monster. I saw that movie, too."

"Not even close. It's an antitank plane," said Cal, laughing. "Okay Ma'am, you asked for it, Alissa. This one is all about me. When FareChina Industries first built the plane in the seventies, I was part of the team that checked into the accounting records to be sure they weren't overcharging the government. Is this more interesting?"

"Actually not. Are you sure you are a colonel? Haven't you done anything exciting like finding the Unabomber or solving the Iran-Contra arms controversy, or do you have any tips on gardening I can use?"

"Negative on Unabomber, affirmative on the Iran-Contra affair, no on gardening, but I can tell you that I haven't always been a colonel. Sometimes my rank was upgraded temporarily, because if I was assigned to check out someone in the military, it was important to have a higher rank than the person I was investigating. I had several aliases for cover. I guess none of this is really interesting," he said, noticing that Alissa was not hanging on his every word. "But I can tell you a funny story about a time Greg and I got *potted* in Hong Kong, and I did learn the A-10 accounting records were *clean*. Does any of that excite you?"

"Yes, tell me about Hong Kong."

"Greg was so drunk he couldn't remember where he was. He started yelling that he was in *King Kong*. He goes ape and starts hanging from the edge of the bar by one arm and shouting for someone to bring him Fay Wray."

Alissa was laughing. It felt so good to have a real, deep, gut-wrenching laugh. She liked Colonel Calvin Zach, and she was pleased that he wanted to amuse her and was not put off by her negative mood. She needed encouragement to reconnect again with life. She wanted to know more about him and asked him to tell her more stories about what he did in the OSI.

"Okay, Alissa, but remember, I have to be cautious about how much I can tell you. Here's one. I didn't have a major role. You wouldn't find what I did very exciting. All I did was shadow this guy Waters. We thought Waters was selling secrets to the Russians. Excuse me, I don't mean Waters. I mean Walters. He was working out of some old building in the Bronx."

Alissa went pale. "Did you say, 'Walters in a building in the Bronx'?"

"Yes." Cal laughed. "Don't tell me you know something about the Walters case. Nobody made a movie out of this one. I doubt if it even made the papers."

"No. It has to be a coincidence. I know someone named Robert Walters who had a building in the Bronx. But he was selling perfume. You can't mean him."

"Alissa, we may be talking about the same person. I am required to ask you: what do you know about Robert Walters? These cases never get closed, you know."

Alissa wasn't amused. "You can't tell me that Robert Walters was selling secrets to the Russians. He made perfume. The Russians would not have enough money to match what he made by selling *Laver Stinken*."

"Isn't that an odd name for perfume?" asked Cal.

"It's toilet water," said Alissa.

"Toilet water? He should have named it Lavatory," said Cal.

"He wanted to call it Wet, but that name was taken by a company that made doggie vitamins. You have the facts wrong on this one, Mr. OSI. Robert's business genius was to find out what people's weaknesses were and exploit those, kind of like what the OSI does. But in Robert's case, he developed a secret formula that caused women to be attracted to the person wearing the product. It was really something. Even meek, insecure men who thought they were losers in the game of love became instantly attractive to the opposite sex by wearing a dab of *Laver Stinken* behind the ear.

"Robert discovered something about the male sweat glands behind the ear that reacted to the product when the man's temperature goes up.

It works. All they had to do was to wear it in a sauna, in the sunshine, or anywhere that would cause their temperature to rise. They didn't have to be sexually aroused. In fact, using a hair dryer would have worked as well.

"It was awesome for men who were afraid of suffering rejection. They were suddenly popular and desirable with the ladies. It was all done subliminally. The men did not need to be able to charm women, be attractive to them, or even suggest intimacy. The reason the ladies were attracted was because the polyphenols in their bloodstream were actively releasing serotonin and dopamine from the brain. It's a sexual stimulant for women that gives them a false feeling of euphoria. You can imagine how much money this brought Robert."

"Are you serious, Alissa? It doesn't sound possible."

"Oh, it's possible, all right. He added some oxytocin to the formula. I know you have heard of that."

"Sounds like something combustible to me," replied Cal.

"Not even close. You probably know oxytocin as the Love Drug."

"Can't say I've heard of that, either. Is this something I should look into?" he teased.

"Oxytocin is a female hormone. It gives a woman the urge to bond."

"I think he was on to something. Maybe we could finally have world peace and make our women happy at the same time," said Cal.

"Don't forget, this is very profitable. Robert Walters got his idea for the product from his travels in Africa. He used the testosterone of the African bull elephant for his perfume. Female elephants are attracted to the males very quickly. Robert hired natives to collect the extract. He had to pay them a lot of money because it was dangerous work. They have big feet, you know. Wouldn't want to start a stampede. But it takes money to make money, and Robert didn't care as long as he didn't have to collect the samples himself."

"I never heard about that one," said Cal, shaking his head in disbelief. "That's one hell of a sperm bank."

"It was promoted by word of mouth. You wouldn't expect it to be on TV at prime time when he started this business. That was before TV brought the bedroom into the living room. What made this so special was that it was a secret shared by all the losers in the world. Nobody wants to admit they aren't attractive to women. Robert chose the name *Laver Stinken* so that it would sound manly. *Laver* means "to wash," and *stinken* certainly doesn't imply a feminine fragrance. It was very expensive. But they didn't have to use much." She paused. "Why would you think he was a Russian spy? Admittedly, that was during the Cold War; this has to do with women being in heat."

"Because we couldn't tell why all these envelopes were being shipped from that boarded-up building on Tuckahoe Road in the Bronx. That stuff was going all over the world under bills of lading that said Secret Formula."

"What spy tells you he is transmitting secrets? Good grief, Cal, labeling it secret doesn't make him a Russian spy. Even Colonel Flanders's chicken has secret ingredients. I'm beginning to think I don't want to ask any more questions about the OSI. Is this your tactic, Cal? Your strategy is not to divulge anything about your military secrets, and the tactic is to make it as uninteresting as heck. If obfuscation is how things work in Washington, how about telling me about your travels?"

"Okay. Have it your way. I spent some time in London, and oh yes, you would be interested to know that I had an assignment in the fifties that brought me to the desert to play a small part in the investigation into the crash of fighter pilot Joe McDonald at Albert Air Force Base. In fact, that was the first investigation I was ever involved with."

"I loved the way June Allyson played McDonald's wife in the movie," responded Alissa. "Were you in the movie, too?" she said teasing him.

"No, I was in the book." He chuckled. "I saw the movie too. Did the citizens of Sunny Hills really build her a house?"

"Beats me. That was before my time. I was in high school and living on the East Coast when McDonald died. Looks like you may be older than me, Cal. Confess now. How old are you? And don't tell me you will have to kill me if you tell me."

"I was born in 1935 and joined the army air corps right out of high school. I immediately joined the OSI as an enlisted man."

Alissa teared up. This man had been born the same year as her first husband, Fred Walters. She began shaking. A sudden feeling of anger came over her that she did not understand.

She removed the dishes from the table. Cal followed her into the kitchen. He was not going to allow her to turn him away.

"I'm sorry," she said, wiping the tears from her cheek. "I know you lost your wife recently, and like me, you are grieving. But being with you brings up more pain that I haven't thought about in years. I'm getting a bit overwhelmed."

"Shall we sit outside?" asked Cal, not wanting to leave. "It's a beautiful evening, and there is a full moon."

"I don't want to go out there. This house is built right on the greens. Roland played golf right there outside my kitchen window. I feel like I can still see him arguing with the guys about the game. It's too close for me, Cal. I'm really sorry about this. Please, let's call this an evening. Perhaps you'll be in LA again and will call me."

"I'd be happy to do the dishes," said Colonel Zach. But before Alissa could answer, the doorbell rang.

Alissa wiped her face on a tea towel. "Do I look presentable?" she asked.

"You look perfect."

Buzz, Al, and Sid were standing at the door. Alissa invited them in and introduced them to Cal.

"We've come back from a committee meeting," said Buzz. "We approved an idea we think you will like, Alissa. We know how much Roland loved golf, and we want to order a commemorative plaque with his name on it. See here?" Buzz showed Alissa a picture from a catalogue. "Here's what it would look like. We think it would be nice to put it on the greens right outside your house. Do you like it?"

Alissa's eyes opened in horror. "It looks like a grave marker."

Buzz turned the book to take a look at it himself. "Hey, you're right," he mumbled. "I hadn't thought about that. Leave it to a woman to see things that way. We only wanted to honor Roland."

Alissa covered her face with her hands and rushed out of the room, crying, "No, no."

"I don't think Alissa is prepared to make that kind of a decision right now," explained Cal politely. "She'll get back to you later, gentlemen; in the meantime, if you would excuse us," he said, hurrying them out the front door.

After the committeemen had left, Cal waited patiently for Alissa. He did not hear her crying and didn't know where she was. He was fairly certain she had not left the house. After a few minutes, he felt it was appropriate to look for her. He went down the hall, looking for doors that were open, calling her name. She didn't answer, but when he got to the bedroom, he found her sitting on the edge of the bed, staring blankly toward the wall.

"Alissa, are you all right?" he said, approaching the room but respectfully pausing at the doorway.

"No, I'm not, Cal. I know they meant well, but I don't need a brick in my yard to remind me daily of my love for Roland."

"I understand. I'm going to leave now, but if it is okay with you, I would like to come back tomorrow."

Alissa could not answer. Her head was bent down, and her thoughts were far away.

As soon as Cal left, she called Jennifer. "I don't understand what happened to me today," she said. Her voice was subdued as she related the events and the anger she was still feeling.

Jennifer listened to her carefully and then tried humor to encourage her. "You are so vulnerable now. You've got PMS, my darling—post-marriage syndrome. You are still angry with Fred. This thread has been going throughout your whole life. It's taken up too much of your life. It's time to understand it and cut it off. Your anger is not with Cal at all or with the men wanting to build a monument for Roland. That was a smokescreen you created to avoid what was really bothering you. You felt helpless, and your anger was because you did not want to feel helpless."

"Helpless?"

"You couldn't control the things happening to you, and you became overwhelmed. You know, Alissa, when you can't control something, you get angry and depressed. It's time to forgive yourself for what happened with Fred. You couldn't do anything about it then, but you can do something about it now. Cal is not Fred. You can depend on Cal. Just because they were born the same year doesn't make them the same. That coincidence is what triggered your emotions. He won't betray you. He won't let you down. But he might try to take out anyone who does. Cut the thread."

Jennifer's words touched her as though the finger was taken out of the dike–Alissa's tears flowed. The phone was still pressed to Alissa's ear, but the words Jennifer continued to speak sounded as if they were far off in the distance, coming through a tunnel.

"It's time to let go, Alissa. Hang up the phone and cry your heart out."

Cal did return the next day and the next, and then he came back to see Alissa every weekend. His visits caused a major uproar in Riverview Estates, but Colonel Cal showed he outranked the major problems they threw at him. Thus, any minor gossip the busybodies could invent was mitigated. Cal took charge. This was true even when the women at Riverview found they could impose on Cal's good nature and willingness to help them when they used their widowhood to garner sympathy.

There were many women living alone and in need of the company of a man, even if it was only to talk. As soon as word got out that Cal was a true southern gentleman who was willing to be called upon for assistance, his time with Alissa became less and less. The imposition started with one neighbor, but the routine got exponentially larger as that one told another.

First there was the hysterical call in the middle of the night. "Alissa, I hope Cal is there. I need to talk to him. I hear a noise in the garage."

Alissa would say, "Don't worry, Cal will be right over." She put down the phone and turned to Cal.

"It's my paranoid neighbor again. This time she thinks there is someone in her garage. It would be good if her doctor changed her meds so she could get some sleep. But if it's real, Cal, I don't want you to put yourself in any danger."

"No sweat," said Cal. "But maybe you should call the police. They will respond more quickly if a woman calls reporting strange noises."

"You want me to call our rent-a-cops?"

"You don't have a police department here?"

"They're sheriffs' deputies. They get switched out so frequently you only have time to say howdy, and they're gone. And when they are here, they don't attend to any duty more involved than a donut/coffee run."

"I'll try to get there before Howdy Doody shows up so I can lend him a hand. Lock the door, Clarabelle, while I'm gone."

When word got to Coco Beignet–the neighbor whose name Cal said sounded like a chocolate dessert–she couldn't resist saying, "Is Alissa getting another man? She should write a book. Alissa changes husbands so often, she must be getting something for recycling men."

◆ ◆ ◆

Cal was always honorable and accommodating. He knew Alissa needed him, and he needed her. That would preempt anything that stood in the way of the love that he felt was growing between them.

Both Alissa and Cal had recently lost a spouse they loved deeply. They were not replacing that love with another person. Four people entered this relationship. Alissa understood Cal when he spoke adoringly of his late wife, and Cal knew that when Alissa spoke of her passion for Roland it did not mean that she loved Cal less. They loved more completely. Just as the love of a parent increases when another child is born into the family, the widow and widower who had loving relationships in their former marriages find love increases when another spouse is taken to heart.

Three months later, Alissa, in a silver brocade fitted dress, and Cal, in his formal air force uniform, were married at the Buddhist Temple in Trickle Creek Valley with friends from Riverview Estates; South Carolina; Hong Kong; Mariposa; Los Angeles; Solana Beach; Greenwich, Connecticut; Long Island, New York; and Washington, DC, joining their families in the celebration of their love and commitment.

Cal absolutely adored her. For Alissa, her joy was evidenced in her paintings, which became rich with vibrant colors again. There were no more wars on her horizon because she had a soldier to stand and defend her. There was no more self-deprecating humor because Cal refused to allow her to diminish who she was. There was no longer a need for Alissa to have to defend her position or ideas because Cal always supported her opinions without diminishing his own. And as she aged and her memory did not always serve her, Cal smoothed out the event by telling her it wasn't a senior moment—she just needed more time to boot-up. All this coalesced to create a life of harmony and tranquility for the couple as they grew old together in loving relationship.

For Alissa, there would be no more burning tears. She had become the embodiment of all that she had yearned for as a child when all she asked for was to be loved. She learned to love herself, and doing this gave her rebirth. She could direct her own life and find the shepherd she was willing to follow. That shepherd was Cal. He was someone she could trust. She no longer struggled to be wanted and learned to accept his unconditional love. In so doing, Alissa had opened her soul to the needs of others and gave comfort and support when needed. Her own destiny was no longer a challenge but an acknowledgment of truth, understanding, and love.

TWENTY-ONE

The Crossover

Some anthropologists of Mesoamerica studying the Mayan calendar discovered what they suspected might be a prediction that the world would come to an end on December 21, 2012, or it might be the twenty-third, or it might not come to an end at all, but in any event, the date might mark a major event. *In other words* they were absolutely, positively, convinced they were not sure. But these possibilities for change were enough for Alissa. Actually, all the Mayans had shown on their long calendar was that on December 21, 2012, the sun would be positioned in the center of the Milky Way Galaxy, and when that lineup occurred, it would coincide with a wobble of the Earth. A wiggle of earthly proportions would get everyone's attention and might shake people up a bit.

Always intrigued with religious myths, Alissa thought it would be fun to have their planned move from Trickle Creek coincide with the date of the Mayan prophesy of change. So Cal and Alissa arrived in Arizona in time for the winter solstice of 2012, but the only thing that moved for them was their furniture. Alissa didn't believe the world would come to an end, but she gave some credence to the idea that the date might mark a new beginning for her. Cal, on the other hand, always the pragmatist, pointed out that the Mayan long calendar was intended to describe events when a new king would rule and great battles would be fought, and the prophecies were meant for their ancient culture. He pointed out that the fact that the Mayan civilization ran out before their calendar only indicated that their advance planning had not included the arrival of the Spanish Conquistadors. Nevertheless, Cal was willing to follow the life he loved on an adventure of her choosing.

Sedona, Arizona, is reported to be influenced by a strong vortex creating a natural geomagnetism that affects human brainwave activity. A vortex, in Cartesian philosophy, is a collection of matter that is rapidly rotating around an axis. Descartes, who is more famously known for his *cogito ergo sum*, also had a divine theory that attempted to attribute the creation of the universe to vortices. This was more than enough science to draw Alissa to Chapel Hill to experience the Sedona effect. Alissa proclaimed her need to be there by adapting Descartes's 'I think therefore I am' to her personal statement of authenticity: "I paint, therefore I am."

The Zachs contracted for an adobe-style ranch house to be constructed on a site where Alissa could look up into the red Sedona hills whenever she needed an extra dose of inspiration. Cal's explanation of the vortex was that the iron in the red hills accounted for the magnetic draw. Whatever the reason for the attraction, Alissa discovered she was most fulfilled while painting at their home in Chapel Hills. Some kind of energy seemed to draw out her inner self and allow her to put it on canvas. She refused to show her work to anyone for fear of having it copied. Certainly in the case of creative art, imitation is not the highest form of flattery. Since so much of her spirit was on canvas, this would be identity theft.

She felt at home there. Alissa asked Cal, "Do you hear my name being called?'

Putting his arm around her shoulders, Cal said, "Maybe it's my heart, darling."

"No, I'm serious. Don't you feel an awesome pulling? My mood seems to be lifting to a higher plane. Don't you feel it, Cal?"

"If I felt something pulling on me and calling my name, I'd be watching my back."

"Oh, Cal, let yourself go. Join my spirit."

"Too late for me, my dear. But I'll stay grounded and be your anchor so that you can fly as high as you wish."

"The colors I use here are a far cry from those I used in the world I lived in before. I never saw all these colors until you came into my life. It's as if you painted them into me."

"I think you are giving me too much credit, Alissa."

◆ ◆ ◆

It was fortunate that they left when they did. The state economy was in shambles after a succession of governors who failed on promises to handle the financial deficit—the state was ostensibly bankrupt when it couldn't sell its bonds at any interest rate. Property values dropped during the housing meltdown in 2007. In 2008, both Alissa and Cal lost half the value of the IRAs and stocks they had planned to use to help finance their retirement years. Federal taxes started skyrocketing in 2020 to pay for interest on the federal debt.

The bankruptcy meant those people who relied on state pensions had to look elsewhere for income, and this impacted many Riverview residents. This resulted in many vacant houses in the community. Fortunately for the Zachs, Alissa's pension came from Connecticut and Cal's from the federal government, and although they were not indexed for inflation, Alissa's home was saved from foreclosure.

But the state bankruptcy meant those schools and prisons that had not been privatized were no longer funded, and inmates were released into communities to join the street gangs of out-of-school kids who had nothing better to do with their time.

"It's starting to look like Dickens's London there," said Cal as he downloaded the news on his computer. "If we had stayed, we might have had to move in with the kids."

"I didn't raise them to take care of me," said Alissa. "

◆ ◆ ◆

One of Alissa's greatest joys was the time her granddaughter, Millicent, came to visit during spring break from the University of Arizona, where she was completing a doctoral program in socioeconomics. Grandmother and granddaughter took an early morning walk when the red-rock country was cool, and they could explore the ideas they held in common.

"I can see why you love it here," said Millicent. "It's peaceful."

"It's more than that. It's majestic," replied Alissa. "It keeps people from getting too full of themselves. Watch where you step; the ground is soft. We are planning to plant a vineyard here. I intend it to help finance my future."

"Are you planning to open a winery?"

"Just a small house winery. I enjoy things that improve with age even though they have been stomped on."

Millicent laughed, but Alissa was deep in thought. "Sedona is a place where we can come to finally forgive ourselves. The majesty of this place has a protective quality that will allow us to take on another day without fear."

"Are you afraid, Grandma?"

"Sometimes, but not often. I think I've learned to let go and let things happen as they will. I've been most fearful when I tried to control things that shouldn't have concerned me. I've come to realize that it was fear that held me back."

Alissa produced her best art during her Sedona period. She took Millicent to her studio to show these paintings to her.

"Show me your most recent paintings. These would be from your Sedona phase, wouldn't they?" Millicent asked.

"I'm calling the latest *Creativity II*," she said, walking toward the studio to show off the painting she most prized. "Don't touch it; the oils are still wet. And I'd like it better if you called this a *period* as artists do, not a *phase*." Alissa laughed.

"Grandma, what a beautiful expression of color. You have accomplished so much." Millicent stepped back to get a better look at all the paintings at once.

"Enough of your flattery; it will go to my head. Are you hungry, Millie? I smell something delicious. Cal must be cooking up a surprise for us in the kitchen. That means he's finished straightening out the files in the den. I think we are finally settling in."

As they moved toward the house, Millicent noticed the flowers in one of the landscaped beds were drooping and looked like they could use a little attention. She pointed this out to her grandmother.

"No, what they need is some good old-fashioned manure. Maybe I should place some soaked political papers around them," quipped Alissa.

"That reminds me of something in the news today," said Millicent thoughtfully. "Did you hear about our former secretary of state's daughter getting paid outrageous fees for lectures about diarrhea?"

"Maybe I should send her my feces thesis."

"What's that about Grandma?"

"Come in and sit down, girls," said Cal. He had prepared a lunch of shrimp scampi with linguini on the newly constructed patio that overlooked a dry riverbed framed by three stately Palo Verde trees. "Your grandmother can tell you about the way she once discouraged an unwanted suitor who didn't suit her." He said laughing.

"I was afraid of him, Cal. It was a *think-on-your-feet* moment."

"And making him sick to his stomach was the best defense you could come up with?" asked Cal filling the wine glasses with Chardonnay.

"I wasn't armed, and I needed to disarm the guy before he got the impression he was getting more than dinner. I was using my BS degree."

Millicent looked back and forth at both of them in a total state of confusion; but neither Cal or Alissa seamed prepared to elaborate.

"I hope you enjoyed your morning together, girls. Family brings its own precious rewards," said Cal, sitting down to have lunch with the women. At Alissa's plate, he had placed an old pouch decorated with Native American beadwork.

"Where did you find this, Cal?" asked Alissa. "I haven't seen this in years."

"Yeah, I know you save everything, but your father's tobacco? Or are you planning on taking up smoking?"

"Only with the peace pipe," said Alissa. "This is the tobacco I purchased in Mariposa to try to call upon the spirit of Crazy Horse. Where did you find it?"

"Filed under Tashunka Witko. I figured if you kept it this long, it must be important."

"It certainly is," said Alissa. "It's fine to show this to Millie, but don't show it to Josh; he always teased me about moving to California and sniffing something to take me to another world."

"Did Josh really believe you would become a hippie when you moved to California?" asked Millicent.

"Josh always teased me, and I adored it. His humor helped keep me sane."

Cal wasn't sure if he should show Alissa and Millicent what else he had discovered that morning. But they seemed so at ease, he decided to broach the subject by showing them what he stored on his 2030Series IzPad. "I'll bet you didn't know about this. You might want to look at this story on XNN news."

Alissa was shocked at what she read. "How is this for poetic justice? It's about your great-uncle Robert. He's not so great anymore."

"What happened?" asked Millicent.

"Seems that 'not so' hanged himself in his cell while he was waiting for his sentencing hearing," said Cal. "After all, as you know from the song by that Russian country singer Dusty Offski, 'Every dog has his day. But today, dog, just ain't yours.'"

"Listen to this," said Alissa as she read from the screen.

"'Robert Walters, Creator of Sex Stimulant *Laver Stinken*, Hangs.' I don't like this headline," said Alissa. "It implies something about his anatomy that I seriously doubt. Anyway, here's the rest of the story." She read:

> Last night in the county jail, the body of Robert Walters was found hanging from a light fixture in his cell. Walters had improvised a

> rope by using his bed sheet. He had been convicted of securities fraud, illegal importation of a restricted substance, embezzlement, perjury, and product misrepresentation. Walters was scheduled for sentencing today. His body was discovered by the guards who had arrived to take him to court.
>
> Walters' crimes triggered a class-action suit filed by the law firm of O'Brian, Sanchez, and Ginsberg on behalf of the thousands of men who experienced itching, redness, swelling, and throbbing pain of the ear. In most instances, the ear lobe became so extenuated that it touched the top of the shoulder.
>
> Other claimants complained that the fragrance appeared to attract flies. Victims described the disfigurement as debilitating. They were unable to work, could no longer wear head-coverings, and confined themselves to their homes in embarrassment.

"Yep," said Cal. "It's a stinking shame. No one wants to be the elephant man."

"They must not have read the warning label. They fared better than Van Gogh. At least they aren't in so much pain that they are cutting off their ears," said Alissa.

"He should have used the testosterone from Indian elephants, and then the ears might not have gotten so big," said Cal with a laugh.

"Poor Uncle Robert," said Millicent–tears welling up in her eyes.

"Poor is right," said Cal. "Sounds like he was broke, and that's probably what killed him."

"Don't shed tears for him, Millie, darling. He brought this on himself. In his mind it was the only thing he could do. He could not live without his money and power. He had no shame and was not concerned about the people he hurt. He probably had exhausted all his legal remedies and knew he would be in prison for a long time. But I'm surprised that he didn't have some money hidden away–it's not like him to be in a powerless position."

"Let's propose a toast for justice," said Cal, raising his glass of lemonade. "And if the court can find all the money Robert had in his offshore accounts, maybe the victims can get compensation for their suffering. That is, if there is anything left after the attorneys get their share."

"And most important of all," said Alissa, "the Walters family is no longer part of our lives." She paused and sighed. "But I'm sorry for those women who were duped into believing they were attracted to these men who were Bob's customers. It wasn't love they were feeling–it was *Laver Stinken*."

"They should have had a hint when the flies arrived in V formation," said Cal, smiling.

A clap of thunder rolled through the valley, and as suddenly as the clouds appeared, large drops of rain peppered the group on the patio. "We had better move this party inside before the storm gets worse," said Cal.

"Liberation from the antics of my former in-laws would be most welcome," said Alissa as they each grabbed up plates and moved into the kitchen. "I won't allow the Walters family to intrude any longer on my life."

As soon as they settled in, Cal went to the windows and bolted them shut. He pulled the inside shutters closed and then joined the ladies at the kitchen table. But Millicent was anxious to leave before the storm made the roads impassable.

"I'm so thankful to have spent this time with you, Grandma. Your mind is so sharp. And you look so great. I think she will live forever, don't you, Cal?"

"I'll do my best to help her do that." He smiled.

As Millicent was leaving, Cal and Alissa waved their good-byes from the kitchen door. "Watch out for washed-out roads," called Cal. "Flash floods can be treacherous."

◆◆◆

The December 21, 2012, date on the Mayan calendar depicting a major change in world order turned out to be an ordinary day for most people, including Alissa, for whom the major change in her life didn't occur on that date. It happened instead in 2032 on her ninety-sixth birthday at high noon. Alissa had long since realized how many of the things she wanted for her life had been accomplished. Her goals were met, and she felt complete, but she was tired, and it was natural for her to conclude her work on earth was finished.

Great-granddaughter Carrie Streeter's struggle with learning arithmetic was only an amusing distant memory as she was graduating from Caltech with doctoral degrees in applied physics and mathematics. Daughter Katie Streeter's third book on constitutional law for dummies was being used worldwide as a textbook in major law schools. Grandson Daniel Streeter was lead tenor at the Metropolitan Opera and reserved seats for Alissa and Cal at each of his opening performances. Son Joshua Walters sold his investment enterprise to a Russian oligarch, and he and his lifelong spouse, Rachel, were living in Boca Raton in the penthouse of the apartment building they built overlooking a world-class golf course. Colonel Calvin Zach completed a degree in psychology, attributing his success to the on-the-job training he received from the years of living with Alissa.

Alissa resolved that either on her own or by influencing her family, she had accomplished everything she wanted to do with her life. Her offspring were all honorable, intelligent, and open-minded. George would be proud, and so was she. Unfortunately, the legacy of her parents and abusive husbands continued to plague her. The years of living with two parents who smoked left a mark. She had developed emphysema from exposure to secondary smoke, and at this stage of her life, every breath she took was painful and labored. The "old goats" had never stopped damaging her.

She took a new blue Lanz gown out of the dresser and put it on, ignoring the pain from the dislocated shoulder that was magnified with arthritic joints. She retired to bed midmorning.

Alissa had become increasingly tired in recent days, and although she was not sick, she was showing signs of slowing down. She wasn't depressed. She was content. She was no longer the driven woman, juggling the multitude of projects that attracted her interest. She had come to the end of another period, and it was natural that she should make another transformation.

She had chosen the option best for her at this moment in time.

Cal suspected something was wrong, but her somber behavior did not alarm him because Alissa seemed not to be concerned with her health. He went to the bedroom to see if she needed assistance.

"Are you okay, Alissa?"

"Yes."

"Is there something I can do for you?"

"No."

"Is there anything you want?" he pleaded, hoping that she would need him. Cal was overwhelmed with the finality her soft, whispered answers implied. He could do no more for her. He was overcome with a mixture of shock and grief as he tried to make the emotional bridge that would allow him to continue being with her into the hereafter.

A tear formed in his eyes. He noticed a faint smile on her lips. She reached for his hand and held it for a moment. Hers was becoming cold and limp, and it slipped out of his tender grip.

"I love you," he said, knowing that she had chosen this time to move apart from him.

"I love you, too." Alissa formed the words on her lips because she no longer had the strength to speak them. She was relaxed and content, and a small smile formed on the corners of her mouth as she was beginning to slip away to join the angels.

Cal remained at her side, watching the color drain from her soft face. His mission was to stay with her to protect her from the *Erlkonig*. His strong hands, which had seen battle and had fought the enemies of his country, held and caressed her, gently brushing away a wisp of her hair that had slipped onto her forehead.

Alissa's lifelong battles were coming to an end. She had dealt with so many years of abuse by consciously denying them and wearing a mask of humor. But now, in the conclusion of her life, all these had to be reconciled. Denial does not go gently into the night. But the damage from it was now was now defeated by her acceptance of things for what they were. She was grateful to the Lord for allowing her to rise above the misfortune. The angst and turmoil left her.

Cal stared at her, not wanting to believe what he knew to be true. There would be no more vitality in her life or his. He gently kissed her for the last time and murmured, "Save a place for me, dearest. We have all of eternity to be together." His mind drifted to a peaceful scene that would please her. He imagined her running through fields of mariposa lilies in a springtime of new beginnings.

She saw the mariposa lilies projected from Cal's thoughts and relaxed as she drifted away from him. She felt she was covered in silk that caressed her gently. Her pains and woes ebbed out of her from a low wave, cooling the heat and struggles of the world and surrounding her in an infinite, beautiful myriad of blues—colors that had never been on her palette. They were all the colors of oceans and lakes and the sky in the moment of creation before they had been separate and apart. Blue chicory and crystals sparkling above her beckoned her forward. Faces of friends welcomed her with inviting smiles, showing her they had prepared an easel for her art. From a distance, she saw her father waving to her and smiling. He was once again a young man, no longer enduring the hardships of Parkinson's disease. The demons in his mind had been stilled, and happiness had taken its rightful place.

Truth and discovery surrounded Alissa. New images came onto the canvases of her mind. This home is where the greatest Father of all time dwells.

"I'm home, Father. Thank you for all you have given me."

Cal felt her leave. He bowed his head and prayed, "Thank you, Lord, for your constant strength and for watching over us. Our lives were truly blessed." He wiped the tears running down his cheek. He understood what Alissa meant when she spoke of the pieces of the puzzle of her life. The pieces had come together to form the final canvas of her life. The dark-colored pieces of her beginning had led upward to bright brilliant shades, and now with her death, they were topped with quiet, peaceful tones that had slipped gently into place in a wisp of mist.

He whispered to her, "I am complete, too, dearest Alissa. I am there with you to see the sunset from the other side," knowing that he was connected to the spirit of Alissa forever.

ABOUT THE AUTHORS

Jessica Oswald, a retired principal and teacher, has written many noteworthy items, including a substance-abuse program stressing responsibility, positive thinking, and self-reliance, while she was a resource teacher for Glen Cove City School District, New York. Due to this program, Jessica was listed in the 1983–1984 *Who's Who in the East*. The program was written up in *Newsday* newspaper and in a five-part series in the local Glen Cove Long Island newspaper. In the capacity of public policy chair and science chair, she wrote columns for the monthly newsletter of the Victor Valley, California, branch of the American Association of University Women. She has been the recipient of several awards for her art. She provided direction, themes, stories, wit, inspiration, and artwork to the creation of *Crossover: Did I Miss My Exit?*

Margaret Furman, a former corporate-tax manager and California teacher, has published in several genres, including a monthly column named "Tortoise Tales" while a columnist for the Hesperia section of the *Daily Press* from Victorville, California. The writing style of her column was touted by the editor as "reminiscent of Erma Bombeck." Her technical writing includes authorship of a weekly column entitled "Overtaxed?" for Jacobs Engineering Group, a multinational engineering firm; and lesson plans for business education with a team fulfilling requirements of a grant obtained by the Los Angeles County Office of Education. When she was a teenager, her poetry was published in a high-school anthology. She is currently preparing several manuscripts for publication, including family poetry anthologies, the history of the founding of the Pasadena Conservatory of Music, and genealogical-research items, including annotated maps of former villages along the Vistula River in Poland and a compilation of her own family research.

Both authors have lectured and have been guest speakers and consultants to professional and civic organizations.